The Adventures of Artie The Whisker

An Autobiographical Novel of
Innocence, Experience and Magic

ARTHUR SPELMAN

The Adventures of Artie The Whisker

An Autobiographical Novel of
Innocence, Experience and Magic

(I love this photo of grandma standing upon this big boulder, we all saw and knew her as that rock itself, full of love and sure footing.)

I dedicate this book to my Grandmother Blanche Louella Ferris Brown who was the very heart and soul of our band of hooligans, and the center core of the Brown Family. Grandmother, you gave us music and dreams and love. I can still smell your lilac perfume. I can still hear your council, and feel your wise, loving embrace. I look up for your wings often. I miss you and there hasn't been a single day I haven't longed for you in this old world. In this book, may we all have a chance to run into your arms, even if only for a moment.

Thank you Grandma.

In your light I learn how to love.
In your beauty, how to make poems.
You dance inside my chest where no-one sees you, but sometimes I do, and that sight becomes this art.

- Rumi

Walter Crawford, Artie Spelman, & Harley Brown

Summer, 1943

Contents

1   Lightning and the Lightning Bug. 1

2   A Towhead In Eden 4

3   A Giant's Band of Angels 8

4   The Gnome Exemplumonious 15

5   Cauchemar. 24

6   The Talisman 29

7   The Tribulations of Tonto. 39

8   The Eagle's Nest. 47

9   Just A Walk in the Sunshine. 50

10 The Alcazar & Dr. Duck (Negotiations). 65

11 The Alcazar & Dr. Duck (An Offer For Sally O'Flannery). . . . 80

12 The Alcazar and Dr. Duck (Skinny Dippers) 83

13 The Alcazar & Dr. Duck (Enlightenment!) 96

14 Love Finds Handy Artie. 114

15 The Red Baron vs. The Greasy Spoon. 125

16 Rembrandt's News 144

17 Muggs (The Celebration) 156

18 Muggs (Arlington on Atlantic) 164

19 Muggs (The Whizzing Ghost) 170

20 Duck Arrests a Tufts 178

21 Stand and Defend 184

22 Artie Takes The Stand 188

23 The Verdict. 193

24 The Hanging 200

25 Mrs. Brown 205

26 Stitches in the Sacred Heart 213

27 The Tiniest Viking (Sharon De Brun; Burial in Icy Seas;
   Kerstin Rydstrom, the Viking Mother) 224

28 Circus Trilogy (Part One: Bring in The Clown) 241

29 Circus Trilogy (Part Two: Hear Those Giants Singing?) 255

30 Circus Trilogy (Part Three: Babes in Arms) 266

31 Duduk (Day One) 290

32 Kanapy (Day Two) 297

33 Flet Boga (Day Three) 309

34 Last Days on Atlantic Blvd. 319

35 Death of a Giant 332

36 The Eighth Life of Orange Pasha (The Dream Triplex) 337

37 The Eighth Life of Orange Pasha (The Winged Heart) 345

38 The Eighth Life of Orange Pasha (Rejection at High Noon) . . 351

39 The Eighth Life of Orange Pasha (Murder Most Deliberate) . 355

40 The Eighth Life of Orange Pasha (The Windmills at
   Gopher Spit Hollow) 363

41 An Armenian, A Drunken Duck, and An Irishman... 370

42 Baptism in the Olive Garden 383

43 The Blasphemist (Hope Springs Eternal) 392

44 The Last Supper (Sunday, December 28th, 1947) 407

45 The Trinitarian Bottle 424

46 Anchors Ah-Waitress 435

Epilogue. 447

Artie Spelman, 1943

CHAPTER 1

Lightning and the Lightning Bug

I T WAS 1943. The "greatest generation" was off dying in a world war. A small boy sat alone in the dark night on an eight man platform swing suspended from the branches of a hundred year old pepper tree. Under the cardigan sweater, knitted by his Grandmother, he wore a black and white striped shirt and his new long pants supported by bright red suspenders.

The moon, gigantic and the color of popcorn, was surrounded by twinkling stars in a cobalt black sky. The boy, Artie, watched the silhouette of a Stearman Kadet biplane cross the face of that orb like a drunken bug staggering in the cold, jasmine-scented air.

Artie stretched his arm toward the moon and the airplane as if trying to touch them. As the Kadet winged westward across the moon's face, he saw the distinct profile of the pilot and recognized him immediately as his Uncle Harley's black and white dog, Muggs McGinnis. The canine warrior dipped his left wing, raised his goggles, winked once, and then waved his paw enthusiastically at the child below. Artie smiled and waved back.

Muggs pushed hard left rudder and hard left stick as the Stearman snapped into a beautifully executed wingover. The aircraft responded immediately, going into a steep dive aimed directly at the boy's nose. Within the trunk of the old pepper tree, Artie could hear the cowardly mumbling of Gnome Exemplumonious, the tree's caretaker and resident. By Gnome's side, a couple of gypsy squirrels indifferently chewed on their nuts, and a nervous French Skunk named Pie waited for the inevitable.

Artie glanced back at his home as shadowy hands lowered the black-out blinds on the windows in preparation for an air raid.

The house lights went out.

The street lights went out.

No DING! Ka-ching! of the traffic paddles.

Artie looked up at the moon and it went out too.

The stars winked out and finally he, the swing and the tree went out. Only his ears were left. They lay side by side, resting on a few blades of damp grass like twin fakirs reclining on a bed of nails. His left ear listened to the tramping of the booted feet of a millipede marching over the surface of the ground. His right ear focused on the sound of the bi-plane's radial motor changing pitch as it plummeted to earth. One ear heard it getting closer. The other ear was distracted by the sound of Grandma's console radio playing in the distance. Vaughn Monroe was singing:

> *When the lights go on again all over the world,*
> *the boys are home again all over the world*
> *rain or snow is all that may fall from the skies above*
> *A kiss won't mean 'goodbye' but 'hello' to love.*

The singing faded and almost inaudibly an old mans voice whispered, "The difference between the right word and the almost right word is the difference between lightning and the lightning bug."

Startled, Artie's eyes opened hard. As vision slowly returned, Artie found himself slumped down in a broken swivel chair with a port list, his bearded chin resting on an unfamiliar barrel chest. His eyes skidded down his chest to an expansive stomach imprisoned by a red T-shirt covered with food stains and moth holes. Below the stomach, his eyes met a pair of unfamiliar hands resting on the computer keyboard sitting on his lap. They were covered with liver spots and were the proud parents of eight swollen knuckles and ten badly-trimmed fingernails. He raised his head to find himself looking through a pair of glasses. The sound of the Stearman's untrimmed radial motor sputtered inside his cerebral cortex then mercifully crashed into his brain pan as the fading Stearman bounced down the runway of his consciousness.

Slowly and painfully, the boy's mind leapt forward sixty-eight years as he came to grips with himself as an old man.

Often when Art fell asleep, he would find Artie waiting somewhere near. His dreams took him back, not by force, but by the will and wealth of boyhood well spent near the pepper tree, next to that small white house in the city of Bell California.

Fully awake, Art stretched his arms and yawned as he felt his ears and uncombed beard. Recalling his dream, he chuckled to himself and shook the cob webs out of his remaining strands of hair. He gulped some cold dusty coffee, swallowing a moth.

Taking in a deep, stuttering breath, he exhaled slowly then took up where he had left off.

"Let's see," he mumbled to himself, "there was a garden…" His old fingers followed his wrinkled thoughts back to the small blond boy who had once thrived on that swing near a garden.

CHAPTER 2

A Towhead In Eden

COME! COME WITH me! Let me take you to meet my friends from childhood; giants, gypsies, wizards, musicians, singers, dancers, poets, tellers of tall tales, god-fearing Grandmothers, funny little gnome-chasing dogs, and the hairy-kneed misbehaving boys that ran with them, and *oh*, the pigeon-toed precocious girls who tormented their hearts.

Yes, there were some who entered uninvited to wound me, but I was always safe next to the heroes who roamed there. Next to my pepper tree. Close to my Grandmothers Arms. My army conquered my fears, nursed my wounds, and their love made all things even.

I sit in front of this magic screen sipping old wine and chasing it with hot chocolate and gout medicine, but my crippled fingers and ancient heart are forgotten and I feel like a boy again. A young adventurer who cannot wait to replay part of his journey for you.

Come, remember with me when we were young and anything was possible. When promising skies were above and scabby knees were below.

Won't you join me there where your mind intersects with the corner of mine? There near Gage Avenue and Atlantic Boulevard in Los Angeles, California?

The most profoundly happy times from my boyhood were in the first house I remember living in. To this day, my heart goes to that spot, and often in my dreams I run towards that place. Those people who loved me and whom I loved so dearly. I can hear and feel and taste those all too few years as if they were yesterday.

My body was born Edward Arthur Spelman, August the 28th, 1938, in a house on Fishburn Avenue in Huntington Park California, one of Bell's neighboring cities, but my soul took some time to grow and was jump started and developed during those nine years at that house in Bell from 1939 to New Years day of 1948.

I lived there with Blanche Louella Brown, my maternal grandmother, Iris Brown Spelman, my mother, and my Uncle Harley Brown. Three of them. A Trinity. Papa Eudie,(a giant, whom you will soon meet), always spoke to me of what he called *The Law of Threes*, in which he claimed all important things in life happen in threes and were written into the sands of time as Trinities. He instructed me carefully in this, and I have been ever watchful for my relationship with threes throughout my life.

Another of the trinities was my Eden; our small white house, Uncle Harley's garage just behind it, and our large pepper tree out front.

Our lives were rich with love for each other. The house was full of song, laughter, mischief and music. Our nightly dinners together brought a treasure of sharing that in this modern age seems all but gone.

World War Two started and ended while we lived there, and we did what everyone else did during those years; we snuggled at night, tied our shoes in the morning and did the best we could in between. Bing Crosby was on the Radio and F.D.R. talked with us during his fireside chats. Often, I was allowed to smash the color dye into white lard giving it the color of butter, or if I was lucky, help knead the bread dough for Grandma. And there were always my chores.

My uncle Harley was my best friend. His brother Jimmy spanked me when I needed it, which was often, but also laughed at my silliness when I craved it, which was continuously. Their older brother, uncle Fuzzy drew the world for me in dazzling colors, opening my eyes to the arts. Uncle Paul, the oldest of Grandmother's four boys was a merchant marine sailor who told us tales of the mighty seas, and of a world at war. Tales of friends drowned or burned in oil-slicked fiery seas after being sunk by U-Boats. Tales of death.

It kept the problems at home in perspective.

Just across the street I had my own Giant story teller with mile wide shoulders I called my *Crows Nest,* and waiting outside our back screen door to play with me was Harley's puppy, Muggs McGinnis. What could be better than that? If this wasn't the biblical Eden Grandma Brown always talked about, what was?

Grandma's house had only one bedroom, my mother and grandmother shared the double bed and sometimes my aunt Veve, who was just six years older than I, slept on pillows at the foot of their bed. The house had a single bathroom a tiny kitchen, and the small front room doubled as a dining room. The entire house had well worn linoleum floors and one of my chores was to help keep them mopped.

The bathtub was my bed. I slept there when uncle Fuzzy wasn't visiting and when he was I bunked with Harley in his garage or scrunched down between my mother and grandma. Aunt Elza Jean (who we called Eddie), sometimes slept on the love seat in the front room. She often cried during the night, worrying about her husband, Carl, on his B-17 fighting somewhere over Germany. She would often come to the tub, drag me out to her makeshift bed on the love seat and spill tears down the back of my neck as she spooned me. Sometimes I would get to crying with her. When Grandma heard us sobbing I told her I was just helping Aunt Eddie cry. She would kiss us both then return to her bed, or sometimes she would go in the kitchen and make us hot chocolate and cinnamon toast and we would talk about the war. On a few occasions Muggs would be allowed to come inside the house and he would lay in a triple spoon snuggling next to us sobbing in sympathy. This always made us laugh. We loved Mugg's funny gentle nature, and we'd go to sleep smiling and thankful for each other and for this very special puppy.

Our home stood almost in the center of a four acre lot owned by the lumber yard next door, but we had the sole use of this property. Next to the house was a monster pepper tree, with a platform swing on it that was constructed by uncle Paul and Papa Eudie in 1936. It was big enough to hold eight adults and was suspended by four two inch diameter hemp ropes, one at each of its four corners.

In the summertime, or when the house was crowded, some of us bunked out there on the swing trying to see the stars through the tree's knurled limbs. The tree was beloved to my family. It had strong arms that held us all there singing and laughing or perhaps day dreaming.

According to Papa Eudie, that tree was near 170 years old when he and his wife Anna moved to Bell from Romania in 1932. Which meant that grand old tree was growing there as a sapling during the time of the American Revolution. Sometimes out on that swing I could hear the sounds of airplanes flying unseen high above me. Their voices were those of old friends and they made me feel safe and secure.

My life in that house was both joyous and painful, but I learned from those extremes, and in the end the residue of it is reborn within me once again made delicious. What I sometimes took for granted as a child I can now see was a tapestry of events so rich, that I can scarcely believe I was lucky enough to have lived through them, or in some cases, to have survived them at all.

CHAPTER 3

A Giant's Band of Angels

THE THEOCARIDES WERE our loveliest friends. They were all extraordinarily tall, stood ram rod straight, and though they towered over everyone they weren't the slightest bit self consciousness about themselves. Grandma Brown used to say that when you stood next to any of them you were in tall cotton, and when both our families were standing anywhere together, we knew how Lilliputians felt. She called their family 'The Giant and his Band of Angels'.

They were all strikingly good looking though everything about them was massive. Their hands and feet were twice the average size and all four of them had heads the size of large pumpkins placed upon tree stump like necks, and their intellect, generosity and sense of the ridiculous matched their magnificent scale.

The whole Theocarides family was wondrously out of place in the real world. I think sometimes they frightened people, but to us they seemed straight from the pages of a fairytale. The world must surely have seemed smaller to them, but they made our world feel much larger and richer. They invited us into their fairy tale, and I think we sometimes took for granted how stunning they truly were.

Eudie was a wealthy man by the standard of the day. He was the mortician and the proprietor of the Theo & Carides Mortuary as well as co-founder of the local savings and loan. He owned the Suekeetchers Drug Store and Soda Fountain caddy-corner to his bank and at least two other restaurants that my Grandma Brown supplied with her famous homemade pies and German noodles.

Mr. Theocarides was the most outrageous man I ever knew. He towered head and shoulders over everyone without exception. Uncle Jimmy used to say that "Eudocio Theocarides looked like a bank vault door with the bust of a Greek God sitting on top of it," and whenever this family walked together in public, my Grandmother said it was like watching a family of polar bears entering a toddler's tea social.

Eudie's wife, Anna, a Romanian woman raised in Greece, was taller than any man in my extended family. That means she had to have been at least six foot three in her bare feet, just an inch shorter than Stavros, the older of their two sons. Because of the Army's height limits, Stavros had just barely made his way into the U.S. Army Air Corps as a P-47 "Jugg" Thunderbolt pilot, one of the few fighter planes that could provide a bit more cockpit space for the larger pilots.

Duck, my Uncle Harley's best friend was the tallest of the Theocarides boys. His given name was Timoleon or Tim, but he was called Duck because by the time he was 14 years old he stood an imposing, six foot seven inches tall and constantly banged his head entering the plank door of Harleys Garage hideout. As a precaution, Harley painted a sign just above his hideout's door that read **DUCK!** and the name stuck.

Besides being the tallest, Duck was the smartest, best looking, most popular kid in Bell High school. He gained the respect of everyone who knew him, and most everyone loved him. Grandma Brown *adored* him (even if he *was* Greek Orthodox), and he in turn *revered* my old first Baptist Grandma as though she were Mother Mary herself. She had been best friends with his mother Anna for two decades and He and Harley were embraced by both families as brothers.

During our time in that house, Papa Eudie was a substitute father figure and mentor for all of us who were drawn to his story telling and, through his stories, to his wisdom, which was considerable.

Eudie loved music and a sucker for someone legitimately in need. On many occasions he paid destitute men for a song. He was also a superb musician himself; he sang Greek, Armenian and Romanian songs to us many times, often accompanying himself on the cimbalom or the duduk. He could speak a dozen languages and sang songs in each at our behest. I loved the sound and nuance of how those flavorful strange languages sounded as they took me into the worlds of powerful and profound ancient peoples.

Papa Eudie never tried to make anyone feel small, in fact we all felt bigger around him, and when any of us were unsure about something we went to him knowing that he would know the answer to most any question we could pose.

And an actor! When Eudie told a story he acted it out with great heart and passion so that you lived it through him. He portrayed each of his characters in minute detail on the panorama of his gigantic, expressive face and used a dozen different accents from strange foreign lands. His theater was so powerful that you could feel a tiger's whiskers brushing against your cheek; a spider crawling up your arm; the chill of a single snow crystal on your nose simply at his telling.

He told romantic stories to all my aunts which left them crying tears of joy and yearning. He knew little girls well and seemed to have a special love for them. Papa Eudie's peerless stories weren't always about light and laughter though. He also had the ability to terrify his audience. His horror stories were legendary. His wife Anna once said he could scare hell out of the devil and my uncle Fuzzy said some of his stories were on the verge of insanity. Eudie understood life and death well, and he could make you taste either at will. He had grown up during dozens of mini revolutions and upheavals in Greece, and had killed his first man when he was sixteen. He had witnessed the unimaginable insanity and cruelty of 1916 Turkey, and retaliated against it. He had seen every corner of evil. Members of his own family had been beaten to death, dismembered or tortured there. He knew the dynamic of light and shadows within the souls of men. During the time of our family he was a mortician, and dealt almost daily with the death side of life.

The only time I ever saw Grandmother mad at him was when he scared my Aunt Veve so badly she wet her pants. Veve was thirteen when Papa Eudie terrified her with a story about microscopic, flesh-eating winged worms. He called them Forlornicapedes and claimed each one had a hundred mouths, and each mouth a hundred razor sharp teeth. The Forlornicapedes, he said, hatched from eggs incubated in the pubic hair and sweaty armpits of another creature he called *Gnome Exemplumonious.* According to Papa's story the bugs would march single file on midnight walks from our big pepper tree, up the stoop steps, under the door, over the linoleum and straight into Veve's bedroom where they'd hide inside her favorite lipstick. Then, while she dozed or twittered away her precious time with pulp romance novels, the bugs crawled from the lipstick into her ears and ate her brains out. During the tale Papa Eudie screamed so horrifically and contorted his face so wretchedly, that Aunt Veve fled in terror, considerably damper for the experience. Afterward, Anna dragged Eudie inside our house and read him the riot act. To make amends, the big man brought his cimbalom and sang "When Irish Eyes are smiling." Grandma gave him a cuff across his head while Anna scowled at him from across the room. Eudie sat on Grandma's bench, the only chair in the house that could support his weight, and expressed his contrition with the devil in his eyes. Veve finally stood on her tip toes, put her arms around his big neck then kissed him on his cheek.

"You scared me Papa Eudie," she said.

"I know," he said, his dark eyes sparkling as he made spiders with his fingers and crawled up each of her arms and shoulders towards her ears. She ran off screaming and laughing and, of course, and Grandma walloped his big head yet again.

"Eudocio, you are a hopeless!" she said.

"The Gnome Exemplumonious made me do it," he said simply, hunching his massive shoulders.

"Oh my... Exmplo-who? Another tale?" Anna asked.

"Oh no," said Papa, leaning over toward where I had been eavesdropping, "it's something important I found out about the pepper tree and I need to tell Whisker about it, the whole world may depend on Artie."

"Hmmm," Anna said, "I'll just bet."

As far as I know, my Grandma Brown never listened to radio soap operas, and whenever she listened to music or the war news on the radio, even she was always knitting or crocheting; something to keep her hands busy. But when Papa told his stories, she set everything aside and leaned forward just a bit with her hands folded on her lap to listen attentively to his every word. Even though Papa was a very busy he always made time for us with his weekly hour of stories. I was a special case and enjoyed many unscheduled stories on his lap as well.

His weekly story telling hour usually concerned itself with two distinct creations. The first was a tale especially designed for Grandma Brown; a serialized story, "The Pie Lady, the Preacher and the Wordsmith." It was about a beautiful woman and a preacher man named Thaddeus who adored her. He was handsome as a fox, but flawed. A victim of the daemon rum. The woman couldn't resist his charms, but she couldn't fight his drinking or philandering either.

The beautiful woman in these stories had many romantic liaisons with the tragic preacher of course, and eventually they produced a beautiful child. Then, inevitably, he would leave her again, running to mistress rum, the Chautauqua tent, sinful flesh; into godlessness drunkenness and debauchery. What he did depended on his fancy and of course the whim of his storyteller, Papa Eudie as well.

Thaddeus would often return to his love, bringing her treasures from around the country. Sometimes they were hidden under chocolate imported from Europe, or perhaps tied inside a silk scarf. Sometimes he brought her a brown paper bag full of dollar bills to help her with their many children.

The tale of Thaddeus and his love was a not-so-veiled retelling of my grandfather Frank Brown and my Grandma with changed names and fanciful renderings, most of which my Grandpa Brown could never have lived up too.

Within this fictitious series, Eudocio introduced another real life character by the name of Wilcoxen O'Connor. During the 1940s, Wilcoxen was a reporter for our local newspaper The Bell Cudahay Farmers Journal. He was also smitten with my grandmother and used every excuse imaginable to get next to her. He was like a love starved puppy and flattered my grandma with flowers, candy and cards for every reason he could muster.

In Papa Eudie's stories Wilcoxen is the adversary of Thaddeus. In one story Papa Eudie even included a duel between Thaddeus and Wilcoxen fighting to the death or minor injury over my Grandmother by tossing Grandma's Pies at each other. Whenever Wilcoxen showed up in Eudie's stories it was sure to make my Grandma blush and fuss and gently smack Papa Eudie on his great head with her fly flap.

This was great sport for our families who teased her endlessly. Sometimes Papa would deliberately pause much to long in the middle of some exciting and important passage and Grandma always took the bait and gave in.

"Well for goodness sakes Eudocio! Then what happened? Darn your eyes," she would say.

Papa Eudie took every advantage to tease Grandmother and she couldn't wait for a week to pass for the tale's next installment.

Eudie's second story of the show was usually some nonsense he created on the wing often he could make stories I had read or heard a dozen times before completely new.

When he told Little Red Riding Hood, for example, he performed a delicate little dance on his tippy toes through the imaginary forest. He was so big that when his Little Red Riding Hood skipped across our floor ruffling her curls his head hit the ceiling of Grandmother's house and made the floor joists tremble while he sang an exquisitely composed song in a perfect. That ridiculous performance would leave me doubled over in laughter rolling on the linoleum.

Eudie was amazingly graceful and agile, but once during the telling of one of his animated stories he tripped and fell over Grandmothers wooden milk stool. He tumbled backwards out the front door onto the stoop, tearing off the front door, the screen and pulling most of the door jam out of the front wall.

Grandma Brown said, "Dear Lord I'm not sure this old house will survive another of Eudocio's stories"

Eudie was the greatest man I ever knew. He touched all the bases of my boyish dreams and longings.

Now you have met the Theocarides.

Later, you will meet a giant cat named Orange Pasha who wore a mouse named Iggy round his neck. Orange Pasha saved Papa Eudie from the electric chair.

But that's yet another story isn't it?

CHAPTER 4

The Gnome Exemplumonious

T HE IRASCIBLE GNOME Pie Exemplumonious was born one day on the lap of Eudocio Theocarides, I happened to be sitting there at the time and helped in the delivery.

One day Papa was telling me some absurdity in preparation for one of his tall tales when suddenly he switched gears and whispered, "Beware."

I looked up and caught a small, wry grin on his face, but his eyes were most serious.

"What?" I said, struggling to hear him.

Again he whispered, "Artie, beware of the *Gnome Exemplumonious!*" This time his voice was audible but only barely. I looked into his face and he said nothing but his lips moved.

"*Beware,*" he mouthed.

After a considerable pause he continued. "Artie, the Gnome lives for centuries at a time within the roots or trunks of trees. God invented him and put him in the Garden of Adam and Eve as their house boy, his duties there were to shine their apples and wash and iron their fig leaves. He also had to de-fang serpents, bring the two lovers grapes and food, and pour their ouzo and such like that"

I hung on his every word. I had no idea what a Gnome was, but his voice was mysterious and serious and I felt as though I was in the presence of privileged and confidential knowledge.

I'll bet Harley or Grandma did know this stuff, I thought to myself proudly. *I'll bet there is a Trinity coming soon I thought.* I took a breath and waited.

Papa Eudie continued in a quiet voice, "You see Artie, since Adam and Eve got kicked out of heaven for eating wormy apples, God fired the gnome as well and from then on why he could only live inside the trunks of certain trees and could only stay outside of his tree for precisely three hours, thirty three minutes and three seconds. As you can imagine this poses a problem when the tree that was formerly his home gets old and dies. Then what is he to do?"

I scrunched up my shoulders and thought about it some with the palms of my hands facing upwards. "Gosh, I don't know Papa," I said, wide-eyed, "Tell me."

Papa Eudie slowly looked around the room, worriedly squinting to see if anyone was listening or observing us from some shadowy corner. When he felt it safe he whispered to me in secretive tones "Artie, that very gnome is living right outside in your big pepper tree."

"What?!" I asked excitedly.

He checked the room once again for a malevolent who might overhear, and then he said softly, "That Gnome lives in the big pepper tree right next to your house."

Papa gave me the mix-nicks and then the shush sign too keep mum, and I looked suspiciously around the room as well. All looked clear to me.

"He does?" I said, amazed and enjoying my new special knowledge.

"Yes sir. He has been there since that big tree was a sapling, during the time of the American Revolution."

"Wait, wait, Papa! What's a gnome look like?"

"Well Whisker, I guess you could say he is considerably smaller than me, and ever-so-much larger than you. He has green and orange skin, and three fingers on each hand with an extra thumb for shooting marbles. He walks with a slight limp and his ass cheeks squeak with a whistle when he walks or runs. You see Artie, that's how I happened to discovered him. One day Anna and I were out on the big swing smooching and as I was giving the poor wretched woman my sugars we heard his arse squeak and then he giggled."

Papa paused and the corners of his mouth turned down. He twiddled his large thumbs and looked like a sad, petulant little boy about to cry. "Now there is a tragic story. You see, during our revolution the gnome--"

"Papa what was that evolution?" I interrupted, "And tell me 'bout the sad story too, o.k.?"

"The revolution was during the time of General George Washington, the greatest man in American history. You see, Artie, before the gnome came here to Bell, he lived in an elm tree clear across the United States in a city named Boston."

"Really? Well what did he do that for and how'd he get here?" I asked.

"Well Whisker, now that's just what I am about to tell you. The Gnome was full of mischief, because you see, in cosmological years he was around one hundred and forty four thousand years old and in Gnome-years that's about same age as you. And, just like you, he sometimes strayed ever so far away from the safety his tree home. On one such occasion he threw an apple at General George Washington just to test the commander's mettle. Now Pie was one of the best apple throwers there ever was, having thrown all those apples in the Garden of Eden and he could knock the bullocks off a flea at a hundred yards in the dark. But guess what Artie? General Washington while on horseback caught it one-handed, took a bite then tossed it back at the gnome while riding his horse at a full gallop. He hit the gnome in the hip which winning the creature's infinite respect but, ever so sadly, injuring his left hip and leg permanently.

"Now you know Artie, before that Gnome Pie could run like the wind. In fact, he can still run so fast it's almost impossible to see him, but since old George thumped him on his arse with that apple he has a bit of a limp. That's what makes his butt cheeks whistle a bit when he skips and such, and if you listen carefully you can sometimes hear his three toned cheek squeak whenever he approaches. Especially if he is in a happy mood.

"He is very sensitive about that you know, and tries always to remain grumpy or unhappy just 'cause for some strange reason that helps to keep his buttocks quieted down a bit. He even had a special shoe made, with a thick sole that lifted his left hip up just enough and his arse quieted down considerably. Unfortunately, it still squeaks and sometimes at the most inopportune times. But with every bad thing comes some good thing and so guess what, Whisker?"

"What Papa?" I asked.

"Well," Papa said, "that special shoe old Ben Franklin made for him made him really sneaky and if he walked on it just right no one could hear him creeping up on them. He became one of the best creeper sneakers anyone had ever heard of, but if he forgot himself and got too happy again his arse whistles still broke out and made people nervous."

"Really?" I gasped taking it all in. "Bet that Gnome is a good sneaker upper!"

Papa nodded his mammoth head, "Yes sir, little Whisker he is a hell of a sneaker alright. There was none better anywhere in Boston and guess what else he did?"

"What Papa?" I asked wide eyed.

"Well Artie, that Gnome helped us all win our nations freedom. You see we were at war with the English just like we are now with Germany, Italy and Japan because we wanted our very own country and so we had to fight to get our freedom just like we do now. And it was our very own Pie Exemplumonious that inadvertently helped us win that war all those years ago to become a free nation."

"What does enrevertontly mean?"

"Inadvertently means by accident or not on purpose."

Inadvertently. I saved that word for a later date to tell Grandma Brown and possibly torment all my Aunts with.

"You see Artie," Papa continued. "Quite by chance the Gnome drank a large quantity of the British Tea supply. Then he used his sneaky foot, crept up on those Brits and pissed directly into their Rum ration."

I giggled so hard thinking about that that my stomach ached. When my tears of laughter cleared I said, "Gosh, that wasn't very nice was it Papa?"

"Goodness no," Papa answered, "but sometimes it takes some naughtiness to win over tyranny. You know what? I wish someone would piss in Hitler's schnapps right now."

I was still tickled and hardly able to catch my breath. "What else did the gnome do Papa?"

"Well sir," Eudie said. "I only heard tell of part of it, mind you, but it was said that he pooped in the Brits gun powder then soaked their hard tack in axel grease and alum."

I could not breathe and doubled over laughing on Papas lap which got Papa started laughing too. Anna came in from the kitchen and found Papa and I both hysterical. She was infected and joined in our laughter. "Eudocio, whatever in this world are you doing to this poor child?" she asked.

"Darling," he said. "I am glad you are here; sit down with us, while I finish my historical story."

She sat down next to her husband and held his hand. I excused myself, telling them I had to run and tinkleate. I ran as fast as my legs would carry and returned within seconds, wondering as I sat down on Papa's lap if I had raised the toilet seat or flushed the toilet or made a mess of their floor tiles. Very casually I glanced down to my fly to see if I had wet on myself and was pleased to find that I had not, but my pants were unzipped so I reached down and zipped them up as casually as possible. Papa winked at Anna then restarted the tale:

"Now let's see Artie," Papa Eudie said. "Where was I? Oh yes… when the Gnome's tree dies it can be dangerous as you can well imagine. Three hours and thirty-three minutes and three seconds is not enough time for a crippled Gnome with an ass whistle, even a fast one, to run from Boston City to Bell California. What if he died out there in Indianapolis, Indiana or the Colorado Rockies in mid-sprint?

"You see Artie at that time Exemplumonious lived in an old elm tree that was called the Liberty Tree and his best friend was an immortal

French skunk named Mouffette Superbe de Pew, but the Gnome just called him Muffy. The Gnome and Muffy were the two best Bezique Players in the new world at that time--"

"What's 'Bezique' Papa?"

He looked at Anna's amused face and then to my confused curious one. "Well it is kind of the forefather of Pinochle. You know, like Duck and Harley play all the time? Anyway, Artie, the king of the Englishmen put a tax on all paper goods coming to us from England which included taxes on playing cards.

"The Gnome and Muffy were not particularly patriots, why hell as far as that goes they liked the English as well as they did most, and they liked the Irish and Scottish better than everyone. But, they didn't like that old tax on those Pinochle cards at all and it really ticked them off so they joined up with the *Sons of Liberty* and their rebellious ways were directly responsible for the British cutting down their home inside that Liberty Tree. But they cooked their own gooses in the process because, that left the Gnome homeless and running out of time and well, he near died."

"How come Papa?" I asked.

Papa looked to Anna as though amazed that I didn't know the simple why of it and said, "You see Whisker, legend has it that the one and only way that Gnome could change homes from tree to tree was if a Towheaded boy child between the ages of 3 and 33 with a very vivid imagination closed his eyes and envisioned three paper boats powered by butterfly wings blown to their new location by the breath of that specially qualified boy's imagination and laughter."

"How did they find that special boy Papa and what qualifications did he need?" I asked having only the faintest idea of exactly what the word qualification meant.

"I'm glad you asked that" Papa said. "Well sir, by shear coincidence (or serendipity or divine intervention) during an argument between Thomas Jefferson and Alexander Hamilton it was disclosed that there was a tow-headed colonial boy by the name of Nathan Picklestock Breitbart, who was the son of Lilly Breitbart. He was just the ticket and they demanded he be summoned for the transfer vision for the Gnome and Muffy De Pew. However, Whisker, there where some problems."

"What kind of problems Papa?" I asked concerned.

"Well Artie, remember the triad! Always remember the triad! There were three things required for the transfer. First, a towhead with a great imagination who was full of laughter and fun, then according to the legend the boy must have a mother named after a flower. Nathan's mother's name was Lilly, which would work, but the third thing they needed was a boatswain's pipe and Nathan didn't have a boatswain's pipe and didn't know where to get one."

"Then what did he do Papa?" I asked.

"Well sir, now Nathan was a savant about ships and such, just like you are about airplanes and the sound of motors, so in the stealth of night and with the help of Pie's sneaky foot he and Pie snuck on board the HMS Peanut Butter and Jelly, one of Lord Sandwiche's newest ships. While Exemplumonious stood guard Nathan stole a boatswain's pipe from round the neck of the drunken old chief boatswain of the PBJ and that was that! Slick as a frog's heinie the trinity was complete. Of course, Exemplumonious had only scant minutes left for the transfer but, as we know, they made it and your pepper now houses that *very* Gnome.

I was captivated utterly.

"Oh yes and one more thing!" Papa said. "The captain of the imagined paper boats must be a French skunk!"

I started to giggle again and pleaded with him to stop it. "Oh Papa, you're so crazy, you're joking me right? You just keep adding more and more stuff. Are you sure that's all Papa?"

"Yep that's the list! Well, wait, there is just that one more thing. The boy must be able to produce three differently pitched toots, a little trinity in homage to the Gnome. So the boy must have a musical ear, a rhythmic arse with great tonality and at least a three note range of flatulence."

"Does that mean farting?" I ask Papa a bit unsure. Papa Nodded sagely.

"Now Artie, we have a few years left yet but Anna tossed the Tarot and read that your pepper tree is in danger and that the Gnome

Exemplumonious will need a new home sometime between now and the end of 1947. So perhaps we can figure who should be on guard to help him make the transfer when that happens. Do you have any suggestions, Whisker?"

We all sat their silently thinking who that boy might be. After about ten minutes, Eudie ask Anna and me if we had any ideas on the subject. I shrugged and Anna said, "Let me cut us all a piece of mince meat pie with a glass of milk while we think it over."

Anna left to retrieve the treats and soon returned. We ate together and pondered this important lifesaving and historic issue. Suddenly, my mind leapt forward to something that had just dawned on me. "Papa," I said, "Guess what? My mother's name is Iris, isn't that a flowers name? And guess what Anna? I know all about boats and dreams and laughter and I can practice farting in three different tones, and maybe if I stick a Kazoo in my arse I could sneak in those three tones pretty good huh?"

Papa could scarcely hold back a guffaw and, still trying to hold himself together, he said to Anna, "Well necessity is the mother of invention isn't it dear."

"Well guess what Papa? Guess what Anna?" I continued, excitedly. "I'm a Towhead. I'm like Nathan from the Revulsion war."

Papa sat down his milk in mid-gulp, slapped his knee and exclaimed, "Why, I would never have thought of that it might be you Artie! Would you have guessed that Mama?"

"Why my no, never in a million years," Anna answered.

"Yep. I'm your man" I said.

Papa smiled broadly then wrinkled his brow a bit concerned. "Well Whisker, we might have one small problem."

"What Papa? What?"

Well, he said, "You also don't have a boatswain's pipe."

"Oh yeah, I forgot." I said.

Papa smiled wryly, "But I *just happen* to have one here right in my pocket that was earmarked for you." He took a red velvet case out of his pocked and inside was the strangest little whistle I had ever seen.

Eudie said that now I was fully equipped and we should all remain on high alert and that I should always be on guard because the Gnome and Muffy's life depended on it.

When we weren't around Papa's mischief, we made our own. Harley, my cousin Walter Crawford and I oft times whiled away the hours lying on our backs on the big swing looking up at the sky through the branches of the big pepper while searching for evidence of Exemplumonious the Gnome.

This story and variations of it went on for years among the families and we were willing to accept most any evidence of the Gnome's presence there no matter how microscopically small. We sometimes saw the blur of something orange and green whisk by, or jump from limb to limb out of sight almost before it came into view. This impressed us to no end and all of us swore we heard his arse whistle. Further evidence was that once in the middle of the night Muffy sprayed Muggs McGinnis directly into the eyes.

"So there's your evidence," Harley quipped.

CHAPTER 5

Cauchemar

INGERSOL-RAND! NOTHING WAS ever as frightening as that black iron, rubber shoed horror. Nothing could evoke such churning desperation, such a gut wrenching feeling of hopelessness; no Frankenstein's monster, no werewolf, no movie creature ever matched the absolute terror of that deathly machine. I knew it waited to devour my small bones and burn my flesh, and I was terrified.

I was just five years old I had been abandoned in my dirty underwear in the middle of some unknown street, injured and running from someone. The street was dark and dusty but the air seemed moist and drizzled with evil and the deep, friendless night was darker still. No sky. No stars or moon. Only Blackness.

Sadness hung over my small bones like a heavy, piss soaked wool blanket. My mind was devoid of the memory of a single smile or loving face. I knew my heart had been broken, but I remembered nothing else. Nothing existed for me but despair.

Something malevolent was after me. I could not see it but I knew it was there. Lurking. Watching me with heartless, yellow, sticky eyes. I moved toward a sputtering filament within the bulb of a single street lamp, and cried out weakly for someone's help. Nothing responded.

Nothing stirred anywhere, only mind numbing echoes. The sound of my ragged breathing and my bare feet slapping the muddy, wet asphalt as I ran toward merged with a distant sound:

bleat... bleat... bleat...

It was overwhelming.

My bladder spilled into my shorts and urine ran down my leg, burning the welts on my skin. Humiliation combined with terror. I stood in the road frozen, wanting desperately to cover my shame. Wanting to run. But my legs trembled, refusing to carry me.

bleat... bleat... bleat...

I did not know what the sound was, but it sounded like screaming to my ears.

I recognized none of the strange, unfriendly houses. There wasn't a light shining in any window, but I felt something malevolent peering out just behind the blinds in the house to my right. Finally, I coaxed my legs to move slowly toward the flickering street lamp. Eventually I stood in the dim light, and I saw the source of the noise: a frightening mechanical beast with one wheel on the curb that sent shivers up my spine. Dark and heavy, with a great appetite for small, disobedient boys. No doors or windows. No steering wheel. No driver within. The terrible sound of that bleating coming from somewhere inside the beast like a plea.

bleat... bleat... bleat...

I tried to escape from it but it sucked me in like a riptide. I did not have the strength to run or resist it. Instead, against my will I moved closer to it. Shaking, my thin little arms reached with outstretched hands for it without my permission. I touched it, and it was cold to the touch, and vibrated menacingly, like a low growl. I moved closer trying to hide myself from the cruel peering eyes behind those window blinds, and tried to listen to the mewling within. As I listened, the sound changed.

t...r...e...a...eye
bleat... bleat... bleat
eye...r...e...a...t...
bleat... bleat... bleat...

It wasn't a human voice but a spitting, gurgling whisper. The letters sounded clearly, but jumbled themselves inside my head as I tried to make sense of them. I began to sob, wanting it all to stop and for someone to find me and take me home. I wanted to lie in someone's loving arms, but no one came. The large metal box moved almost imperceptibly closer toward me and I felt it was ready to spring.

bleat... bleat... bleat...

A small yellow light began to blink on it's side as it bleated, then I heard the voice from within it say;

"T...r...e...a...eye..."
bleat... bleat... bleat...
"A-are-tea-eye-ee"
bleat... bleat... bleat...

"Arrrtieeee... Artieee! Artie! wake up! You've wet the bed!"
It was my Grandmother's voice.
She helped me out of bed, and I could smell the pungent aroma of warm urine rising off the mattress. Mother staggered out on the other side of the bed smelling of whiskey. Her eyes were red, and tear-streaked mascara ran down her puffy cheeks. Someone had slapped her face hard enough to leave finger marks on her swollen cheek. Veve got off her cushions at the foot of the bed and stood by the window. I pulled off my wet pajamas and shorts and ran into the closet throwing them

on the floor on top of my mother's shoes and sat my naked, ashamed, burning body down on the cushion I had just made for myself, partially closing the door behind me. I peered out as the three women flipped the mattress and changed the bed sheets. The sliver of light from the bedroom shone on the remnants of broken wooden coat hangers on the closet floor next to me. The memory of my mothers beating came flooding back to me, and I felt the welts on my chest, arms, and legs. Mother had come in from a date, caught me jumping on the bed, and the beating ensued as it always did when she drank and was unhappy. She went through every single one of the supply of wooden hangers.

As they worked on the bed, I heard Grandmother talking to my mother, angrily reproaching her in no uncertain terms for her drunken disgraceful beating.

"What else did you expect Iris?" she said.

I didn't understand it all, but Grandmother was clearly not happy with her daughter. Veve ran my bathwater and bathed me like a loving older sister. Before long I was in new dry underwear, PJs, and out into the garage snuggling with Muggs and Uncle Harley in his loft bed. I told Harley about my dream and at first he said nothing. I knew he was seething. Every time I had wet my bed in the past it had come from a similar incident. But pretty soon he got me laughing, and I felt safe and loved once again. He explained to me that the thing with wheels that had so frightened me in my dream was an Ingersol Rand construction trailer. Probably a generator or an air compressor. It was just a machine he assured me, adding that once when he was a very little boy just like me, that those same trailers scared the bejesus out of him too.

"But I have something special to help cure your fear of it forever. Something magic. Something that very few people know about." he said.

He Jumped down from the loft bed and retrieved a large fist sized chunk of smooth, cold, shiny black tar.

"I got this from Wilford Dobbit, a construction worker. Now this man knows near all there is to know about working on streets and machines and stuff. He told me that time back when I was afraid, that if you chew it--but don't swallow, just chew it then spit it out--he told me that chewing it could take away the power of those old trailers to frighten me. He said, 'Now Harley Brown, those tools won't never scare you ever again'," then Harley told me as an afterthought, "…and guess what fartster? It will also protect you from getting Juju Bees and other sticky things stuck to your teeth. Now just remember Artie, Wilford knows near everything about that stuff. Plus it's fun!"

"Really, Uncle Harley? No joke?" I asked.

"No Joke!" he said, "I have his word for it and after all… he works for the city!" Harley watched my reaction, then said seriously, "I wonder why they make those darn machines so frightening in the first place. It doesn't seem right does it Artie? Maybe Papa Eudie or mother should write a letter to someone and complain."

"Maybe!" I said, feeling worlds better.

I chewed on Harley's sage advice and on the mysteries of the tar. Harley chewed some with me that night and we spit it in a steel bucket when we were done. It tasted rubbery-clean and good. I felt safe and loved it there chewing away 'the evil' next to my snaggle-toothed poet.

I did get over my fear of those Ingersol Rand trailers, even though deep down I knew the cure was just a little love and a small chunk of black Tar. Although, those machinery monsters still show up in my dreams now and again, but I just wake up and take a mental chaw of street tar and smile at the memory of my Uncle Harley's love and his sweet mendacity.

CHAPTER 6

The Talisman

ANNA THREW THE Tarot. This flew in the face of all my Grandmother's Baptist proprieties but she vowed to love that portion of Anna which was loveable and ignored the rest.

Reverend Wall, on the other hand, claimed Papa and Anna were both Godless devils filling all our empty heads with silly stories and Ouija board mystical fairytales of dubious origin. He said Papa and Anna were both nothing but nickel and dime mystics spewing bargain basement rubbish from an ignorant catholic doctrine and that neither of them would ever enter the kingdom of heaven.

The Preacher also opined that something was not right with Papa Eudie. He said, "God must have made Eudocio that unnaturally large so that he could see him easier and thereby keep a close eye on him."

Mom Brown bristled at this assessment. The Theocarides, as far as she was concerned, may have been a bit flawed because they weren't Baptist, but they were her beloved and she stood by them. She told revered Wall, "God doesn't need glasses Mr. Wall! God sees things just fine."

Grandmother simply would not truck with meanness from anyone even him and she told him so. The good reverend Wall left the house in a huff and did not speak to Grandma or return again for a month.

According to Anna, Papa Eudie had second sight. I don't know about that, but I do know he did many amazing things and was a part of strange and unexplainable events which stayed with me over my lifetime. Some are still a mystery to me to this day. He was indeed in all ways a different sort of man, but most considered me the strangest of kids, so I think we were a perfect fit.

One unexplainable event involving Papa coincided with one of the ugliest events of my life.

One day, in the winter of 1944 as I sat on his lap listening to some crazy wonderful story, he stopped his in mid-sentence, his face changed, his gaze became introspective and his eyes seemed to change color.

He asked me, quite seriously, if I knew what a verbal talisman was. I was 6 years of age and did not recognize either of the two words. When I said I didn't know, he tried to explain.

"Artie," he said patiently, "there will be times in your life that you will be in harm's way. Put there, perhaps by people who have broken souls, or who have lost their moral compass, perhaps some who wish to harm you. Artie some in the world are sick and wish to infect you with their own sicknesses. They are evil."

I still didn't really fully understand why he was telling me, but he continued. "Perhaps one day, you will be far away from Papa and I won't be near to help you, so I want to give you something, something that in ancient times was called a Talisman. This can sometimes generate a special blessing or protection."

I thought immediately about the chunk of tar I always carried in my pocket and nodded.

"If you remember it, and listen to what Papa tells you, it can help bring you through danger, understand?" he asked.

"Yes Papa," I said in wonderment. I was fascinated but still quite unsure, waiting and trying to understand as best I could.

Papa Eudie continued, "If you ever feel in great danger, as though something or someone is about to harm you, run from those devils as fast as your legs will carry you and as you are running you must say this talisman three times to yourself. The words are *Oculi sub umbra alarum tuarum proteges me.* Remember now little Whisker you must say it three times."

"A trinity right, Papa?" I asked.

"That's right Artie. Always the trinity," Papa answered.

Then he had me practice it, slowly going over and over its pronunciation until I had it memorized correctly. I repeated it perfectly several times before he was satisfied. Papa seemed to be relieved as though a great weight was off his shoulders and he put his arm around me hugging me and kissed me on the top of my head. "Good job, Artie," he said.

Then he gave me a large red grape inside a tablespoon of ouzo. I swallowed it and he made a benediction, the sign of the cross starting in the middle of my forehead down to my chin then cheek to cheek with his thumb. He said something in Greek and then, "Receive this blessing in the name of the Father, the Son, and the Holy Spirit. Remember Artie, three times. Always remember what Papa told you about the trinity of things. "

"Papa, if I say that those words what will it do?" I asked.

"It will make you invisible to the eyes of evil for a short time and you will not exist to them for a while."

"But Papa," I said, "what if that doesn't work?"

"Do you doubt your Papa Eudie?" he asked, smiling down at me warmly.

"No Papa," I said contritely, hunching my shoulders and looking sheepish, "but I'm just saying--just in case."

"Whisker, if it doesn't work scream at the top of your lungs and yell bread, butter, shit, jam! Make a sandwich if you can! as loudly as you can and then kick the bastard square in his nuts as hard as you can, three times if possible, and run like the wind to the first person you can find to help you!"

"Aw Papa, you're joking me right? Reeeally?"

"Really." he answered.

"Papa" I asked, "why three? Why is everything three?"

"I will explain more when you're older, but for now just remember what I have always told you. Anything of importance in your life should be measured in threes. It is a special number throughout the world of religion and philosophy. You know about the Father, the Son, and the Holy Spirit, right?"

"Yes, from Grandma," I answered.

"Well how many is that?" he asked.

I counted and held up three fingers.

"Now between say, a Mama, a Papa, a child, how many is that?" He asked.

"Three," I said again.

Papa smiled approvingly, "What about Gnome Pie, where do you suppose his threes would be? Remember Whisker, look for threes in everything."

I thought about his question for a while and said, "Gosh Papa, I'm not sure but could it be, his own self and Muffy and the Pepper Tree?"

"Could be," Papa said with a broad smile, "not a bad guess at all. Always look for those threes and think about them, then come tell Papa what you found, and your ideas about what they might mean, will you?"

"Okay Papa, I will," I said.

I thought about threes a lot, three even took the place of nine as my favorite number. I had learned many times over not to doubt Eudie, and felt a bit ashamed about challenging him with my what ifs. In any case within a few days I had the opportunity test the talisman he'd taught me.

I had turned six in August; and the test took place a few weeks before Christmas of 1944. I had squirreled away a token stolen from my mother's purse and decided to take the yellow street car into Huntington Park, about four miles away, to look in the windows full of Christmas toys and talk to all the people on the sidewalk. I didn't bother to tell anyone where I was going nor how long I might be.

That was common for me. I was forever running the streets and being brought home by a truant officer or the police for being way too young to be out alone or after curfew. I wasn't a thief, and I didn't have a delinquent's reputation. My crime was that I loved to talk with everyone, look at everything in detail, and try to figure the world out by eavesdropping on the conversations of strangers.

On the street car, I spoke to every single person I could, going from empty seat to empty seat and asking way too many personal questions. I am sure I was really cute for about three minutes, and then most people could not wait to get rid of me. In fact, some just ignored me from the start.

When I arrived in Huntington Park, I sat on every bus bench and looked in every storefront window. I picked up aluminum foil from dozens of discarded cigarette packages, folded them into little silver paper boats and looked for gutter water rivers to send them on their journey. Some times as they floated away, I saluted them by creating my kazoo sounds out the side of my mouth to the tune of taps. I always kept a half dozen of those tiny aluminum foil boats in each pocket as possible gifts for anyone who would engage me in conversation.

Soon it was night time. It was cold and a drizzle was turning into a light rain. I stood shivering and damp in the painted loading zone area next to the streetcar tracks in the middle of the main street of Huntington Park waiting along with a few shoppers for the street car to return home. Then I realized that I had no return fare. I got a sick feeling in my stomach and was mad at myself for not thinking about a way to get home. I put my hands in my pockets and tried to look casual as I watched everyone else get on the trolley bound for Bell. I was going to have to walk and would be another couple hours late getting home.

As I stood there all alone, fidgeting to keep my hands warm, a car pulled up. It stopped in front of me and the driver leaned across to the passenger window rolled it down. "Would you like a ride," he said. "Aren't you cold?"

Grandma had admonished me about riding with strangers, but I was never really quite sure why I wasn't supposed to accept a ride. Still, I kept her words in mind when I replied to the stranger. "No thank you," I said. "I just live a few blocks away. I can walk."

The man drove off and turned at the corner while I crossed out of the loading zone over to Gage Avenue. I began walking in the direction of my home. I walked leaning forward and with my head down at a brisk stride to keep warm. Then the same car pulled up beside me once again and the man said, "Little boy, what are you doing out here all alone? Does your mother know where you are?"

"Yes," I said trying not to make eye contact. "She knows."

I looked straight ahead, walking on as the man drove slowly alongside of me.

"Well listen," he said. "It's getting late and starting to rain hard. You look like you are freezing cold, get in and I'll give you a ride to warm you up okay?"

At that second it started to pour and the man opened the passenger door, pushed it open and patted the passenger seat. It was a good long walk home and I was cold and hungry, so I jumped up on the seat and shut the door after me.

The man was dressed in a suit and tie, with combed back hair and wire rimmed glasses. I noticed that his left and right eye were different colors and that he had a chunk the size of a small button cut out of his right nostril. He did not smile much and seemed fidgety. That made me uneasy, so I started my Artie quest for knowledge thru communication.

"My name is Artie, what is your name?" I asked.

He didn't answer right away but within a few blocks he finally said, "Here, sit over here just next to me in the center of the seat, it's warmer over here." He motioned me over and I scooted over toward him a bit more happy to feel the warm air blowing out of the little heater in the middle of the floorboard.

After a while he said, "Move over just a little closer, because I have to shift and your knees block my shifting gear."

He demonstrated his supposed problem by putting the floor shifter into neutral, then up in to second. I considered what he said and must have looked doubtful because he said, "Nunyur, my name is Nunyur."

His being conversational disarmed me and I became more relaxed and moved a little closer.

"Artie," I said once again, "My name is Artie Spelman. I am six years old."

Reaching in my pocket I pulled out one of my Aluminum foil boats and handed it to him.

"I made this myself," I said. "You can have it." Then I asked, "What's your other name?"

"Bennis," the man said after a pause. "My name is Nunyur Bennis." He tossed my little boat on the floorboard by his feet.

"Oh," I said, wondering why he hadn't liked my boat. "Do you live near here?"

"No I live very far away."

"I live near the Alcazar Theater," I said.

Suddenly he shifted into high gear, bringing his gearshift down directly between my knees and pushing my legs apart. Then, his right hand came off the shifting knob, palming me between my legs and directly into my crotch.

I didn't know what to do. I sat paralyzed and scared to death. I looked out the window, just numbly ignoring it and holding my breath, pretending nothing was happening and not daring to move.

He began rubbing my thigh.

Nothing like this had ever happened before and I didn't know a great deal about this variety of human behavior. I knew men had testicles and that it hurt when they were hit there, and I did have the vague idea that no one else was supposed to mess with me there, but that was the sum-total of my knowledge on the subject.

I searched within my arsenal of Artie knowledge to its deepest core and could recall just two events related to my genitals at all. Once I was trying to balance a penny on the end of my 'peter' to act as a base plate to see if I could then stand one of my tin soldiers on the balanced flat penny. This was a balancing act that required considerable skill I thought. My grandma walked in and asked;

"Are you working on an act Artie, are you off to join the Circus or something?"

"Nooo," I said as the tin soldier plopped off, "it's a penny perch into sudsy seas."

"Perhaps you will go far with that act." She left the bathroom smiling.

The second time she caught me flicking my penis with my spring loaded thumb held middle finger of my right hand as if I were shooting marbles. I delighted as my little member sprung back and forth at each flick as it stuck above the surface of the water like the periscope of a submarine. I made the *Pah-Que! Pah-Que!* Rifle report sound as I flipped it a couple of last practice times.

"Artie if you play with Peter too much he might turn purple and break off. I think it's best for now just use him to peepee."

I considered that briefly, but flicked it a couple more times just so I would remember how I had done it for future reference.

I snapped back from my memories when Mr. Bennis squeezed my thigh hard enough that it was starting to hurt and held me right next to him. I couldn't move or slide even an inch toward my door. "Be still," he said. "I'll take you home to meet my sister. She has toys and ice cream."

I was terrified but I had walked or ridden this route dozens of times, and at a glance, I knew I was about half way home. With both hands, I pushed the car's shifting lever straight up as hard as I could. The gears grinded badly and the car lurched and stalled, distracting the stranger.

As he braked and clutched, I slid to the passenger door as fast as I could. He grabbed my left wrist and held me hard, hurting me so I bit his fingers so hard it drew blood. He pulled his hand back and I bit him again, harder, and felt the bones in his hand crush between my teeth. He screamed and swore to kill me but he released his grip on my wrist. I jumped out the door, with the car still rolling a bit and landed face down on my knees and palms. I jumped up then ran in a low crouch to the back of his car and squatted down behind it out of his sight.

I looked around, pondering my situation and saw the familiar space between the Five & Dime and the old State Theater. The two buildings did not have a common wall which created a pathway between them that was just wide enough for a small animal or small boy to squeeze through. I quickly squeezed through it sideways.

In a flash the man was out of his car after me but the opening was too small for him to squeeze through. As I got to the end of the squeeze-way into the alley behind the buildings, I caught a glimpse of him walking away, and could hear him cussing. I ran down the alley as fast as I could and crashed headlong into an Ingersoll-Rand air compressing monster.

I fell flat on my face and cut my shin wide open on its trailer hitch and screamed in pain. Eventually I gathered myself and continued to run down the alley.

"Oculi sub umbra, Ah, crap!" I said to myself, "Er, ah, unbra, tuarum..." I couldn't remember Eudie's words. My memory was failing me as adrenaline ate those special words out of my brain, faster than a frog swallows flies. Eudie had failed to mention that when the devil was chasing me I would be scared to death, and find it difficult to remember Latin. I just needed to get home!

I saw the back door of an above-garage apartment that faced the alley and then ran to its wooden stoop. I banged on the glass of the door with one hand while leaning on the buzzer with the other. I could hear the sad little bleat of the buzzer within the house and it reminded me of the *bleat... bleat... bleat...* of my Ingersol nightmare. I buzzed again but nothing stirred inside the house.

Then the last of the Talisman rang in my frazzled brain "Proteges me!" I said.

I said to out loud to myself out loud. protégés me. I knew that part meant protect me. Papa Eudie had told me that much.

As I turned on the stoop to continue my escape I saw the beams of headlights a block up on the intersecting street approaching the alley going north. I knew it was him, Mr. Bennis, and when he turned to the right in my alley to go east his headlights would shine directly onto me running away down the alley. He would be on top of me within seconds.

I jumped off the three steps and ran headlong into several empty aluminum trash cans, without thinking I jumped into one and pulled its lid into place over my head. I heard the motor as the car came my way and suddenly I remembered the entire talisman. "Oculi sub umbra alarum tuarum proteges me," I said and then repeated it twice more to make the trinity.

Oculi sub umbra alarum tuarum proteges me.
Oculi sub umbra alarum tuarum proteges me.

Closer and closer the car came and I held my breath, shut my eyes and waited. I pulled the piece of the tar from my pocket to chew on but I dropped it. It bounced off the side of the barrel and hit the bottom between my legs. To me, it sounded like a hand grenade. I thought I was cooked.

All my senses were heightened as I heard the car slowly coming my way. Its tires crushing the gravel

I could smell the exhaust.

I crossed my fingers, closed my eyes, and took another deep breath trying not to move. I waited. Waited for my fate. I felt my heart's loud thumping inside my chest and wondered if the evil man outside could hear it pounding.

I didn't hear anything for what seemed like forever. Then I heard the car door open and click shut softly followed by slow footsteps. One step, two, three, coming closer. The lid of the trash can came off and I looked straight up into Mr. Bennis' pale, cold face. It wasn't three feet away from mine.

I looked right into his mismatched eyes as he looked down at me. *Straight down at me.*

I held my breath and waited, paralyzed. He squinted as though he were looking directly into the sun or into profound shadow and then he replaced the lid on my garbage can and walked away. I heard him get in his car, cussing and mumbling as he slammed its door and then he drove away.

I released my breath in a single large gasp. I stayed put in that barrel chewing my recovered chunk of tar for what must have been the better part of a half hour in case it was a trick and he was still out there somewhere waiting. Then I got out of the barrel, looked in both directions and bolted for home as fast as my legs would carry me.

CHAPTER 7

The Tribulations of Tonto

I DRAGGED MYSELF THROUGH the door about a quarter past eight. I was dirty, cold, wet and hungry with tar-stained teeth and the fiend's dried blood down my chin and shirt front. The first thing I saw was Grandma's tear-stained face. Muggs was on her lap and for the first time in memory he ignored me and looked away. My mother, still in her uniform from work at the drug store, stared at me lividly.

"Where have you been Artie? Tell me. Now... "

She was cold as ice.

I told.

The only thing I left out was my use of Eudie's talisman. I don't know why I left it out, maybe because I had no real idea how to explain it and I still wasn't sure what exactly had happened.

Grandma said nothing. Mom reached for me, then changed her mind and refolded her arms. I broke and ran to her with tears in my eyes, and she finally gave in just a bit and hugged me rather coldly. Grandma drew a hot bath for me and brought me some hot coco, but refused to give me anything to eat. As I sat soaking in the tub, Mom snuck a hard blueberry muffin into me saying, "Here is some hard tack sailor and this isn't over yet Mr. Spelman."

They sent me to bed in their bedroom.

Just after I awoke the next day, Harley bounded through the front door. Grandmother had sent him across the street to see Papa Eudie with a note. Harley went to Grandma and handed her Eudocio's response. She read it and said, "Artie, go over with Harley to see Papa Eudie and officer Stavros Zambetes. They want to talk with you. And Harley, don't forget to bring back a few of Anna's good strong switches for Jimmy. He's coming over later in the afternoon for Artie's ass warming."

As we walked across the street to Papa's, Harley said, "Artie, you're in the shaa-eat house now Tonto. Your little farty fanny is getting fried, and brother Jimmy Brown is the fry cook!"

Red-faced, I hit Harley on his arm as we walked in the door and then I ran as fast as I could for the safety of Eudie's lap, but in the middle of my sprint Anna snatched me up in her arms and bit me, almost painfully, on my ear and said, "Artie, you little whisker! Do you want to get yourself killed and break your Grandma's heart in half!?" Then she smothered me with her usual barrage of kisses, took me to Papa and set me on his lap.

Papa looked into my eyes, then looked me over, lifting me up and inspecting me closely, like he was inspecting an injured possum. There was no anger or disappointment in his face like those of my Brown inquisitors, only an expression of relief. He gave me a kiss on the forehead and then sat me down. Patting me on the fanny he said, "Go say hello to the Sergeant Zambo."

I knew Sergeant Zambo. He was Anna's brother, but unlike her, he spoke with such a heavy Greek accent that it was sometimes hard for me to understand. several times in the past he had sheparded Muggs and me home from the streets. He had a nice face that was round and kind, but his eyes were fierce and he was built like a bulldog. He was almost as wide as he was tall.

I walked over to the seated Sergeant Zambetes and offered my hand. "Hi, Officer Zambo "

He smiled broadly, shook my hand, and motioning for me to sit down close beside him said, "Artie, can you tell me what happened to you last night?"

I sat down and related the entire story in minute detail, just as I had to my family the night before, leaving out the part about my talisman. He listened carefully taking notes on a small note pad. When I told him the man's name, his eyes smiled as he looked to Eudie. "Nunyur Bennis, was his name?" he asked, making sure.

"Yes," I said.

Harley, listening from the corner laughed out loud and then put himself in check.

Then Zambo asked, "Do you know what's kinds ah car eet was?"

"It had four doors."

"Was it a Ford or a Chevrolet? What *kinds* ah car eet was?"

"I don't know exactly," I said, "but it was just like the Reverend Wall's car except Mr. Bennis's car was black not green. It was a six cylinder though. I can tell by the sound of its music, but only it misfired and I told him he needed a tune up during my ride"

Harley chimed in, "The Reverend owns a '37 Dodge Brothers Sedan six."

Zambo wrote that down on his pad then continued, "Artie when you was crowchink down behinds da car did you appens to notice da license playts?"

"Yes," I said.

"Do you ramamber da numbers?" he asked.

"Not all of 'em, but one of the numbers was a nine and I think there was a three also. I like nines and threes," I said and made a nine and then a three in the air with my forefinger.

"Did you notice 'nyting else Artie?" he asked.

"Well, the license plate had that metal thing with the star on top of it just like your funeral car Papa," I said looking at Eudie.

We all went out to the garage and stood behind Eudie's hearse and looked at the bracket on its plate. Mounted on top of the plate was a slide bracket that held a pot-metal round wreath with a five pointed star inside. It was the symbol indicating a chamber of commerce member.

"Artie, was there letters 'roun dat wreath like dis?" he said, pointing to Papas plates.

"Yes," I said.

"Whats color were dey do you ramamber?".

I thought for a moment then answered tentatively, "I think they were red."

Zambetes looked at Eudocio.

"Den eet have to be Cudahay, Sout' Gate, Bell, or Huntington Park. Dey are de only chambers dat have the red letters."

Eudie nodded his head in agreement, and Zambo scribbled on his pad.

"Can you tink of 'nyting else that appened?" Zambo asked.

"No, I don't remember anything else."

"Tank you Artie," Zambo said and offered his hand again.

I shook his hand, then reached into my front pocket, removed one of my little foil boats and handed it to him. "Here. You could have this Sergeant. I make them all by myself." I said proudly.

"Oh tank you," he said warmly, "Eats's ah leetle party hat right?"

"No," I said, "It's a boat. I gave one to Mr. Bennis, but he threw it on the floorboard."

Zambo wrote that down in his notepad then folded the little boat and tucked it inside. "Tanks you leetle Artie."

"You're welcome." I said.

I watched from my perch on Poppa's lap as Harley selected the four best sticks from a group of Anna's flower and vine braces, testing each one of them carefully for Uncle Jimmy's switches, Anna told us that the Theocarides would all be in Lake Arrowhead for Christmas with Zambo's family this year and that she would drop bye to see Mother Brown before they left. Eudie bent down and whispered to me, "Take it like a man, Artie, you deserve it little fart, but bear up. Be strong." Then he pinched my chin and winked at me. I loved that Papa thought me a man.

As we crossed the street, Harley shook the switches at me mockingly. "Guess what Tonto? Brother Jimmies gonna brand your silly little heinie!"

I punched him in the arm and he ran off ahead of me into our front yard.

"Catch me if you can little red ass," Harley taunted.

As I gave chase, he jumped up on the swing, leapt off the back side and escaped through the back door. He ran through the kitchen, into the front room and skidded to a stop in front of Grandma who was sitting in her rocker. He was laughing as he handed her the switches.

There was no smile on Grandmas face.

Uncle Jimmy showed up within the hour. Grandma Brown told him briefly some of the sordid details. I knew the drill and dropped my pants.

Uncle Jim said, "This is going to hurt me more than it does you"

"Bet it doesn't!" said Harley.

"Harley. Never you mind," Grandma scolded.

I glared at Harley.

Jimmy wasted no time blistering my little ass, raising three thick six inch long welts on the back of each leg just below my buttocks. I bit my lip but did not cry out, although it damn well hurt. I pulled up my pants, hitched up my suspenders, and ran for my Grandmother's arms. She did not embrace me but looked at me with moist serious eyes.

"Do you know why you were spanked?" she asked.

"Yes," I said, "because I left without telling anyone."

"That's right," she said. "You *know* you are not supposed to leave without telling someone where you have gone. You are just six years old Artie Spelman. You have *no business* that far away from home by yourself! Didn't you know that you must ask to do something like that? Didn't you know that we all would be worried sick about you? That fiend could have *killed you*, Artie!"

I scrunched my shoulders, "Yes," I said looking down at my shoes.

Grandma released a deep breath and said exasperatedly, "...And this isn't the first time Artie. Do you know that in the past the authorities have threatened to take you away from your mother?"

"No" I said, eyes brimming.

Grandma held me in front of her by my shoulders and looked directly into my eyes.

"You will learn, as you grow up, that you can behave any way you wish to. You can lie, steal, cheat and disobey. The truth is, no one can really stop you, Artie, but you will have to pay for your actions eventually. Sometimes you might only be a little hurt, but sometime you might have to pay with your life. That means you'd be dead and never see any of us again, and that we won't ever see you again. Is that what you want?" she asked.

"Dead?" I asked

"Yes, dead! It's not just old people who die you know. What is more, you will kill me too. Because I'll die from a broken heart for the loss of you. So remember little boy, you are not the only one who pays or suffers when you don't do as you *know* you should. We *all* pay when you misbehave and are hurt."

Tears filled her eyes. She put her knuckles to her lips and bit her lower lip then looking away from me she said, "Can you imagine how your mother, or Harley, or the girls would feel if something happened to you? Or that big old Greek across the street? Why it would break Papa Eudie's heart in half. How do you think he would feel, Artie Spelman, if he had to prepare your broken body and lift you into a casket with his own two hands? His stories would die because of your disobedience. Your actions affect us all Artie. *What you did just wasn't fair.*"

Now she had my attention.

I looked at my grandmother's bereft face. Her look of disappointment cut my heart out as surely as if her glance were a knife. I started to cry and my six year old brain even understood a bit. Harley had been listening carefully to Grandmother and was fighting to hold back his own tears. For the second time in a few minutes I felt *really* bad.

The whipping I wore proudly, dropping my trousers to show the welts to anyone who cared to see them and a good many who didn't. To those who showed great interest I gave a complete tour showing the gash from the Ingersol monster on my shin as an extra bonus. I showed Veve and Eddie several times, and several times they complained vociferously to Grandma Brown about it;

Arties, got his pants down again, showing everyone his welts Mama! Sometimes he forgets to wear his underwear!

Gosh Mom! Jeeze Louise, can't you control him?

Honestly Mom!

We know he is brave and all that but JEEZE Mama won't you tell him to give it a rest?

Honestly it's so embarrassing! Isn't there something you can do?

I even showed the postman and the iceman.

Grandma would scold me, and reluctantly my pants would come up. I waited longer in-between demonstrations for each subsequent victim, and eventually tapered off but was not able to quit entirely for quite some time.

I always loved cuts, scratches, injuries and all that. Bruises were priceless things to me. One time I asked Eudie why that was so and he told me that boys just are that way. He said *we wear bruises like badges of courage.* They were the signs of a man, he said, and that I was just growing up and could take it. After that talk I felt older, and some how taller.

As much as I loved my triad of welts, Jimmy had done a good enough job that I did not acquire a taste for more whippings. Plus the memory of Grandma's sad face was for me the cruelest cut of all and was a beating unto itself.

I did backslide several more times of course, but with each ass whopping as well as Mom Browns subsequent lectures, I felt an inch or so taller and loads wiser each time. My fanny was gaining useful knowledge by leaps and bounds as well because of its marvelous continuing education.

Sometime later, I talked with Papa about why I was proud of my welts from my Uncle Jimmy and yet ashamed by the marks from my mother's beatings when she drank. Papa said,

"Well, because one is from love and you deserved it and you knew you did. The other is from your mother's lack of understanding and misguided anger. Her beatings are from self-loathing. One has nothing to do with the other. I believe we all, boy or man, know the difference between *just* punishment and *undeserved* punishment. Every parent and every child knows when they have crossed the line, and that is why you wear your wounds differently. Know that those wounds from your mother are not your fault and you should never allow them to defeat or humiliate you, because life has a ways of wounding us all anyway and we must learn to recognize which of our wounds are of our own doing, and which *are not.* and not whine about them without understanding why. Do you understand?"

"I think. Papa, what is loathing?"

"That means your Mother doesn't like herself sometimes."

"I see," I said thinking hard about what he said.

"Your momma is a bear with a thorn in her paw, Whisker."

That image stayed with me for the rest of my life.

A bear with a thorn in her paw...

CHAPTER 8

The Eagle's Nest

I WAS ON THE front stoop cooling the lead soldiers Harley had poured a few minutes earlier when Eudie's shadow fell on me. He was wearing a beautiful double breasted suit and looked, to me, like large block of navy blue granite blocking out the sun.

"Artie," he said. "Do you want to come with Papa Eudie to see Sergeant Zambo?"

"Yes, Papa," I said enthusiastically. "Right now?" "Yes" he said, "Go tell your Grandma."

Mom and Harley heard the booming voice and came out onto the stoop with broad smiles.

"Eudocio, you look very nice," Grandma said.

"Thank you Mother Brown," he answered politely.

"Zambo has the fiend in custody, but he needs Artie to identify him. Can I borrow him for a minute?"

"Can I go Mama?" Harley pleaded.

"*Mr. Brown*... you need to clean up that disgrace of a Garage for our Christmas guests. The police don't need your help."

"Holy Moly!" Harley grumbled and pushed a lead soldier over with his toe, "I wanted to see that creep."

"Get to work Harley Thomas, *and* you need to practice for your glee club. Besides, Eudie has a funeral for you to sing on Tuesday.

As we left, Grandma told Papa to keep an eye on me, knowing full well that I was as safe with him as though I were in the arms of Patton and the 3rd Armored division.

"Don't worry," he said winking at her, "Artie will be in the Eagles Nest." He swept me up, spun me around, and sat me down on his massive shoulders. Grandma smiled looking up at my happy face.

My six lashes from Jim still smarted, chaffing against Eudie's shoulders and neck but I would not have complained for the world nor all the gold in it. To me, nothing was ever as grand as my walks up Gage Ave upon Papa Eudie's shoulders. In those moments, I felt like the biggest, strongest man on earth.

I was connected to the stride of a real giant. I was taller than anyone that we passed on our journey and I could see the tops of everyone's heads. His being was my being, I would never be so tall or powerful again. I was fearless. I was the Talos-protector, protecting the gates of Bell California.

As we walked across the back lot past Harleys Garage toward the police station, Eudie told me Sergeant Zambo had arrested Mr. Bennis and they needed me to make sure they had the right man.

I was scared, I leaned down and said, "Papa Eudie... proteges me, okay?"

"Nothing will happen to you when you are with Papa," he said. "Just look at the man closely and tell Zambo if this was the man or not. Then we will go for a long walk looking in windows, talking to people and maybe have an ice cream. Okay?

"Sure Papa Eudie," I said.

We crossed through the small parking lot in front of the station and I recognized the black car with the Chamber of Commerce Star and red lettered wreath on its license plate. I started to feel a bit anxious.

"Proteges me, Papa Eudie," I said again, holding tight to two big handfuls of his long wavy hair.

Within a few of Papa's long strides we were at the front door of the station. Papa Eudie swung me down from his shoulders and made a seat with his left forearm. It fit me perfectly. Our special code for this modified traveling arrangement was called "The Beanstalk." Eudie had to do it for us to go through doors.

Inside, the desk officer recognized Papa immediately. He pointed to the office and said, "Mr. Theocarides, Sergeant Zambetes is waiting for you."

We entered the room. Sergeant Zambo and Mr. Bennis were sitting across from each other at a small oak table. Sergeant Zambo greeted Papa Eudie in Greek, but Eudie was distracted by Bennis, who was nervously fidgeting.

Eudie bent over to stare into the eyes of The Fiend. Bennis looked up at the mammoth Eudie, and his mouth fell open wide. When he recognized his former prey sitting up there in the eagles nest, terror filled his eyes and all color left his face.

Eudie didn't sit down. He towered over Mr. Bennis and glared down him. Judging by the look on his face, I think Mr. Bennis was on the verge of wetting himself, just as I had there in that trash can. I relished in him feeling some of the terror he'd inflicted on me.

Sergeant Zambo stood and handed me one of my little foil boats. "Leetle Artie, es dis ah-one dem baughts you make?"

"Yes," I said.

"We find dis en the flurboard of this gentleman's car." He looked at Eudie then down at Mr. Bennis adding;

"How Youah sappose et got dare?" Then he asked, "Artie is dis dah man who gives a-hue da ride?"

I knew it was him, but I remembered Papa Eudie telling me to be sure, so I looked carefully into his mean pale face then at the hair straight back, the glasses, then the piece missing from his nose. I saw his puffy swollen knuckles and my bite marks on his hand and I said, "Yep, that's Mr. Bennis alright! We saw his car out there didn't we Papa?"

Eudie answered affirmatively then I added, "Guess what Sergeant? The license plate had a nine and a three in it!"

"Oh I know it deed!" Zambo said with a grin.

Papa, handed Sergeant Zambo one of his business cards with something written on the back of it and said something to him in Greek, while pointing at Mr. Bennis.

Papa Eudie patted my shoulders, and we resumed our beautiful walk.

CHAPTER 9

Just A Walk in the Sunshine

PAPA COULD WALK for miles, covering a lot of territory in a hurry. As I looked down at the sidewalk from my perch in the rarified air of my eagle's nest I could see the astounding difference between one of his long strides and those of the folks we passed. Eudie was walking at his normal pace, but we were passing others as though we were running slowly by them. It was amazing.

One day a few weeks earlier, my uncle Fuzzy was at the desk in his alcove working. He was painting an oil on canvas from an old photograph of Eudie and his oldest son Theo, then a boy of about seven, riding on Papa's shoulders. As I watched Fuzzy at work, I told him that I, too, rode on the big man's shoulders four or five times a year and that I was about due for another voyage soon. I elaborated on how much fun it was to be near eight feet tall sitting up there. Fuzzy grabbed a little sketch pad and drew me on Papas shoulders as Superman with a cape and goggles. It was amazing how he could draw the most wonderful things so fast and seemingly out of no where. Within fifteen minutes he handed me the completed sketch. I asked him to keep it, explaining that I wanted to give it to Papa after Christmas and that I didn't want it all smooshed up. He said he would embellish it a bit more then give it to me when he had finished. As we continued our conversation I learned that Papa was nearly sixty four years old. I could scarcely believe it. Uncle Harley and Duck were just fifteen but even they seemed terribly old to me so I could not imagine anyone being as ancient as sixty four.

I also knew that both my Grandma and Anna, Eudie's wife had both just turned what seemed to me a very ancient forty nine years old. I knew this because their birthdays were close so they celebrated them together. I saw those two wonderful ladies as grandmas and somehow, they always seemed far older than Papa Eudie. But sixty four? How could anyone be that old?

Ruminating on this as I traveled down Gage Avenue on Papa's shoulders, I feared briefly that maybe he could not bear my weight and he might topple down dead from old age, killing me in the process. It was a long way to the ground and I briefly thought of getting down and walking, but I was having too much fun and Papa seemed to have the energy of a boy and the strength of an ox. He still had full head of coal black wavy hair without a touch of white in it and his youthful face and demeanor baffled me. The man just didn't age. He looked the same to me then as he had twenty years earlier in that photo Fuzzy was working from.

Fuzzy had told me he thought Eudie was a Magi, or perhaps some special wizard who never grew old and never died. (Uncle Fuzzy loved Eudie just like all the rest of us, but had said several times that under-takers in general were just sort of creepy, and that he sometimes felt uncomfortable around Papa and didn't know exactly why.)

As we walked down Gage Avenue, a little old lady dressed completely in black, and wearing a black veil waved at Papa.

"Mrs. Manfrianni," he greeted her. "How are you today?"

"Imma justa fine," she answered with a heavy Italian accent then looked up to the Eagles nest. "Whosa dis Mr. Theo, you Granah-son?"

"No," he said. "This is Iris Spelman's son, do you remember her? She works in the fountain at Suekeetchers."

She shook her head a bit. "Hesa not ah so pretty, but hesa kinda cute." She reached up to touch my foot but couldn't reach it.

*L to R: Iris Spelman, Harley Brown, Artie Spelman,
and Carol Brown at Sukeetchers, 1940s*

"My name is Artie," I said and handed down three of my foil boats.
Papa passed them over to the surprised little woman.

"Merry Christmas," I said as Papa set the boats in her hand.

"Why tanks you little Marty," she said.

"My name is Artie," I giggled.

"O.K. Marty," she fumbled in her change purse, putting the little foil boats in and then removing a penny which she handed to Papa the penny to pass to me. "Dis isa foe yu Christmas foe bye yuself somating nice."

"Thank you," I said. She started to say something to Papa, but I interrupted. "Mrs. Manfrianni, guess what? I got a whippin' and I got two triads of big red welts on both my butts, want to see them?"

"My goodaness Marty! Wachu get ah so spank foe?"

"I left the house without telling Grandma and a fiend gave me a ride home and touched my peter. Then I hid in a trash can."

She made the sign of the cross then shook her head tugged on Eudie's sleeve. "Mr. Theo puttah dat Marty down here en I givum onea moe spanka myself." Then she looked up at me and said loudly with her cranky little voice, "Whatsa matta you Marty? Donta you know how behayfe youself?."

Eudie was shifting on his feet. "Well, it was nice to see you Mrs. Manfrianni," he said.

But before he could get away, she reached grabbed the bottom of his coat sleeve once again. "Mr. Theo tank you so mucha onesa moe time, fo what you didah fo my Antonio. He looka'd so beautiful. You do so nice ah work an you sing ah so beautiful. Like a da angel. Tank you Mr. Theo. Mr. Theo when I die Ima gonna justa walk ah straighta ova to you funeraley parlah, 'n axe ah you tah fix ah me up justa like you dida my Antonio den you puts me justa next to hem o.k.?"

She kissed the back of Papa's hand, patted his coat sleeve, took two steps back, raised her veil, and looked up at us both as if she were trying to remember the sight. She nodded her head in approval then she put her veil down again, turned and walked off.

"Artie," Papa asked as we walked away, "Why did you give Mrs. Manfrianni three of your boats instead of just one?"

"A triad Papa, a trinity. I am working in threes now just like you told me," I said proudly. "Don't worry Papa I've got lots of boats."

"Little 'Marty'," Papa said, teasing me. "A single ah bot tah to a tree people isa a triada too!"

"Oh yeah, I forgot-ah," I responded, sticking with the accent mockery and going with the flow. "Yourah oh ah so funny Mista Papa."

"Papa?" I asked as we continued our walk, "Why does Mrs. Manfrianni wear that piece of black cloth tied around her arm?"

"A lot of people from the old country wear those. It's what is called a mourning cloth," he answered.

"From the old greasy countries?" I asked.

"Yes, some in Greece," he said, "but she is from Italy."

"Do they wear it just in the morning in Italy or in the afternoon too?" I asked.

"Not morning, Artie, mourning. The word sounds the same but is spelled differently, it is m-o-u-r-n-i-n-g. People wear the black cloth to show their pain over the death of someone they loved. Sometimes they also rip their sleeve or clothing as well, to show their sorrow."

"Papa," I said. "If that Fiend had killed me, would you and Grandma wear those black arm things?"

"Artie," he answered, "There wouldn't be enough black cloth in the world to cover our suffering. That's why you have to learn to behave little Whisker, even if we have to beat you to death before someone kills you."

Chuckling, he pinched me on the side of my leg. I squealed and laughed with him. After I squiggled back to comfort, I asked, "Did someone just die in Mrs. Manfrianni's family?"

"Her husband Antonio died sixteen years ago, she is still in mourning."

"Oh" I said, and wondered about that for a good while.

The sun was on my face, I could smell flowers and the exhaust of the passing cars. It was a delicious mixture to me and I inhaled, through my nose, The scent of Eudie's aftershave lotion, his pipe tobacco and hair oil were delicious. Hey, there is another triad, I thought. I must tell Papa about that later.

I was near to bursting with happiness. Surely, I thought, nothing would ever be this grand again. I was a giant striding down my own personal road. This was my journey and I owned it. Nothing could harm me up here, nothing could defeat me. I looked up at the puffy white clouds sure I could touch them, I reached up with both my arms to try while Papa held my ankles. I was closer, but could not quite reach so I grabbed my reins once again then I whispered, "Thank you God."

I don't know why I said that, I was always a heathen. I ditched church at every opportunity and hated Sunday School. The only church I knew or cared about was next to my grandmother's bosom. That was my holy space, the promise and frontier of heaven itself. Nothing held a finer or greater spirituality for me, than her embrace and her rocking chair and arms where my refuge from all harm. That and being up here on Papa's shoulders.

As we walked toward the Alcazar Theater, I got to running my fingers through Papa's hair. I put my arms around his forehead, clasping my fingers together and making my arms into a band around the barrel of his forehead.

"What are you doing Whisker?"

"I want to see if I can feel some trinities going on in your brain," I said.

"Did you feel anything moving in there?" he asked.

"No Papa, but I did feel three dents in your head. One is a big one." I stuck my fingers in a considerable dent in his skull, just behind the hair line over the forehead above his left eye. "Did you know you had a big hole in your head Papa?"

"Well," Papa said, chuckling. "Anna tells me I have plenty of holes in my head".

"But Papa where did you get this one?" I persisted with my finger still in place.

"I got that during the war, Artie." he said.

"Papa, were you a pilot like Theo?"

"No son, this war was another war. Back 1916 in Turkey."

"Was it a greasy turkey Papa?"

"Artie, I got a few holes like that one. They were given to me by men who were sick like Mr. Bennis only they had guns, knives and torches."

There were so many questions I wanted to ask him but in another few steps we were in front of the Alcazar Theater. I pulled hard on Eudie's reins bringing him to a halt. I reminded myself to ask Harley or Duck about those holes in Papas head and why, no matter how hard I pulled

Papas hair, he never once winced or complained. *I'll ask the boys later about his tough hair* I thought, *they'll know.*

"Oh look Papa, look!" I said excitedly peering at the photos through the glass. "It's Muggs McGinnis and the Bowery Boys. What's it say, Papa?" I could read but mostly Papa did it better.

"It says Christmas time trio of fun! Join Muggs, Glimpy and the entire Bowery Gang in three new holiday hits! Million Dollar Kid, Follow the Leader and Block Busters. Matinee today only! Box office opens at two PM."

"Oh Papa! I love those guys. Gosh, I would love to go see those movies!"

"Artie," Papa said, "I will see if Timoleon and Harley would like to go with you this afternoon. We won't be together for Christmas this year so perhaps the boys would like to enjoy a movie and take you along. Papa might treat you, we will just see, but we have to ask Grandmother Brown first. The theater doesn't open for three more hours so we have time."

"O.K." Papa I replied.

"I have to go to the office of the Savings and Loan then we will go across the street visit your mother and have a nice soda or a sundae O.K.?"

"Sure, Papa!" I said excitedly. I gave his reins the giddy up and he followed my lead at a quicker pace to the old bank building just on the corner.

We walked east to the corner of Atlantic Boulevard and Gage Avenue through the very tall bank doors. It had been the Bank of Italy before the war, then the building was sold to Papa and his partner for their Savings and Loan business. I did not have to go to the bean stalk or even duck my head to clear the ten foot tall double doors. As we walked into the bank all heads turned. Everyone recognized Papa immediately, the employees all smiled broadly at the sight of the two of us. They greeted him warmly and wished him merry Christmas.

Papa and I went to a lady sitting at a large desk and he asked her for the envelopes. She handed him a canvas bank bag full of envelopes which he passed out to each employee. He thanked them by name and wished them each a merry Christmas and prosperous new year.

There was Christmas cheer and all round and happy smiling faces. Finally we walked upstairs into what Papa told me was the office of his friend and general manager, Yahudi Edelstein. Papa sat me down in an oak-armed bank chair just across from the man, reached into his suit pocket and removed another, thicker envelope. He gave it to the Mr. Edelstein and said, "Thank you for your hard work Yahudi. This is the first time we have been able to do this in a while."

"Yes Sir, we've had some sparse years, but things are getting better. God willing this war will be over soon." He looked over at me. "Who's this, Eudocio?"

"You remember Yahudi, this is little Artie, Iris Spelman's boy. She works just across the street at the Soda Fountain?"

"Oh yes of course. My he's getting so big. Yes I know her, she's a pretty lady." He looked at me, "I have lunch there once in a while. Your mother is quite nice."

"Thank you!" I said, then I got up, went around the desk and handed him three of my foil boats. He took them appreciatively, setting them in a careful line on top of his oak desk.

"I love these little boats, I used to fold them myself as a child," he said with a broad warm child like enthusiasm. "This is a flotilla" he said to me, smiling down and looking proudly at his grouping.

"No Sir," I said. "They don't float 'til you put them in water. It's a trinity, or a triad or trio. Do you have children?"

"Yes, two," he said, with his brow a bit wrinkled trying to follow the thread of my reasoning.

"Maybe you could give one to each of them and keep one for yourself," I said. "Then you could flotilla them all at once."

Mr. Edelstein looked to Eudie a bit confused.

"I'll explain later, Yahudi. We are working on threes," Papa said with a wink and a smile.

"Ah yes." Edelstein said.

He shook my hand and thanked me profusely for the boats telling me that he would endeavor to distribute as well as float them properly as per my instructions.

"Oh good," I said. I was about to ask him if he would like to see my welted triads when I noticed he was wearing a beanie on his head.

"I like your beanie," I said.

"Thank you Artie, this is called a Kippah."

"Neat, I love hats but I am always losing them."

Mr. Edelstein looked in both of his suit pockets and pulled out another little black Beanie and gave it to me. "Here son, you can have this for your collection."

"Thank you, gosh, that's great!"

He smiled and said, "Seems a fair exchange to me, three silver boats for one skull cap, that's good business."

I put on the beanie, still thinking of showing Mr. Edelstein the trinity of welts on my arse but Papa read me, turned me around and reinstalled me on the Eagles Nest. "Lets go see your Momma," he said.

With me sitting on his shoulders, Papa offered Edelstein a handshake. His hand was so large that Mr. Edelstein's was like a child's inside it, almost disappearing in Papa's palm. Things like that never ceased to amaze me. I was around Papa so much that I sometimes forgot how large he really was.

Yahudi Edelstein looked up to Papa, "Thank you for this Eudocio. Ruth will be very pleased this year."

"You earned every Penny of it," Eudie responded, "Thank *You*."

We turned went out the big doors, crossed two lights, and were in front of the Suekeetchers Drug Store and Soda fountain. Eudie set me down on my feet as we walked inside. I entered first, Eudie followed struggling to get his mass through the normal door.

My Mom looked up and saw me. "Hi honey," she said. I ran behind the counter and gave her a big hug, then we sat down at the counter. Eudie was on his specially constructed stool at the very end of the counter, I on the swivel chair next to him.

"Hi boss!" Mom said to Papa Eudie.

"Mrs. Spelman," Eudie said. "You look very nice today."

"Thank you," she answered. "Are you men out on the town today?"

"Mom," I blurted out. "Guess what! We saw the fiend and Papa gave him a business card, then we talked to Mrs. Manfrianni. She gave me a penny and then we went to the Alcazar and saw Muggs McGinnis. After that we went to the Bank and saw everyone. I talked with Mr. Edelstein and, guess what Mom? I taught him how to float a tillah but he couldn't because he didn't have any water on his desk but guess what? He gave me this beanie. Now we are here and we are going to have some ice cream, aren't we Papa?"

"Really?" Mother said smiling and a little confused. She looked to Eudie, who nodded his head in agreement, verifying my account of the day thus far.

I ordered a banana split with everything on it including hot fudge and Papa ordered a large strawberry float. As we sat eating, I noticed Mom staring at Eudie with her lips parted just a bit but trying not to be too obvious. His long soda spoon and tall soda glass was hidden and had virtually disappeared behind the wall of flesh and bone that was his cupped left hand. Momma looked at me smiled, I knew why she was smiling, I had just witnessed something similar at the bank. Papa was like a Saint Bernard that we were just used too somehow but who never ceased to delight us. He was the biggest kid on the block and we were his pals who just sometimes took him for granted.

As we were ready to leave, Momma said to Eudie, "Mr. Theocarides please let me treat you two to these sundaes, as my Merry Christmas for you both O.K.?"

"Thank you, Iris," he said. "We accept. And here is a little something for you." He handed her an envelope with her name on it.

"Thank you," Mom said. "But I haven't been with you for a full year yet."

"Well I'll be darned," he said winking at her. "How could I have missed that? Well better give it back to me then." Mother stood there clutching the envelope to her chest with a silly grin on her face.

"Excuse me just a minute," Papa said as he got up and walked through the archway into the drugstore side of the building. y.

When he left the room, Mother anxiously opened her envelope and her eyes lit up. There was twenty one dollars in cash, the equivalent of a full week's salary plus tips. She put it in her apron pocket smiling like a cat with a new mouse.

Papa returned prepared to leave. I took out my Manfrianni Christmas penny and left it beside our dishes. Papa smiled, and set a quarter beside my penny. Just as we got to the door I turned and ran back. Placing one of my foil boats on the counter I sat my penny and Papas Quarter one at each end of the boat, then looking to my Mother I said, "This is a boat with two rowers. The penny is me, and that Quarter is Papa, cause he's bigger. See Mom? Merry Christmas Momma!"

She noticed my skull cap but said nothing, then she kissed me and I ran outside to catch Eudie and remounted my eagle's nest.

We walked to Papa's house behind his funeral parlor. Harley and Duck were there playing chess.

As we entered the library we heard Harley say, "Check!"

Duck smiled and said nothing. Harley was preening like a peacock in heat.

"You big ass Greek, now I know why you are so damned big!"

"Really?" Duck said, concentrating on his chess response, "Why is that Brownie?"

"You are so big Timoleon, because you need the space to keep all that dumb!"

Harley smiled ever so proud of himself, but within two moves he was checkmated. Duck looked at him casually.

"Brownie... You were saying?"

Harley threw a sofa pillow at Ducks head, and looked up at Papa.

"Your son cheats, Papa!"

"I know," Papa said. "The only way I can beat him is if I use three queens and an extra knight."

"I need to see Zambo again," Eudie said to the two boys. "I told him I would drop back by. Want to come with us to the station again for about ten minutes?"

"Sure Pop," Duck responded.

We all walked out through the Meditation Garden around the driveway to Atlantic Boulevard and crossed the street to the sidewalk just in front of our house. As we stood on the sidewalk facing the little white house, Harley teasingly said to Eudie, "Hey Papa, why don't you put Artie in his eagle's nest and race Duck I to the edge of the far lot?"

I think the boys were stunned when Papa said, "Well lets see, I think we can beat these boys don't you, Artie?"

"Do we get a head start Papa? You're pretty old." I said.

The big man balanced himself on one foot and took off his shoes. Then, tucking a sock in each, handed one shoe to Duck then the other to Uncle Harley. "If I have to carry Artie, then you each have to carry one of my shoes."

Papa swung me up into the eagle's nest and told me to hang on to his hair as hard as I could and not to let go under any circumstances.

"But Papa," I said. "Uncle Fuzzy told me you were 64 years old. Heck, Papa you might fall down dead for old age. Who would glue a smile on your face and lift you into that ole coffin with their bare hands, Papa? You can't undertake yourself can you?"

I knew it was coming and there it was. He pinched my poor calves once again as I squealed in delight. I was sure I had another triad of pinch marks and couldn't wait to show the abuse to Veve or aunt Eddie.

Papa stood there barefooted in his beautiful double breasted suit. He didn't even bother removing his tie or unbuttoning his coat. "Ok, here are the rules. Artie gives us the go." Papa continued, pointing a hundred twenty five yards or so across the adjoining fields to a bush. "We will race to that bottle bush there near the end of the Clarkson street lot just at the end of the lumberyard fence. That way we'll have a few yards to slow down before we run out into Clarkson Street and all get killed by some car. The bottle bush is the finish line O.K.?"

Duck and Harley nodded.

"If I drop Little Artie on his head, or if either of you drop a shoe we lose the race, no matter who crosses the finish line first o.k.?"

"Yes, Sir!" the boys said with big smiles.

"But Eudie, what if we drop only one of your shoes, and you drop Artie, do we still win the race? " Harley asked.

Papa winked at the boys and said, "If Artie gets killed in the fall, yes, then you win. But if he is still clinging to life, or only has a broken spine after he hits the ground, then the Whisker and I win the race..."

"Don't kill me Papa!" I said yanking his hair, "It'll make Grandma awful mad and you won't see me anymore. You'll have to paste my broken body then bury me with your own two hands."

"O.K. Whisker," he interrupted. "Get ready."

We all lined up at the edge of the sidewalk looking toward past our house down and behind Harleys Garage, past Grandma's garden across the second lot to the bottle bush. As we started to line up, Grandma Brown, aunt Veve and uncle Fuzzy came out to the stoop to watch the spectacle.

Eudie said, "On Your Mark! Get Ready!"

Then squeezed my leg and I said, "One, Two, Three Go!"

Papa took off on the count of one, Duck was a couple strides behind him and Harley a pace behind Duck.

It seemed to me, from my position on the nest, that Papa and I were moving slowly, but in fact we were covering a great deal of ground. As we passed the outside of the swing side of the pepper tree, Eudie ducked us under a branch and bumped Duck with his left hip knocking him sprawling onto the platform swing. Harley, who was just behind Duck was forced to jump onto the platform swing, over the top of the prostrate Duck, who fell to the ground on the back side of the swing with a thud and a groan but managed to hang on to the big shoe. Soon both boys were back on their feet, close behind us and gaining ground rapidly.

"Go Papa! Go Artie!" The gang at the porch yelled. Grandma had her fingers to her lips and Veve was jumping up down like an excited goose.

All racers and passenger eagles had reached the back lot and were in the last half of the foot race when Papa stumbled in a chuck hole. I waited for the long fall but Eudie regained his step and ran on. He was a bit slower and seemed to be hobbling just a bit, but his strides were still long and we were still a few feet ahead.

As I glanced back over my shoulder I could see Duck coming on fast. Uncle Harley was well behind but doing his best. Behind the boys I could hear the Brown clan's voices as they rooted us on.

Soon we were nearing the bottle bush finish line and as I looked to my right I could see that Duck was shoulder to shoulder with his father.

Duck crossed the line a foot ahead of Eudie but at that moment Papa reached with his right arm and pushed Duck down laughing robustly. Duck dropped Papa's shoe then ate some dirt. Papa and I managed to barely stop before we hit the curb of Clarkson Street.

All the racers were laughing as we looked back to our audience who were walking toward us waving. Papa asked me, "O.K. Arty," he said still laughing. "You had the best observation point, so tell us who won the race?"

"Oh Papa, gosh. We did!" I said over enthusiastically.

When Papa spun me around I saw on his face an expression of such pain and anguish that for a moment I was frightened. At first I thought maybe he had twisted his ankle in our pot hole or was in pain, or maybe he was sad because we had lost the race. But this expression of pain even I knew, was triggered from his heart. From something only he knew. Perhaps something dark from long ago in the greasy turkey I was old enough, even then, to imagine a fleeting memory was breaking his heart. You see I sometimes saw an expression similar to that when Grandma talked about Grandpa Brown and sometimes I saw it in my mother's face, when one of her boyfriends broke her heart.

When Papa saw me staring at him with my mouth wide open, he smiled, covering his pain up quickly and jostling me playfully to the ground.

As Papa put on his shoes, Duck and Harley grabbed me, holding me face down into the ground. Then they rolled me over and raised my shirt to put dirt, rocks and grass on my stomach. They packed my navel full and pulled down my T shirt. Harley turned me onto my stomach again, found a potato bug and put it down the back of my underwear. "You little liar!" he said tickling me.

I was giggling so hard I near wet my pants. I looked up at Duck's face and squealed, "Well yeah! You crossed the line first, but you dropped Papa's shoe. So guess what? We won! Right Papa?" I asked.

"We sure did, Whisker. Fair and square!" he said, winking at his son.

CHAPTER 10

The Alcazar & Dr. Duck (Negotiations)

W E STRAIGHTENED OURSELVES up as our *Brown* fans joined us at the finish line to congratulate the victorious Duck, the winner in spite of Papa's shoe rule which Uncle Harley verified with his comment, "Even a man who couldn't see out of one eye and was blind in the other or even a person with bleeding ulcers in their eyes and wearing sunglasses at night during a lunar eclipse could see clearly who the obvious winner of *that* footrace was."

Papa asked Grandma Brown if he could treat "those disgruntled Champion foot racers and his own jockey, Edward Arthur, to the movies?"

She said that would be just fine. Mother Brown and the track fans returned to the house in good cheer as the four of us walked across Clarkson Street to enter the Bell police station, Papa and I for the second time that day.

The *'fiend'* was no longer in police custody which disappointed my Uncle Harley as he had not yet in his young life actually seen a genuine perverted fiend.

Fox Alcazar Theater, 1940s

The news according to Sergeant Zambo was that Nunyur's attorney had him released and that by now Mr. Bennis was threatening to sue the city of Bell, California, *as well as* bringing a lawsuit against Mr. Eudocio Astraeus Theocarides, proprietor of the Theo & Carides Funeral Home. It seemed from what I could understand of it and from what Harley sometime later explained to me was that according to Papa's brother-in-law, Sergeant Zambetes, the recently arrested Jonathan Bruce Brittlewhite, a.k.a. Mr. Bennis, was released from custody due to the efforts of his high-powered attorney, Marvin L. Tufts.

According to Zambo's accounting of the subsequent events, Mr. Brittlewhite, while in police custody, had accidentally fallen up three flights of stairs causing himself two black eyes as well as several broken teeth and lacerations. The Attorney Tufts pointed out to the police captain that the Bell police station stood on a *single floor* and that it in fact *had no stairs* either going up or down.

Zambo went on to tell us that the fiend's attorney had also claimed that the business card the defendant had received from "**that very large menacing man**" was nothing less than a *veiled threat*, because although it was a normal business card on the front, on its reverse side Papa's handwritten note was deemed a threat to his client since Papa had written a promise and offer for free embalming and burial services. Attorney Tufts further stated that both Mr. Theocarides and Sergeant Zambo also suggested to Mr. Brittlewhite **that death** was not *necessarily a prerequisite* to receive the full value of the gifted service. Zambo further added that, according once again to Nunyur's attorney, the sergeant had also verbally threatened his client by telling him never to drive within the borders of Bell, California, again or that the aforementioned free embalming services might well take place pre-mortem. He also claimed that Sgt. Zambo had whispered in Brittlewhite's ear, "That big undertaker across the street will bury you facedown with a large sunflower sticking out of your nasty ass so that the hogs can find your bastard guts when they find you rotting there in hell!"

Attorney Tufts was not pleased and left the station in a huff with Mr. Bennis in tow saying, "We'll see you *all* in court!"

After telling us the details, Zambo said something to Papa and Duck in Greek, and Papa's face grew very drawn and angry. Duck's expression also changed to one of astonishment as the three Greeks stood there looking at each other shaking their heads slowly back and forth incredulously.

We soon walked out to the parking lot where Papa asked the boys if they would like to go to the Alcazar with his winning jockey.

I oversold the irresistible fair of Leo Gorcey as Muggs McGinnis and they bought it. Papa handed us each a dollar bill and we took off for the movie house richer than lords.

There was a line of three or four hundred youth standing four-wide from the Alcazar box office all the way past Papa's savings and loan bank around the west corner. We joined at the end of it laughing as we waited, full of chatter and excitement about our upcoming Christmas, our loved ones and some of Papa's ideas and tall tales about some gnome he called Pie Exemplumonious possibly living inside our pepper tree but they did not elaborate on it they just said, "Papa said Beware!" I did not bother to tell the boys of my special inside knowledge and my possible future duties regarding the gnome, though I wanted desperately to brag about it. I somehow managed to keep mum.

We returned to talk of war and to the recent news of Duck's brother Captain Stavros Theocarides having just shot down his third German ME-109, as well as my Auntie Eddie's husband, Technical Sergeant Carl Agajanian, on his B-17. We all talked about if they would live through it all to laugh with us once again, each of us speculating on how many Christmases more it would take before they came home and if they would have their arms and legs when they returned.

We stood there shifting on our feet playing rock-paper-scissors for *noogies*; I mostly lost, but even when I won, Duck's head was so far from the earth that his penalty was difficult to deliver. To make it worse, Duck refused to bend down to pay his price for my few victories, so we switched to *wet willies*. I only fared slightly better, so I soon sued for less-painful entertainment.

Duck spotted Sally O'Flannery, a Bell High School junior cheerleader, up ahead in the line and then said something to Harley in a low, inside voice saying something about her giving him a big woody. Duck tried to assuage and deflect my curiosities, as they laughed at my inquisitive naive face and he said, "*Woody Woodpecker ew who ah ha ha!*" looking down at me trying to understand and take it in.

I guessed they just liked cartoons and I wondered why that was funny. Then I heard Duck telling Harley, as he elbowed him, that Sally had mentioned that since Duck planned on going to medical school to become a doctor someday, she wanted to be his private nurse knowing "*just exactly the right place* to take his blood pressure."

Finding great interest in each other's company, the two fifteen-year-old boys were having exaggerated fun punching and horsing around with each other, and I loved watching them and feeling part of it all.

As we stood there killing time I got to thinking about the day's activities and Papa's advanced age and his stumble during our footrace.

"Duck, did you hold back and *let* Papa almost win our race because he is really old and might have fallen down from old age and killed us both?" I asked most seriously.

"Are you kidding me?" He answered, looking at me intently. "Two years ago I couldn't have beaten that old man in a foot race if he had been carrying your Grandmother Brown on his shoulders."

"You're joking me right, Duck?" I asked.

"No," the big boy said. *"I am quite serious,* I promise you."

"But, Duck, Duck," I asked earnestly, "Isn't 64 years old pretty old? That's way older than my Grandma Brown and guess what? Papa is just a *regular Father;* he is not even a *grandfather yet, is he?* Shouldn't he be a Grandfather?" I asked, giving it some careful thought.

"I suppose," he said, "but my dad is from a different cut of cloth. Sure, Artie, there are many men my father's age who are grandfathers that cannot even walk very well, much less run, while still others a decade younger than he shuffle and fart as they walk along or are in wheelchairs," he added with a broad, proud smile. "My dad is still physically the most powerful man I know."

I knew that Papa and his son Duck sometimes wrestled in the gym room behind their garage. Papa had taught Duck how to wrestle from an early age. Those two men throwing each other down reminded me of two great bulls banging heads. Amazingly, Duck with considerable effort could lift and pin his massive father and move him around the mats surprisingly well. The energy between the two large males was so intense that I could hear it and feel it crackling through the air like static electricity giving me goose bumps at the sheer physical power in front of me. He taught us all how to box a bit and how to defend ourselves, even some of the Brown girls learned how to defend themselves. He explained how to be a good sport lecturing each of us about cowardice and courage and the degrees between the two.

As we continued to stand in line, Duck looked at Harley and asked, "Did I ever tell you, Brownie, that when my dad was about eighteen or nineteen that he worked in a Spanish circus in Madrid, Spain, as a strongman? Momma showed me an tintype of him crossing the finish line once when he'd beaten a horse in a footrace."

"Really?" Harley and I responded at the same time.

"Yes, Momma didn't know him then; she didn't marry Dad until he was near forty, but Papa's twin brother, Anthanasios, and others told her many stories and she has some photographs from those early years. It seems that Eudocio and his brother, whom they called Ant and was just two inches shorter than Papa, wrestled and boxed each other for the amusement of the circus patrons as part of the sideshow attractions.

The circus posters said *"Duo Rapash en Boxeo"* or some read *"Niños Gigantes"* or *"Los Hermanos Diabolicos!"*

I looked at Uncle Harley and asked, "Can we go ask Mama Theocarides about Papa's life sometime? Then guess what? Maybe we could see those pictures."

Duck answered for Harley, "She'll be happy to tell you two what she knows about the circus days. Papa might too if you ask him just right, but just don't ask him about the **Armenian genocide**, that was a war he fought in Turkey in 1916."

"Harley! Harley!" I said remembering as I tugged on his shirt sleeve, "Guess what? This morning when Papa and I took our long walk up Gage, while I sat up on his shoulders I felt some holes in his head and when I asked him about them he told me about some mean, sick Turkey people who did it during the war with those *Armenians*. Bet that was it! Bet that was that war."

Duck took a breath as if questioning himself about just what to share with Harley in front of my little pitcher ears and tender sensibilities so close at hand. Finally he said, "Yes, the Turks got him and made him and others dig their own graves. After stabbing Papa, the Turks propped him up to make him watch while they killed the other captured Armenians, some of them were his friends and his wife's relatives. When the others were dead, they stood him blindfolded, bound him and stood him near the edge of a trench then shot him in the head.

"Harley and I both remember those holes on Papa's head, don't we, Brownie?" he asked Harley warmly.

Harley said looking at me, "Yes indeed we do; he used to carry us on those walks riding on his shoulders when we were little, just as he does with you and Artie, and we also felt those holes."

"Why did those Turkeys want to shoot Papa?" I asked innocently.

"Well," Duck said, "there are lots of legends about that within our extended family circles, and I guess even among the Armenians who during that war mistakenly called him The Armenian Giant not knowing he was actually of Greek descent.

"My brother Theo once told me that in part it was because sometime during the fighting, one of the stories was that Dad had literally once tore the head off some Turkish captain with his bare hands then Papa grasped the decapitated captain's head by the beard and beat the Turk's sergeant to death with it by wielding the captain's skull like a sledge hammer.

"You see Papa was married before he married my mother. During that holocaust, Dad lost his Armenian wife and two little girls who were killed. They were, they got, well, well… just never mind *what* they got," he said glancing down at me but he doesn't like to talk about it so I only ask about the circus and not about tearing heads off the Turks.

Duck went on, "There were many stories told by the Armenians about Papa and he was a feared warrior; some say he went insane when he lost his wife and children and tried to kill everything in sight."

I didn't quite understand it all and wasn't privy to most of those stories until many years later, but my eyes were wide open as I thought about that. And I asked Tim, "Duck, do you think it's true?"

I saw Duck thinking about his answer. "I guess it's possible, but Papa always warned us about exaggerated stories and such. From a medical standpoint, tearing a head off using only the strength of hands and arms would be problematic because of the subject's neck bones and flesh and muscle and so on. A cutting edge would have done a much better job but my father certainly had the kind of strength to have done it, and snapping a soldier's spine would have been child's play for Papa at that age. Even now he could do it to the average man, and Uncle Ant told us that Eudie killed many Turks with his bare hands during that war, so who knows?

"Papa is a loving and kind man, and he is a very wise man, but the term Gentle Giant has never in anyway been applied to describe my father. My dad as you both know can be quite fierce and frightening, particularly when someone meets him or sees him for the first time at his full height and width and at his most hostile. As you know, it can be both funny and frightening for sure."

The box office wasn't open yet but the line started to compact slowly as we shuffled around the corner once again to a stop.

I asked Duck what had made him, Papa and Zambo so angry inside the police station and what they had talked about in the "*Greece*" language.

The big boy looked at us. "What Zambo and Dad spoke of, Artie, was that he found out that your Nunyur Bennis, along with his sister, were the co-owners of Cudahay Kiddy Coral, a nursery school and day care center for little children seven and under, and that Nunyur's sister *also* had a criminal record in the state of New York for mistreating and abusing children. In fact she also had an alias and was naught but a fiend herself. So that was what angered them. Papa said it was like two drunkards owning a liquor store built over the basement of an opium den."

"What's an alias?" I asked.

"You do understand, Artie," Harley asked me quite seriously, "that your mad fiend's real name was *not* Nunyur Bennis, don't you?"

"Really?" I asked, rather surprised because I could not imagine *why* someone would lie about their very own name; I had started to have some creeping doubts about Mr. Bennis's name because every time I mentioned it, someone in the room always laughed, but I just didn't get it and hadn't yet gotten around to asking Papa or Grandma Brown about it.

"An alias, Artie," Harley continued, "is when someone uses a false name, makes up a name, or uses someone else's name. Get it?"

"Yeah, I think so." I said, "Like Superman and Clark Kent, right?"

"Something like that," replied Uncle Harley.

"What was *her* alias?" Harley asked Duck casually.

Duck answered, "Zambo said that on her New York City arrest record she had the name a.k.a. Mrs. Ippy."

Harley smiled looking down at me asking, "Do you understand that, Artie?"

"Yeah," I said. "Her husband was Mr. Ippy, right?"

Uncle Harley sighed, shaking his head exasperatedly. He then said, "Nephew, I swear to God, you will not live long enough to see your tenth birthday."

I tried unsuccessfully to extract the mysteries of what I was misunderstanding about those names, but the boys steadfastly refused me enlightenment by saying only, "Think about it, Artie. Think About it!"

Duck reached down giving me a bonus noogie saying, "Brilliant, Artie. Brilliant." Then seeing my feelings hurt and the disappointment in myself written on my face, Duck said, "You'll work it out, Artstir. Just think about it; just pronounce those names slowly. Listen to yourself when you say those names out loud… you'll get it eventually."

"Yeah," Harley said. "When he's thirty-five, if he's not dead yet."

Now Duck who was taller than a redwood and could see all the way to the box office said to me, "Artie, isn't that your little friend Leslie up there about third in line from the box office window?"

"I can't see," I said. So Duck picked me up putting me on his shoulders as I looked down the line. Leslie saw me and smiled broadly, waving to me and so I waved back enthusiastically.

"Yeah, that's my friend," I said happily as Duck sat me down on the sidewalk.

Duck sat me down, then said; "Well, here, Artie, take this dollar to him and tell him we will treat him to the movie if he will buy all our tickets so that we don't have to fight this line to get good seats, OK?"

"But, Duck, what if he doesn't want to do it?" I asked.

"Make a deal, Artie! **Bargain** with him! Think like Papa Eudie would," he said, chuckling. "Negotiate, Artie, Negotiate!"

"OK, Duck," I said, taking his dollar and running to meet Leslie at the front of the line. When I arrived, I hugged my friend as we always did, and Leslie said; "Hi, Artie; come to see Muggs?"

"Yes," I said, "A trinity of three movies; pretty neat, huh? I love those guys; don't you?"

Not waiting for his answer, I made Tim's proposal to him. He responded, "Well I am here with my friend Sol Rubinstein," he said, pointing to the pleasant-looking older boy standing just next to him. "He is taking me to the show, see; Sol is thirteen and he is now a man cause he got his bar mitzvah last week so he's in charge."

Sol offered his hand and I shook it introducing myself. I liked him right away; he had the same intelligent, kind eyes that Leslie had but I was crestfallen because when I offered him one of my paper foil boats he refused it saying he was too old for such things. Anyway, after some stiff negotiations regarding the addition of free mini bubble gum cigars, a French chew, Jujubes, and a jumbo salted popcorn for both boys as well as their admission, we came to an agreement. I gave Tim's dollar to Sol and when the box office opened he purchased all our tickets. I told them to keep the change for the candy. Sol's eyes lit up at the forty cents in change.

"I like your yarmulke!" he said pointing to my beanie which I totally had forgotten about and had stuck with me through the footrace and all.

"Mr. Edelstein from the savings and loan gave it to me," I said proudly.

"Yahudi Edelstein?" the boy asked me.

"I think so," I said. "I traded him three of my boats for it. Do you know him?"

"Yes, he is my uncle's cousin. We go to Temple Beth El together."

By this time Harley and Duck were there, and as the theater opened its doors they took their tickets and walked in front of us into the theater.

They gave their tickets at the front door to a freckle-faced girl with huge blue eyes and dimples. As her eyes met Harley's, she dropped the tickets stumbling over her own feet. Picking them up, she flushed then tore them in half until the stubs turned into confetti, giving all the tiny pieces to Harley completely ignoring the tall, strikingly handsome Duck standing at Uncle's elbow. She said, looking giddily to my uncle, "Hi, Dreamboat."

Harley smiled a silly grin showing his crooked teeth in all their glory.

Tina, the freckled-faced ticket girl, gave Harley a little folded note then she said dreamily in a sweet little voice, never taking her eyes from his, "Give this to Timmy T. It's from Sally O'Flannery." Harley took the note smiling.

"I'll find you later, Brownie, OK?" Tina said. Harley made no reply but with the satisfied grin of a canary who had just swallowed a cat, he nudged Duck who had been by his side all along.

"Harley, you are as happy as a clam in heat." Duck teasing him, as the mismatched pair walked into the theater. Harley handed the note to Duck who said, "Jeez, I was standing right there next to you, Brownie. Why didn't Tina just give the damn note directly to me? Is she blind or something?"

"Simple old man, she only has eyes for me. Like it or not, Timmy, you are not the only big man on campus around here." Harley added, doing a really miserable imitation of Cary Grant, "When you got it, you got it. I just got it!"

"Yeah! Cooties!" Duck responded.

Harley nudged Duck, then sang the line, *"If she's got dimples on her butt, she's pretty."*

Duck opened Sally's note which said, "Dr. Lover Lips, meet you on the balcony." She had signed the note with her red lipstick kisses and over the top she signed it *Nurse Sally*, followed by three little hearts with ME + U -written within each of the hearts.

He showed it to Harley, then said, "Brownie, it's time for my amazing linguistics demonstration. Doctor Duck Timoleon Theocarides will perform an exploratory tonsillectomy with his tongue and perhaps save this girl's life!"

The boys waved to us pointing up to the balcony staircase indicating where they were going. We nodded our heads in understanding and waved.

As they walked up the semicircular staircase, Harley elbowed Duck saying, "Oh man, it'll be a *hot time* in the old town tonight!" Then Bell High's Mutt and Jeff flew up the remaining steps disappearing into the balcony delighted at their good fortune to be males on this promising day.

Waiting for Leslie who was already getting his candy, Sol and I sat on the little upholstered bench next to the popcorn counter. We were discussing what treats we wanted and talking pleasantly getting to know each other. Leslie purchased his bootie, then returned offering me some jumbo popcorn; I took three kernels and told them I would get mine at intermission because the counter was too crowded now. Sol agreed.

Then Leslie said, "Well OK then, I'd better get inside and save us seats in the front row, OK?" then he ran off.

We sat there a couple of minutes; finally Sol asked me, "Can I see that little boat again?"

"Sure," I replied looking for the best of the three I had left and gave it to him.

"You can have it," I told Sol once again. "I make them myself and I can make others."

Sol looked at the boat with the lovely face of a wise old man then said seriously, "I am sorry. I can't take one, Artie, because I am now a *man*," he said matter-of-factly, "but I would like to buy one from you."

"But *guess what?*" I said imploringly, "I can just give you one!"

"Thank you, Artie, but I now have to consider ethics, so I cannot accept it," Sol repeated.

"Well," I said, "I have never actually sold one before. I just mostly give them to people I talk with."

"Yes, well," Sol said, pausing as he looked closely at the boat I had handed him then asked, "How much would you sell me this one for?"

"I don't know," I responded in a bit of a quandary. I thought about it for a while thinking that Duck's admonition to negotiate might apply here as well, then said, "Mrs. Manfrianni gave me a penny for three of them, but these are my last ones 'til I make up some more, so would two cents for the three be too much?"

Sol looked at the boat closely then said, "How many did you say you have, Artie?"

"A trinity," I said smiling, holding up three little fingers.

"I'll tell you what," Sol said, "I'll give you four cents for all three boats plus twenty-five cents if you show me how you make them."

I thought longer and harder than I could ever remember regarding such things, finally responding, "Make it thirty-five cents total," I said smiling, remembering again that Tim told me I had to bargain.

"What about thirty cents?" Sol responded.

"Sure!" I said enthusiastically, giving him the contract of my offered hand. "Sol," I said proudly, "we have negotiated."

"Shalom!" he said shaking my hand, adding, "Yes, Mr. Spelman, we have indeed!"

I remember feeling so old, so proud of myself at my new sense of adulthood and financial independence.

Sol and I exchanged boat money as well as insights and instructions into paper boat construction, then after missing the first 15 minutes of previews and short features we entered the theater to find Leslie in the front row center saving us a seat on each side of him.

As we entered the theater, the *MovieTone News* had just started: *"Dah da dah…da da da da da da ti dah dah!"* the music sounded, followed by a scene of British soldiers marching with rifles somewhere in war-torn Europe, then the announcer's voice-over saying, "October fifth, British forces now in Greece; England is on the move; nine days later, Athens is liberated!"

"Dah da dah… da da da da da da ti dah dah!" the music sounded once again.

"November fourteenth, American B-29 bombers, from their fields in the Mariana Islands, bomb Tokyo taking it to the enemy." The bombers were shown flying in formation with stock footage of bombs dropping somewhere. "Now how do you like that, Tojo? And there is plenty more where that came from!" the baritone voice-over said proudly.

The news reel ended followed by a dozen or so cartoons, then the first feature *Million Dollar Kid*, followed by the second feature *Follow the Leader*.

As I sat there, I realized that during my *high financing* that I alone had forgotten to buy myself candy. As I toyed with the money burning a hole in my pocket, it occurred to me that I still had the original dollar given me by Papa plus my negotiating money from Sol and this was more money than I had ever had at one time in my life. For reasons only known to the angels, I imagined the tears of joy and amazement streaming down the faces of Grandmother Brown and my mother as they opened some costly, superb Christmas present from the totally unselfish and saintly Arthur Spelman — *man and master negotiator!* When I came out of my fantasy, Muggs McGinnis and his mother, Mary McGinnis, were on screen in some touching scene that reminded me of my own *Granmudder.* That did it for me. I took a vow of *confectionary abstinence,* swearing not to spend a single penny on candy but save it all to buy two spectacular gifts, one for Grandmother and one for Mother. I thought ever so briefly of a life of self-sacrifice, perhaps even the priesthood or as a Baptist preacher... maybe eventually sainthood, although I did not know exactly what that entailed. I just knew it was something good and you deprived yourself of everything that you liked but were happy.

As the three of us sat there in the front row, Leslie and Sol offered me some of their candy and popcorn. I have no idea why, but something had happened to me that day. Remembering back on it now after all these years I think it was likely my observations of the young Sol struggling with his manhood passing before me moment by moment that had so impressed and inspired me. So, I refused my friends in favor of my great and noble sacrifice by saying to them both that I could not take their treats when I had money for my own in my pocket. Then I added to Sol's surprise by saying proudly, "I found an *ethic,* and I can't negotiate on this." We three were having great fun. Leslie taunted me amidst listening to my soul-searching prattle; while like a greedy little squirrel he stuffed his cheeks to full capacity with a combination of popcorn and malted balls, chewing them slowly and mockingly making funny faces at me as he looked into my yearning hungry eyes.

Leslie always made me laugh and I knew that I had a wonderful new friend in Leslie Dow, who I found out on *that very day,* sitting there with my arm around him, that he was in fact my first cousin. You see, we had run into each other many times before, usually in a Danny Kaye movie at the Alcazar or up the street at the State Theater, and we had always created this mysterious bond. Finally I now found out that it was likely because his mother, Carole, and my mother, Iris, were sisters. Something happened with his parents, just like something had happened with my mom and dad. That's all I knew or needed to know. That was the quiet part of our brotherhood, the core of our inner bond and love and yearning. But God had given me Eudie and my Grandmother Brown, so I hoped Leslie had someone special in his life just as I did. I know he loved his mother, Carole, because he told me so many times. I loved her too, but I guessed that she and Mr. Dow just didn't like each other anymore. I must remember to ask Grandma Brown about that I thought.

I remembered that my Auntie Carole's face was like sunshine breaking into a dark room. She was a special person and so for me it stood to reason that her son Leslie was special too. I think he was younger than me, but I always remember him somehow as older and wiser than I am. He had the demeanor even then of what they decades later called *an old soul*. I remember feeling even as a child that somehow Leslie was a being that had been here in the world before, somewhere in the long ago. A person who just knew things that I didn't know, and I felt safe with him just like I always had with his mother. Leslie and I only saw each other perhaps 15 times within those years but I cannot remember one single other friend my age from those times whom I loved nearly as much. As I pondered about this, I looked over to my cousin and said, "I Love you, Cousin Leslie."

To which he answered, "I love you too, Cousin Artie." We both giggled but kept our arms well around each other anyway not caring what anyone thought of us.

Sol watched and listened to our silly chatter carefully and finally he looked at us, smiling with his warm countenance, and just said, *"Oy vey!"*

CHAPTER 11

The Alcazar & Dr. Duck
(An Offer For Sally O'Flannery)

MEANWHILE ON THE balcony of the Alcazar, according to Uncle Harley's later account of the details and what I remember, this is what happened: Harley and Tina were sitting in the row just behind Duck and the Irish in the section on the far right of the balcony. Harley had his arm around her as she lay with her head near his shoulder looking up at him dreamily. Harley was whispering sweet nothings into Tina's red, freckled ear that had the besotted usher squirming nicely.

Duck and Sally were in the row just in front of them a few seats to their left and were firing up the motors of their sexual triage. Duck had seated himself in the seat next to the aisle to make room for his long legs. The doctor and his nurse were petting heavily while exchanging chewing gum between installing multiple hickeys on each other's necks like hummingbirds on a bottle. Both were thoroughly lost in their study of pubertal chemistry with the Theocarides-O'Flannery sexual thermostat on high, when a loud voice from across the aisle said belligerently, *"Hey, I know you!"* Neither Duck nor Harley looked up.

"Yeah, I know him too!" another, louder voice said.

"That's that queer-ass freak wrestler from Bell High School!" the second voice said, addressing Tim. No one responded. Duck went back to fishing for Sally's bubble gum with his tongue.

"Hey Betty Boop," the first voice said addressing Sally loudly enough for the balconies audience to hear him.

"When you're through with that *big fairy*, I can show you the thrills of being with a real man. Can you handle that, sugar britches?" The second voice added.

"I'll bet she can handle us both," the first voice jeered.

"Maybe we'll let the big goon have sloppy thirds," the second boy said even louder to Duck.

A group of other boys sitting somewhere in the dark behind the two could be heard exhorting them on, laughing and cheering in approval. "Go Showalters! Go Garfield High! Go Bulldogs!"

Duck ignored it all, but after their next rude commentary he responded, "Well listen, fellows," he said calmly, "don't you think the lady has something to say about your magnanimous offer? Why don't you just *ask her* about how she feels about it before you skitter me away, crying myself to sleep, as you two *thrill* her with all your obvious charms?"

"Good Idea!" one of the big boys blustered. "What about it, Honey Buns?" he said to Sally. "How about a couple of 17-year-old senior varsity men instead of an overgrown 15-year-old sophomore wrestler?"

Duck sat up, then smiled as Sally straightened herself out looking over at the two boys pondering their question as though she were carefully considering their proposal.

"Well, let's see," she said, pausing thoughtfully while taking a deep breath. "Well, Yeah... Yes, you know... I can sort of see it. You are both kind of cute, in a, clumsy, pimply and immature sort of way and besides, I see by your lettermen sweaters that you play football."

"Yep, Sweet Cakes!" the first boy responded proudly. "We are Garfield High senior varsity linemen, first-string, all-state selection, board-named players... both of us."

"*Wow*, that's pretty impressive; I must admit," she said looking back and forth between them and Duck.

"I know I'm Impressed," Duck chimed in, not looking up as he kissed the tip of Sally's nose, and then went back to gnawing her neck a bit.

Then Sally kissed Duck on his eyelids, then his lips, while speaking in broken sentences between exaggerated breathlessness as she poured it on for the benefit of the footballers. Continuing the show, she began running her fingers through Duck's hair, moaning and accentuating her every move.

"Now then," she said as she sat up straight once again, making eye contact with the two boys, "I just this moment gave your proposal some serious thought and it might work out if you two were only *undefeated* heavyweight wrestlers."

Sally paused, looking at them both directly, then said, "You see boys, I like to wrestle with men who know how. The *rah-rah* stuff of you loudmouth types never really interested me very much; you boys enjoy playing with your balls a bit too much for me. Plus, *boys,* I prefer men who act like men, not bullies. Besides, I like men who don't smell like bad cheese or goat shit, you know? Men who don't belch or fart just before they kiss me. So, I'm afraid that I'll just have to suffer through as best I can with this beautiful wrestler for now, but who knows, one day I may just switch *to real men* if you can show me you are better, smarter or nicer-looking men than this one."

Many on the balcony audience applauded her response appreciatively. She finished her assessment with, "Thanks for the offer, *boys.*" Then she and Duck went back to work exploring the limitless boundaries of teenage sexual discovery by mining each other's mouths for bubblegum.

The boy's entourage mumbled occasionally, lofting an insult or catcalls to no effect.

CHAPTER 12

The Alcazar and Dr. Duck (Skinny Dippers)

I WAS SO PROUD of myself! You see, I had determined not to back slide. Maybe one day, I too could get to a Bar and get Mitzvahed, perhaps becoming a man like Sol. But damn, as I sat there playing with the fortune in my pocket, watching Leslie gobble huge mouthfuls, that Popcorn smelled ever so good. Leslie looked at me a bit strangely; perhaps he saw my inner struggling, so of course he taunted me more by offering me bites every few seconds then laughing at my suffering. The movies went on and on. Finally we got a bit restless with all the cartoons and cliff hanger serials.

I said to Leslie, "I like your shoe!"

My cousin Leslie was taken aback.

"What?" he said.

"Your shoe," I repeated, "it's thick. I like it."

"Oh yes, it helps me walk much better since my operation," he said.

"Neat," I said sincerely. "I know all about those shoes and injuries and such. See, the Gnome Exemplumonious has a shoe just like that one. Bet you can sneak up on people better cause you can scrunch a big step then a little silent one. Neat!"

"Never thought of that Artie," Leslie said as he put his arm around me once again. "Who did you say had a shoe like this?" he said chewing his Abba-Zaba.

"The Gnome that lives in our Pepper Tree, his name is Pie. Papa Eudie says that gnome is forty four and a thousand hundred years old and was one of the best sneaker uppers of all time. He even snuck onto the sandwich ship and pissed on the hard tacks of the HMS Peanut Butter and Jelly owned by the boatswain Smith Kennedy. He practically saved the revolution from the tacks collectors. Guess what Leslie, did you know Grandma Brown collects buttons?"

Leslie looked at me strangely. Mystified he asked, "Who's Papa Eudie?"

"Oh," I said casually, "he's a Giant story teller."

Now Leslie was looking at me as if I was getting stranger by the minute. He asked, "Does he live in the Pepper tree too?"

"No," I said. "He lives across the street in the Funeral Parlor and he fixes dead people, then Harley sings for them then Papa Eudie lifts them with his own two hands and puts them into their ground. Then people wear black until the next morning then they tear each other's sleeves. And guess what," I added. "I ride up on his high shoulders and pull his hair hard."

"You ride on his shoulders during the funeral?" Leslie asked.

"Naw, just sometimes when we can, but when we walk I pull his hair really hard."

"You do?" Leslie said with some interest.

"Yes, and he never says ouch," I said. "And guess what. He has bullet holes in his head."

Leslie said, "Really?"

Then I remembered something and said, "Really. And guess what Leslie, once he tore the head off a turkey and hit a greasy sergeant with it."

I guessed Lesley didn't believe me because his eyes got a bit glassy, so we changed the subject.

Sol had been listening to my palaver and just looked bemused.

We talked a good deal and paid little attention to the movie. I convinced Leslie that having one great shoe like his was a real advantage in the world of boys. I think he felt genuine pride and real love in my commentary and in the sincerity of my ignorance, so he just smiled and did not seem to take offense. I was on the brink of bragging about his very fine left foot and special shoe to some of the kids in the rows just behind us by extolling the virtues and advantages of his sneaky foot. I told him so, but he advised me not to.

He said, "Let's just keep that to ourselves. Might scare them and spoil our secret if we should need to do some sneaking about of our own."

"Okay," I whispered back, "that makes sense. Mums the word."

Soon we were bored with the endless movies, but the worst thing was that by sitting in the front row the back of our heads were being used as targets for theater rubbish, small candy pieces and spit ball practice by the five hundred or more kids seated just behind us. Plus we were stiff necked and blurry eyed from being much too close and looking almost straight up at the big screen.

"Hey," I said to the boys, "let's go upstairs and spy on Harley and Duck." The boys agreed and I whispered to Leslie to use his sneaky foot to lead us up to the balcony in the quietest way possible.

Leslie just said, "Sure." Then he added, looking at me as though it were his first view of me, "Artie you are so weird!"

I believed whole heartedly in the powers and grace of Leslie's special sneaky foot. I warned Sol to keep quiet and to be really silent like "The Shadow, Lamont Cranston" on the radio.

As we walked up to the balcony, I followed Leslie and tried my best to imitate his slight limp. It made me invisible, or at the very least, silent. Sol, just behind me, was clueless as to our secret and started to laugh at me as I seriously tried to imitate Leslie's limp.

If Leslie was self conscious of his crippled foot, he owned it and looked back at us both and said, "Follow me. And for gosh sakes, be quiet."

I looked at Rubinstein just behind us and said, "Sol, walk like us and just watch Leslie carefully in case those girls are in there. They might be giving Harley and Duck 'cooties' and some of those girls' cooties could get on us!"

Upon hearing my warning, Sol said, "From your lips to Gods ears, may God smite me with such cooties." He rolled his eyes to the heavens saying out loud, "May those cooties engulf me and smother me completely!"

We trinity of voyeuristic detectives headed for the balcony. Upon arriving we slouched down in our seats. We were at a safe spying distance for watching the love birds and the movie in equal proportions. Some funny moaning noises were coming from Duck and Sally. Leslie and I giggled. I whispered to Sol that maybe she was sick.

"No," he answered in a low voice, "she is not sick yet, but if they keep that up, in about three or four weeks from now she'll be sick every morning and crave pickles with Aunt Jemima syrup and mustard on them."

Leslie and I looked at each other and were about ready to ask what he meant when Sol, looking across the Isle from Duck, said to us, "Uh oh, I've got trouble."

"Where?" we asked, looking around.

"Over there," he said, pointing to the two large, muscular boys sitting across the isle from Duck and Sally.

"That's the Showalter brothers, Danny and Denny," he said, showing concern on his face as he continued with his head lowered, speaking to us in a very low voice, "I go to school with them; they play football at Garfield High School and are real trouble for me and others. They have been after me for the past semester and have beaten me up twice. Once they tore off my pants and threw me in the girl's locker room."

The two big boys were starting to look our way. Leslie got us on our feet, motioning for us to follow. We three left the upstairs theater and moved into the balcony foyer. Sitting down on the large velvet bench in between the two upstairs bathrooms we continued our conversation.

"Sol, why did they pick on you?" I asked.

Sol said, "Perhaps because they are bullies or because I get good grades and I am on the honor roll or because I am a thirteen year old junior instead of just a thirteen year old eighth grader in junior high.

And I always have a little money, which they steal from me when ever they can. Other than that, I really don't know exactly why," Sol said, thinking about it. "I have wanted to ask them that for some time now. They are the toughest kids in the school and they run that campus. They have most of the Garfield Varsity football team at their disposal, so it's hard for me to figure out what to do about them."

"Why don't you tell your teacher or the School Vice Principle or someone?" Leslie inquired.

"No, I think it is my responsibility," he answered. "I have to deal with them on my own, particularly now that I have become a man. If I don't, my father says there will always be those that are ready to bully me and that it will never end. Father said it just gets worse. I'm just not sure what to do?"

Leslie and I looked at each other not knowing what to do either.

"Well," Leslie said, "let's just go back down stairs and watch the last feature and stay out of their way."

We all agreed and got up to leave when the double doors from the balcony into the foyer opened with Duck filling the doorway. He walked out towards the men's bathroom and when he saw us he smiled and was about to say something when he saw me staring at the large bulge in the crotch of his pants. Now I had seen my Uncle Harley stuff a pair folded stockings in the front of his pants then laugh at himself as he looked at his profile in his garage mirror, but I looked at Ducks feet and he still had his stockings on.

Duck looked at the three of our incredulous faces like deer caught in the headlights. Then pointing to his own fly he said, "Sally invited this "wood pecker" into the balcony and right now I have to take him in to peepee."

Sol smiled knowingly, but Leslie and I were simply clueless. Duck went in the bathroom as we waited there in the foyer.

I told Sol and Leslie, "Let me tell Tim about those brothers. Bet he'll know what to do."

Sol said, "Well, he's a fine large lad that's for sure. If he is our friend, I feel a whole lot safer already."

Duck came out the bathroom door within five minutes without any evidence of the woodpecker. I guessed he had just left it inside the boys' room. Sol and I, well, mostly the clear headed clear thinking well spoken Sol, had laid out his dilemma to Duck and the two scholars understood each other quickly.

Duck told us that he had just had the pleasure of meeting the Showalter boys and had some ideas on the subject.

You see, we all knew, through years of us watching the movies of Muggs McGinnis, that Muggs had developed a system in which he would say to his gang, "Routine three!" or "Routine nine!" or some arbitrary number which would cue each member of his gang to perform a specific function. They would spring into action battling the villain whenever Leo Gorcey called one of his 'routine' numbers. Well then, accept on faith that that is precisely the way Duck laid out part of his master plan, carefully instructing each of us about what to do when called upon.

Wow! Leslie and I were so excited to have our dreams come true in real life. We were now instantly transformed from Artie and Leslie into Glimpy, Freedhoff and Lefty. Sol, was our gang's newest member and Tim was, of course, our own personal leader, a much larger version of 'Muggs McGinnis'. Our dreams come true, right there, right then in the balcony of our Alcazar Theater exactly at the same time as the real Muggs appeared on our big screen. Man oh man!

"Tim," Sol said, "I am not afraid to fight. I am not an athlete. Actually I am a chess player," he said as an afterthought, "but I have courage and since my first encounters with those two, my father has taught me a bit of Savate. So if you need me, I am willing to try and help. I will endeavor to give you the best I can."

"Thank you Sol," Duck said warmly, "but I need a man to supervise Artie and Leslie, making sure they get their part right and don't get hurt. Just cover them okay? I can handle these boys just fine."

Sol smiled broadly and braced himself, throwing his shoulders back at the ready. Sol lacked neither intellect nor courage.

Tim said, "Let's all go in, then when you see me make my move be ready to spring into action when I call the routine numbers. Be sure and remember the duties I have assigned each of you, okay?"

Before we turned to go back in, Duck said to Sol, "Perhaps, if we can give these devils inside the raspberry, a bit later I can give you a few pointers in chess. That's my game you know."

Sol said to the big boy, "Yes, perhaps so, I would very much enjoy learning more. I am always eager to become more proficient and I seem, day by day, to be slowly getting a bit better at that infernal game."

Finally, Duck looked at us then admonished, "You guys all stay well back till I need you, okay? Do you all know what to do?"

We all nodded our heads affirmatively.

We entered the balcony once again and found our seats. One of the Showalters was sitting in Ducks seat next to a squirming, unhappy Sally O'Flannery, who was pushing him off, saying something about his bad breath.

Duck looked down at Showalter and said, "I think you have my seat. Move it or lose it."

Showalter replied, "Really?"

Duck answered, "Really!"

Our little gang held its collective breath. A half dozen of the Garfield footballers were now on there feet mumbling their support to the Showalters.

Danny and Denny Showalter were now standing up alongside Duck, but soon the two large Showalter brothers were dwarfed, not only by Duck, but by yet another boy who had come to support Duck. Both Tim and the new boy were five inches taller than Danny and Denny. Standing next to Duck's shoulder was an equally large black boy, about seventeen, who was almost exactly the same height and build as young Tim.

"Mr. Tim," the other big boy said, offering Duck his hand. "My name is Butter Guest. Yo daddy buried boaf my gran folk lass year. He a really good man 'n he hepd us out a lot when we dent have much. I 'members you from dat funeral 'n I knows you from yo wrestling, cause I likes dat stuff." Butter paused looking directly at the Showalter boys and their supporters saying in an unmistakable voice of authority, "Now, I don't know what all ya'll got in mind here an taint none ah my bennis!"

"Bennis," I repeated to myself. *I got it! NUNYUR BENNIS!* "None of your business." *Oh man, I got it! I got it!* I wanted to scream it out loud to Uncle Harley, but kept mum.

Butter went on specifically addressing the Garfield footballers just behind the Showalter boys, "Ya'all knows me from Manual Arts High School football. Ya'll are gibbin footballers a bad name 'n you mouf is gonna get you in a wuld ah hut talking like dat tah nutha man's woman, but that's you Bennis. But what dis 'bout, is weis gonna keep dis betwixt jus Tim here 'n ya'll Showalters. Ya'll understand me over dare," he said addressing the Showalter friends then looking right in the eyes of Showalters. "Cause," Butter went on, "if not, you sho nuff gonna have dis Mississippi Negro to whup too." With that, Butter Guest said to Tim, "Mr. Tim I'm right up yonder and I'll be watchen 'n ifn you needs some hep?"

"Thanks Butter, I appreciate that, but we aren't going to have any trouble here," Duck said looking at Danny and Denney. Besides I've got my buddy Harley Brown here."

Now we all looked over at Harley and Tina and saw Harley gulp and start to squirm uncomfortably in his seat.

Butter put his forefinger on his eyelid then pointed to the Showalters as if to say, I'll be watching. Then he did an about face and went back up to his girlfriend in the upper balcony loges. He sat next to her watching for any untoward move from the other footballers. The Showalters grumbled and sat back down. Duck sat down and held Sally's hand, but was on guard.

Mrs. Ippy. "Miss is sippi." Holy Moley, Mississippi. Oh man I got that, too. Ever since I met Sol this afternoon, I had been learning all kinds of great stuff. Oh man, I just can't wait till I tell Uncle Harley and Duck. But this wasn't the time. I was anticipating an explosion. I was also busy reviewing my "routine" duties and numbers given by the Duck. We were all on high alert.

Harley was suing to go home and said something to Duck about just leaving, but Danny Showalter, the older brother, heard Harley's words as something provocative and spoiling for a fight, said to Harley, "Hey, you pansy ass little queer peter pounder coward, what are you looking at?"

Uncle Harley started to answer him, but before Harley's first syllable scratched the ether, before the next thousandth of second passed, Duck sprung up like a panther tossed through the air from a catapult, stunning everyone. He was so fast and furious and so sure of himself that no one had even a second to react, certainly not the Showalters.

They didn't know what had hit them. Duck was used to lifting and slamming big boys to the ground. After all, he trained with his father Eudocio who oft times weighed as much as three high school footballers combined, so these big boys were just light exercise for the Duck. He threw Danny head first with great ease, ass over teakettle and head first in between two rows of seats.

In the blink of an eye, Danny was standing on his head, trapped in the foot space between two rows with his buttocks and legs bent over the back of the seats just behind him. He had no room to twist or extricate himself and for thirty seconds or more was just plain stuck. In two yanks, Duck removed Danny's shoes. Then he removed the boy's pants in one fell swoop by yanking them by their large pants cuffs.

Denny, the younger Showalter, could scarcely believe the speed at which young Tim worked. Finally he was on his feet slugging Duck in the back of his head as hard as he could. Duck spun in one fluid motion landing two crackling rock hard punches to Denney's face that flattened his nose and bloodied his mouth knocking him out cold within the span of a breath. Several additional blows sent him tumbling back into his brother who had only just gotten back onto his feet. They both fell back down again into a heap.

Duck tore off the other boy's pants and shoes as quickly as he had the first, tossing them back over his shoulder. The Showalter boys were not yet back into the fray because by design or fashion Danny had chosen not to wear any underwear and was by then completely naked from the waist down. His brother Denny had quite visible, brown peckerwood tracks in the crotch of his underwear. Both bothers struggled to cover themselves.

Sally looked up at the naked Danny. He saw she was blushing and giggling as she viewed his manhood. The hapless boy tried to remove his lettermen's sweater to use as a makeshift kilt. He was trying desperately to reverse this indignity by getting out of the line of Sally's sight while trying to figure out what the hell to do about the possible on coming violence of Duck.

Sally was now having a wonderful time said to him loudly, "Hey there ALL STATE, was that a pimple I just saw there between your legs or was that your 'big thriller'? Come on big boy, uncover that great rascal and give all us love-starved girls up here a look at your man berries." Then she said to his younger brother, "Hey Sugar Britches, it looks like you spilled some of your chocolate sugar in the crotch of your BVDs. Want a Kleenex? Or maybe Dr. Tim can wipe your ass for you."

The kids in the balcony were having great fun at the Showalter's expense.

Duck gathered the Showalter's pants and as he tossed both pairs to Sol he said to us, "Routine Three!"

We sprang into action immediately, knowing exactly what to do. Leslie grabbed the Showalter's four shoes and tossed them over the balcony. The audience of kids below got into the spirit of the event, throwing the boys shoes back and forth to each other, hooting and hollering up to the balcony for more treasure to fall from the balcony skies.

Duck tossed me the boys' wallets and I emptied the contents over the edge of the balcony, floating all their possessions down to the curious and rowdy crowd who were enjoying the hail of objects peeled out of the billfolds. There were a few dollars that rained down, coins, papers, a photo of a large breasted naked woman, little bits of paper with girls' names and phone numbers on them, and a driver's license.

All the articles were happily consumed then redistributed or destroyed by the mass of screaming kids below. As I tossed over the second wallet, I saw two strange things, soft rubbery things in packets that had fallen onto the edge of the balcony from the wallet tossing. I yelled to Uncle Harley, asking him what they were before I threw them down.

He said, "Those are party balloons fartnick. Just put them in your pocket and save them for us for later."

I did as I was instructed then I tossed the wallet over the edge, watching it quickly get ripped into shreds below.

Sol took the Showalter's pants and ran out to the foyer then into the bathroom. After cutting the crotch of their pants open with his Swiss army knife and tearing the boy's pants in half, he took each leg and stuffed them in separate trash cans. He found in one pocket a set of car keys and flushed them down the toilet and then he returned to the fray.

After I pocketed the balloons, I ran directly to Tina, the little freckled face ticket girl with Harley, and told her that Tim said for her to call the police and ask only for Sgt. Zambo or Captain Malloy. I said to be sure tell them the call was from Timoleon. She complied immediately.

Now then, the Bell police department was not more than five hundred yards from the Alcazar Theater and both Zambo and the Captain were there within minutes. Duck's entire operation had lasted no more than ten minutes start to finish, and it was over almost as fast as it had begun.

Captain Malloy heard from all the witnesses, none of which had a kind word to say about the Showalters or their minions. Within another ten minutes the Sergeant had everything down on his report. Zambo and the Captain took the Showalter boys to the station on a charge that Zambo called, "Skinny dipping in the balcony of a movie theater without the benefit of water."

We later learned that within an hour of the boys' arrival at the jail, Mr. Showalter, accompanied by his sons' football coach, arrived to find them red faced, bruised and bloody and still in there letterman sweater kilts. Both were very unhappy with the behavior of the big boys. The boys' car had to be towed and their Garfield supporters had abandoned the theater like rats off a sinking ship.

"So much for team loyalty and spirit," Sol said.

Danny and Denny were suspended from football for six weeks and their car was temporarily taken away from them.

It was ever so glorious! I thought, and I commented to Uncle Harley and Duck that it all happened so fast, that we used only one routine number and guess what; it was a three, my trinity number. I couldn't wait to tell Papa and Grandma about threes.

Our matinee experience ended a little early and all of us were standing outside as the unhappy Showalters were taken off to the station house. Harley and Duck paid little attention to the semi naked miscreants. However, Sally waived and blew them a kiss. Harley and Duck then said good bye to their sweethearts as Sol, Leslie and I impatiently waited for them.

"I'll see you in school in a few weeks, dreamboat," Tina said waiving to Harley as she jumped onto the street car headed for home. She blew him kisses out the window.

He waived back to her, watching till her street car was out of sight.

Duck asked Sally, "Will I see you in school in January?"

"I hope so. If I can figure out how to hide these hickeys from my dad," she said flushing a bit and looking troubled.

"Your father doesn't like me very much does he?" Duck asked.

"Not at all," she answered. "Of course he doesn't really know you, but he doesn't like anyone for me who's not Irish. He just knows you are a Greek and for him that is what he calls 'Predigested Whap Shit'. He likes the fact that you are Catholic alright, but the Greek part he can't quite handle. He wants a good Irish, Catholic boy for me."

"What about your mother, does she like me?" Duck asked.

Sally said, "Oh my God Tim, she loves you. She told me last week that she thought you were the best looking man she had ever seen. She used that word 'man' not 'boy'. I swear to God Tim, I think she is beguiled over you. How do you think I get out to see you at all? The only thing she ever says to me about you when I leave to meet you somewhere is, 'Keep your knickers locked high and dry and in the upright position!' So far I am managing to do that, Tim," she said, stretching up on her tip toes to kiss him on his chin. Then, as she turned to leave, she smiled and said coyly as she winked at him, "But, Doctor Tim, remember darling, I got an eye full of Danny Showalter's 'thriller' so you just never know, I may switch too 'a real man' soon, so watch out big boy," she said, shaking her finger at the

Duck, who spun the blushing Irish round, lifting her off the ground just like in the movies.

He placed his very best kiss on her saying, "Frankly Scarlet, I do give a damn, so damned well behave yourself you beautiful Irishwoman."

She sighed and said, "Okay, Doctor Theocarides, maybe not just yet, but you also keep away from those damn Greek girls who wish to cook for you and give you an even dozen babies."

We all stood together in front of the Alcazar smiling at each other over a job well done. We were the living, breathing embodiment of Muggs McGinnis and his newest chapter of the West Coast Bowery Boys.

I renamed our gang the Alcazarians.

CHAPTER 13

The Alcazar & Dr. Duck (Enlightenment!)

SOL OFFERED HIS hand to Duck saying, "Thank you, Tim! This was an interesting experience to say the least. I will either be killed when I return to Garfield High in January or those guys won't bother me anymore. God willing it will be the latter. May I show you my appreciation by allowing Leslie and me to treat us all to an ice cream sundae over at Suekeetchers Fountain? It would be our pleasure to treat you all."

We all enthusiastically agreed, especially me. But Duck said, "Nah, let's all just go up the street to my house and I can give you some chess pointers as we play a game of chess."

"Hold your little horses there, Kimo Sabe," Harley interrupted. "What's in that for us? Who is the 'we' you are speaking of here? Are you two going to play chess with Artie and Leslie, too? No, I don't think so big man." Harley was defiantly poking his buddy in the ribs. "Let's take a vote on it."

Of course, Les and I agreed with Harley. Besides, we intoned, the soda fountain would only be open another half hour or so.

Akiva Rubenstein, Polish Chessmaster, Sol's Grandfather

Sol said, "We can wait till we get to your house or play tomorrow if you wish?"

Duck protested, "Oh no, now I'm in the mood. All that action there in the balcony has my warrior blood itching. After all, chess is naught but mental war."

Harley Brown rolled his eyes skyward and said to Duck, "Tim, you've used that old warrior axe for everything from adding extra syrup to your hotcakes to necking with your accursed, all-Irish girlfriends. Irish lips and other sundry body parts also apparently get your warrior blood growling. And by the way dorfus, have you ever in your goofy life had a single girlfriend that wasn't Irish?"

Tim ignored him then changed the subject by saying, "By the way Brownie, thanks for all the help with the Showalter Boys. Where in the hell were you when the fan hit the shit?"

"For your information Theocarides, I was otherwise engaged doing a very important academic experiment regarding freckle transference through passion and heavy breathing. Besides, what the hell am I going to do, sing those big ass Showalters to death? They are the ones who needed help to kick your show-offy warrior buns. Hell, I knew their asses were grass from the start. Jeeze Duck, it was over before I even knew it had started. Besides, you big dumb ass Greek, watching you potentially get your fanny kicked is the only recreation I ever get, so why would I want to jump in and help you? Anyway, you guys didn't even bother to include me in your master plan, so you at least owe me five minutes here for a sundae before you destroy poor Sol to inflate your warrior's ego, okay?

Harley just shook his head and waited for a consensus.

Duck finally gave in and we slowly walked along toward the drugstore.

Sol considered this thoughtfully then asked, "Well Tim, how good of a chess player are you?"

Now Tim was extraordinary in every way, save one. He was by no means humble or self effacing so by this time his rhetoric was as Grandma Brown would have said, full of 'pride and pickle juice' as he answered Sol's question by asking Uncle Harley his own question, "Harley Brown, did you hear that? He wants to know how good a chess player I am. Why don't you tell him?"

Duck was grinning ear to ear, well satisfied with the sure praise to come from the young Mr. Brown. He wasn't disappointed.

"Nobody ever beats him," Harley said. "I've never beaten him. No one at Bell High has ever beaten him. He is the president of the Bell High School Chess Club and well," Harley said with finality, "he's just a phenomenon. Tim is as good at Chess as he is at wrestling and science and everything else he does," Harley said factually.

"I see," said Sol, considering it. "Well, the reason I asked you Tim, is that if you want to, we can play a game right now as we walk along toward the soda fountain and then when we arrive, over our sundaes. Then also as we walk on to your house, and if we haven't finished the game by then we can finish on a board at your place or, if I manage to last that long, we can finish it over the phone should it go on a bit longer?"

Tim gulped just a bit, but said, "You mean to play it descriptively in our heads."

"Yes, if you wish to," Sol replied, "but I like to play algebraic notation."

Now Tim had played a little bit of 'descriptive chess notation', one move at a time using the U.S. Mail service or on the telephone with a chess board in front of him over several weeks or months. But he had yet to play any real algebraic notation and was only vaguely familiar with the concept through chess books. He certainly had never tried to play a game entirely in his head. But Tim would never admit it to this rather small, thirteen year old boy; after all he had just been the hero of the day and saved the boy's life. Certainly he was not willing to relinquish his new hero ship and all the adulation just yet.

"Err ah, well sure... yes," Tim said, "algebraic will be just fine."

They asked me to pick a number between one and ten and the closest guess to my number would go first, get the "white chess pieces" and first move. I picked it and Sol won by guessing the number three.

Harley chided Duck about me and my 'Trinities', querying as to why in the world the great, Greek genius chess player would not have guessed Artie's famous number three.

Harley observed, "Christ man, Sol has known Artie now for what, four hours, and you know full well that silly kid would have three fingers on each hand and three toes on each foot, but you forgot about Artie's famous threes? That's brilliant, Duck man. That was just freaking brilliant!"

The trinity of us walked directly behind the chess players toward Suekeetcher's Soda Fountain, and Sol said "E-4" to Duck without hesitation.

Painfully slow, Tim responded, "C-5."

This went on until we reached Suekeetcher's. As we walked into the soda fountain, my mother looked surprised to see me. Bedraggled, she seated us all at a bent-wire ice cream table made for four.

Noticing Leslie Dow, my mother came around the counter, giving Les a kiss and a warm embrace. Then she chatted with him a bit.

I introduced my new friend Sol to my mother, who said, "Hello, Sol. Nice to meet you."

Sol smiled at her and replied, "It's a pleasure to meet you too, Mrs. Spelman." Then with almost no pause, he glanced over to Duck. "N-F-3," he said.

After awhile, Tim answered Sol, and on they went. Duck had no time to concentrate on our idle conversation. It was very slow and painful for him. A drop of sweat started forming on his upper lip as the battle continued. After every move came Sol's response, and so on.

At the next table there were three people celebrating a birthday. A dimple-faced baby girl of about two years old was sitting in a high chair between the older woman — whom I'd mistakenly assumed was the mother of the baby, and perhaps the sister of the younger teenage girl — sitting next to her. I often failed to understand the obvious, and this was no exception. I didn't know that the fourteen-year-old girl, whose innocent face looked far younger than my Aunt Veve's, had become pregnant by a young Marine corporal who had died somewhere called Saipan.

All I wanted was to make these sad women happy. While I was showing Sol something about paper boatmanship, I secured a small rectangular piece of paper from my mother, creating yet another one of my paper boats. Sol watched me very carefully and asked, "Do you mind if I try something, Artie?"

Duck interrupted us, giving Sol his next move.

"No," I interjected, as Sol took the newly-constructed paper boat and refolded it just a bit, making it more symmetrical. Then he used the tiny scissors on his Swiss army knife to cut around the gunnels of the little boat in such a tight pattern that it resembled a boatswain's half-hitch rope. Those ropes were often used to dress up the rails aboard ships, just like the ones that my Uncle Paul had showed me on the arm of a chair. It was really beautiful to watch this boy, I'll tell you.

And then, after he dashed off his next chess move in response to a frustrated Duck, he took the tip of his little scissors and created four perfect portholes fore and aft on each side of the boat. With Mom's pencil he made the inside of the portholes black with the lead, which made it look like there were cabins inside the paper boat. I was really impressed — I had never imagined that level of skill from Sol. It was almost like something Uncle Fuzzy might have created.

"Gosh, that's neat Sol," I said. "Where did you learn to do that?"

"Just something I've been thinking about for a couple of hours," he said.

Sol handed me his modified paper boat. I glanced over to Leslie to invite him to come with me on my mission, but he was speaking to my mother — something about the operation on his foot and her son and his sneaky foot ideas — and so I went alone to the birthday table, sitting down uninvited between the baby and the younger of the two girls. I brought the boat with me, along with one of my party balloons from the Showalter wallet toss.

"Here is a little boat we made," I said, showing it to them. "You could have it for your baby. And here is a party balloon." I held up the little packet, dangling it between my thumb and forefinger, and swinging it back and forth in front of the young girl. Then I set it back down next to the boa, right in front of her.

The older of the two women looked down at my gifts and scowled. The younger girl turned red and covered her face. The baby grabbed the boat, putting it in her mouth and spitting it out. Sol, who had taken it all in while waiting for Duck's next move, understood the dilemma in an instant. He scooped up the balloons and handed them to Harley, who started to laugh.

"Artie!" Harley said to me.

"It's nine, cousin! Nine, Artie! You won't live to reach your ninth year of life."

"Oh, yeah?" I said. "Well, Mississippi and none of your business. What do you think about that?"

"Alright, Spelman," Harley said. "That's pretty impressive — twelve or maybe thirteen, God willing!"

Sol received Duck's chess move and parried without hesitation. The woman at the ice cream table got her trinity to their feet and they stormed out en masse without saying a word.

My Mother stood dumbfounded as they walked out the front door. "Hey!" she cried. "They forgot to pay the bill! They stiffed me $1.05."

She slumped down on her little stool behind the counter, looking weary. Duck's face had the weight of the world on it too. He had forgotten where he was in the game, and Harley whispered to me that he believed Tim was ready to concede. He knew Duck was utterly humiliated.

Grateful for the rescue from the Showalter brothers, Sol saw the despair on Duck's face and asked, "You know what, Tim? I am having a bit of trouble keeping track of our chess moves. Would you mind if we just waited and set up the board at your house to finish the game on a live board? What do you say?"

Duck said, "Well, I guess so." He paused. "Sure, but only if you have the energy to do that. Make it easy on yourself, and if you are just too exhausted we can finish tomorrow or you could just concede the game now. We can do that if you want to."

"No," said Sol. "After all, I am a man now, and I must see the things I start through to the bitter end."

Sol paid our check and left my smiling mother a thirty-five cent tip. At Sol's suggestion, we helped my mother clean up the back counter and sweep, and helped her shut down the soda fountain. Just before we all walked out the front door I ran to my mother, sliding a nickel folded inside my dog-eared dollar bill. I placed it down into her apron and said, "Mama, this money is for those stiff people that left. I'm sorry, I think my boat made them sad, so this is to make up for it. This is for you Mom, okay?"

That was when my mother told me about the young girl's loss during the war.

Mother kissed me on top of my head and hugged me warmly before she left the building. The pharmacist locked up as we watched Mom cross Atlantic Boulevard at the light. She walked in front of the lumberyard through the lot, past the big swing and up the dirt path, right into our little white house. We waved to her, and then we walked up the other side of Atlantic toward Duck's house.

As we entered the Theocarides home, we saw Papa sitting next to Momma Anna on the sofa. The two of them were holding hands. Papa had on his house slippers; I noticed that one of his ankles was all swollen, and a bowl of Epsom salts sat on the end table.

As Papa and Anna stood to meet Sol and Leslie, the two boys almost fell backwards. Sol didn't quite lose his composure, but Leslie was speechless, looking almost straight up into Papa's smiling face, while Sol remained wide-eyed but restrained. Anna quickly removed the soak bowl, and looking at Papa, she said to the group, "My little boy has done too much playing today, racing the other children with a great weight on his neck. I guess his jockey was just too heavy for him."

Papa chuckled at Anna's words, while I grinned from ear to ear, looking at Sol and cousin Leslie. I proudly pointed to myself, indicating that I had been his jockey during the race. Duck explained the track scene to the guests and Sol nodded his head appreciatively.

"I would have loved to have witnessed that," Sol smiled.

Leslie's mouth was still agape as he whispered in my ear. "Artie boy," he said. "You weren't kidding, man. That is the guy that lives in the beanstalk! I thought you were fibbing me."

I said, "No, I didn't joke you and I don't lie unless I have to. Now see, once Uncle Harley lied about some tar, but that was only to help me. But our Grandma Brown says, 'Never lie when the truth will do, and that the truth will always do.'"

Leslie hesitated and said finally, "Jeez man, I can't wait to meet your gnome and see his special shoe!"

"That may take a bit longer," I said.

Anna left to get some pasteli and milk for her guests. Sol, Papa and Duck soon began conversing about chess, with Duck trying to explain to Papa that he and Sol had been playing a game in their heads on their walk home, and that he had been trying to explain the finer points of the game to his new friend, but that Sol had just gotten too tired, so they decided to play next week. Papa nodded his head, but he knew his son well and said with a wry smile, "Well, we have a chess board right here. Why don't you two play another game right now? I would enjoy watching you teach this young boy a lesson."

"Well Papa," Duck said. "I think Sol is just too tired from today at the Alcazar."

"Yes," Papa Eudie said. "Zambo phoned a few minutes ago to report all your Bravura."

Meanwhile the milk and Pasteli circulated the room as everyone went over the day's happy events with Papa and Anna. There was good fellowship all around. We all told our versions of the fight story, exaggerating it more and more with each telling.

Sol painted Tim's balcony heroics in glowing colors, expressing great admiration and gratitude, stating unequivocally that young Duck was nothing less than a shinning Sir Lancelot, and that he was honored to know him — and now, by extension, his wonderful family. Tim, trying to steer the conversation away from chess, said, "That big boy Butter was there, and offered to help me with those goons. Remember Dad, you buried his grandparents a while back. Pop, I didn't know his name was 'Butter', though. I thought it was T.J. or something."

Papa said, "Yes, nice kid. I remember him and his lovely family very well. I think it was his daddy who once told me he got that name because whenever the Manual Arts football team and T.J. Guest flattened an opposing quarterback, before he could get the ball thrown the players would yell 'Have some Butter with that pancake?' to their opponents, and that's how T.J. got the name of 'Butter'."

"Yeah Papa, he mentioned that you helped them a lot."

"Well, I don't remember that, son. You know, sometimes you do the smallest things and people still make a big deal out of them. But I do remember them all very fondly."

Harley was not going to let Duck escape, and without a word he was on his feet, setting the oval table with the chess board between the teacher and the student.

Before Duck could say another word, Sol instantly removed some pieces from the board and reset others. Before Duck could say anything, Sol said, "Here is our game exactly where we left off."

Duck looked surprised and trapped, but he still queried,

"You remembered after twenty moves?" He tried not to appear impressed.

"No, it was twenty-one moves," Sol corrected. "And it's now your move."

"Oh yes, of course!" Duck said, smiling as though that had just slipped his mind. Then he made his move.

Within scant minutes, Sol mercifully delivered the coup de gras to the befuddled Duck. The cold steel checkmate dumbfounded him, Duck's lower dropped to his chest.

Sol, ever the gentleman, explained to Duck and Eudie and Anna that perhaps the evening was merely a matter of luck. He wanted to assuage the big boy's ego.

Eudie looked over at his son's defeated face. Duck accepted his loss like a good sport, but he could not get a grasp on how this young kid had destroyed him so thoroughly in a game that Tim knew and played very well. Finally, Papa couldn't hold back any longer and had mercy on his son. He hobbled a few steps to his bookshelf, returning to Anna's side with a large beautifully bound book. Papa flipped to a photograph and showed it to Sol.

"You say your name is Rubinstein," he said. "Is this fellow of any relation to you?"

Sol looked at the photo and said, "Yes sir, he is my grandfather."

Eudie laid the book on Duck's lap and said, "Don't feel bad, son. This was not me or Harley. You were playing Sol tonight, and that's saying something. In fact, I doubt that many people could beat your new friend Sol here in chess. The man you are looking at in the book is the boy's grandpa, Akiba Rubinstein, Poland's Grand Master Chess Champion. He is considered by many to be one of the greatest chess players who ever lived.

"By the way son," Eudie continued, looking at Sol. "I recognized you as soon as you walked in the door on your own merits, and this is the reason why I goaded my son into finishing the game. He showed us a news clipping, which featured a photo of young Sol in South Gate Park, playing and defeating thirty of the best chess challengers from all over the state of California.

The news clipping said:

Young Solomon Rubinstein, progeny chess wizard with a bloodline of world class chess genius, takes on all comers at South Gate Park!

The article went on to explain Sol's relationship with Akiba Rubinstein and spoke of the brilliant thirteen-year scholar from Garfield High School who was now a junior at Garfield High School, having skipped forward almost two years. He would graduate at the age of just fourteen.

Papa said to Tim, "You saw this clipping too, Tim, don't you remember? We even commented on this article over breakfast a few months ago!"

"Of course!" Tim said excitedly, slapping himself on the forehead with the palm of his hand. "I knew I had seen you somewhere before!"

Duck's face lit up with relief as he embraced Sol. "Thank you, my friend, for a damn fine lesson," he said. "I think I might have needed this, and somehow I knew my dad would be there for it."

They were enjoying each other's company as Papa gave the boys a pat on the back.

"Tim, I'll trade chess lessons for wrestling lessons with you anytime," offered Sol. "And by the way, Tim, no player I have ever known of is undefeated. That is a myth. If this is your first defeat, it won't be your last, I promise. I have been defeated many times, as has my father. And I suspect that although I have never met him, my grandfather has been defeated as well. I have read about some of his defeats — and we all lose sometimes.

Sol added, "Hopefully not too many times. Because that is the point after all, isn't it?"

Harley said to Sol, "We are going to give you the nickname of 'hot syrup' in our gang, because you just melted the ego of our big Greek warrior hotcake here."

"I'll get you for that, Brownie," Duck said. And then we all teased the defunct Bell High School chess wizard, who laughed at himself more than anyone.

We returned home soon after that. I was praying Anna wouldn't give me her usual shower of kisses the way she usually did — not in front of my new friend Sol, who was now a man after all, and might have no interest in spending his time with kissy-face little boys. Anna read my pride perfectly and let me escape unscathed with a formal handshake, which stunned me. Papa offered to take Sol and Leslie home after some discussion about wartime gasoline rationing. Papa explained that he had a 'T' unlimited gas sticker and that he would be happy to give the boys a lift.

Eudie had four vehicles: three he used for the Mortuary and a fourth. Anna said the last one was Eudie's toy, and that before the war he had only used it on special occasions. Papa pulled the gorgeous Jet Black 1932 V-16 Cadillac Limousine around to the front of the house, and we all watched as Papa sat sporting a chauffeur's hat behind the wheel. In the front convertible portion, the Cadillac was huge, very long; but those V-16 '33 Cadillac's weren't all that wide. Papa was wide, and even when he was in the sitting position in the open air of the chauffeur's seat, he was so big that he looked like an elephant in a tea cup ride at the fair. He stood a full head taller than the top of the windshield, and almost the entire width of the front seat.

"He looks like a grown man riding on a child's peddle car," Leslie said.

It was wonderful to see this. Sol was enthralled, and as Papa brought the car around he said, "Oy gavalt, I hope Mother and Father see us as we pull up. I feel just like King David."

"No, Not David, but Solomon," Duck corrected, smiling at his new friend.

Sol said, "With two Menchen like you and your father, are you sure it's not David?"

"Well, you might be right, King David. You slew an arrogant big-mouthed giant Greek tonight in chess, that is for sure," Tim smiled.

"Yes," Sol said dramatically. "Well, then I must remember that glory is fleeting, and so on to our chariot, young Goliath!" Leslie struggled to open the heavy carriage door.

Reaching for the door handle, Duck said, "Allow me, gentlemen." And he opened the door for us all.

Everyone had a smile on their face as we took off down Atlantic toward Beverly Boulevard, dropping off Leslie first. Sol dutifully walked Leslie to his front door, turning him over to someone standing in the darkness of the doorway.

When Sol returned, Duck said, "Don't worry, we will give your parents a real show when we arrive at your house."

As we arrived at Sol's house Papa skidded the limo's big tires into a dramatic halt, designed to attract as much attention as possible. Then he revved up the powerful sixteen-cylinder engine and sounded a toot on the three-tone horn. He pressed another button several times, sounding an "Ooga" horn. Within seconds, Sol's parents were out on their doorstep, watching the commotion. Papa got out of the limo and in his most dramatic form, he stretched to his full stature and opened the door, removing his black chauffeur's cap and placing it on his chest.

"Your majesty, King David of the Alcazarians, the wise slayer of arrogant Greek youth," he announced. "Your multitudes await you at the wall."

Then as Duck instructed, I got out with my boatswains pipe and sounded "Flag Officer Portside". Sol joined in on our charade with verve and stepped out, grinning at his astonished parents. Hw walked toward them with slow, ceremonial steps, almost as if he were on his toes. Sol's father shook his head, bewildered, and his mother put her hands over her mouth. Sol continued walking, accentuating each step up the royal path to the front gates of his kingdom.

I sounded "Cast Off" on my boatswains pipe. Duck came around to open our door, and we both reentered the limo, while Papa remounted the drivers seat. That was great theater in itself as he sounded the dual horns, and then the ooga once again. We tore off, peeling rubber down the road.

Sol's parents still stood staring at us in disbelief. On our way home we all talked about the questions Sol's parents must have asked him about his day.

You see, I was pretty sure that God had made Grandma Brown's arms, lap and bosom out of leftovers from heaven, as they felt too good to just be regular body parts and stuff.

Once in a blue moon, as she used to say about things, everything would work out just right. I would be there in those arms talking with her, rocking there in that perfect space reserved for the two of us alone. Of course I never knew for sure when or if it was coming. You knew you couldn't always make it happen, and I knew that sometimes when I tried to make it happen that there was a little fire in the kitchen, or Muggs had caught a rat in the front room — or maybe Anna had come for a visit, redirecting my grandma's attention.

But I just knew that this evening was my day. Today was mine and I owned every second of it, so of course it had to end in Grandmother Brown's arms.

We would talk about everything. I could tell my grandmother anything; she always listened carefully, responding when she could, or kissing the side of my head and ear when she was speechless.

After I sat down on her lap Grandmother said, "I'll bet your tired. Boy, you've had a big day."

I answered, "Oh Grandma. It was so much fun. I'll bet I'll never have another day this much fun. And know something, Grandma? I've been thinking about it a lot today, and I am pretty sure that I must be the smartest six-year-old boy in the whole city of Bell, California." Grandmother's eyes glistened as she absorbed my immodesty.

"Really?' she said, tracking my thoughts with interest.

"Gosh yes, Grandma," I said, hunching my shoulders and putting my palms up to emphasize the obvious truth in what I was saying. I raised my eyebrows as I leaned back against her chest. I took in a deep breath and released a long self-satisfied sigh, saying, "Just look at all the things I learned today. In just one day!

"Grandma," I continued. "Did you know my brain is hurting from all that I learned since Papa and I left the front porch this morning? And what happens when your brain runs out of room and you've got no more space to put stuff?"

"Well, that could be a problem," Grandma answered. "But I don't think I'm there yet." She chuckled and added, "but I can see how it could happen, all right."

"You know, Grandma," I continued. "The day started out really great. Guess what, it just got betterer an betterer. First Harley and I poured our lead soldiers, and now what could be better than that first thing in the morning? Then Papa took me out. Oh yeah, and then we went for our walk on his crow's nest — that's what we call Papa's shoulders."

"Yes, I know," she said, patting me on my stomach.

"Oh Grandma, gosh Grandma," I said. "How many other six-year-old boys ever get to be that tall? Not many, I'd say. I am pretty sure I'm the only one who does, you can bet."

Then I said, "Guess what, Grandma? I learned that some greasy Italian ladies wear black in the mourning because they are sad about having to die at night.

"I talked to a real bank guy who knew about my boats, and then I traded some boats for this beanie. And then we got an ice cream sundae… then guess what, Grandma — 'member, Papa and I ran like the wind this morning. Gosh, Papa's so wonderful. Know it, Grandma?" I asked.

Remembering something important, I interrupted myself and said to Grandma,

"Oh Grandma, guess what? I forgot to tell you…Guess what? While we were standing in line at the movies, Duck said that if you wanted to, that Papa Eudie could just put you around his neck on his crow's nest, and then run with you on his shoulders in his next foot race if you wanted to. Do you want to, Grandma? I'll bet you two could win."

I spoke enthusiastically. Grandmother exploded with laughter and said,

"Goodness gracious! Dear lord have mercy, where would Tim ever get an idea like that? My, my…."

I looked back up at her face, and her eyes sparkled and were full of amusement.

"But Grandma," I went on, "you'll have to wait probably till summer 'cause Papa sprained his ankle and Anna's got to fix it before he can play again. But then you could run, I'll bet...."

Grandma was still tickled.

"Now that would be a sight to behold, my Lord," she said. Joy infected me and we laughed together,

"Oh dear," Grandmother continued. "I have got to tell that to Anna".

Then I said, "And Grandma, you'll never guess what, but did you know that once Papa Eudie tore a turkey's head off with his own bare hands and beat somebody with it till it killed them? He must have been really mad. Do you suppose they ate that turkey afterward?"

I said, "Grandma, did you know that Duck and my new friend Sol played a game of chess, but only in their heads? And guess what — they didn't even use a chess board or any of the pieces. Then Duck lost his mind and forgot his moves, and then when we got to Papa's house, Sol reassembled the whole game again from his very own memory. And then they replayed the whole darn game all over again, right there on the regular chess board. Sol won again.

"Gosh Grandma, you know the Duck was really surprised. He kept looking at Sol, and then at the chess board. Then back at Sol again. Now Grandma, Sol is a Jewish boy who only a few days ago got Mitzvah-ed at a Bar, and so, see, that made him into a man and everything. Gosh Grandma, now that Sol, he is really smart and that's for sure. Why Grandma, that's how I got so smart today, just by being around him. He gave me an ethic and so I gave almost all my money to Mama 'cause one of her stiff customers cried over the boat and didn't like my balloons. And then the trinity of them left without paying.

"Gosh, I like Sol," I continued. "Did you know Leslie was my cousin? His name is Leslie Dow. Did you know that he is Auntie Carole's little boy? But he lives somewhere else 'cause he has a crippled foot that needs attention. Guess what — he wears a special thick shoe just like Pie, and walks with a little limp. But gosh, that kid can sneak good. I want a shoe just like his because it makes us sneaky. I tried to walk just like Leslie, but I couldn't.

"Guess what, Grandma — we love each other and we laugh all the time, and his face lights up just like my Auntie Carol's. And Sol said, 'Hoy-vee' and teased us about hugging. What does 'Hoy-vee' mean?"

Grandma kissed me on the cheek and said, "Slow down, Artie. Slow down, darling."

I shut my eyes and leaned my back against Grandma's chest, pulling her arms around me tighter. I sat there for a minute or so, rocking quietly. I'd always hated church, but I knew there was a God. I could feel his arms around me as Grandma and I rocked.

After a bit, I couldn't hold back anymore.

"Guess what, Grandma," I said. "We all got in a fight at the Alcazar. Duck tore off two boys' pants, and said, "Routine Three". Then they were naked and, well, that Irish girl Sally saw the boy's peter. She called it a 'little tiller'. And guess what, Grandma. Duck caught a Woodpecker in his own britches from somewhere up in the balcony. It had to pee so he hid it in his shorts, and then he took it into the bathroom, but I think he forgot about it because he left the woodpecker inside. And then Sally got sick while she chewing Duck's bubble gum, and then I threw some wallets over the balcony. The police came afterward. Gosh, Grandma, it was so much fun. Now, that Duck is tough!"

I took a breath and continued.

"Grandmother," I said. "What does 'impressive' mean?" "Well Artie, you know what it means to impress someone, don't you?' Grandma asked.

"I think so," I said. "It means you did something good, or showed off, right?"

"Yes, something like that," she said. "Why do you ask?"

"Well," I said, "because twice today Duck and Harley told me that I was impressive. They told me when I told them I found out about Mrs. Ippy and Nunyur Bennis."

Now my Grandmother had no idea what I was talking about.

I saw it in her face and said, "Well, you see Grandma, I learned all 'bout Aliases from the fighting. And from Harley and that tall Butter kid. So on the way to the soda fountain Duck said I was impressive. And guess what, Grandma? I went there twice today — I had two banana splits all in one day. I think that's impressive, don't you, Grandma?"

"Why, my yes," she said, kissing me on the side of my face.

I leaned my head back and whispered,

"Pssst! Pssst!"

I motioned for her to come closer with my forefinger, and for her to bend her head down so that I could whisper something special to her. She complied.

"Grandma, know what?" I said. "I made up some aliases of my own. I figured them all by myself! 'Donut Botherme', 'Ima Lost' and 'Artie de Smarty'! I like that last one the best!" I said, "So, see Grandma, I am really getting smart 'bout stuff. Sol taught me how to negotiate and bargain and everything.

"Grandma, I'm going to sleep now," I added. I could hardly keep my eyes open.

Grandma held me tight as she rocked me in her arms. Then just before my brain shut down, I said, "Grandma, know what?"

"What?" she said.

"You are impressive," I replied.

CHAPTER 14

Love Finds Handy Artie

NO DAISY IN Bell, California stood a chance. I had just jumped out from behind a bush, kissing Lorna Green. Lorna was a fellow second grader and the object of my besotted fervor. After I kissed her she slapped me across the face, and her friend Lulu Fogg kicked me in the shins and hit me over the head with her lunchbox. I thought this was encouraging. I planned to do it again the next day.

Homeward bound with a handful of hapless daises, I began to tear the petals off.

"She loves me?" I said. "She loves me not. She loves me? She loves me not."

When I didn't like what I saw, I selected a new bouquet and hoped for more cooperative daisies, trudging along and repeating that process in an endless liturgy.

"She loves me! — I knew it!" I cried. Something in the little girl's eyes had destroyed me, and I wanted ever so much more to be ruined by her once again. I could not for the life of me imagine how this was happening; I had never felt this way before, and I vowed to myself to speak to Grandmother Brown about my feelings. She would most certainly know what to do. After all, she was a girl, and she had seven daughters, so I reasoned she must know something about the subject.

But first I wanted to test the waters just one more time — to make certain Lorna Green felt the same way about me as I did about her.

The next day after school I waited behind the same bush. This time I enlisted the help of Tubby Belew. We decided that after Lulu Fogg gave him a pot knot on his head he might catch a little kiss of his own. He was less than enthusiastic because he said that Lulu had lips like a mallard and a face like a kangaroo. He added that she was as silly as a "twizzle," but I gave him two of my paper boats, three pieces of double bubble gum, six bottle caps and two ice cream sticks to secure the deal.

We hid behind the bush like two quails waiting for a passing potato bug. As the two girls passed the bush, I jumped out in front of Lorna Green, poised to plant a big one, but Lulu threw down her lunchbox and grabbed me instead. She pushed me against a tree and delivered a wet sloppy kiss right on my mouth as Lorna looked on.

Tubby Belew casually walked out behind the bush, and without a care in the world he picked up Lulu's lunchbox and walked to the curb. He sat down and rifled through it, looking for treats. I, on the other hand, was still pinned against a tree. Suddenly Lorna shoved Lulu — who was slobber-coating me — aside.

"No," Lorna said. "He's my kisser! Those kisses are for me — stay away, Lulu!"

Lulu jumped back as though she'd been hit by a lightning bolt. Then Lorna gave me two soft kisses, one on each cheek, and I fell to pieces. Both giggling girls ran off as fast as their legs could carry them. Lulu had forgotten her lunchbox, and when I looked around I saw Tubby sitting on the curb, eating what was left of Lulu's lunch.

"Hey Artie, want a bite of banana and mustard sandwich?" he asked. I answered him.

"No Tubby," I said. "What I want is my all my stuff back! Where were you when that crazy little girl was attacking me?"

"Nah ahh," Tubby said. "A deal is a deal. You got your kisses, didn't you?"

I thought about it and replied, "Well yes, but I got scrunched by Lulu, and she wet me all up! Give me back at least one of the double bubbles and my two boats?"

Tubby got up and reluctantly handed me the two ice cream sticks. "There," he said. "Now we're even."

I thought to myself, *Well, there go my negotiating skills.* I would need to visit Sol and see what he thought about all this.

Then Tubby turned and walked away with the lunchbox, six bottle caps, two paper boats and three double bubbles, most of which were already filling his cheeks — and for nothing! But I understood that I couldn't negotiate with Tubby like I could Sol because Tubby hadn't Mitzah-ed at the Bar, nor did he have an ethic, so I turned on my heels and concentrated on picking daisies. My mind was consumed with the sweet memory of Lorna Green's kisses.

"She loves me not... she loves me...thought so!"

When Grandma Brown arrived home she looked beaten and tired. I wanted to talk to her but she sat down in her rocking chair and released an exhausted sigh before I had the chance. I went underneath the sink to retrieve a chipped blue-and-white porcelain bowl she used for soaking her feet.

I put a kettle on the burner to heat some water. Then I went in and removed my grandmother's shoes and carefully setting them aside. Her feet and ankles were all swollen, and she had large mean corns that gave her great pain. I didn't know what her work was, exactly, but she was on her feet all day — and on concrete floors, that I knew.

"Why Artie," Grandma said. "What an angel you are today. Have you done some mischief, little man? Do you have a note from your teacher?"

I thought for a moment and said,

"Oh no, Grandmother. Today Mrs. Perry gave me a 'most cooperative' on her star-board. It's just that I need some advice."

Grandma adjusted herself and said,

"Well sweetheart, sit on Grandma's lap 'til Mom gets her feet soaked a bit. Then I'll see what I can do. But for now, dearest heart, turn on the radio and let me rest just a bit, okay?"

"Sure Grandma," I said as I clicked on the radio. It took awhile for the tubes to warm up as I returned to my work in the kitchen. I remembered to bring in the Epsom salts for Grandmother's foot bath.

A voice on the radio said, "Today the Russian Army liberated the death camps at Auschwitz, Poland, revealing unspeakable horrors of torture and starvation. Jews, priests and political dissidents were murdered wholesale by the Nazis, leaving the few who survived emaciated beyond recognition — a visage of the living dead.

"Meanwhile our military campaign in the Ardennes has come to an end. God willing, the war will be over soon and our boys will come marching home."

I returned to Grandma, who had tears in her eyes as she listened to the news. I had the foot bath prepared at just the right temperature, and I lifted Grandmother's tired feet into the soothing water. She reached down to kiss me.

"Why Artie, that is just perfect," she said. "Lord knows my poor old feet need this, Now come sit on my lap while I soak and we'll listen to the radio awhile. Then we can talk a bit."

I hopped up on her lap and we listened to some music. I leaned my back against her chest as we listened to Vaughn Monroe and Bing Crosby. Finally, "The Adventures of Ellery Queen The Green Turtle Mystery" began.

We sat slowly rocking until the music picked back up. I could hear Grandmother snoring, so I got off her lap as quiet as a mouse. Then I retrieved a towel dabbed her feet dry, removing them from the bowl. I went into the bedroom and got Grandma's big torn slippers and a blanket, and after carefully putting the slippers onto her poor sore feet I quietly got back into her lap and pulled her arms around me. I managed to pull the cover up over us both, right to our necks. I joined her not long after that, sleeping in the heaven of her arms.

When we woke up, the sun had gone down and it was nighttime.

Grandma said, "Goodness, I don't remember soaking my feet or putting on these slippers?"

Grandma Brown, Early 40s

"It must have been Muffy Superbe du Pew or Gnome Exemplumonious," I said with a big smile.

"I guess so," she said, "but I think it was a small boy that loves his grandma. That would be my guess."

Then she kissed me on the top of my head. Only the two of us were home that evening. Veve was spending the night at the Waterman girls' house, and Harley and Duck were rehearsing for the Bell High Schools production of "Our Town". Mother was on one of her hot dates.

So I had Grandma Brown all to myself. Grandmother straightened up the living room, returned the blanket to the bedroom and walked back to where I was sitting in the living room.

"I know a certain angel that can have most anything he wishes for supper tonight," she said. "What can Grandma fix you, Artie?"

"Gosh, Grandma," I said. "You are awful tired, heck. I can just fix a peanut butter and jelly sandwich, my 'Artie special', and then we can just rest."

"Well, I need a little something too," she said. "Why don't I fix us grilled cheese sandwiches and some tomato soup? That will be easy on my feet."

I nodded, excited about Grandma's grilled cheese.

"Then later," she added, "if you help me, we can make up a batch of fudge, How does that sound? You can bring the step stool into the kitchen and talk to Grandma about your day, okay?"

I got the step stool and positioned it near the end of the counter, just in front of the back door. Grandmother stood in front of the sink, washing her hands in scalding hot water. She scrubbed her nails with lava soap and a short bristle brush. As she wiped her hands dry, I heard a scratching at the back door, and when I opened it I found Harley's pup Muggs McGinnis with a pair of Harley's dirty shorts in his mouth. Grandmother told me to let him in, and then she told me to toss the shorts into the wicker hamper in the bathroom. I returned to the end of the counter and Muggs lay down at my feet. As Grandma started cooking, I told her about my day down to the last detail, leaving nothing out — including my bribe to Tubby Belew and the loss of my recently acquired negotiating skills. Both those things gave her a chuckle.

I laid out my heart's dilemma about Lorna Green, who I said in all seriousness was the only girl I could ever love. And that I just wanted to be near her and that I wanted to touch her without getting clobbered or kicked. I said that I couldn't think about anything else — not Muggs and not my Stearman flights, nor Papa Eudie's tall tales; nothing, just Lorna Green. Then I went on to explain that Lorna paid no attention to me in class, and that she had in fact ignored me, chattering with the other boys and fluffing her hair, and then glancing back at me with wicked dark eyes.

"Well," Grandma said taking a deep breath.

"Day after next Wednesday is Valentine's Day. Didn't I hear you say that your second grade class was going to exchange valentine cards again this year"

I had forgotten about that.

"Well, yes Grandma," I said, "but Lorna doesn't know I love her yet. And last year I only got one valentine card, from a boy named Roland, and one from my teacher. Everyone else in the class got zillions of them. I don't do too well with valentines."

Grandma thought about that as she flipped the grilled cheese sandwiches. Then after awhile she plated them, and after pouring each of us a bowl of tomato soup, she gave Muggs a wedge of her grilled cheese, which he devoured in one gulp.

"Did Lorna get you a Valentine last year?" asked Grandma. "Did you get her one?"

"Well no," I said, "'cause see she was not in my first grade class. She just came to Bell from somewhere called Missoula, Montana. Grandma, she's the most beautifulest girl in the world. Bet she'll get two zillion valentines next week. Shoot Grandma, I'll bet she don't care any about me."

Grandma asked, "Well, she kissed you twice, didn't she?"

I responded, a bit surprised at her logic. "Well yes, Grandma, but it was only once on each cheek. And that only count as once, I think."

Grandmother smiled and said, "Oh yes, well, I wasn't quite sure how they counted kisses nowadays, but it sounds like twice to me. Even so, you have a whole week — including the weekend — to make a beautiful Valentine for her."

This fired my ardor and I asked, "Really, do you think I could win her over with just an old Valentine?"

Grandma said, "Well Artie, remember this: 'Faint heart ne'er won Fair Lady'. I think if you make her something with your own hands, she surely couldn't help but be impressed. I'll bet those other boys will just give her one of those little ten-for-a-penny valentines. Why Artie, if Lorna Green has any sense at all she couldn't help but fall in love with a boy like you. Now that's what I say about it. I looked into her eyes and said, "Really Grandma, you're not joking me?"

"No I am not joshing, Mr. Spelman, Give it a try, and tomorrow I will bring home some crepe paper and glue, and then we'll see what supplies we have around the house. We'll gather some scissors, pens, pencils and such, and then we'll fold out the card table and you can get to work. What do you say?"

"Oh gosh, Grandma," I said. "That would be great."

Three days of school passed before the weekend began. While there were no more "Star Boards" from Mrs. Perry, I did get one dunce cap and had to sit in the corner, plus I got three reproaches and a letter to carry home to mother. I had flown my Stearman in class again.

Then thankfully, my wonderful valentine-creating weekend came. Both Harley and Walter had warned Grandmother about letting me anywhere near glue or paste, but obviously she paid no attention to them. I think by Sunday I had glue in almost every orifice of my body, but my card was the most elaborate, detailed Valentine ever created. It had eleven full pages of drawings and cut-outs, including an image of a wedding dress clipped and pasted from a magazine. I also through in pictures of how I wanted our cake to look. I had written out a marriage license for her to sign by the X on the signature line. I described Leslie as my best buddy who would give her away, whatever that meant and I added a detailed sketch of his sneaky shoe. Muggs McGinnis would be my best man, and we would own a car and have an eleven babies that we'd order from God. I had pasted cutouts from a dozen magazines of the pets that we would have, with dash scissor lines for cutting, so she might put them on her mirror. A cat named "Prissy Thunderbolt" and a Dog named "Ruff P-47" were two options, and then there was a pet squirrel named "Chipper Nutballs".

I had written several poems for her. The one I can remember went something like this:

ROSES ARE RED
VIOLETS ARE BLUE
YOU LIPS ARE NOT STICKY LIKE LULU'S
THAT'S WHY I AM IN LOVE WITH YOU.
SIX REASONS WHY I AM IN LOVE WITH YOU—
You smell just like bubble gum.
You don't hit me anymore.
You make me tingle when I am close to you.
I feel funny when you kiss my cheeks
Your slap on my face didn't hurt much.
I like girls when they are skinny. My mother is really skinny.

Then I thought of something else I needed to tell her:

Oh yeah, you'll love my Grandma Brown. But if you don't,
don't cry, but I won't marry you.

Soon I was through with my masterpiece. Grandmother looked at the pages in astonishment. Then smiling, she asked,

"Artie, are you sure this is going to be enough?"

"Yep," I said, "she'll see that I am a good planner."

I took the card, which I'd slipped into a huge envelope On the outside was a large heart with an arrow through it that said *A.S.* + *L.G.* right underneath.

For the first time in my life I got to school forty minutes early and sat on the steps. I fingered my envelope, rehearsing what might happen when I gave her this special valentine. I visualized the avalanche of love and affection that would come through when my future wife saw this wonderful card. I had even woven an engagement ring out of one of Papa Eudie's multicolored pipe cleaners. Grandma said it was beautiful. I had taped it with scotch tape on all four sides, just under the image of "Chipper Nutballs" with an arrow pointing to it that said:

Remove tape then place on finger. This is your engagement ring. Wear it to Church, oh yes…. and show it to your daddy, Mrs. Perry and Lulu.

Love, Artie Spelman.

The school doors opened and I was so excited I ran into the bathroom, hiding inside a toilet stall. What if she hated me and was just tricking me? Maybe she gave me those kisses just to torment me. Tubby had told me that sometimes girls just did that, that they tricked boys. The bell rang and I sat there for another fifteen minutes. Finally I trudged through the door to my classroom late. Everyone stared at me. By this time each student had a pile of valentines on their desks. On my desk was a single valentine in a small white envelope, sealed with a lipstick kiss. My heart skipped a beat when I saw it, and for a moment I couldn't breathe. The teacher announced that we could take some time to read all our cards aloud, and then chit chat with each other a bit until she called the class back to order.

The lipsticked envelope gave me courage, so I took my own massive heavy envelope to her desk and laid it on top of her other cards. She looked up at me and asked, "B'wats this?"

"It's your Valentine," I said, "I made it just for you. Open it, it's got lots of good stuff!"

"B'wat is it? I non't want it, I non't like it!"

"Just open it," I pleaded. She slowly tore the envelope open without care and started to rummage through the many pages of my card, totally disinterested.

"I non't know bwat this is," she said. "I non't like it!" And without further adieu, my beloved Lorna Green swept my heart onto the dirty floor.

I was ruined. I remember actually looking at my chest to see if it was bleeding. I returned to my desk with my head hanging down to my ankles. My heart was obliterated.

As I sat down I saw the lone envelope on my desk, and my heart briefly skipped a beat. *Ah yes, Lorna's card,* I thought as I opened it. It was a pretty little card, and inside it had a two-inch photo of Lulu — her school picture. On the card she had written **Be my Valentine, I Love you, Lulu**.

Lulu sat two seats in front of me. I stepped forward and thanked her for her card, the only card I had received.

She said, "You're welcome Artie." Her smile was nice. I walked to the next row, right by Lorna's desk, and without saying a word I scooped my pages up off the floor. I took my engagement ring and put it in my pocket, and then I threw the rest of my work into Mrs. Perry's trash can.

As I passed by Lorna's desk on the way back to my own, she said, "Go away, Artie!"

The rest of the day was relatively uneventful, but I was numb and I had just one petal left on my last daisy.

"She loves me not…thought so."

CHAPTER 15

The Red Baron vs. The Greasy Spoon

FROM THE FIRST days that I can remember there on Atlantic Blvd, the industry of choice for we three miscreants, Harley Brown, Walter Crawford and me, was primarily building paper and balsa model airplanes from model kits of all varieties.

Harley was a wonderful model maker who never encountered a balsa model that he couldn't build to perfection. My cousin Walter, who was just six years older than I was and four years younger than Harley, was not far behind Harley in his quality of apprenticeship and was superior to Harley in engineering.

I, on the other hand, was a disaster, but Harley and Walt humored me until I aggravated them, which was usually often and sooner rather than later. Therefore, they would allow me only to unfold the plans or, perhaps, help attach the plans carefully with straight pins to the thick cardboard support that was on top of the folding card table or, perhaps, allow me to pin one of the thicker pieces of Balsa wood together or occasionally glue a strut or two to the plans. I always over-glued everything that stuck to the struts or spars onto the paper template, which soon became an ironclad glob of crystallized rock-hard glue that forced the boys to cut the wood away from the face of the plans with a razor, tearing little chunks of the paper blueprint in the process. I was a mess, and should I get on a tare before being caught, more than three quarters of my work had to be redone by the boys.

When their good humor ran out, they moved quickly to either avoid me or redirect my energies by keeping me occupied elsewhere with harmless or trivial tasks. Even when I tried my very hardest, I still managed to get glue in my eyebrows, ears, hair, and most everywhere except where it was actually supposed to be applied. One day, as the boys were hard at work, I returned from the bathroom and said proudly:

"Hey Walt, Hey Harley, I got a trinity on my peter."

"What?" They answered simultaneously.

"Yep I just went pee-pee and guess what? I saw some Peanut Butter, some Jelly and some Deco model airplane glue on my peter. A Trinity! Neat, huh?"

"Holly, Molly," Walt said, and Harley just shook his head and returned to their project, speechless.

I mostly just watched, assisting the boys by handing them the pieces or struts as a happy participant, like a nurse handing a brain surgeon a scalpel or swab. That combination seemed to work out nicely for all.

Harley and Walt built all of the varieties of model kits of the day, but the most frequently constructed were Piper J-3 Cubs with a twelve inch wing span because they were just twenty cents for the kit, were quick to build, and included almost everything in the kit for their construction. When they were completed, we almost always immediately got on the roof of the house, winded their rubber band propeller motors to the maximum, set them on fire, and then sent them flying somewhere into oblivion on a flaming Kamikaze run. Then, as soon as we gathered some money, we repeated the process again.

Uncle Harley was often commissioned by the R & T Hobby shop on Gage Ave. to build the larger, four to seven feet wing span, motor powered models of P 51s, Air Cobras or P47 Thunderbolts, to display in the model shop's front windows. The money that he garnered from such endeavors and from his singing at funerals at the Theo & Carides Mortuary mostly went to Grandma for food and household expenses, but if there was any left over, she oft times allowed Harley to keep for his beloved model construction.

Over the nine years there, he built for himself only about fifteen of those more costly, complicated models that took hours of delicate, precise, and thoughtful work to create, and those few made it unscathed into the "Harley Brown Museum of Aviation," hanging safely in the private sky just above the loft bed in his garage hideout.

A P51 Mustang with a 36" wing span was very rare and mostly sponsored by Uncle Paul or by Uncle Fuzzy if he sold a painting or, on occasion, by Eudie or Duck because they loved to see us happy and were naught more than children themselves mentally.

If it came between us eating, paying the rent, or model building, surviving during war time always won that contest.

To us, the sight of that burning plane gasping for its last breath of flight brought the war home to us in a way that no MovieTone or Pathe news reel at the Alcazar Theatre could. When the burning models flew off of our roof to the ground, we imagined Carl Agajanian or Stavros Theocarides shooting down an enemy. It was always a somber, yet exciting moment for us, and if we managed to get two flaming aircrafts to crash into each other in mid-flight, it was cathartic. On one such occasion, aunt Eddie ran in the house, complaining to Grandma, crying her eyes out, and cussing about Harley. You see, in her mind, she saw Carl in one of those planes and didn't care for our theater. Eddie called Harley and Walter ghouls, as well as bad influences on me. I knew that I would receive a teary summons to spoon with my aunt Eddie that night.

Anyway, Grandma didn't like that exercise much, either. She said it was terribly wasteful, which of course, it damn well was. Besides, a little fiery piper cub once caught some dry grass near the Lumber Yard fence on fire that spread so fast that it gave us a bit of a scare when we came precariously close to having to call in the Bell Fire Department. Grandma put the three of us on hard tack and tepid water that night, or punished us somehow, I can't remember what the punishment was. I think it was withholding her bread pudding, but I just remember that she was very displeased.

Walter Crawford and Model Plane, 1940s

The one and only exception to never setting fire to an expensive scale model was disastrous. Harley and Walt had worked every waking hour for the better part of five days to build a beautiful scale, 42" wing span model of a German Stuka dive bomber.

There were no model kits for German aircraft during the war. I think, if I remember, it was just a custom made Brown/Crawford Creation that they improvised as a Stuka dive bomber from the American Corsair kit that had a similar wing design, but it was gorgeous to look at, whatever it was. It was painted with six coats of black Dope Lacquer, and Uncle

Fuzzy created a little flower and water paste pilot and painted all of the Luftwaffe symbols and numbers on it perfectly. Then, on a sugar coated almond, he painted the face of der Fuhrer, complete with his little black mustache, a leather helmet, and goggles. It was a master piece. Walt had received the gift of a large size CO2 Motor as a birthday gift and volunteered it for this mission.

We test flew the plane several times. It flew perfectly, and if one caught sight of it just right in the correct light at a distance, it looked exactly like a real plane flying through the air and flown by a real live pilot. It was a wonderful work of art and craftsmanship. Walter had set the trim rudder stabilizers so that they flew perfectly about thirty feet off the ground in a high, lazy circle about sixty feet in diameter. Then, when the CO2 ran out and the propeller stopped, it glided in so beautifully balanced that it landed itself perfectly, stalling just above the ground and coming to a stop without damage.

Walter could always figure out how to make these planes fly, and many of the kits where designed not to fly, but just to hang or sit on a shelf and look pretty. Walt was mostly always able to get any kit flying, or at least gliding, in a straight line.

Now, then on its last flight, it was a sunny Saturday afternoon. Walt installed the last of the gas canisters to the motor, started it up, -lit its tail on fire, and released it from the usual spot on the roof of our house. A summer thermal caught the mock flaming, German Stuka JU-87 dive bomber/ pretender and carried it aloft into the afternoon traffic in the center of Atlantic Blvd., where it dropped, burning out of the sky and crashing into the windshield of the Huntington Park deputy mayor and his family, bringing their car to a screeching halt and scaring the Bejesus out of them, very nearly causing multiple car accidents. Horns honked on both sides of the Boulevard as cars skidded to a halt, forcing a large dump truck over the curb and into a light post.

It must have been particularly disconcerting for all of the traffic involved, particularly for deputy mayor's car, because the Stuka, with its detailed Nazi swastikas, smashed their windshield into a hundred pieces, and the very loud screeching sirens of the L.A. air raid alert system went off on its weekly war time test schedule at precisely two P.M.

Harley always tried to flame one of the smaller models at precisely that time because he said it added to our fiery, realistic show beautifully. We boys thought that was great fun. Grandma Brown was not in the least bit amused when the police showed at our door. We didn't know it then, but that event almost cost us our precious home. Eviction was on the minds of many. Grandma Brown had several official visitors from both Bell and Huntington Park. She was livid and forbade any further flaming aircrafts of any sort for a period of lesson shorter than forever, and, well, we obeyed mostly.

Grandma put a crimp in our model making for a while, but when we unionized ourselves and did all of our chores like a band of dutiful, sugar sweet angels for a couple of weeks, she finally relented and let Harley start building once again, but she insisted;

"Only those little Pipers, do you hear me Harley Brown, just the small ones and no more fire, understand me, Mr. Brown? No More Fire!"

Harley said, "Yes, Mother," and nodded his head, but as the weeks passed, the models got a little bigger. Now, on one of our particular Bullish financial cycles, Uncle Harley Brown and Walt decided to buy a medium size kit of the WWI Fokker DF1 tri-plane of the Red Barron. The bottom of the three wings was only 11 inches, and the boys could claim that the Fokker wing was even an inch shorter than the Piper cub's wing, and, well, the two boys decided that they just wouldn't mention that the bottom wing was the smallest one of its three wings and that the two upper wings spans were a good deal larger. After all, Harley said,

"If we can't go out in wing span, we'll go up in wing count." Besides, he reasoned that the stubby length of the tri-plane's small fuselage wasn't all that much longer than a Piper's. Harley and Walter juggled those lies and created a clever deception and partial truths, here and there, while coughing up a few justifications and coming to the cockeyed conclusion that not only was this the right thing to do but that they were, in fact, doing Grandma Brown a favor, she just didn't know it yet.

Walter, after taking the money for the project into account, decided that we had enough left over in the kitty to afford a CO2 motor and five compressed gas canisters, which were enough to propel the tri-plane on four separate, one minute test flights and then one final, one minute flight. It was then that the fine engineering mind of Cousin Walter Crawford came into play. He suggested that he could install a pack of one hundred fire crackers inside the fuselage and light the fuse that was sticking out just under the vertical stabilizer upon take off. There would be no actual fire as Grandma had insisted, but only something sounding like a machine gun firing created by the sound of firecrackers would be heard.

Darned if all of this planning didn't make me hungry, so I went in for a piece of pie and a council with the baker. Harley and Walt wisely took that opportunity to start the project without me.

As I sat there eating Grandma's Apple pie, I casually mentioned to her that the boys were building a tri-plane, and she glanced at me as she sat down with a glass of cold milk.

"Really?" She said.

"Yep," I said, "and guess what, Grandma, they are not going to light it on fire, but Walt is putting a real motor and a machine gun in it. Neat, Huh?"

"What!" She said, raising her voice just a bit. "You go and get those boys right now and bring them here to me!"

Only Walter, the negotiator, reported as requested, and he took her objections stoically, answering her sincerely and diplomatically, overcoming each of her objections matter-of-factly. He said,

"Grandmother, we are not going to flame this airplane, it will only have the sound of machine guns as it flies. See, Grandma, we are going to fly it several times because you see, we will have several CO2 canisters, so it will have several test flights. You can come and watch the tests, O.K. Grandma?"

Walter hugged Grandma, then told her in confidence,

"Grandma, Harley just wants to impress you by being a bit more responsible, and he has some fancy plan to gain back his good name with you and within the community. Please, please, give him a chance, o.k. Grandma?" Walt pleaded.

Grandma's sparkling eyes looked down at Walt, the scoundrel diplomat, and she agreed somewhat reluctantly, but smiling just a bit, and dismissed him with a hug. As he left the room, she smacked him lovingly on the fanny with her fly flap and insisted,

"Just remember, Crawford. NO FIRE! Or some pilots and their co-pilots," she said, glancing at me, "will get their landing gears blistered. Might be you!" She warned him.

"O.K. Grandma, don't worry, everything will be fine," he said with an air of authority.

"It better be," Grandma said, as Walt returned to the garage.

Now Harley, as always, had a master plan ready to unfold to us.

He was determined to repair the damage to his good name caused by the flaming mock-Stuka JU-87 windshield bombing incident. He laid it out to us as we walked down Atlantic towards the newspaper office.

As we walked north up Atlantic, we chattered away about airplanes, machine guns, and Walter's engineering ideas, and Harley retold Walt the story of when all of us Browns and other families had, only a few years earlier, stood near this very spot to watch a sea of American military aircraft fly in formation overhead, filling the sky like roaring thunder. Hundreds upon hundreds of every variety of American fighting plane flew overhead as we all stood there, watching in amazement. Then, trailing behind the bombers and fighter planes came the Stearman, Travelaires, Wacos, and various trainers, then cargo aircraft of all varieties. Some towing gliders filled the sky with thousands upon thousands of planes in total, flying south at slightly different speeds and at layered altitudes two or three levels high and half a mile wide. They flew maybe only fifteen hundred feet overhead, going straight down Atlantic Blvd., southward toward Signal Hill, and over the oil wells to the ocean. The roar was deafening and exciting. Cars pulled over and hundreds of people got out, looking upward, waving, and cheering toward the sky. This went on for the better part of forty five minutes, letting up only in spurts of a minute or so until the next wave of aircraft arrived. That morning, the sun went dark because it was blocked by the mass of aircraft in the sky. This happened sometime in January of 1942. I was there when it happened, but I only just remembered during Harley's retelling to Walt that my Auntie Carole was holding my hand. I was not quite four years old at the time. I just remembered the sunshine and sky being full of airplanes that flew overhead for what seemed like forever. When the last little trailing gaggle of piper cubs passed overhead like hovering sparrows, there was silence. The silence was more deafening than all of the motors combined. The people below started to breath again, embraced each other, and then got back into their cars or continued walking on their journeys. Harley reminded me what Papa Eudie later said to us all.

"Remember this day," he said. "We will never see this many aircraft in the sky at one time again."

I had been there to witness it. I remember Uncle Jimmy was there, holding back tears. He had tried so hard to go into the army air service, but a perforated ear drum kept him home and out of the war. It broke his heart, and he never took his eyes off the passing planes and stood there, watching them until they flew out of sight.

Jimmy said nothing, and he just looked up at the empty sky.

"Where were those planes going?" I asked Harley. He said,

"Well, Papa Eudie said they were flying to hundreds of different locations. Some would turn around at the ocean and then head back due east, and some would go south into the Virginias or Carolinas or to Louisiana. Some would touch and go in several states, eventually landing in Pennsylvania or New York or Florida to be loaded onto ships bound for England or somewhere in Europe. Papa said this was our little surprise for Hitler and his minions. Some of these, he said, will land in San Pedro or San Diego's North Island to be sent into the battles in the Pacific to circumcise Hiro Hito, and he told us that at least as many as we saw flying overhead would also be loaded onto the flatbeds of cargo trains and sent to the respective ports."

Now, after our historic reverie, Harley said to Walt and me,

"I mention this story because we are going now to see Wilcoxen O'Connor and invite him to attend our Fokker Tri-Plane's maiden voyage. I want to get Duck in on this deal because he is always the fair haired boy. Duck's ugly mug is always in the local news every other week for winning a science fair or a wrestling match triumph or for his chess club or high school debating club win." "Shit," Harley said, looking quickly behind him and checking his mouth to see if his mother was, by chance, following him with her bar of mouth soap, "If I ever got in the God damned newspaper, it would say:

'Harley Brown, son of Blanche Brown, abandoned mother of eleven children, deliberately crashes flaming Nazi dive bomber into windshield of the Deputy Mayor, killing the entire family. Or Harley Brown, dishonored by burning the Alcazar Theater.' That," he added, "would doubtlessly be followed by: 'Brown? Isn't that a German name?'"

Walter couldn't help but laugh and said,

"Well Harley, I saw your picture in the paper once when you sang at a funeral. It said something about the lovely baritone voice of young Harley Thomas Brown, and it even had your picture there singing next to the casket."

"Yeah," Harley said, "me singing songs for the stiffs. Boy, that really gets the girls. Then, of course, there is all that lively applause from the mourning audience and weeping guests. Besides that, Walt," Harley added,

"my stupid brother Fuzzy Von Rembrandt got a hold of Grandma's newspaper first and changed the face on my photo into a perfect monkey's face, and of course, he refolded the newspaper before Artie or Muggs brought it to Mom. Boy, I was so proud of that 'till Mom opened it and started laughing so hard." Finally, as we continued our walk, Uncle Harley started to laugh at himself and said,

"That bastard Elwood, I'll get him one of these days. When he visits here again, I'll stick a beetle in his ass crack while he sleeps."

"Oh, can I watch ... or help?" I asked Harley. "Grandma said he might be coming to spend the night. I'll go dig up a potato bug when we get back home."

"Never mind," Harley said.

We joked and walked and talked. There would never be a gaggle of three knot-headed boys like this flying down Atlantic Blvd. again, either. The sun shined on our happy faces, and the street, the earth, and the exhaust from the passing cars smelled just like love and boys on a mission. I had great fun visualizing my uncle Fuzzy running around the pepper tree tomorrow with a Beetle stuck in his BVDs.

There was often a shortage of not only rent but things for school. Clothes had to last, and we had few, if any, luxury items. Our tummies were many times not as full as they could have been, but we were never short on belly laughter or good humor and playfulness. On that, we dined with kings.

As we walked, I stretched my wings into my Stearman mode. You see, I always morphed into a Stearman aircraft whenever I was either very sad or very happy. My entire body and being became a bright yellow and blue Stearman bi-plane doing maneuvers. If I was hopelessly sad or hurt or desperate, I would fly around the room with my arms outstretched like wings, crashing myself into the walls as hard as I could, hopefully knocking myself senseless or landing in a belly flop outside on the big swing. I would crash with a thud and sputter 'till my motor restarted or the plane toppled over the edge of swing, propeller first, face down into the dirt below, gurgling up from the ashes like a phoenix, taking off once again and returning into the house to find Grandma's big arms as I ran face first into her lap. She always recognized my moods by my motor sounds or my wing angle.

On this trip to the news office, my yellow Stearman was doing happy wingovers and inside loops, even a zoom climb or two. Everything was new and fun and exciting in my world, and on that day with no stall speed, I had a nice tail wind. My trim tabs were set perfectly, and I flew straight and level. Harley was so clever, and I wondered what he had in mind on this journey of ours.

Wilcoxen O'Connor was a sure thing, and Harley damn well knew it. Harley was sly as a fox, and he knew exactly what he was doing. You see, Wilcoxen was in love with Grandmother Brown, had been utterly besotted with her for years, and didn't bother to hide it. Harley knew it. Hell, everyone in the family knew it and teased her endlessly.

This seemed ever so odd to me that at Grandma's advanced old age that someone might think of her as a "girlfriend." After all, my Grandma was near forty-nine years old. "Now," I reasoned, "who in the world ever had a boyfriend at that age?" No matter how hard I tried, I could not imagine Grandmother and Wilcoxen necking or exchanging cooties or hickeys in the balcony of the Alcazar Theater like I knew Harley and Duck did with their girlfriends.

Doctor Wilcoxen O'Connor had something they called a PhD and was the assistant editor and feature writer for our local newspaper, The Bell-Cudahay Industrial Journal. Wilcoxen had tried every trick and every excuse in the book to get close to Grandmother Brown, but he had little success.

As Harley unfolded his idea to us during our walk, it turned out that his plan was that, with the help of the newspaper archives, we could create a photographic homage to our fighting boys in the war, complete with a fly over of the legendary Red Barron's Tri-Plane with machine guns ablaze. He further said that he wanted to remember the day of that great flight spectacle down Atlantic Blvd. by, perhaps, suggesting to the paper that they write about that massive flight we had just chatted about as a feature article. As we walked through the door into Mr. O'Connor's office, he recognized Harley as Blanche's son immediately and almost jumped up out of his swivel chair. He shook Uncle Harley's arm, using it like a water pump and nearly disjointing him. I started to laugh at this spectacle, but Walt nudged me. Before Harley could say a thing, the office intercom came on, and a woman's voice said,

"Dr. O'Connor, Mayor Fletcher Bowron is on the phone." Without hesitation or the slightest pause, he answered her, saying,

"Tell him I'll call him back soon, or let him hold on."

"Yes, sir," she said, with some surprise in her voice as she clicked off.

After brushing off a dozen questions about his mother's health and well being, Harley presented his idea about the fly over and, perhaps, Wilcoxen's newspaper's homage to our troops at war and so on. The widower was glassy eyed and looked like a school boy staring off into space. He started saying yes to Uncle Harley just after the third word of his proposal and called in his secretary, instructing her to listen carefully to the boy and take note of Harley's plans and ideas, as well as jot them down and then arrange a date and time. Then, he asked her to call his tailor and barber and to make an appointment before the proposed event. She turned to leave, and we followed to make the arrangements. Harley had completed the negotiations in less than twenty minuets.

All of Grandma's kids teased her endlessly about Dr. O'Connor, to which Grandma protested,

"Oh Poof, why, that's the silliest fool man I ever saw. Oh, he's nice enough, but I swear he doesn't know the difference between a flea and a bald eagle."

Aunt Eddie said, "Well Mom, he's a Doctor, after all. He must know something." Grandma responded,

"Why, he couldn't give a snail a tonsillectomy! Doctor? Humph!" she said, chuckling as she often did at her own attempt at humor.

"Well, he just likes you, Mom. What's wrong with that?" Veve asked.

Grandma said, calmly and with a sweet smile,

"Well, he must or be twitter-patted or Adel-brained."

"Mom," Eddie reasoned, "give the poor guy a chance, will you? He's attracted to you, and why shouldn't he be?"

"Yes, and me with all of these kids and swollen ankles. I'm not exactly Marlene Dietrich, you know, and he's no Tom Mix either. I don't trust him. He's got something on his mind, and whatever it is, I don't have time for it. I've got the Red Cross and mouths to feed. Why, the fact that I'm still a married woman apparently doesn't bother him or any of you kids. What in the world was Harley thinking?" she asked.

"Yeah, Mom, Dad might catch you two kissing or playing paddy fingers near the pepper tree when he comes round five or ten years from now to ask you for something. Oh boy, now that would be something."

"Never you mind about that, young lady," Grandma said.

Eddie protested, preparing some hair treatment for her, she said,

"Well, Mah-amma, for goodness sakes. He hasn't asked you to marry him. He just wants to be friendly."

"Humph," Grandma said,

"Friendly is as Friendly Does."

Of course, as she was arguing with her girls and those standing about her, Veve and Eddie were industriously bending her head into a porcelain pan full of warm water and putting some solution on her hair. This conversation about Wilcoxen's virtues and possible debilities went on for a half hour or so, and as the ladies worked over the kitchen sink, giving her hair a final rinse under the faucet, aunt Eddie said,

"Well Mom, why did you have us do your hair and lay out that green velveteen dress for tomorrow if he is so bothersome?" Mom Brown said,

"Well, I can't be rude, now can I? And cleanliness is next to Godliness."

The girls looked at each other, and Grandma's cheeks flushed just a little.

The stage was set for 10:00 a.m. the following morning.

The next morning everything went off without a hitch. Wilcoxen showed up thirty minutes early with a bouquet of a dozen or more beautiful mixed flowers and a huge box of "Mary See's," candy which was almost unattainable during those war years because of the prohibitive cost and sugar shortage.

When I saw my Grandma, my mouth fell open. Why, she was beautiful, and I had never seen her like that, not even in church. I was stunned. I flew my Stearman-Artie over to her, and she grabbed me, putting her hand over my propeller mouth to quite my engine sound, and then held me in front of her like a shield as I folded my wings.

She said, "Mr. Wilcoxen, now, this is not an airplane. This is my Grandson Artie."

He paid little attention, and his eyes never left Grandma's face. He said 'hi' to me off-handedly and then handed the flowers and candy to Grandma.

She thanked him politely and then excused herself to put the flowers into a vase.

The show went off perfectly. Harley, Walter, and I had drug out all fifteen models from Harley's museum collection and laid them out on display on the big swing, using it as the tarmac for the models.

Wilcoxen paid little attention and had Grandmother, Aunt Eddie and Veve cornered near the stoop, trying to charm them while his secretary took copious notes and photos of the airfield and then of Uncle Harley and Walt holding up various beautiful models, one in each hand. Finally, it was time for the flight of the Red Baron.

The boys brought out the beautiful, bright red, meticulously crafted tri-plane and showed it to Wilcoxen and his secretary, who admired it and its superb workmanship. Mom, the girls, and Wilcoxen were directed toward the front of the lot next to the fence, standing with their backs to the greasy spoon restaurant that was just next door to the north side of the property.

The building, I think, was called "Marie's Sandwich Shop" or something, but it was, in fact, the third of three bankrupt and abandoned greasy spoon restaurants that had tried and failed in that location. Word was that the building was to be torn down. It was a good thing because it had been the hangout for every freeloader in the area. There were drunks and fights, and many a customer walked out without paying their bill. Anyway, I can remember that we just called those various efforts in that spot: "Greasy Spoon One, Two, and so on." This was just "Greasy Spoon Three" to us. The day was almost over, and it looked like a smashing success.

Now, it was time for the Grand Finale. The boys positioned the tri-plane on its preplanned Trajectory, then lit the machine gun fuse, which released the plane from our usual spot on the roof of the house. The tri-plane flew beautifully, except it wouldn't fly straight and level because Walt had added the weight of the string of firecrackers for the final flight and had not taken into account the extra loading on the wing in his previous tests. It flew like a bronco pony as the machine gun went off in a long, long "rat tat tat tat." At first, it was really impressive, and Wilcoxen and attendants had large smiles on their faces. Finally, due to there being too many fireworks and too much paper and balsa wood near the gunpowder and dope, the airplane caught on fire from the explosions inside of it and headed directly for the noses of Mom Brown and Wilcoxen, who hit the ground with Grandma falling spread eagle directly on top of him, in what aunt Eddie later called "The most inglorious, ungraceful position imaginable," while they were struggling to regain their footing and pride. The flaming tri-plane regained some altitude and made a slow right turn over the top of the bamboo fence as the port side of one of its three burning wings fell off just behind "the Greasy Spoon Number Three."

It wasn't over yet. The Fokker made a slow base leg turn, returning to our property. Passing over our heads, it headed directly for the Brown Airfield, crashing in the middle of all of the planes from The Brown museum collection. Almost instantaneously, in less than ninety seconds, every single plane in his collection was in flames, burning themselves out like spent match sticks, leaving little cinders of tissue paper and chard chunks of balsa laying on the tarmac swing. They burnt so fast that nothing else on the swing or tree caught fire. It was over before it had begun. I looked at Harley's face, and it was bloodless as hundreds of hours of his best work went "Poof!"

Walt was in shock. Grandma and Wilcoxen had managed to get to their feet, and as poor Wilcoxen was trying to brush Grandma off, he nervously and innocently brushed some leaves and dirt off of her dress and from her bosoms, and she gave him a wallop that had no effect other than to embarrass them both. The aircraft on the tarmac was done for. Kaput! The Red Barron, without a pilot, had become a Triple Ace in a single flight, completely eviscerating fifteen of Harley's most precious aircrafts and perhaps nearly a thousand total man hours of the two boys meticulous work in one fell swoop.

It was so quiet that one could hear a pin drop. Then suddenly, something that I immediately thought might be the Gnome Exemplumonious skittered along the ground from somewhere near the big swing, moving rapidly toward the girls' feet. Was it a rat, or a wounded squirrel, or perhaps a rabid cat? Veve naturally screamed. No one knew for sure exactly what the "flop flit flit flop- flit flit flop" sound along the ground was, but it was skittering toward them at a rapid, crippled thumping pace, kicking up dirt chunks of grass and small pebbles. Whatever it was, it was coming on fast. Poor Wilcoxen bravely stood in front of Grandma Brown to protect her. I thought it must have been a dying animal or perhaps some wounded field critter flop flit fliting bravely toward us. First, it thumped left, then to the right, but it always wound up heading and thumping directly for Grandma and Wilcoxen. When the skittering beast finally came to a halt just in front of Grandma's gallant knight, it was discovered to be the broken detached CO_2 gas motor that was attached to the broken half of the propeller, still turning on its last gasp of compressed gas, skipping through the dirt and grass and limping down the yard on its journey towards Wilcoxen.

Finally, every one gathered their composure, and we all went inside the house. Mom offered Wilcoxen and his secretary chairs. There were only a few, so the rest of us stood as we all chatted and drank punch. Grandma Brown passed around the most delicious chocolates I had ever tasted. She smacked my hands as I reached greedily for my fourth piece while she was passing them around the room. I went over and stood next to the front window, shuffling on my feet and listening to Wilcoxen talk about how wonderful the event was as he found new, inventive ways to compliment Grandmother on the grandeur and excitement of the event and for having such a wonderful, talented son. Grandma asked Harley to sing, and he sang:

Off we go into the wild blue yonder,
Climbing high into the sun;
Here they come zooming to meet our thunder,
At 'em boys, Give 'er the gun!
Down we dive, spouting our flame from under,
Off with one heckuva roar!
We live in fame or go down in flame.
Hey! Nothing'll stop the Army Air Corps!
Off we go into the wild sky yonder,
Keep the wings level and true!

If you'd live to be a grey-haired wonder,
Keep your nose out of the blue!
Flying men guarding the nation's border,
We'll be there, followed by more cause-
Nothing'll stop the Army Air Corps!

Now, this was not one of the touching songs that Harley usually loved to sing, but his beautiful baritone voice filled the air, and all of us had goose bumps, and it was the perfect choice for the occasion and a perfect occasion for me to salute, once again with both hands.

Wilcoxen's secretary was in tears, and both she and Wilcoxen applauded Harley enthusiastically. Almost at that moment, Duck was banging on the front door. Harley had asked him to drop by to impress the good Doctor. However, he was banging loudly. I opened the door, and Duck flew inside saying, "Brownie, the Greasy Spoon is on fire! Dad has called the Fire Department!"

We all rushed outside to see a tall flame coming out of a fifty gallon drum that apparently had some grease or lard in it that must have been lit by the flaming wing tip of the tri–plane.

When the fireman arrived, the restaurant was in flames, and finally, a second engine showed up. I later learned that the firemen just allowed it to burn down in a controlled burn because there was no saving it, and later, the property that was also owned by our lumber yard had been condemned. The Greasy Spoon Number Three, all of Harley's Air Force, and, of course, the tri-plane were no more. Kaput!

I saw Grandmother Brown, who had daggers in her eyes as she looked at my cousin Walter Crawford, who was slowly inching his way toward the back door.

What would the newspaper say about the Brown's tomorrow?

FAMILY OF FIREBUGS ARRESTED ON ATLANTIC BLVD!

Harley Brown, Walter Crawford, and Arthur Spelman sent to serve a trinity of life sentences in Los Angeles County Juvenile Hall!

Aunt Eddie and Uncle Carl Agajanian, WW2

CHAPTER 16

Rembrandt's News

NOW MY UNCLE Elwood Brown, who everyone just called 'Fuzzy', was one of the finest artists I encountered over the course of my life. I have viewed few, if any, technical artists better than uncle Fuzzy. It is only now, as an old man having attended with interest some of the great art museums of the world, that I have come to fully understand and appreciate the depth of his talent. Fuzzy was proficient in most media, but oil paints, pencil, pen and ink were his preferences. Throughout my life I drank in his amazing works of art. They ranged from recreating the simplest cartoons to the creation of family portraits in oil in the style of the masters for wealthy clients.

Most of his life's work was rooted in "realism". He sold his work by the piece or by contract to many national magazines.

It is fair to say that I never saw him do what they call impressionism or modernism, so I would not compare his work with Vincent Van Gogh or Picasso. Fuzzy's art was not intellectually clever.

He added greatly to my childhood, which was already filled with laughter and mischief. He had a happy, smiling countenance, a great sense of humor and was a natural tormentor of all of us. We adored him and he loved us back equally. We could not wait for his visits.

When Fuzzy stayed with us on Atlantic Blvd., he was already a married man near 24 or 25 and making a living with his art. As a young boy, he had been adopted out to the Reverend Osgood and his family. Later, when he was in his teens, he once again found his siblings and real mother, who was my Grandmother Brown.

Between 1943 and 1947 Fuzzy visited us about four to seven times a year. When he did, I would sit with him near his alcove desk watching the magic appear from his easel or sketch pad. His hand would move back and forth or in a circular motion just above the page as life and beauty appeared magically beneath his pencil. It was like looking at a photo developing in dark room chemicals. It seemed so effortless. It was amazing.

Muggs McGinnis and I oft times ran a frantic foot race to retrieve the early morning newspaper. You see, Fuzzy's favorite entertainment was to get hold of that daily newspaper before we brought it in to Grandma and, with pen and ink or pencil, change the photos in small, or sometimes drastic, but always entertaining ways. His doodling was nothing less than fine art. Whatever he did when he was done, his modified art looked exactly as it would have in a photograph of the real thing. One was hard pressed to tell that someone had fooled with the photo at all. That's what made it funny and genius.

One morning I brought Grandma the paper, and there on the front page was a photo of some city officials with a totally naked woman standing between them.

With the strokes of his mighty pencils, Fuzzy had disrobed this lady who was previously in a white dress. With a bit of his magic he rendered her completely naked. Right there, in front of God and everybody, in all its glory, was an extremely detailed, anatomically correct vagina with pubic hair. He also gave her an ample bosom. What was even worse, standing next to her in the photo was the Mayor of Los Angeles, Fletcher Bowron, with a bulging woody showing through his light brown suit pants, just like the one I had seen on Duck at the Alcazar. Grandma Brown later hit Fuzzy with a broom or took the refolded newspaper to his laughing head. But he mostly out ran her and it had little effect other than our uncontrollable laughter.

Now it would be fair to say that I was always sexually what they then called a "Late Bloomer". This was painfully true until I reached the age of about seventeen. Back in the forties it was worse -I had never paid attention to the reproductive process. There was some silliness about storks and babies in baskets left on doorsteps, but no one had yet bothered to explain to me how babies were born let alone how they were conceived. I did not grow up on a farm and I had not paid much attention to humping dogs or the nightly caterwauling of cats in heat. Oh, of course I knew about that and had seen it all right, but I just thought those cats and dogs were playing with each other and having great fun. I gave them no further thought.

Until my Uncle Fuzzy created that naked lady, I had, in fact, not ever seen the working parts of the female human animal up close. I was quite fascinated. I looked at it with great admiration and interest for a good while before Grandma hit me with her notorious fly flap and snatched the newspaper from me.

You see, previously I had just assumed that the basic difference between boys and girls, men and women was that women had fatter chests, were softer, a bit smaller and just smelled better. Of course, Harley's "naughty books" showed some things and I had my suspicions, but there was never a clear view of most of the lady stuff - certainly nothing as educational as Fuzzy's naked woman. I was stunned to find out that the female was bereft of a "peter and balls" -shocked in fact. I could not understand the design of it nor imagine why God had neglected to give the female those vital items.

I think it was Uncle Jimmy who explained to me something on the order of:

"Artie, when God, up in heaven, was designing and producing human beings on his assembly line and getting them ready for distribution here on earth, his order of peters and testicles was shorted by the supplier and permanently put on something called "back order". So God, in order not to lose business, just passed a single set to every other unfinished being in line. Those that got "the package" he called man. The ones that were shorted he called woman. You see Artie, Jimmy went on, God intended to give a set to everyone but because of the shortage in the supply chain, was unable to."

God help me. This somehow made perfect sense to me. I thought for sure that Jimmy Brown would never have lied to me.

Now I know this all seems unbelievable by today's standards, but I swear it was true.

Many wonderful things happened with that newspaper. Some disturbed me. Others delighted me. Some made me laugh till I wet my britches.

That newspaper always landed on the front porch if the news boy was on his game. But we were always woefully unaware if Rembrandt Fuzzy Von Brown had gotten to the paper first and made his mischief within its pages.

When Fuzzy was not in residence, Grandma always read me the cartoons, especially "Henry" and my favorite of all "Andy Capp" who, for reasons that elude me to this day, I found hilarious.

She would always read portions of the paper to me while I sat on her lap, slowly dressing for school. Dreading socialization, I tried to kill as much time as I possibly could. This was our daily morning ritual.

On one such occasion I managed to read, on the front page, a headline that I thought said:

WORLD ENDS TOMMOROW!
WORLD COMES TO AN END AT 2:00 PM FRIDAY SAYS FAMED BIBLICAL SCHOLAR!

My eyes lit up and I asked Grandma if I understood it correctly. I then asked her to read me the rest of it. She held me on her lap putting my socks on as I held up the newspaper for her to read. She read the first few lines over my shoulder saying, "Well Artie, let's see. It says:

"World will come to an end at 2:00 PM Friday, October 27, 1944 says Dr. Reverend Aaron Beauchamp, renowned philosopher, bible scholar and Baptist prophet."

I was absolutely petrified and went numb. I wanted to grab Muggs up in my arms, jump into my Stearman mode, put the throttle forward and head into a slag pile, killing myself before the world died taking away my beloved Grandma, Harley and the rest.

Of course, I planned one last flight over our little white house and pepper tree before crashing. And maybe just a brief landing to refuel with Anna's Greek pastry while saying goodbye to Papa Eudie and his family. Not even big Eudie could save me from Dr. Beauchamp. After all, Papa was just a Catholic, I thought, but I wanted to sit on his lap one last time, and I have no idea why, but I wanted Anna to kiss me all up and fuss over me, slobbering her lipstick on me just one last time.

Grandma sensed my misery as I started sobbing. She held me fast on her lap and with absolute assurances she calmly said, "Artie, the bible says that when the world comes to an end, not the wisest or smartest man among us will know exactly when it will happen."

She spread the newspaper out in front of us and pointing to the prophet's photo asked me, "Artie, does this man look like the smartest man in the world to you?"

I looked very carefully at his face but said nothing.

Grandma said, "Does he look as intelligent or as wise as say Uncle Paul or Uncle Clayton or Papa Eudie?"

"Nooo," I answered slowly, putting the palms of my hands face up, stretching it out as I thought about it. But then I added, "But Grandma, he's a preacher and talks to God 'n stuff!" I scrunched my shoulders, tears running down my face.

She assuaged my fears by saying, "Artie, some people talk to an apple and think it's a sausage. That doesn't make it so. There is a fool born every minute and six other fools that hang on their every misguided word."

Grandma hugged me and kissed me off to school saying, "Now don't be late. This old world is not ending anytime soon. Your school is just a ten minute walk from here -we always send you off forty minutes early and you always arrive at school fifteen minutes late- so get going and don't stop to talk to everyone."

She asked me if I had any paper boats to give out, knowing that it would slow me down to give them out and talk to folks, so she made me turn my pockets inside out just to check. All was ready, and so I left on my dreaded, daily epic journey. I arrived 18 minutes after the bell.

I had run into Cousin Leslie sitting on a bus bench, so naturally I had to talk with him about the Lone Ranger and, of course, fornication.

Now you see, that biblical scholar in the END OF THE WORLD article had gone on to say that because of man's evil ways, as in the days of Sodom and Gomorrah, we would all be destroyed and that the end of times, according to his calculations, was set for tomorrow afternoon. The cause of it, according to him, was man's lying, cheating and greed as well as mankind's distance from God's word, but, he went on to say, the most serious of all was the "fornicating and fornicators in the world". I had no idea what fornicating meant. When I asked Grandma, she just told me it meant "misbehaving". I think she realized, almost immediately, that she had made a mistake in giving me that definition but could not backtrack and wanted to get me off to school.

I was on that new word like a hobo on a hot jellied biscuit. I gathered that delicious sounding word into my Artie repertoire and did not hesitate to use it frequently and with great authority and verve. After all, its definition had come directly from my Grandmother and, according to the newspaper, from God himself.

On my walk to school I stopped at a bus stop and announced to a man and lady that I had given up fornication altogether and that they should not fornicate either or the world might come to an end. I gave them a paper boat I had hidden inside my underwear and wondered to myself if I had unwittingly fornicated by the act of slyly hiding some of those boats from my very own Grandma.

When I got to school, I stood up and confessed in front of the entire class. By the grace of God I vowed to give up all future fornication so that the world might be saved. I confessed that I was pretty sure that I had recently fornicated with a man and lady near a bus stop by pulling a boat out of the front of my underpants.

The teacher called me up for a private conversation regarding that word.

I just knew that I was personally determined to keep my own fornication down to a minimum and wanted to confess and change my wicked ways. Nothing could stop me once I got on a tear, and as the next couple of weeks passed, all those around me received the benefit of my many lectures on the evils of fornication including the indifferent ear of Muggs McGinnis, our ice man and of course the mailman as well as milkman.

I even vowed to repent of my habit of lying on the linoleum floor, looking up under my aunts' and their girlfriends' dresses at their panties as they walked by.

It was to me a veritable kaleidoscope of joy and I felt perfectly at ease doing it. I had no idea what I was looking at or looking for and less of an idea "why". It was just wonderful what ever it was, and besides, it just looked "neat".

They, of course, would kick me calling me a little pervert and then run complaining to Grandma Brown. This made no sense to me what so ever because I only had a vague idea of what a pervert was, but I knew I was misbehaving and therefore a fornicator. But I couldn't help myself. I just thought it looked really entertaining when they walked by and thought it strange that there were no bulgy parts in their shorts. Of course Jimmy's explanation had enlightened me some, but I did devote some thought to wondering if girls also caught wood peckers in their panties like Duck and the Mayor of Los Angeles?

Truth was they needn't have worried about my mental state. Hell, I didn't have enough sense or education to be a pervert and no inclination for it.

When I vowed to quit fornicating, my ever aggravated Aunt Veve and Aunt Eddie went, once again, sniveling to Grandma Brown about me embarrassing them by the misuse of that "stupid word" in front of their girlfriends and telling poor Grandma, yet again, about my continued looking up their dresses. They further whined to her that I had added a new twist to that loathsome act because I had recently taken to song with each viewing by singing:

> *Down in the meadow in a little bitty pool*
> *fwam three little fiddies and a mama fiddy, too.*
> *"Fwim," said the mama fiddy, "fwim if you can."*
> *And they fwam and they fwam all over the dam.*
> *Boop boop dit-tem dat-tem what-tem Chu!*
> *Boop boop dit-tem dat-tem what-tem Chu!*
> *Boop boop dit-tem dat-tem what-tem Chu!*
> *And they fwam and they fwam all over the dam.*

The girls further complained to Grandma, "That little pervert is counting something up our skirts. He points his arm and forefinger up under our dresses like he's counting cooties or something while he sings that stupid song."

"Honestly Mom!" Veve declared. "Can't you talk to the little monster?"

Grandma told them she would have a talk with me, but of course, she never did.

It turned out that Grandma simply ignoring me was the cure. A few weeks later I gave up my viewing from the linoleum but kept the song, discovering, quite by accident, that it was associated with something naughty to my aunts and their girlfriends. It, of course, meant nothing to me. I could not for the life of me see what they heard in that silly song to object to nor what the connection was to them, but knowing that it bothered the girls I used it till the words wore down. What fun! Life was ever so grand, I thought.

I did not look up another skirt in such a way until almost 13 years later in Mama San's Rising Sun Bar in Sasebo Japan, courtesy of the U.S. Navy and Wild Turkey Whiskey. I did at that time enjoy it ever so much more and was much better educated and far better for the experience.

Anyway, when the "End of the Earth" day came, I was looking at the clock and holding my breath as the minute hand clicked forward to doom. At precisely two p.m. the air raid warning system went off and scared the living hell out of Mom Brown and yours truly. Both of us came up out of her rocker eyes wide open. The air raid warning sirens had previously only been tested on Saturdays at 2:00 p.m. This test was an off-schedule fluke. Grandma and I breathed easier when 2:05 p.m. came around and the alarm stopped wailing. I waited 'til 4:16 p.m. before I relaxed completely and a few weeks later gave myself the "all clear" on the end of the world stuff, returning to my cussing and recreational fornicating once again.

Later, Grandma Brown told Papa Eudie and Anna the story of the article and the siren's unscheduled test time. Papa Eudie looked at Anna and said, "God has a great sense of humor doesn't he?"

"Yes, he does," Anna said. "After all he created Artie Spelman."

I liked that "God had a sense of humor" and got to quoting that to everyone whenever possible, usually seven or eight times a day to Veve and Eddie just to watch their eyes roll up to the sky.

That was back then, but now, five months after the above event took place and the world refused to end, we all breathlessly waited once again for the news boy. Perhaps, when the newspaper arrived it would really end our world just a little bit by destroying poor Uncle Harley who simply had wanted to please his mother.

We were all up early, sitting around the table in the front room as Grandma Brown fixed six of us flap jacks and eggs with homemade, brown sugar maple syrup. It was well past paper time and we were all growing impatient. Finally, we heard the thud against the screen door. Harley held back Muggs and I ran to retrieve the paper, handing it directly to Grandma Brown. I didn't say anything, but I did not see Skip, our usual paper boy, and could have sworn I'd seen Uncle Fuzzy's car driving off.

She opened the paper slowly, almost fearful of what she might find but saw nothing.

"Look Grandma," I said, "on the front page!"

The headline read:

GERMAN DEFENSE IN NORTHERN ITALY
FINALLY COLLAPSES!

Just below that:

LOCAL FAMILY PAYS HOMAGE TO
OUR FLYING HEROES!

There was a news archive photo of all those planes Harley had mentioned, the ones that had flown down Atlantic Blvd. The article went on to say that many of those airplanes had, in fact, been flown by the Women's Auxiliary Ferrying Squadron (WAFS) and went on to explain that these grand women flew many of those planes so that our boys abroad could, "Take it to the enemy!" It said these women were fine pilots and were helping to win the war as surely as or lads "over there". The article ended with:

GOD BLESS THEM ONE AND ALL!

The article described the wonderful demonstration flight of a perfect copy of the World War One Triplane built by Mr. Harley Brown and Walter Crawford. Next to it was a photo of Walt and Harley, smiling broadly as they stood near the pepper tree with beautiful model airplanes held high in each hand.

Nothing appeared anywhere in the paper, not a single word about the fire or demise of the Greasy Spoon number three.

Amazingly, almost all of the copy was given to the "superb baritone voice of young Harley Thomas Brown, patriotic youngest son of the lovely and gracious Mrs. Blanche Louella Brown."

Then Dr. O'Connor went on to explain that Harley's voice could, in his opinion, one day rival the great baritone voices of the world. He then went on to describe his personal knowledge and interest in opera and the human voice and so on, elucidating about other baritones of his acquaintance by the names of John Charles Thomas and Thomas L. Thomas. Dr. O'Connor quipped:

"And now we have the young Harley Thomas Brown. Thomas seems to be a good name for baritones."

We all looked at Grandmother Brown whose face was beaming with pure pride. Her eyes were moist. She called Harley over and kissed him on the lips, then both cheeks. Smoothing down his hair with both hands she said, "God gave you that beautiful voice son, use it. You've made me very proud of you Harley Thomas. That was a lovely thing you did."

Duck came by to check in and, of course, Grandma invited him to breakfast. This big boy, who had a hollow leg, accepted, gratefully digging in. After breakfast Duck looked through the paper smiling at his best friend's smashing success and said to him with a big smile, "A star is born Brownie!" Then turning to the back page Duck said, "Hey, did you guys see this?"

"What?" Everyone asked.

"Listen," Duck went on, "it says:

"Sunday, April 29th at 3:00 a.m., fire units from the Bell and South Gate Fire departments were called to fight a fire at The Cudahy Kiddy Coral, 1541 Lorella St., Cudahy California. The building was completely destroyed, but there were no casualties. The owners and proprietors Jonathan Bruce Brittlewhite and his sister Elizabeth Rose Brittlewhite cannot be located and are being sought for questioning. Authorities say arson is suspected."

Then Duck said, "Mother Brown, take a look at this" and handed her the paper. Just under the fire notice was a cartoon strip, obviously but artfully drawn and pasted there by Uncle Fuzzy called:

"STEARMANBOY & MIGHTY MUGGS by Elwood Brown"

The title character of the cartoon was called "Artie Fartie" and was a perfect cartoon characterization of me. In his cartoon, I was dressed in a costume that resembled a yellow Stearman biplane with double, two foot wings on each of my hips. In front of my pants was a propeller cowling with a little spinning propeller a bit lower than waist high. Behind, attached to my fanny, he drew large feathers like a peacock's in the place of the rear end of the fuselage -tail and rudder section of a bi plane. Where landing gears would normally have been, were my skinny, little legs and knobby knees, both shown with little white crossed bandages.

In the cartoon I was accompanied by my super side kick, Mighty Muggs. He wore a little cape with an MM on it just like Superman's. I was shown with blond hair sticking up in all directions and wearing goggles. On one of my legs a "trinity" of three little red welts could be seen. Artie the Stearman hero flew around a flaming building, releasing flaming farts under his tail feathers and setting the building on fire. The building bore a burning sign that read: "Kiddy Coral". The caption read: "Burn you fiends, burn!"

In the next frames of the cartoon a man and a woman are standing outside the Kiddy Coral looking up at Stearmanboy silhouetted in the moonlight, running across the top of a plank fence yelling encouragement to Mighty Muggs who is pissing on the couple's shoes as the building burns down around their ears. The caption out of the dog's mouth said: "Whoa! Ruff, ruff, ruff, you fornicators. Gurrrr!"

The couple yelled up to the Stearmanboy, "Who are you and what do you want?"

To which Artie the STEARMANBOY, still releasing flaming farts, yells back, "Nunyur Bennis you Fornicators!"

With roll ends from the local newspaper, Fuzzy had created a perfect cartoon, then meticulously pasted it there on the last page of the paper. In the last frame of the cartoon, a police Sergeant, looking very much like Zambo, is seen chasing the couple out of town, waving his billy club.

CHAPTER 17

Muggs
(The Celebration)

I WAS JUST A couple of months shy of seven years old. I remember May 8, 1945 as if it were yesterday because it was V.E. Day, the last day of the war in Europe, and the whole neighborhood was celebrating. The news was all over the radio, which we had turned up so no one would miss a word since our windows were opened to a cacophony of sound. People where out celebrating on every corner. The traffic on both sides of Atlantic was thick with folks cheering and honking their horns and holding up their fingers in the "V for Victory" sign or standing on the sidewalks with the American Flag. It was a day filled with happiness and promise. Our men and women were coming home! The world was celebrating and we were a part of it.

Grandma Blanche vacillated between laughing and crying. My Aunt Elza Jean's husband, Carl Agajanian, would be flying back to her arms soon, relieving me and Muggs of our billets as her crying snuggle buddies.

Artie and Muggs, VE Day, 1945

Everyone was happy. Me too. I was laughing that kind of laugh only little boys know. It was the kind of joy that is born in the center most pit of little boys' stomachs, just behind their navels, that churns up like an earthquake of molten, teary eyed silliness. Do you remember how as a child you could just lie on the grass, rolling and laughing, neither knowing nor caring why? Just glad to be alive? This was that moment for me. It was brought on partially by the energy of the day itself, but mostly because of the pranks of Muggs' Uncle Harley's pup as we played together in the grass. We ran and chased each other, and I fell down when I didn't have to, knowing this would bring the dog running to lick my face or pull at my shoes or pant leg. He loved pulling off my shoes, then socks, and he did it very well. The shoes and socks translated into a chase for Muggs as soon as they were free of a foot. He would take off running across the backyard at full speed with me close behind him. Muggs loved the chase most of all.

I didn't understand exactly why everyone was so happy, but I remember having the feeling that I would never be this happy again. Getting up, I tried to catch Muggs once more, but he was just too smart and too fast. As we played in the field behind our house, Grandma and the family waited inside for the Theocarides family to join them. The Theocarides were bringing Greek food, musical instruments and stories. Laughter and love were surely to be plentiful at this hurriedly-put-together, celebration party. Just out of sight of the house and the group assembling there, Muggs and I were oblivious to it all. We were lost in our own little world of chase and catch. What a wonderful day, I thought!

Now there were these kids that lived somewhere near Huntington Park High School whose last name was Tufts. They were four brothers that Grandma called, "The Devil's Knuckles", or "Tufts Boys". Being a kid, I heard it as "Tough Boys". Ranging from age nine to fourteen years of age, they were all capable of great mischief that was not harmless but full of a brooding brutality that was often violent and always mean spirited.

They had been messing with me for a couple of years, but I had always managed to escape with only a few cuts and bruises. I would often run from them hiding somewhere in the lumber yard next door or escape into Harley's garage, bolting the door behind me. Bruce Tufts, the eldest and most vicious of the four, carried a bull whip around his neck and was deadly accurate with it. He was forever hitting dogs and killed cats by the dozens. He loved to go for their eyes and blind them, cackling as he inflicted pain on anything that did not move aside quickly enough, including me.

Grandma had chased all of them off the property at one time or another. They rode their new Schwinn bikes through her garden several times, destroying it. Other times they tore down her clothes line filled with clean wash, grinding it into the dirt and mud as they rode over it with their bicycles. The Toughs terrorized anyone they could with very few repercussions. They were bullies and uniformly hated by the neighborhood, but no one could quite catch them at their cunning, nefarious deeds.

Muggs possessed one of the happiest souls of any dog I ever knew. He lived to play and what I remember most about him was that he was never mean and possessed a lovely, gentle nature. When we weren't playing in the big vacant lot behind our house, he entertained himself with an old shoe or ball. Several times Muggs had turned up with whip cuts on his flanks, and once there was a cut or two just above his eyes, but the small dog's speed had always saved him from a harsher fate. Harley was livid when he saw the cuts on Muggs' face. He knew the Tufts boy had put them there, but neither Harley nor Duck were ever in the right place to catch him. "Duck and I will fix that guy one of these days," Harley said, gritting his teeth.

Ironically, at the very moment I thought the world was my oyster -hell came for a visit.

Sitting in the grass, laughing at Muggs as he ran off with my sock, I failed to notice the four boys on their bikes cutting across the back of the lot. When I looked up, the "Devil's Knuckles" were on top of me. My first instinct was to run. Scrambling to my feet as fast as I could with one bare foot, I hobbled towards the lumber yard and the safety I'd always found there. Closing me in with their bikes so I couldn't veer away from my intended destination, I tried to remember Papa Eudie's Talisman Trick for evading enemies and fiends. He had given it to me several months earlier, but I couldn't remember it. Besides, it was too late. The Tufts boys were just feet away. Nothing could save me now and I knew it. Just as I reached the hole in the lumber yard fence, Muggs shot through ahead of me and I followed. The boys were off their bikes and through the hole just seconds behind us. This time all four of the "Tough boys" were there -not the usual one or two I'd contended with before. They caught me and dragged me screaming behind a pile of lumber. There was no escape. Muggs, in his determination to defend me, was trapped, too.

The pup was darting between me and the boys, snarling and barking in his effort to protect me. He managed to bite Bruce Tufts on the leg several times, but he was just too little a dog for such a big job. Bruce grabbed two pieces of scrap wood about the size of baseball bats and tossed one to his brother. Using them as clubs, they went after Muggs. The dog held, but could not get close enough now to retaliate. Yelping and wailing with each blow, the brave dog stood his ground as they beat him mercilessly.

"Don't hurt Muggs!" I pleaded. "Pleeease," I cried, "please don't hurt him!" My pleading fell on deaf ears. Pinned under the weight of the other two boys, they turned my head and held it, forcing me to watch every detail of the vicious beating. Howling and whimpering with pain as each blow struck him, Muggs refused to retreat. He put himself in harm's way again and again.

In time, Muggs fell. His spine shattered and his body broken from repeated trauma, he lost control of his bowels and his hind-quarters. Bruce and his brother were still laughing, but they were deadly serious about their intent now. Laying there in the dirt, helpless and paralyzed, Muggs' mouth was still moving slowly, snapping at them -trying hopelessly to defend himself and me. That's when they went to work on his head. They took turns beating the little guy, crushing his skull. Finally, after what seemed to me an eternity, it was over and Muggs passed from life into my memories. He died there next to me, trying to protect me on the last day of his life on the last day of war in Europe.

Sobbing, I lay there in the dirt as helpless as Muggs had been. I was sure I was going to die and I hadn't even misbehaved. I hoped Grandma would know that I had been a good boy and had done nothing wrong and wouldn't blame me for Muggs and I dying.

The pup's death was not enough. Bruce had not tired in his torment of Muggs. Glancing over to make sure I was still being forced to watch, Bruce started kicking him in the ribs so hard that it raised his small, lifeless body off the ground. With each kick I could hear the pup's ribs cracking. They then repeated this several times, hooting and laughing like baboons.

After tiring of their sport, Bruce yelled to his brothers, "Watch this!" He positioned Muggs' head where it pleased him, stepped back, then took the bull whip from his shoulders and popped out Muggs' eyes. Turning toward his brothers, he bowed deeply receiving their thunderous praises.

I reached my free hand toward Muggs to try to touch him. I wanted to thank him and love him with my finger tips before I died, but one of the boys who had pinned me to the ground jerked my arm back. I soon realized that Muggs was just the beginning and that it was now my turn. I can remember that somehow I was at peace or perhaps just numb or resigned, but I recall thinking that I wanted to tell my family goodbye and that I loved them all. I knew Papa Eudie would fix my crumpled body and lay me and Muggs in a pretty place. Maybe under the Pepper tree, I thought, or perhaps at Gopher Spit Hollow next to the windmills. Yes, that's it, I thought, between those windmills I loved so much. That gave me some peace. Maybe I could say goodbye to him in the funeral parlor.

Bruce kicked me in the face and my nose exploded as blood filled my mouth. The Tufts boys were only warming up. Fortunately, my ordeal didn't last as long as the one Muggs had just endured. All four started to kick me at the same time and it wasn't long before a well placed kick to the side of my head sent me spinning down into oblivion. The last clear memory I had before waking up in Blanche's arms was of seeing Muggs lying there so still in the dirt. His torn, eyeless and bloodied body had a couple of ribs sticking out through his skin and fur.

Much later, the night watchman from the lumber yard found me as he made his rounds. Muggs' body had been thrown over my unconscious one. After calling the police, the night guard had picked me up and carried me to Grandma who, along with family and friends, had been searching for us for more than five hours since discovering we weren't in the backyard playing.

I don't actually remember that part of it. What I do remember is the smell of Grandma's lilac perfume as I regained consciousness. I tried to open my eyes, but they were swollen shut. The night watchman had laid me in the arms of my Grandma and I pressed the side of my head against her bosom. I was alive and at home, safe in my church. She gently put her wonderful big hands on me. I tried to tell her about Muggs, but my jaw was frozen shut. My throat was swollen and my voice had vanished completely and was replaced by a gurgle when I tried to speak.

She shushed me and told me everything would be all right. I knew we would never see Muggs again and that it would break Harley's heart as it had already broken mine.

She rocked me, singing "Rock of Ages" as we waited for the police. I was covered in the pup's blood, brains and excrement as well as a great deal of my own blood. I had several broken ribs, my jaw was fractured and I was bleeding from my ears. My nose was broken and full of blood, but somehow I could still smell Grandma's perfume. I remember thinking nobody can hurt me now.

Doctors were not as readily available in those days, and they cost money. There was no such thing as billed emergency services, you paid up front or you got no service. Grandmother, apparently, had angels because the night watchmen, an old Marine named David Abadjian who knew and loved Blanche Brown, had a son who was a doctor, and he sent him over to our house.

Doctor Abadjian told Grandma that I was very lucky to be alive. I had a severe concussion and several open gashes across the top of my scalp. I had broken ribs, a fractured forearm, loose and missing teeth and split lips. I had been kicked in the throat and I had also lost a considerable amount of blood from my rectum. The doctor had no clear idea what that was from. One or all of the boys had kicked me between the legs so hard that it drove my ruptured testicles back up into my abdomen and my little "Pistol Pete" was nearly torn in half, bruised and seeping blood. My shirt and pants had been ripped into shreds by something and my back, arms and legs were covered with dozens of welts that looked like someone had beaten me with a belt or whip. A couple of them were open and bleeding. The doctor was quite concerned about possible internal injuries, but his biggest fear was that I had been unconscious for so long.

Doctor Abadjian told my Grandmother that whoever had done this clearly wanted to kill us both and by the grace of God had failed. By the next morning most of my body had turned a deep shade of purple, blue, yellow and black.

Years later, I learned something from Harley that I had not known then. When the night watchman brought Muggs to Harley, he told him that the pup was soaking wet because, when he found us, someone had pissed all over both of us as we lay there. He also said there must have been more than one attacker because we were both completely drenched from head to foot in urine. As a kindness to Harley, he had wrapped Muggs body in a blanket.

It took me almost three months to recover enough to go back to school. I couldn't even stand or walk for a couple of weeks because of my injured testicles. Of course, as soon as I could speak, I told Harley and Grandma who did it. They were not surprised.

The next morning, the Theocarides family paid for me to go to the City of Angels Hospital to be checked out more thoroughly. They also provided caretakers to nurse me at home for six or seven days. I don't remember any of the nurses clearly. I just remember faces fussing over me as they gave me medications or liquids through a straw. The doctor had instructed them to shake me awake every few minutes because of the concussion, and I hated that. I was so exhausted that I just wanted to sleep. I did lose most of the sight in my left eye. None of that hurt as much as the loss of Muggs and not being able to help him.

Those bastards showed no mercy to that happy, lion-hearted soul. They enjoyed it. The "Tough" Boys were my introduction to real evil.

This event affected and disturbed Papa Eudie profoundly. I would find out exactly why it had five decades after the fact.

Duck was scared to death of his father's reaction and possible reprisal for my beating. Eudocio was furious. Duck was concerned about his dad's mental state because of Eudie's past experiences with such cruelty. He had lost his first family to such brutality and worse in Turkish occupied Armenia.

"God help us all if Papa catches those boys," he told my grandmother.

Grandmother just said, "Well God can help them, but I'll not."

CHAPTER 18

Muggs
(Arlington on Atlantic)

HARLEY BURIED MUGGS by the side of his garage the next day. Duck and Eudie had meticulously worked on pup's body and brought him from across the street into Harley's garage. I was still a lump of beaten flesh from the previous night as Grandma Brown told me about how beautiful Muggs looked. She said Duck had bathed him with a special solution and Eudie fixed his eyelids shut as well as visually restored his bones, skull and fur. Grandma said Muggs looked like he was just sleeping when Harley laid him to rest in the little casket he'd constructed of pine.

Eudie produced a small vial of Ouzo, a Greek Liquor, for the boys, and they had a little wake for Muggs. Harley and Eudie sang while Duck played the cello. I could not move around, but I could hear the music from Grandma's lap. It was so beautiful, a symphony for a little pup. How wonderful, I thought. Grandma had snatched me up onto her lap and I leaned back against her chest with my head just under her chin, as I always had, as we listened from inside the house to Papa Eudie Theocarides' cimbalom dulcimer and basso voice joining Harley's baritone. Their music rang into my heart, healing it and destroying it at the same time. While the wake was unfolding, Grandma and I heard the most beautiful of all the music. Papa Eudie sang what we later learned from Harley was an ancient Greek Chant, something called Gregorian. Eudie's voice seemed to pierce the distance between the garage and us as his warm, full base voice shook both the rafters of our small, white house as well as our souls. I squeezed Grandmother's hand, feeling something I had never experienced before. I could still not open my eyes, but I reached up to feel Grandma's cheeks and felt moisture on them as we listened silently. I remember thinking being there in Grandma's arms and listening to that music was almost worth my beating, but I could never forget the cruelty shown to Muggs who would never hear music or his Harley sing again.

Uncle Harley put one of his tennis shoes in the casket with the pup, and then installed the lid and they buried him. It took my uncle several weeks to carve Muggs a pine headstone.

About five weeks later, when I was recovered enough to stand next to Grandma, a funeral service fit for any Dutch Irish Brown was held at the foot of his little grave. It was attended by an even dozen mourners, which included Grandma's four sons: Harley, Fuzzy, Jimmy and Paul and just two of her seven daughters: Veve and my mother Iris. In the back row, towering behind the Browns like four Redwoods stood the entire Theocarides family including their oldest son, Captain Stavros Theocarides. Everyone called him Theo. He was still in his Army Air Force uniform and had only a few days earlier returned from the war in Europe. He was a Jug pilot who had won the Bronze Star and was home on leave en route to fight, yet again, in Japan.

Harley placed his pine headstone on the grave. It said:

IN LOVING MEMORY OF
Lance Corporal Muggs McGinnis Brown
Who died at the Hands of Cowards!
Born: Around Easter Sunday 1941
Died: On V.E. Day 1945

All stood in somber silence, respecting a simple and wonderful creature that had done his best.

This was more than the burial of just a pup with a great heart. Had it been another pup during any other time it would have been just a sad footnote in the life of the Browns and one of their pets. But today it was part of the culmination of years of following the war on the radio, Grandma Brown and Anna Theocarides working with the Red Cross, attending to the parents of some fine soldier who had been killed, Anna worrying about her own son Theo off fighting in that war or the red stars in people's windows being changed to gold, another son gone to the grave. It was about all those years now grinding to an end, of not being able to really change anything and feeling helpless because of it, of worrying about gas rationing, or Grandma fixing a meal that had even a glimmer of a meat in it or giving your used lard to the grocers. It was about Mom Brown's girls painting a stripe up the back of their legs to imitate the look of nylons and waiting for their men to return. It was a special time of remembrance of lots of brave souls who gave their all. This funny little dog was now, to us, a warrior pup. In the middle of it all was a sad and beaten, tow headed, small boy who had lost his buddy and a great deal of his innocence. Muggs' gravesite was a focal point for all of our hearts and minds to now come together. We needed it. This just felt right somehow.

Uncle Paul, Grandma's oldest son, was home from almost five years as a Merchant Marine. He had survived two sunken ships. He stood in between Harley and me, putting an arm around each of us. Looking at Grandma Brown he said, "Mom, I knew a lot of good men who died during these last few years." Then he looked affectionately at Captain Theo and Grandmother and continued, "Cap'n, I hope you don't think my suggestion disrespectful here, but a bunch of those lads that died were my friends. I believe many of my mates would have been proud to stand here for this small pup and would not resent our prayers and kind thoughts for him. We all know he was a silly, black and white puppy and not a real soldier. But Mom, it is his spirit and courage that we wish to honor here today, so if it's o.k. with you and Theo, I want to offer something here that I have always loved. You may have heard it. It was written for our soldiers during the First World War. I just thought it applied to Muggs' effort to protect and defend one of us and I offer this now in the memory of the best in all of us." Mom Brown touched him on his cheek in approval and Theo nodded his head. Uncle Paul then recited the following from memory:

> *In Flanders fields the poppies blow*
> *Between the crosses, row on row,*
> *That mark our place; in the sky*
> *The larks, still bravely singing, fly*
> *Scarce heard amid the guns below.*
> *We are the Dead. Short days ago*
> *We lived, felt dawn, saw sunset glow,*
> *Loved and were loved, and now we lie*
> *In Flanders fields.*
> *Take up our quarrel with the foe:*
> *To you from failing hands we throw*
> *The torch; be yours to hold it high.*
> *If ye break faith with us who die*
> *We shall not sleep, though poppies grow*
> *In Flanders fields.*

Paul looked down at the little grave and said,

"We do not break faith with those we've lost in our war and those still dying in hospitals and we, the Brown and Theocarides Families, do not break faith with our Artie or your wonderful, little heart Muggs. God bless you and God keep us all from the hands of the cowardly."

Harley and Jimmy played Last Call, then Taps on their harmonicas. Captain Theo saluted. I did too, twice, once with each hand as I could never remember which hand to use.

Finally Harley Hugged his big brother Paul then took a piece of paper out of his shirt pocket and read from it:

"Muggs, this is Harley. You were just a little dog. You were my pain in the ass with a broken tail. You never learned a trick from me, but you had plenty of your own."

Harley was trying to keep it under control but losing the fight from the start as he continued:

"You never paid attention to any one -only my Mother and just maybe God. You were a dirty, flea bitten, stupid, little pup that made me laugh and all of us glad to be alive. You never met a postman or a milkman that you liked, but you loved the iceman for his gifts of chunks of ice. You never met a cockled burra you didn't wear proudly, and all the fleas in Bell found a happy home in your neck. You forever hid my tennis shoes…"

It was hard for Harley to continue and his voice cracked as it changed pitch. Grandmother started to step in to comfort him, but Uncle Jimmy shook his head and gently held her back as Harley continued:

"You marked everything in my garage twice and once again for good measure. I chased you out more times than I can remember, and you'd run to Mom and sit on her lap: listening to the radio, eating a larded biscuit, waiting for me to call you back."

Then, wiping his nose on his sleeve and coughing up a deep sob, Harley said:

"Mom told me that when you'd hear my garage door slam, your ears would perk up and you'd jump down, burst out her back screen door and fly up into my arms, licking me. That's what I will remember most and best about you Muggs."

Harley fought hard to continue. Finally he said:

"Muggs, I loved you and I will never forget you boy. I miss you. You were the best dog I ever knew." Uncle Harley's voice was cracking and barely audible. "I will see you in heaven and I'll sneak another tennis shoe past God for you to pee in."

Harley started to say good bye, but he couldn't get all of it out. He turned and ran into his garage, locking it behind him. He put on his John Charles Thomas record. His sorrow was only partially muffled by the great baritone singing "Bendemeer Steam". Everyone left the little grave site saddened by Harley's pain.

Duck went to the garage door and knocked, but Harley just said, "Go away Tim, I'll see you in a while."

Grandma told us all to just leave him alone for a while. No one saw him until the next day.

As the rest of us walked, in absolute silence, toward the house for Anna's coffee and cakes, I was thinking a bit about how Harley would actually go about sneaking the other tennis shoe past God and asked, "Grandma, Preacher Wall says that there are no dogs in heaven, is that true?"

It was so quiet and somber because of Harley's exit that within the group my voice must have sounded as loud as a truck horn. My Grandmother never cussed a day in her life and she was loath to anger, but her face turned red and she gritted her teeth and clinched her fists, trying her best to hold back, but it couldn't be stopped. "Well," she said thinking about it. "Well, well…" Then finally she blurted it out in exasperation, "Reverend Wall, well, Reverend Wall is just a Farter!" she exclaimed with great ferocity.

We all broke into spasmodic laughter. Eudie and Fuzzy both roared. Our tears of laughter melded like a sweet, spirit lifting spice into those of our sorrow. Grandma raised her teary face, smiling she reached over and slapped Fuzzy on his arm. He was just the closest. The entire mood changed from one of sadness to loving joy and laughter as everyone teased Mom Brown. Veve threatened to inform the good Reverend Charles Wall that he had been demoted from Reverend to "Pastor Farter" by the pronouncement of the good Mrs. Brown.

CHAPTER 19

Muggs
(The Whizzing Ghost)

THE NEXT MORNING Harley awoke in better spirits and for the first time, I was allowed to move around a little more. After we hugged Grandma good morning she gave us a package to deliver to Anna, who was expecting us for a special breakfast in honor of 'Harley and the Whisker.' When we arrived across the street, they served us breakfast as if we were royalty, which was nothing new. Anna picked me up like a little rag doll and gave me her usual dose of big wet kisses, leaving lipstick on my face from port to starboard. Then she said something loving to me in Greek. As she carried me to the table, she squeezed the breath out of me, and eventually sat me down on Eudie's ample lap. I gave her the set of doilies and a toaster cover Grandma had crocheted for her, and Harley gave Theo his perfect Replica of a P47 Thunderbolt Balsa Wood model, accurate down to the last detail, exactly like the plane Theo flew in the War. It had four Nazi insignias that symbolized his kills, proving that Theo was just one enemy shy of being an Ace. Just under the model's sliding canopy read 'Captain Stavros "Theo" Theocarides'. Theo passed the model to Eudie, who admired it.

Papa noticed a little hard rubber figure of a Monkey Harley sitting in the cockpit and Eudie's big voice boomed over my head as he said,

"Yes, the pilot looks like you, my Theo!"

We all smiled and Eudie looked down at me at me and asked, "Do you like this airplane, Artie?"

"Yes, it's a P47 Jugg. And guess what, Papa?" I turned to him proudly. "I helped uncle Harley build it."

He said,

"My, what a talented boy you are, my Artie."

"And guess what, Papa?" I said. "I am getting less and less glue in my eyes and ears, and one day I am going to build you a airplane all by myself!"

"Whisker, that would be wonderful," he said as he kissed me on the cheek, his rough morning beard making me giggle. Eudie smelled like leather and pipe tobacco. This great man represented everything to me that was masculine, everything strong and lovely and fine; I loved him as I would have my own father.

We visited for a while at the table listening to Anna singing in some foreign language as she worked at her stove in the next room. Finally we all ate our breakfast, laughing and visiting just as we had in days gone by, with Anna fussing over us all. After breakfast, I climbed back onto Papa Eudie's lap while they all drank thick Greek coffee served in a glass, and we listened to Anna tell Harley funny stories about Blanch Brown. She spoke with heartfelt appraisals about what a wonderful woman and friend Harley's mother was; the two women were a colorful pair, to be sure. Grandma was as short as a munchkin, while Anna was a tower. The two represented pure love balanced precariously on swollen ankles, but they were always laughing. Eudie used to say, "Some folks have religion, those two have God." Sunlight follows both of them wherever they go.

As I sat there on the Eudie's lap, listening, it made my heart light and happy that others admired and loved my grandmother as much as I did.

Then, speaking to all of us but addressing me directly, Papa said, "Artie, someday soon Papa Eudie is going to have a talk with those bad boys who hurt you and Muggs. I think they are not going to like

171

your Papa Eudie so much. Just you wait and see, Papa is going to show those bad boys some things about hell's wages." He glanced at Harley and Duck, who looked concerned. Papa was smiling, but there was fire burning in those huge black moist Greek eyes. Even I could see it, and it frightened me a bit. Papa was so large that I had to stand up to my full height on the upper front of his left leg and reach up all the way up to hug this mammoth man around his trunk-like neck.

I said, "Okay, Papa Eudie, and thank you for breakfast." Then I turned to the others and thanked Anna for the delicious food.

"You're welcome, Artie," they both intoned. They spoke at almost the same time as Papa sat me down, as though I were made of porcelain. He patted me on the fanny and scooted me on my way.

Just before we left, Theo gave Harley his good conduct ribbon and said, "Harley, put this on the pups' grave from Captain Stavros." We hugged Duck and Theo, and then Anna swept me up for a second time. I closed my eyes and gritted my teeth in preparation for the second onslaught of lipstick laden kisses. She put me down and gave Harley a big hug, during which his entire face disappeared in her ample bosom. This made Papa and Duck laugh as she kissed Harley on the top of his head.

We left with a large basket of Greek pastries earmarked for Grandma. Anna gave Harley and me a generous tin of her homemade Pasteli and Anomola candies, with instructions for us not to eat any of them until later (I will admit, a couple of pieces came up missing by the time we crossed the street and arrived at our front door.) Grandma caught our gluttonous sins straight away and admonished us both with a love tap for ignoring what she knew Anna had told us. We were contrite as all get out, yet we did not hesitate — in our youthful arrogance — to beg Momma for yet another piece. It did not work. She refused and put the candy up in one of her special places that were out of bounds for hairy kneed hooligans.

For Mom Brown, those places were as secure as though she'd tucked them away in a steel safe box. Harley and I both loved and respected her too much ever to ever violate that space, and at any time I would have happily taken another beating from the devil's knuckles rather than ever think I had displeased my grandmother. A single look of disappointment on Grandma's beautiful face could destroy me. We would receive our next treat when she told us we could, and not a moment sooner. God, I swear the taste was made more delicious for the waiting.

Our small house was at maximum occupancy from the previous days' guests, and that night I went to the garage to sleep with Uncle Harley in his loft bed, which he'd built between the rafters. Sometime in the middle of the night, Harley must have gone outside to pee because I could hear a linear cacophony of urinary whizz-ardry that sounded like a bull relieving himself on a tin shed; the sound seemed to go on endlessly. I knew that I was sort of asleep but did not for sure know exactly where I was anymore. I was somewhere very dark and cold, that I knew. I was alone but not afraid, and there was no Ingersol Rand about, only a strange longing within me that was painful and unfamiliar.

I sat by myself somewhere outside the concept of time. Where was I? I was profoundly sad and did not know why. I wanted to wake up and tried to force myself awake, but couldn't. I called out Harley's name trying to wake myself. I yelled as loud as I could, but no one answered. Then I found myself in a large lot and somewhere, just behind and to the left of me, was a house with a small stoop. I knew the house, but like a friend grown old, it took me a moment to recognize it. I looked at my knees pulled up in front of me and saw that I was sitting on my butt in the exact center of a very large platform swing. I'd folded my arms around my knees and clasped my hands together, holding them in place to support my back. Sitting in this way seemed so familiar. "I know this!" I said to myself.

I still heard the loud whizzing sound of thundering against tin. *This is really strange*, I thought. Then I heard Grandma singing softly from inside the dark house. "Grandma! Grandma!" I called to her, but she didn't respond either.

There was no light shining anywhere, save the half moon in the sky and the street lamp in front of the lumberyard next door. Searching for the direction of the whizzing, I looked to my right and saw Muggs

McGinnes with his back leg hiked high and heard him marking his territory on the bottom of the large Tin that said *Atlantic Lumber Company*.

"It's Muggs! It's Muggs!" I exclaimed. I quit sniveling and started laughing. "Harley!, Grandma! I yelled as loud as I could. "It's Muggs! It's Muggs!" I was overjoyed. "It's Muggs," I said softly to myself, wistfully pointing to him, hoping he was real. I wanted to touch him.

Before I could call him over to me, he jumped up on the big swing and sat down beside me. There were half-empty sockets where his eyes had once been, with only fragments poking through. His head was cracked open and I could see into his skull. He made no sound but at all, and I saw he wasn't breathing, only wagging his tail.

"Muggs," I said, putting my arm around him. I could feel his broken spine. "What are you doing here?"

He just looked at me with his strange distorted face. I felt no horror, only gratitude and love for the sight of him filling me once again. I could still hear Grandma's voice singing her hymns from inside the house.

My heart was laughing and full. I didn't want to awaken now. I never wanted this to end. So I ran as fast as I could directly back into the center of the dream. I started to pet his head; I squeezed him and kissed his matted bloodied nose. I pushed his brains back into his skull and as I petted the top of his head, all the blood vanished and the skull and fur closed under my thumb as though it had a zipper. I touched his smooshed eyes and sockets and wiped the tears matting from both corners of his eyes with my thumbs just as I had seen Harley do so lovingly whenever he groomed him. His eyes became true again. Petting down his back, I could feel each vertebrae snap into place as his spine righted itself; click, click, click, click. At precisely the last click I heard a *ding*! I heard the *kach-ing* of the green light from the stop sign at the corner of Atlantic and Gage. A single, pre war black and white 1937 Ford police car drove slowly to the curb and stopped just in front of us. Officer Zambo shined his flashlight on us and rolled down the window. Ignoring me completely, he said to Muggs, "Is everything okay?"

"Woof!" Muggs said.

The officer was Anna's brother, Sergeant Zambetes. He waved before driving off.

Muggs just looked at me. He sat there for a good long while, just looking curiously into my eyes. His tongue was hanging out the side of his mouth and he was now panting, just as he had always done. He looked as silly and as gentile and as funny as he always had. Somewhere from within him, a voice said, "Are you okay, Artie? "

"Yes," I answered.

His mouth was open, but his lips didn't move.

"Oh good," the voice said, "because you know I love you, little boy." He paused for a bit before adding, "I would die for you, Artie, did you know that?"

I replied, "But Muggs, you *did* die for me!"

"Oh yeah, I forgot" he said as he licked his balls.

"Well, I would do it again!" I cried.

Then the voice within him laughed and said,

"Heck, maybe not. Those mean little bastards sure know how to make a guy feel unwelcome, you know what I mean? But I would damn well run to get you some help from the big Greek boys," he said as he reached up to lick my bad left eye.

The voice in his throat asked me, "Harley wasn't mad at me, was he?"

"Why gosh, no, why would he be mad at you?" I said.

"Well," he replied, "I couldn't help but notice that on my 'Grave Pine', he only gave me the bleeping rank of Lance-bloody-Corporal — now that was cute as hell — but for Christ's sake, Artie, what would I have had to do to make the grade of Sergeant: re-capture Poland or bite Hitler's nuts off? Jeeze, Artie! Sergeant, Sergeant, I have always loved the way that sounded. If I told you and Harley once it was a thousand times that I wanted to be a Sergeant, just like Sergeant Zambetes or Sergeant Agajanian.

"Sergeant!" he continued. "Honestly, would Sergeant McGinnis have been asking too much? Besides, it takes so much more carving to whittle out Lance-Freaking-Corporal than it would have the gah-damned single word Sergeant. What in the hell was Harley thinking?"

"I am sorry, Muggs. I had nothing to do with that. I was broken and laying on Grandma's lap, holding my chunk of tar when Harley did the carving," I answered cowardly. Ignoring me, he went on, a hearty chuckle coming from somewhere just under his panting tongue, and he said, "Guess what? I chewed up a block of his balsa wood, instead of watching you that day like he told me to. Then I pissed on his pile of dirty socks, twice. Soaked 'em a good one. Why, I just couldn't help it, Artie. I felt terribly guilty. And then, well, then I ran out to the lot to play with you as I promised him; and that's when those 'tough boys' got us. I thought maybe he was mad about those socks."

I noticed Muggs' eyes darting back and forth and looking away, probably thinking he had disappointed Harley. Then he added, "I couldn't protect you, Artie. I was so happy not to find you in heaven because I knew you had made it through and were still alive."

He licked me on the face and whined just like he used to, the way he did when he was hurt or sad or had been scolded. Then he whimpered, "I am sorry Artie. I really tried my best, honest."

I rubbed his ears and his left leg started its automatic involuntary scratching, just the way it always had. Then I said, "Oh my, no, Harley was so proud of you. He loves you, Muggs, did you know that? We all know you did your best. Weren't you there at your funeral; didn't you hear our praises?"

"No," Muggs said, "but I heard that pretentious Greek music sung by the big man on the day I was buried. Boy, it scared the shit out of me, yah know it, Artie? It near ruined my first day in my heavenly home. Don't those dumb ass Greeks no any Dixieland or swing?

"No, I couldn't attend the funeral," he said. "I was hung up with a pretty little Pekinese with a lovely red tail. Reverend Wall was wrong; life is sweet here in the bye and bye, for we naughty puppies and my dance card is forever full. I get my self tied to more tail here than a hurricane kite in a thunderstorm."

I ignored his bragging, confused by his chain of thought, and said, "Grandma says God loves you, and that you were as brave as any soldier. She said you gave it your all."

"She did? Really?" the pup said brightly, ever so pleased. "Gosh, I love that old woman," he added.

"I would love to live again just for one of her biscuits."

Then I said, "Muggs, Harley could never be mad at you. He cried for a month."

"Yes, I know. I can hear it in the sound of his harmonica, and when he sings. I am with him often, but maybe he just can't see me. I will never leave either of you, I promise," he said as he jumped down and started toward the big back lot.

As he passed Harley's garage and his own grave in the moonlight, he hiked his leg and pissed on his pine headstone. I could see his well aimed whiz as it ran over the word "Lance Corporal." Muggs looked back at me and winked, then said, "I love you, Artie Spelman. Lick Harley in the nostrils and ears for me when you see him. His left ear — you know, the one with the bad eardrum — is particularly delicious, and he likes it when you lick him there. Bye Artie, We will meet in the great bye and bye."

"Bye 'nd Bye, Bye 'nd bye we will meet in the great By'nd bye...." Muggs' voice was replaced by the sweet sound of Grandma, her voice filtering from that little white house next to my pepper tree, beside the rest of my dreams on Atlantic Boulevard.

Bye and Bye, we will meet on that beautiful shore. I sent the dream to "save" on my Microsoft Publisher. But alas, I was on a roll and could not stop. I wanted to jot down a few notes about The Duck and Judge Harley's trial, and the conviction and hanging of the Tufts boy.

Oh, those happy days!

CHAPTER 20

Duck Arrests a Tufts

D UCK AND HARLEY were inseparable. His garage hideout was not only where he slept, but also where he built me model airplanes and sang with his John Charles Thomas records, or practiced his harmonica, and where he and Duck expressed their inner thoughts, if for nothing else than just to hear how they sounded. In between their rhetoric, they built things or fixed machinery. It was that special place where those boys bonded, discussing the war and girls, and simply laughing and teasing each other over many a game of pinochle.

Harley's garage, was almost the size of the little white house. Its entrance faced the screen door in the back of our little house about eighty feet away.

VJ Day had come and gone. The war was now over on all fronts. It was about fifteen weeks after my celebratory beating from the "Toughs," and I was on the mend. It was summer vacation and I was sitting in our lot, leaning against the wall of Harley's garage, taking in the sunshine next to Muggs' grave. I placed two of my favorite marbles and one of my old socks with holes he had torn in the toe, and carefully stuck the head of a little plastic squirrel eating an acorn out of the toe hole. I figured that if Muggs' spirit saw this, it would make him happy and bring him a little smile. The squirrel was a "prize" from a Cracker Jacks box. I had been thinking for some time about what to leave for him. This was only about the second or third time I had been out of bed and away from Grandma's curative arms for very long.

I was enjoying the warm sunshine, remembering Muggs and me and Harley in happier times. I looked up at the clouds floating by on that beautiful day, and I could hear Harley and Duck in the garage, laughing and clanking away as they tinkered, working on something. In my peripheral vision, I something that made my blood run cold. About thirty yards away, on the sidewalk of Clarkson Avenue — the street just behind Harley's garage — was the oldest of the Tufts boys out on his bicycle. He didn't seen me. I rolled over on top of Muggs' grave, dashing around the corner and bolting into the garage. Gasping for breath, I found Harley and Duck working on the old rusty rifle Harley had dug up in the big back lot a year or so earlier. As I tore through the door, I was as white as a sheet, weak kneed, sputtering and stammering.

Harley and the Duck came over to me immediately.

"What's wrong, Artie? What happened?" they asked.

"That big tough kid is out there," I said, pointing in the general direction as I tried to catch my breath. My heart struggled to pound its way out of my chest.

Harley smiled broadly, reminding me of Sylvester in the cartoons, just before he swallowed Tweetybird. He said, "Stay here, Artie, and bolt the door behind us. And don't move until we get back."

Grandma wasn't home, Mom was working at the drug store and I was not going anywhere.

"Okay," I said. Then I asked, "Where are you going?"

They didn't answer. Both flew out the door immediately. Duck went up to Atlantic in front of the lumberyard to the corner of Gage and Atlantic. Then he made a sharp right turn, heading back towards Clarkson Street and coming around to the right again, head on with the Tufts boy.

Harley cut through the back lot to flank Tufts, who was pedaling up Clarkson towards Gage Avenue. He saw the trap and started his getaway, but he could not get up to speed before he ran directly into Duck, who reached out and stopped him cold. Harley came up behind him with his old malfunctioning rusty rifle in hand.

He would not escape this time.

"Hey Tufts," Harley said casually. "Just in the neighborhood?"

The boy was Harley's age and size, only more muscular, but he was no match for Duck. Harley also had his rifle at the ready. Tufts, of course, didn't know the bolt was rusted shut, and Uncle Harley didn't know that a bullet was rusted in the chamber, ready to go off. But looking at Duck and the rifle, the boy knew he was outmatched. He stood there straddling his bicycle and feigning a superior confidence. He knew his goose was cooked.

I had positioned myself at a knothole in on one of the planks on the back wall of Harley's garage, taking it all in. I could hear them talking.

"What do you morons want?" Tufts demanded.

Harley did all the talking.

"What do we want?" he repeated. "We want you dead, Tufts, that's what we want. This is the last day you will use that whip hanging around you neck to hurt anything. I hope you kissed your Mummy goodbye before you left your house this morning because you are going to die today, Mr. Tufts." Harley spoke coldly and factually. "But first you have to go to court."

"Court? What court?" Tufts blustered, ever the tough guy.

"Judge Brown's Court," Harley responded, pointing to himself with his thumb. Tufts, still trying to feign control, said,

"You don't scare me Brown. And who's that big goofus asshole — your girlfriend?" he said, pointing to Duck?"

Harley was smiling and as cool as a cucumber.

"He's your friendly undertaker. He's your jury and he's the Brown court bailiff, and he and his father are your worst nightmares," Harley answered. "And after you're found guilty on all charges and hung, he is going to churn your guts, brains and eyeballs into a milkshake with a little machine at his father's mortuary. And then he'll pickle the rest of you in the Los Angeles sewer system, right where you belong. How do you like that, tough guy?"

Tufts started a retort, but he suddenly decided to bolt instead. He tried to escape, desperately peddling, but he became clumsy when he straddled his bike at a stop. That was when Duck yanked him off his bike. Harley picked up his Schwinn Autocycle and tossed it off the sidewalk and into the lot. Then he picked it up and tossed it twice again, deeper into the lot; and yet again, it bounced each time, breaking a pedal and some spokes, or tearing off a mirror and reflectors as it landed.

Tufts started to snivel.

"You guys can't do this. I'll tell my dad on you! I'll call the police," he threatened, looking just across the Clarkson Street toward the Bell Police Station. You guys better let me go or you'll be sorry," he said with supposed authority.

"Not as sorry as you, Tufts, because you'll be dead," Harley answered.

Brightening Bruce Tufts' spirits considerably, his eyes lit up when a Bell police car turned out of the station drive way and onto Clarkson, moving slowly toward the boys. Tufts' troubled state overtook him before the officer stopped in front of the group. The sergeant said, "Hi, Marley." He spoke with a thick Greek accent.

"Hey, Zambo" Harley said warmly, not bothering to correct him. Sergeant Zambo had always called him by the wrong name.

Then the officer stared at Bruce and asked Duck in Greek, "Diabolos apothneskos?"

Duck nodded his head affirmatively, and then they spoke together for another five minutes in Greek. Duck, all the while was still holding on to the back of Bruce's neck. Duck, who had noticed the momentary look of relief on the defendant's face, said to him, "How rude of me, Bruce. Excuse my manners. I would like you to meet my uncle, Sergeant Astraeus Zambetes."

"Nice to meet you," the Sergeant said politely to Tufts. Tufts grumbled something inaudible and tried once again — albeit unsuccessfully — to break away from Duck's iron grip.

181

"You boys have a good time now" Zambo said. Then he looked at the trio and said, "Chust clean up dah blood after youselves." And as the police car inched forward, Zambo added,

"My Nephew tell me you gaw na to meet Papa Eudie soon?…Dat gaw na be so nice for you, Eudocio take so nice care too you, so lung boys" Then he drove off, shaking his head as he laughed out loud at his own commentary.

Bruce, seeing and hearing this indifference to his plight, could scarcely hold back his tears or his anger.

They started walking across the big lot over toward me and the garage. Tufts tried several times to escape, but to no avail. Duck held him fast by the back of the neck with one hand and marched him ahead like a marionette. Duck's hands befitted his size. They were quite powerful as he squeezed the back of Tufts' neck so hard that the boy had little choice but to walk in the insisted direction, or be brought to his knees in pain. I watched through the knothole, petrified at every step Tufts took in my direction.

At Harley's secret knock I unbolted the door. When they entered the room and I looked at Tufts, and as he passed me, he scowled down, looked directly into my eyes and said, "You're dead!" He spoke only inches from my face. I started shaking and wet my pants. I ran out and peed on myself and the side of the garage in equal proportions. I waited outside for awhile, too frightened to return. When I finally came back in, Harley and Duck had Tufts bound completely, sitting helplessly in a chair. He looked like something from a scene in one of those old cliffhanger weekly movie serials. He was tied to his chair with about ten perfect coils running from just below his shoulders to below his elbows, with one of Harley's many ropes given to him by his oldest brother Paul. Bruce's legs, from just below the knee and ankles, were bound in similar fashion. Tufts could neither stand up nor move any pat of his body other than his fingers and toes. But his mouth worked just fine and he said, "You Sons ah bitches better let me out of here. My dad is Marvin L. Tufts, and he's an attorney who knows important people. And I am going to tell him you did this, and I mean it. This isn't funny.

"I know this house is where all you trash live," he continued. "I can bring the real police here, you know — not that Hungarian-goat cheese shit head sergeant of yours, and he will be summoned to a real court by my dad and fired for not doing his job. You assholes are all in real trouble, did you know that?"

Tufts almost tipped over his chair trying to free himself, but nothing worked.

CHAPTER 21

Stand and Defend

HARLEY AND DUCK created a makeshift judge's bench by placing an old hardwood door onto two oak barrels. Uncle pulled the old piano stool to his bench and plopped down behind it. With his mother's walnut cracker and meat tenderizer in hand, Judge Brown's makeshift gavel proclaimed its authority, and Bailiff Duck announced, "Quiet in the courtroom! The Honorable Judge Harley Thomas Brown presiding…."

Harley looked at Duck most seriously and asked, "Bailiff Tim, what is the charge brought against this criminal?"

Duck stepped to the bench and said in a formal voice, "Your Honor, this thug is accused of both cowardice and brutality, and for the cold blooded murder of one Muggs McGinnis Brown, a puppy! He is further accused of beating and injuring a seven-year-old second grade School boy for no apparent reason and leaving him bleeding for dead. Your honor, he is also accused of killing, blinding and maiming dozens of helpless critters, including cats, and we additionally accuse him of vandalizing the personal property of one Blanche Louella Brown. Shall I go on, Judge Brown?" Duck asked.

"No, Bailiff, that will be quite enough to hang this miserable bastard," Harley said.

Tufts took this in with a look of defiant disgust. But as the trial progressed, he couldn't help but notice Judge Brown meticulously tying a completely functional, perfectly correct hangman's noose. His eyes never left the judge's hands. As Harley worked at his art, he said to Tufts, "While we are summoning your defense, how much do you weigh?" Harley kept his eyes on the noose.

"None of your goddamn business," said Tufts. "You assholes better let me the hell out of here. You can go to jail for this, do you shit for brain pricks know that?"

Ignoring Tufts' defiant screams, Harley said calmly, as if he didn't have a care in the world, "I think Tufts here weighs about the same as a hundred pound bag of pig shit, don't you, Bailiff?"

After feigning thoughtful pause Duck, finally answered, "Judge, it really doesn't matter if we get his weight just right because if we are wrong, and his pathetic neck doesn't snap at once, both of us can hang from his ankles until his sorry ass is dead, so lets don't worry about details until after we convict him."

"Good point, Tim!" Harley said, banging his gavel as he added, "So stated and so ordered!"

"You guys are crazy, know that!" Tufts yelled. "And you better untie me and let me out of here if you know what's good for you." He tried to lift himself and the chair up on his tip toes.

I was really afraid that if they hurt him, Harley and Duck would get into trouble; and golly, I thought, what if they killed him? Oh man! Grandma would be really mad at all of us. I was worried and felt pretty sure we'd all get a real ass whipping for this.

I thought about Uncle Jimmy having a lot of work ahead of him. *Nah*, I reasoned. nobody was going to whip the big boy Duck, except maybe Papa Eudie.

Judge Brown banged his gavel and spoke.

"Bailiff, please swear in this thug for his testimony."

The Duck walked to the captive with a bible in hand and started his spiel, "Bruce Tufts do you swear to tell…" Tufts interrupted the Duck, screaming at the top of his lungs as he desperately tried to escape from his restraints. He said, "Yes, I do swear, you dick brain big queer ass wipe. Go fuck your Bible, then go fuck yourselves!"

"Fuck our bible?" Harley repeated mockingly. Then he told me to fetch Grandma's bar of Lava soap. I ran into the house and retrieved it within minutes, and returned anxious to see what might befall my nemesis. Duck cut some slivers off the soap with his pocket knife, and after a bit of struggle, he managed to get some of the Lava chards into the defendant's indiscrete mouth.

Bruce didn't care for the flavor and spit it out in Harley's direction. Judge Brown continued very formally;

"Is there anyone in court today that stands in defense of this worm?" he asked seriously, looking around the court as if some defender might actually be there. Even I looked around the garage. I thought that was really funny because, besides the defendant, there were only three of us inside Uncle Harley's court.

No Answer.

"Is there anyone that can speak to the prisoner's good character? "

No Answer.

"Is there anyone that gives a shit about this cadaver?" Harley asked?

"What cadaver?" Tufts blurted out.

"Oh, sorry," responded Duck. "That is what we in the mortuary business call a dead-stiff, but some morticians just call them units."

"You dick wads," Tufts screamed, "let me the hell out of here!"

Finally Harley looked directly into Tufts' eyes and said, "There is a slim chance for you, Tufts."

Uncle Harley paused and asked Tim dramatically, "Bailiff, is there an Artie Spelman in the courtroom?"

Once again, Judge Harley and the bailiff both looked around as though there were five hundred people whose faces they had to sift through. I was scared to death, and when Tim called my name, I actually looked around the room myself to see if maybe there was another Artie that could have entered the garage, and that I had just missed it.

After Duck asked formally for "Artie," I still said nothing in fear. Then Harley hit his gavel and repeated the question.

Finally, I raised my hand timidly and said, "That's me — I'm Artie."

"Would you please take the stand, Mr. Spelman," he said with an air of authority.

Hunching my shoulders, I held my palms up questioningly. "Where is the stand?" I asked in a whisper.

Bailiff Tim smiled at me broadly and set an apple box and beside the bench.

"Sit here, Sir," he said formally.

Wow! That was so neat, I thought, forgetting my fear for a second. No one had ever called me Sir before.

I took my seat and looked up at Harley, trying to avoid looking at Tuft's scowling face.

After I was dually sworn in, I sat on the apple box, waiting.

CHAPTER 22

Artie Takes The Stand

"**M**R. SPELMAN, DO you know this Boy?" Judge Brown asked, pointing to Tufts.

I slowly nodded my head in the affirmative, but I could not bring myself to look at the boy's face.

"What is his name?" asked the Judge.

"Bruce Tufts", I answered, still without looking at him.

"When was the last time you saw Bruce?" he queried.

I said nothing but pointed in the direction of the lumberyard next door.

"Where you by yourself?" Harley asked me.

I shook my head no.

"Who was with you?" asked the Judge.

"Muggs McGinnis," I answered.

"Where is Muggs now? " Harley asked.

My eyes filled with moisture as I shrugged my shoulders and double pointed to the wall of the garage just behind Harley, indicating the pup's grave just on the other side of it.

"What happened to Muggs?" he continued.

I bit my lip hard, almost causing it to bleed. I shrugged one shoulder so much that it nearly touched the side of my face. I looked down at my untied shoes and without lifting my face to look at the accused, pointed in Tufts' direction and said quietly, "He killed him."

Harley looked directly into Tufts' eyes and asked the accused if that was true.

"Sure, it's true" he said proudly. "That stupid mongrel was always chasing us on our bikes and once he bit at my ankle as I rode by, and he tore off my shoe!"

Harley turned to me and asked, "Did this boy and his brothers beat you up, Artie?"

I hunched my shoulders and said,

"I think so. They knocked my face shut and my brain went out, but I mostly don't remember."

"Did you do anything to them?" Harley queried.

"No," I said, slowly shaking my head.

"You're lying, you little shit!" Tufts yelled. "You gave us the finger and cussed at me. You threw rocks at me, you damned liar!"

I looked at his face for the first time. I was still frightened and started to cry as I pointed at him accusingly.

"Only after you hit Muggs with that whip," I said, drying my eyes with the palms of my hands. "That's when I did it. That's when I threw those rocks, Uncle Judge. Honest."

"Did you hit the defendant with the rocks? " Harley asked me.

"No. I missed," I said.

"Too bad," Bailiff Tim chimed in.

By this time I was crying openly. Harley looked at me and winked with a smile before putting his hand on my shoulder.

I wiped my nose on the back of my hand and arm as Harley said formally,

"Mr. Bruce Tufts, in summing up this case, you have admitted that you killed Muggs and beat Artie half to death."

"I shoulda killed all you pussy Brown sons a bitches, and next time I will!" Tufts said. He cleared his throat and spit a large wad of phlegm as far as he could. It fell short, landing on the bench just in front of the judge, next to the formerly spit chards of soap.

"Contempt of court," Harley said as he gaveled away. "Mister Tufts, after all the evidence has been presented, the court gives you one final chance to plead for your life. Do you have anything you wish to say to Artie?"

Tufts looked directly at me and said, "Yeah, next time I'll kill that fucking stupid little pansy, too, and his ugly fat ass Grandma, then bury them facedown in that stupid garden of hers."

My mouth fell open when I noticed Duck's expression at the mention of my grandmother used so poorly by the accused. I thought for sure that Tufts was about to die right there on the spot by Duck's hands, but the bailiff's rage was briefly distracted by the defendant's struggle.

Tufts yelled and screamed in futility, trying to get free. His face was beet red with anger as he struggled against the ropes, rocking his chair violently from side to side. Finally in the struggle he toppled himself and the chair over. As he lay there on his side, Harley got off the bench and down on his hands and knees, moving his face inches away from Tuft's, saying,

"It's not so funny now, huh, Bruce? Why aren't you laughing? Don't you find this funny, or do we need to beat a helpless little dog to death to get a laugh from you? You know, Bruce, after your sorry dead ass is turned into worm food, we are going after your brothers and hanging them, too. You are a maggot malted, did you know that Tufts. Not so Tough now, huh?

"I am going to pass sentence on you soon, Mr. Tufts. You better pray my sentence is just a hanging. Bruce, you are so damn stupid that you didn't even realize that the old woman you just spoke so foully of is not only my mother, but what is more dangerous for you, you damned fool, is that my friend Duck here — Greek Orthodox — sees her as fondly as though she were the Virgin Mary, and he would love to pull your guts out through your ass. I might decide to release you and see how you fare against Duck here, or his Father, an even larger crazy ass Greek, instead of a helpless small dog fighting for its life. After your trial, and before we hang you, we have a special treat for you. We are going to introduce you to Eudie, the man himself. He is half-crazy and one hundred percent dangerous, and he's the bailiff's father. Now *that* will be really funny; you'll laugh your ass off, Bruce, just wait. You better just pray for the hanging Tufts."

Harley, ever ready to use the gavel, and in the midst of a brainstorm, resumed his calm legalese voice once again. He adjudicated, "For your recent contempt of this court, I sentence you to lie there on your side until the sentence is passed. Meanwhile, the bailiff will gag your sorry ass and the court will adjourn for lunch. Or hell, maybe 'til day after tomorrow, so you can just lie there and piss yourself, toughster!"

Duck picked up Harley's filthy sock off the floor and walked toward the judge's bench, wiping Tufts' fresh goobers off the judge's bench. He carefully wiped up the boys' spittle with it, adding the largest chards of the spit soap — ironically, because of Harley's sorry housekeeping skills, it was one of the very dirty stinking socks Muggs had pissed on multiple times several weeks before on the day of our beating. Duck then managed to shove it into Tufts' mouth, taping it shut with the medical tape. The judge, the bailiff and their only witness left for the house, and Harley locked his courthouse door from the outside.

The three of us entered the house through the back door into Grandma's kitchen, and Harley fixed us tomato and banana sandwiches with some lime Kool-Aid.

As we ate, Harley and Duck discussed Tufts' fate. I really didn't understand much of it and had lost my appetite, so Duck ate my food. After a while we returned to the garage to find Tufts lying exactly where they had left him, still struggling in vain to free himself.

Duck removed the gag and sat Tufts and his chair upright. Then he said to him, "We had a nice lunch. Did you enjoy yours?" He pointed to the rancid piss soaked sock he had removed from Tufts' mouth, which was now filled with soapy saliva foam.

Before Tufts could answer, Harley said to him, "It's now time for sentencing. Does the prisoner have anything to say for himself before this court passes sentence?"

Tufts looked at us, his face calm and deadly serious. His eyes darted menacingly from one of us to the other, and he said, "Yes, I have something to say: You are all going to pay for this. My father will see you all in Juvenile court or in prison unless you release me immediately."

Harley paid absolutely no attention to this threat. Looking directly at me, he asked, "Artie, should we hang Bruce Tufts?"

I shook my head emphatically no, begging him not to. "No, No, Uncle Harley," I pleaded. "Please don't kill him. Let him go, Uncle Harley, Pah-leese don't hurt him. You'll be in awful trouble."

"OVERRULED!" Harley exclaimed as he slammed down the nut cracker.

"Mr. Tufts," Harley said pointing to the defendant, "You, sir, have been hoisted by your own petard!"

Upon his last word, Harley raised his left ass cheek on the side closest to the defendant and cut a fart so that the biggest devil's knuckle might receive the full benefit of its effervescence.

My Uncle Harley loved to fart; there was nothing quite as delicious nor poetic as flatulence, particularly his own, and he loved the word petard. Duck had explained to him that according to one of Eudie's stories, that when one was hoisted by their petard, it meant that their own farts were so powerful that it lifted them off their chairs. Whether that was true or not, this was a pure gold addition to Harley's prurient repertoire, and he used it at every opportunity. Now it was time for The Verdict.

CHAPTER 23

The Verdict

ARLEY SAID, "WILL the prisoner please rise for sentencing."
The bailiff replied; "Your honor, the prisoner is still tied to his chair.

"Oh yeah, I forgot," Harley said. "Okay, the prisoner will just sit there looking stupid, then."

Tufts looked like he wanted to say something, but he just glared at Judge Harley Brown with a murderous look of hatred in his eyes.

"Mr. Bruce Tufts," said the Judge. "This court finds you guilty on all charges. You are sentenced to the following:

"Count A: With regard to the vicious beating of seven-year-old Edward Arthur Spelman, your punishment is that you be taken across the street to the Theo & Carides Mortuary for a tour of the facilities. Assistant funeral director Duck and his father the mortician, Eudie, will demonstrate the various tools that will be applied to your guts, brains, stomach and testicles. He will show you how after you are hung this afternoon and pronounced dead, how your internal organs will be liquefied then removed through your ass with a special vacuum. The court will of course make every effort to make this delightfully educational. I am sure that you will find the experience quite amusing. The bailiff and I will do all we can to make it as hilarious for you as we can.

"Count B: With regard to the death of one Muggs McGinnis, in exactly one hour, or whenever your tour with Eudie is done — should you live through it — you will be brought here then hung there by the neck from these rafters until you are almost dead."

The Judge had finished the hangman's noose and tossed it to Duck. Harley got up from his bench and retrieved his 78 record player from its spot in the corner, setting it on the Judge's bench.

Harley now had Tufts full attention. The defendant's cockiness and bravado had dissipated to an occasional slow drip of expletives and mumbling. Judge Brown put on a thick one-sided 12 inch 78 record. It was a laugh track full of nothing but laughter of different enthusiasms. Mostly, according to Harley's drama teacher, this had been used in the sound departments on radio shows and was called canned laughter.

As the recordings' laughter filled the courthouse with guffaws and giggles of every sort, Harley continued speaking as they listened to the laugh tracks.

"Bruce, just before you are about to die," Harley said, "I am going to play this recording. Then, after we give you a glass of vinegar, we are going to hang you again and again, hanging you each time until you pass out, allowing you to regain consciousness each time, just like you beat Muggs again and again. We are going to play this laugh record so that you will feel at home before you die.

"You know, Bruce," Harley continued, waxing sincerity, "we want you to get into the spirit of the thing. Artie has told us what a great sense of humor you and your brothers have."

Tufts said nothing.

As the recorded laughter filled the garage at full volume, Harley looked over to the record player and said, "Pretty appropriate, don't you think, Tufts?"

Harley looked at me and said, "Artie, we don't wish to be unfair to the defendant. I want to make sure of the facts of this case before we kill him, but didn't you tell me that when Tufts was laughing when he murdered Muggs?"

I shook my head in the affirmative and said, "ALL of them laughed, Uncle Harley."

In an instant, the horror of it all came flooding back to me and I ran out of the garage, remembering it vividly. I ran to the big platform swing at the Pepper Tree and threw myself face down onto it, sobbing with the sight and sound of that laughter and Muggs' beating reborn in my mind.

Harley came out after me. Duck re-secured the tasty sock into the condemned's mouth and followed Harley. I was in the middle of the big swing with my heart, which was broken once again. Harley and the Duck got on the swing with me and put their arms around me. "What's wrong, Artie?" they asked.

I stopped crying. I tried to speak in gasping spurts struggling to catch my breath. I wailed with the deep heaving sob of a child who does not understand and whose knowledge and feelings about revenge are conflicted. With a broken heart, I pressed my face deep into Harley's chest.

"Oh, Harley!" I cried. "Please don't kill that big tough bully, Uncle Harley! Just let him go home, please! Please don't hurt him," I pleaded. "Oh PLEASE, Harley, I know he killed Muggs and beat my face up, but I feel loads better now, Uncle Harley. Honest, look!"

I begged with him, trying to straighten up a bit, throwing my shoulders back in an attempt to demonstrate my much improved condition. That way I could convince him.

I was terrified. I didn't really know what this business entailed. I was terrified that something really bad would happen to Harley and Duck. And when Tufts had previously admonished Harley and the Duck about being in trouble, I believed him. All I could see was the vision of my poor grandma's face as the police took off with her beloved son and Duck.

Finally, Duck said quietly, "Artie we are not going to kill him. We are not even going to hurt him as much as we would love to. That would disappoint your Grandmother Brown and others too much. It's not our job," he said in a deep, soothing voice.

"Besides," Harley added, "his punishment will be his sad life, and that is up to God, not us. That's what Mother says.

"It says in the bible: 'The merciful man doeth good to his own soul: but he that is cruel troubleth his own flesh.'

"It also says 'Thou shalt not kill,'" added Duck, "but it does not say anything about 'Thou shalt not scare the living shit out of some vicious little bastard.' And my Dad says that revenge may not always be sweet, but it sometimes can be very tasty indeed."

"Huh?" I said. I had no real idea what they were speaking of and it must have been all over my face.

Harley looked at me, then to Duck, and back to me again. He said, "Never mind. We promise not to hurt him, Artie, but we do want to scare him."

I looked into Harley's face searching for some sense of it that I could understand.

"Remember at Halloween about three years ago at Papa Eudie's, when we tried to scare you and played with you?" Harley asked.

"Yeah, sort of," I responded, nodding my head and wiping away my tears and runny nose.

"Well, Artie, this is something like that, except we don't love this kid and he doesn't tickle us like you do. We played with you on Halloween, and it was a game, and no matter how scared you got, you knew it wasn't real. And then we'd all laugh and tease each other, remember?" Actually, I had a hard time remembering. Because of the war, we hadn't had a Halloween in several years, and those memories were fading.

"Are you playing with him, too?" I asked, red eyed, still sobbing a bit as I tried to catch my breath.

"Well, sort of," Duck answered. "But we don't want him to know we are. We want him to really believe he is going to die today, so that he will feel just a little of what Muggs and you felt. We are not going to laugh with him and hug and tease him afterward like we did you at Halloween. Do you understand?"

I must have had a blank look on my face because Harley took over and said, "Do you know, Artie, when Grandma washes your mouth out with soap, why she does it?"

"Yes, I think so," I said. "She doesn't want me to cuss or fornicate so that I can go to heaven."

Harley said, "That too, Artie, but she wants to teach you a lesson. That is what we want to do to Tufts, to try and teach him a lesson."

I thought about it for a good long while as Harley and the Duck watched my response carefully.

"I think I understand," I said.

Now I had stopped crying and I was beginning to cheer at the game and my future role in it. Harley and Duck looked at me and knew from my response that after my moment of enlightenment that having me anywhere near Tufts or the rest of their charade would assuredly spell disaster and ruin the terrors they had planned for Bruce.

Harley looked at my now mollified enthusiastic face and said, "Artie, do you trust us?"

"Yes," I said, unenthusiastically and slowly, as some of my own ideas flew into my head.

"Okay then," he said, "You must not be in court with us anymore, because if you are there and he sees your cheery little face, he will know that he may live through this day. Do you understand, Artie?" Harley asked.

"Yes, but look, Uncle Harley!" I said as I demonstrated my alpha and omega of the 'un-cheery facedness with dozens of expressions that I had learned on Papa Eudie's lap. After my most convincing arguments, Duck looked at Harley and said, "We are doomed!"

They smiled at each other and Harley said to me,

"Artie, I am afraid you will spoil it all if you go back to court with us."

"I won't," I insisted, "I won't spoil it. I begged Uncle Harley, honest. I can play, honest. I want to watch that 'farter' squirm!"

Duck remarked to Harley with a wry smile, "Well, well, Mom Brown. it seems to have been a bad influence on our young Artie."

"Yep," Harley answered, "Looks like Mom is hoisted by her own petard."

Duck smiled and said, "I'll get the soap ready for her dear old heart."

Duck had a proposal.

"Artie, why don't we do this," he said, trying to reason with me. "As soon as I talk to my father, we are going to take Tufts across the street to visit the mortuary and give him a little Eudocian demonstrational tour. While we are gone, Artie, get the judge's little stand. The one that you sat on in court, remember?"

"Yes," I said. "The apple box."

Duck continued, "Yes, that apple crate, okay. Then set it up at the knothole outside the back of the garage. Then come back here to the swing and wait for us to return. When you see the three of us pass you returning from my house, wait a few minutes until we've reentered the courthouse. Then you go to the back of the outside of the garage, stand on your apple box and just watch, okay? But Artie, don't say a word or yell out, no matter what it looks like, okay?"

I nodded my head in the affirmative.

After a few minutes Duck returned from across the street and said to Harley, "Okay, Brownie, everything is ready. Dad and Stavros are finishing the preparations."

They both went to the garage and in ten minutes or so, they came back with Tufts in tow, marching him past me across the street to the Theo & Carides Funeral Home. Harley carried Tufts' whip coiled up inside a brown paper bag.

I placed the apple box as instructed, then returned to sit on the swing and wait for the boys' return. I waited a good while wondering what was going on. As time passed, the soft little seven-year-old gears in my brain mooshed and churning together and I came up with a great plan.

Man, this would be a real surprise for Harley and Duck! My plan was that when the three came back past me on the swing, that I would put on a bit of my theater. Demonstrating, pleading and groveling for Tufts' sorry life, perhaps even falling down screaming and kicking, I even imagined perhaps hanging onto one of Duck's ankles, visualizing him as he dragged me by my face, pulling his ankles with each step as I pled for the boy's life all the way back to the garage. *God, this would be so great*, I thought. I joyously imagined the sure results of my plan. *Boy, pretty neat*, I thought, *my high drama begging for his life would convince Tufts that he was surely about to die.* Now I wanted with all my heart to hurt this bastard by scaring him. I wanted him to cry like I had when Muggs died. I wanted him to feel helpless and alone and useless and as scared as I had been.

I didn't understand why Harley and Duck were so preoccupied with my participation in the Tufts matter. I was sure the boys would be so pleased when they saw my plan in action. I could hardly wait.

As I sat there on the big swing for what seemed like forever, I saw something that stunned me crossing the street, walking toward my large perch.

CHAPTER 24

The Hanging

A S I LOOKED at the three crossing Atlantic Boulevard walking toward me, my plans for brilliant theatrics vanished into thin air. Harley and Duck were dragging a person between them. Tufts was barely recognizable to me, his face ashen and bloodless, and his eyes rolling up into his head. His forehead and upper lip were sweaty, and the tip of his tongue was sticking out like that of a village idiot. His knees were so weak that he kept collapsing, forcing Harley and Duck to lift and drag him between steps. He had no physical injuries that I could see, but his affect was one of a person who had just seen hell and only barely lived to tell of it.

This boy's face was frightening. I didn't realize it then at seven years old, but looking back on it now, I believe that Tufts was likely going into shock. As the three passed me going past the swing toward Judge Brown's garage courthouse, I was almost paralyzed at the sight of Tufts. He looked directly at me with eyes that had gone from pleading too lifeless. Among the horrors of Muggs' death and my ordeal, that boy's face walking past me was almost equally as frightening, and I will remember it until the day I die. Bruce Tufts was the walking dead. Amazingly, seeing the wretched bastard's state, I wanted to run to him and hug him and tell him it would be all right, and that Harley the Duck and the rest were just playing. Of course, I didn't. I couldn't. Muggs' brutal beating was not far away and those memories did not take long to bounce straight back into my tiny head, so my compassion soon vanished.

When the three boys passed me there on the swing heading back to the court, my theatrical ideas were completely gone, so I did exactly as Duck had instructed. By the time I reached my knothole and mounted my apple box observatory, Harley and Duck were working feverishly to talk Tufts back from the dead. There was no promised vinegar, or laugh line from the record player; but rather, one of them had secured some white bread with a little jam on it and a glass of Kool-Aid with some chipped ice inside. They were feeding it to the wretched condemned. Frankly I think whatever Tufts had gone through inside the funeral parlor had scared the hell out of the judge and his bailiff. So while they were not friendly to Bruce, they were at least trying to make it nice for him a little, by not letting him go into shock and die before they had a chance to hang him. I think the wind was out of the sail for the boys, and that killing Bruce did not seem nearly as enjoyable as it once had.

I think Harley and Duck just wanted to get it over with, but they could not forgive Tufts — and they were not going to let him off just yet.

Harley said without enthusiasm,

"Bailiff, you may proceed with the sentence."

Duck put the noose around Tufts' neck and threw the slack over the rafter. Harley grasped the other end of the line and Duck pulled up an old junky, severely weak coffee table with spindly fluted legs that was long past its prime, at least two of the table's legs were wobbly and the top was a thin, cheap veneer.

The judge took up the slack and Duck lifted the pale and shaking Tufts boy onto the coffee table like a toy. Bruce didn't know what to do; his trembling hands were now freed, but he was in a panic as he desperately tried to remove the noose from his neck. Harley, however, kept the slack out of the rope. As the boy struggled, I could see through my knothole that the table was going to give way. No sooner had I observed this than it happened — the table broke into pieces and Tufts tumbled down along with it. The rope had not constricted because Harley had tied a block knot in it to keep the noose from inadvertently killing the unsuspecting Bruce. Also, the end of the rope was not secure, but rather just held loosely in Harley's hands. However, the force of Tufts' fall pulled the rope out of Harley's hands. While it did not break Bruce's fool neck, he was choking a bit from the unforeseen fall, and it did briefly cut off his breathing. The subterfuge, accidentally, could not have worked out better or been more frightening for Tufts. I am sure the boy thought he was a dead man, He lost most of his breath, all of his bowels movements sank into his pants and he wet himself as well. No laugh line was ever played and as Tufts crashed to the floor he fell directly on top of Judge Brown, knocking them both down and tumbling the judge's bench over. He broke Harley's record player as the boys cracked their heads together like a couple of coconuts.

Duck took charge and stood up the dizzy hangman and the babbling hanged, then removed the noose from Bruce's neck. Harley had a pot knot on his forehead. After Tufts realized he was still alive and Judge Brown regained his proper decorum, they marched Bruce outside through the lot to his crumpled Bicycle. Duck held Tufts as usual by the back of the neck and Harley had the brown paper bag where he contained the chopped mini pieces of his whip.

Duck instructed Tufts to mount his crumpled bicycle and the boy did so, trembling and pale as he tried to straighten out his askew han-dlebars. Harley then straddled his front wheel in the opposite direction, holding on to his handlebars, and helped him straighten the bars. He looked directly at Tufts, head on.

Harley said to him, "Bruce, I am glad we had this visit. I hope you enjoyed it as much as we did. Be sure to tell your brothers about our hospitality and ask them to drop by to see us. And before you go, tough guy, I want to tell you something. You are not a man, Bruce. You will never be any sort of one. There is nothing genuinely tough about you; you are just a loud mouth Nazi or a young Turk coward, just someone who looks for the small and the defenseless and the vulnerable. Your life will not be an honorable one, and your death — which, God willing, is soon — will not be an honorable one either. But the truth is we want nothing to do with your nasty ass in this life, and even less with your nasty self in death. We wanted to send you a message and now you have it. The message, in case you are too dense to have gotten it, is that you are a human turd, a deviate and a psychopathic coward, and that that is all your mummy and daddy need put on your grave stone when some son of a bitch finally does kill you."

Harley paused and said, "I am sure Duck would like to say something before we let your mushy, stinky ass peddle down the highway."

Duck stood up at his full height, towering over the seated Tufts. He had no idea Harley was going to give him the stage, but he — ever the high school orator — was always ready for the opportunity.

"Mr. Tufts," he said theatrically. "My family goes back 3,000 years to ancient Greece. We come from a long line of warriors. I have not done you the honor of beating you to death here today because there would be no challenge in it for me; and while you are deserving of it, you are not worthy of me doing it. When the Theocarides historically did battle, it was with those we may have hated and even killed, but we respected the warrior in them. As you leave here, you deserve the shit that's now in your britches, and nothing more.

"Bruce," he added slowly and clearly, "you are too pitiful to hate." Reaching into the brown paper bag, Uncle Harley grabbed a handful of the whip pieces, pulled the back of Bruce's pants by the his back of his belt and stuck the remains of his whip down inside his soiled underwear, using his ass crack as a guide. Harley dropped some of them slowly and carefully, one at a time into Tufts' soiled underpants, shaking the boy's belt and pants as though they were a flower colander, ensuring that each little piece received some sauce as they gathered uncomfortably in his shorts.

Harley's spoke his final words to Tufts.

"So, you are free to go back to your family and your life. Your tour of the Brown judicial system is now complete. When you die, it will not be by our hands — unless, of course, you decide to return here. Never let us see you again. Not Ever! If we do, Bruce," he said accenting each word, "we will let Papa Eudie give you the final waltz into hell. Next time you're meeting with him won't be as much fun for you because Duck and I won't be able to contain him or stop his rage the way we did today."

At the mention of Eudie's name, the boy looked ashen and he peddled off and away on wobbly wheels.

CHAPTER 25

Mrs. Brown

GRANDMOTHER WAS TO me what her church and Jesus were to her.

She was the core inside me, that place where my heart hid when it hurt; her bosom created the valley down which my tears of sorrow and laughter traveled. She was that spirit that kept my worms at bay and my spiritual apple from rotting.

She and my mother shared April 18th as their birthday, but to me they could not have been more different personalities. My poor mother had devils that could not be quelled and thirsts that could not be quenched, and she often took them out on me in the form of severe and brutal beatings that had absolutely nothing to do with discipline.

I, of course, realize now as a grown man — and I think I realized some even as a child — that Mother was just profoundly unhappy with herself and her life. Her drinking didn't help, especially once my Dad had left her for somewhere or someone else. Every man in her life seemed to treat her poorly. She was alone with a child in the 1940s, and in those days that was like hanging fish guts around your neck while swimming with sharks. She might as well have had a sign on her that said:

Divorced mother of one. Easy in bed, eager to wed. Son wants a father and needs to be fed. Apply within.

There were some good men out there in the forties, but many were away at war, and so her pickings were thin. The attitude of the average single male in those days wasn't the least bit warm to the idea of courting single women with precocious children. Besides, Grandma said that Mother looked for companionship in all the wrong places.

Mom was miserable. What made it worse was that she was almost emaciated, and so she did not feel beautiful at all. She was 5'7" and weighed only a little more than 85 pounds. She ate like a horse, but she could not gain a single pound.

Grandmother Brown was the buffer between my mother's terrors and me. Grandma protected me and tried her best to just love the misery out of my mother. Sometimes she succeeded, but the road was long and muddy.

I have done a great deal of thinking about my grandmother over the course of my life, and have only now resolved why I constantly rebelled against the religion of the God of her Reverend Wall and his Sunday School, or his hell fire message, all of which I hated. I resented and rebelled against him in equal measure, yet I always found God and heaven just inside the loving arms of his loyal servant, my Grandma Brown.

She never condemned or destroyed my exuberance and energy, nor corrupted my innocence with biblical facts. Rarely did she lecture, nor did she preach. If Grandma disciplined, she often assigned the task to Uncle Jim. It was always fair. I always knew the difference between Mother's beatings and Uncle Jimmy's spankings.

Grandmother could handle a 'sinner' and the 'wayward', because she considered herself the same as anyone else, and so she forgave most things easily and without rancor; but she could not abide a liar, thief or fraud, in that order, nor did she tolerate thoughtlessness or meanness in anyone. Grandma could not handle anyone — even preachers — who claimed superior knowledge of God to the exclusion of everyone else; she had no guile and worked on herself constantly, and although she never claimed to be one, she always tried to be the example — even though by her standards she sometimes failed. She never failed in her kindness or loving ways, however, and her generosity was legendary. If she didn't have a gift for a beloved, she made one with her own hands — a pie or treat or candy, or she'd sew or crochet something. She was a pushover for a hug or kiss. It killed Grandma Brown if there were genuine tears or sorrow from any of us, but God forbid that you should contrive a crocodile tear on that good woman. If you did and you waxed false, you just did so just once. Grandmother abhorred insincerity and she recognized the disingenuous immediately. All of us knew that there was a line you did not cross with foolishness or with your treatment of others. None of us knew exactly where that line was, but we damn well knew when we were getting close to it.

Grandma Brown, 1940s

My Grandmother would have had a little trouble with the Judge Harley Brown, Bailiff Timoleon and their courthouse antics with the Tufts boy; and while she had no love at all for those "Devil's Knuckles," she would have disapproved of us punishing those boys, and condemned the Theocarides family's willingness to participate in that mock trial. To this day, I am not actually sure how much she actually knows about it.

Papa's views were less charitable than Grandmother's. Jimmy and Fuzzy had always believed that Eudie was still a little crazy from the Turkish Armenian business, and that he had never fully recovered from the horrors of that conflict that had butchered his family in 1916 Turkey.

Most of us agree that Grandma would not have criticized Eudie too harshly, even if she had known about poor Bruce's trial. You see, she had a loose cannon of her own, and her loving nature made her own breach of conduct shocking I some ways, and certainly more surprising than Papa Eudie's glitches.

You see, on the south side of the Atlantic Lumber Company stood a small store; it had a butcher counter and several shelves full of canned goods and sundry supplies, and limited hardware merchandise, too. It was the only store for five miles, so of course it was our store of convenience. The proprietor of the market was a German man of about fifty years, who went by the name of Hans Bearwalt. He had mostly been cheerful and funny and more or less well-liked by all, but of late he had turned into a large, red-faced, belligerent man who spoke English with a thick German accent, which led of course to neighborhood speculations that he was a member of the bund, and by extension a German Nazi saboteur. Whatever he was, he was certainly cantankerous, rude and unusually mean to some of the local children and customers.

One of these customers was my Uncle Harley Brown, who one day came bursting through our front door trying to hold back tears as blood flowed from his left ear and dripped down his neck. The left side of Harley's face was swollen and he had a large, red hand print clearly visible on the left side of his face. Harley was made permanently deaf in his left ear from a perforated ear drum due to that slap to the side of his head — or at least the German's slap hadn't helped matters much. All of Grandma's four boys had perforated eardrums from an early age, which kept them out of the War.

Now Harley had stolen six half-penny tootsie rolls to bring to me. That was his crime.

Grandmother went pale as a ghost as she grabbed Harley by one hand and Aunt Veve by the other, marching them down to the little market on the corner. I waited alone out on the swing, just as I'd been instructed to do.

There are several stories that vary a bit, but Aunt Veve's telling was firsthand, and according to her story:

Grandma, who was not even five feet tall, walked in, reached up on her tiptoes and grabbed the big German's ear, nearly twisting it off as he pulled back. He writhed in pain and cussed at her in German. Eventually she released him, and seeing a large meat clever close by, she grabbed it and slammed its blade - *Cah-hwang!* - burying it two inches into a solid oak butcher board. Now here is where the story varies a bit:

Veve said that Grandmother told the big German as she threw down a nickel to cover the three cent bill with one hand and buried the meat clever in the chopping block with the other.

"You son of a bitch," she cried. "If you ever touch my son again, I will cut your Nazi head off."

However, my Aunt Eddie claimed that Veve later told her that, "Mother actually said, 'F -dot -dot -dot -dot -dot -G Nazi head off.'"

I do not know which version actually happened. It was almost unthinkable for most of us to believe that Grandmother would ever use that famous "F" word — none of us had ever heard Mom Brown utter anything stronger than "heck" or "shoot," or the vaunted "farter" description of Reverend Wall during Muggs' funeral; and there was neither a mean, unkind or violent bone in her body.

That is, until then.

But Veve did say that, "Mother was livid and far more furious than I could ever have imagined her being."

So who knows? A few days later all of us took a playful vote on the issue, and even the Theocarides unanimously voted no, that she had not used that word. We did agree on "You S.O.B." as a slight possibly, but the F-word was unthinkable. That scenario didn't get a single vote, and even Veve later recanted her story. We all got a real kick out of thinking about anyone messing with the Mother Brown.

Uncle Jimmy Brown and His Fast Mercury, 1940s

Grandmother always tried to forgive; she later made Hans an apple pie and had Harley take it to him and apologize for being a thief, and for making Harley wash his store windows to make amends. It turned out that Hans' son was a member of the Nazi youth party in Germany and had recently been killed in battle flying in his ME109 Stuka after only hours of training. Hans hated Hitler and Hitler's Youth program and all he stood for, and blamed his son's death on both Hitler and his own wife, who had kept his son. She'd refused to leave Germany with him before the start of the war.

Sometime later, when Harley hit his old rifle with a ball-peen hammer while he was trying to get the rusted bolt open, the rifle discharged and nearly blew Harley's thumb off, and it was Hans Bearwald who took him to the hospital and paid his bill in full. This was no small thing in those days.

Hans sent little baskets of groceries and candy to our front door many times after that incident. He and Harley eventually became fast friends, and Hans taught Uncle Harley how to sing something called Schuman Lieder. Harley and Hans often sang duets there in the little store, surprising and delighting the customers.

All this, to my grandmother, was proof of the existence of God — and of forgiveness and redemption.

During many of our conversations with Grandma Brown, my grandmother said that when anyone's religion made them righteous to the exclusion of all others, that it could eventually result in genocide. Eudie agreed with that, and both agreed that whenever that happens, God is no longer anywhere in the picture. They agreed that whoever lets their sense of righteousness get the best of them is the destroyer, and is worshipping a small and evil god.

I am, I suppose still a heathen but I am one who is still sitting on my grandmother's lap. I can still feel her arms around me and smell her lilac perfume. I still know the words to every spiritual she ever sang to me, and while I am a heathen, I still feel those songs deeply.

She taught me but two prayers: the Lord's Prayer and this one, which most people know at least some version of. I said it almost nightly, sleeping there between my Mother and my Grandma — or in my bathtub bed or with Uncle Harley in his loft:

Thank you lord for another day,
The chance to learn, the chance to play.
Now as I lay me down to sleep,
I pray the Lord my soul to keep.
Please, guard me Jesus through the night,
keep me safe till morning's light.
But if I should die before I wake,
I pray the Lord my soul to take.
Should I live for other days,
I pray that God will guide my ways.
Amen.

I have been saying that prayer for years, and I hope my son teaches his son this prayer one day. However, I used to change it up a little bit, and sometimes it came out like this:

> *Now I lay me down to sleep,*
> *I pray the Lord won't hear me peep;*
> *If I should cry and then awake,*
> *I'll ask my grandma for chocolate cake.*
> *Up in heaven I'll just wait*
> *till she walks trough that pearly gate.*
> *She'll bring some pie and rock me there and sing her songs — thank you,*
> *baby Jesus and oh yes, and by the way, God, this is Artie, and I promise*
> *to be good and never to be bad, unless I forget; but if I backslide, remem-*
> *ber Uncle Jimmy lives just down Atlantic in Compton City and has a*
> *pretty fast Mercury sedan and a good switch. He does good triad welters*
> *on my ass and he'll do a good job for you, okay God? Amen.*

CHAPTER 26

Stitches in the Sacred Heart

S OMETHING WAS ABOUT to happen. Static electricity was in the air, we were all anxious and none of us knew why, but we talked some about it. Our hearts seemed tender, like we were waiting for some important unknown.

I remember that the feeling was like waiting for the mail to come with an important package, a parcel whose contents are unknown. Finally, after much waiting, the postman will deliver the package — but never when you expect him.

This was one of those rare days when Grandma Brown was home on a weekday. Now I can't remember why, but all of us were home from school.

Grandma loved "Mother Peppercorn" and its large platform swing, but due to her center of gravity it was difficult for her sit on it — or even to board it — and because she could not sit without her back supported, she had never really been a passenger on board. Harley had an idea; we all helped her onto the swing, and then Harley showed his mother how to sit back to back with her on one side and him on the other. She was delighted. I remember looking at her childlike face bursting with happiness at that joyous event. Veve dramatically, and with great flair, brought her Mother some lemonade, just as Grandma had done for all of us so many times before. I selfishly got up on the swing, and like a greedy little pig on the teat, crowded onto her lap, not giving much thought to her comfort. Of course, the back to back weight ratio had gone to hell, because now poor Uncle Harley needed some more mass on his side, so Veve got on board and sat next to Harley with both their backs supporting Mom Brown and me, and the world was back in balance once again.

She asked us if we would sing "The Old Rugged Cross" with her. It was her very favorite, and not even Harley could sing this song with more love or feeling than Grandma Brown; she felt the song in her foundation.

She started singing. Then Uncle Harley did the same:

> *On a hill far away stood an old rugged cross,*
> *The emblem of suffering shame;*
> *I love that old cross where the dearest best*
> *For a world of lost sinners was slain.*

Veve joined in and then me; we all knew every single word of a hundred of these spiritual songs. Of course Harley's voice made the fuzzy little white hairs on my arms stand on end as all our voices came together.

Grandmother's voice had absolutely no vocal quality in it, save her great heart, but it was gentle and full of love; and that more than made up for her lack of intonation. She shone to me like the North Star.

As we ended the singing we all told Grandmother we loved her, she responded by whistling and we all chuckled.

"Mother", Veve asked, giggling as she elbowed Harley. "Does Harley get his voice from you or Daddy?"

"Well, he gets it from God, but Frank could sing beautifully as well when he wanted to. Your Papa could do many things very well when he took to doing it. I think some of it is from his dad — certainly not from me."

Grandma Brown and Frank Brown, Early 1900s

Upon hearing this and sensing the play and mischief in Veve's voice, I immediately said, "I love your voice, Grandma. Harley is a boy but you are my favorite girl singer."

She laughed and pulled a few long hairs at the nape of my neck and said, "Oh my, you are such a little storyteller. Artie, now the devil will take you for sure."

After an hour or so of conversation and singing, the Gnome Exemplumonious threw a peppercorn at me, and it bounced off my head and hit Grandma.

As Grandma stepped off the swing, assisted by all of us on firmer ground, she picked up a peppercorn and tried to throw it back at him in the direction of his home somewhere within the branches. But she released the missile a bit too soon and the peppercorn actually fell behind her back by the heels of her shoes.

She must have seen her toss as hitting the mark because she said, "Now let that be a lesson to you — you scoundrel."

"Momma, you missed the tree altogether," Veve said. "Look, you dropped it there just behind your feet."

Grandmother looked behind her and said, "Well, for goodness sake!"

Then she picked up another peppercorn, and laughing at herself, she threw it at Veve, missing her by a mile.

Harley tried for the tenth time to teach me how to play chess, but I only liked the horses and castles, and could not be bothered with the other foolish pieces. I was curious as to why the King was such a lazy bastard. Upon hearing this, Grandma sent me for a taste test with a bar of Lava soap. Veve searched for some music on the radio while Grandma fussed in the kitchen with some remnants of stale white bread and knockwurst sandwiches without dressing, served with cherry Kool-Aid with the last grains of sugar for all.

The cupboards where bare, but she made do. We all knew she would have fed us her own broiled kidney if she had to, and that for now she simply didn't have it. Grandmother used to love to tell us all,

"If it's on your plate and it's not moving, eat it no matter what color it is; and if it is moving, eat it before it jumps ship."

When our cupboards were bare, she told us that we were just a little short and that it would be better soon; and it always was. We ate what was put on the plate to the very last crumb. I remember that the lava soap taste in my mouth gave that knockwurst a rather interesting flavor.

We ate our lunch. I helped Grandmother in the kitchen, breaking a glass and a plate in one fell swoop. Then I helped her clean it up by holding the dust pan, and she said, "Arthur, you'll never be a head waiter."

We finished the cleanup and I asked her to come and let me sit on her lap.

After awhile, Harley went to his garage and Veve tired of the radio and took her pulp romance book to the front stoop. I assumed my position on Grandma's lap as she took up her knitting; then she started to whistle some funny little tune — she loved to whistle but had no aptitude for it — and her whistling sounded like air escaping from a party balloon. Uncle Jimmy used to say her whistling sounded like fly farts; her whistling always made me laugh the most, and when I did she would gently place her fingertips on my lips to shush me with a little pat on my mouth. When she resumed the whistling, I laughed even harder and she'd say, "It's not polite to laugh at someone's artistic endeavors." I could hear her smiling, and I reached up and back to pat her cheek.

Presently, for some reason — which to this day I cannot explain — all sound outside seemed to disappear like before a storm.

Suddenly, and with a loud bang, Aunt Veve came bursting through the front door and announced,

"Mama! Fathers here!"

"My gracious," Grandma said softly, straightening herself.

Veve ran back to the garage to gather Harley for the event.

Through the front window we watched the gaunt, pale man walk very slowly, one dreaded step after the next from the sidewalk twenty five yards away. He moved toward the house, his head bowed along the path to our front door. It was like watching a man leaning into a sixty mile per hour wind, forcing each painful step, and dragging one heavy leg after the other towards the gallows. Grandmother straightened her dress again and pushed her hair back with a nervous hand as she readied herself, holding her breath and waiting to answer the door. Finally we heard a soft, timid knock and she opened the door.

"Hi Mother Brown," he said with a tinge of a smile. "Can I come in for a minute?"

Grandma said, "Of course," and she opened the screen door for him. He entered the little house cautiously.

I stood in front of Grandma and leaned back against her. She put her arms around me and clasped them just under my chin, right against my upper chest as she rocked me lovingly back and forth and said, "This is Artie, Iris's son. Do you remember him?

He nodded his head tentatively, but he said nothing.

Veve and Harley soon bolted through the back door and ran upon the scene, coming to a screeching halt in front of their father.

Frank looked at them with moist eyes and asked Grandma, "Are these our babies?"

Grandma said quietly, "Yes, our two youngest."

He was silent and uncomfortable. He hadn't shaved, and his clothes were a mess; he wore scuffed shoes over bare feet with dirty ankles.

The smell of whiskey was on his breath, but he was not drunk.

"May I hug you?" he said to Harley and Veve. They both stepped forward and put their arms around him.

He embraced them and struggled to contain his emotions, doing so just barely.

"Sit down," Grandma said. "I've got some coffee and I can fix you a sandwich."

"Well, I just wanted to say hi," Frank said. "I am not staying long, but I wouldn't say no to a bite or two." He kept looking at the floor.

Harley and Veve were now sitting side-by-side at the far end of the room, watching and listening.

"How have you been, Mother Brown?" Frank asked Grandma as he reached out to touch her hand.

"Fine," she said looking down at his hand, which was covering hers. "We're doing fine."

There was a long silence.

"And you, Frank. How are you?"

"Oh, I'm okay, Lou," he said with a sigh. "I work some, hanging paper — you know people don't know how to hang paper good as me anymore. But I am temporarily out of work at the moment."

"What's in the bag?" Grandma asked.

We all looked at each other, and I at least was thinking that perhaps it was like in Eudie's stories. Maybe it was full of money or exotic trinkets for Grandma.

Frank opened his little brown bag and withdrew a single pair of white socks. They were badly stained and the heels and toes of both socks were out.

"These are my work socks," he explained. "And I need them for work. I was wondering if you'd fix them for me, Mother Brown, if you could."

"Veve, get your dad a kitchen chair while I prepare his sandwich first."

Harley nudged Veve and she shot up to get the chair. Frank sat down and said nervously,

"Thank you, Valera."

The silence was deafening and everyone just looked at each other, and for a long time no one said a word. Then Grandmother said from the kitchen,

"Thomas, why don't you sing for your father?"

Harley did not respond; he looked past his father and turned his face to the kitchen, looking directly at his mother, and singing the song for her as she stood. She began preparing the last of the food, cutting out the mold from two heels of bread, and spreading the last bits of lard and knockwurst onto it. Harley looked at her face as she worked and started his song:

> *There's a spot in my heart,*
> *Which no colleen may own.*
> *There's a depth in my soul,*
> *Never sounded or known;*
>
> *There's a place in my mem'ry,*
> *My life, that you alone can fill,*
> *No other can take it,*
> *No one ever will.*

Sure, I love the dear silver
That shines in your hair,
The brow that's all furrowed,
And wrinkled with care.
I kiss the dear fingers,
So toil-worn for me,
Oh, God bless you and keep you,
Mother Machree.

Ev'ry sorrow or care
In the dear days gone by,
Was made bright by the light
Of the smile in your eye,

Like a candle that's set
In the window at night,
Your fond love has cheered me
and guided me right.

Grandpa Frank did not look up, and before the song had ended, he excused himself, asking directions to the bathroom. Veve pointed just past her mother in the kitchen, who was wiping her eyes with an old dishtowel as Frank walked behind her. At the sink, he laid his large bony hand on her little round shoulder and I watched him squeeze it affectionately. He struggled to say something, his mouth moving with no sound; then he continued his arduous voyage toward the back door and made a left into the bathroom.

Harley had moved the little lamp table in front of Grandpa's chair, where and the sandwich was waiting for him. When Grandpa Frank returned, his eyes were bloodshot; his hair was wet and his face was drawn. He looked like he had been beaten.

Frank put his hand on Harley's shoulder and said, "Thank you, Thomas. Why, that was beautiful." Harley was pleased, but he did not respond as he moved the little table with the sandwich a bit closer to his dad.

Within seconds the sandwich was ravenously devoured. Grandmother said, "I am sorry we don't have a bit more." Then Frank interrupted and said,

"Oh, that's fine, Lou. I don't know why I was so hungry, that's fine. I'll eat a bit later." Frank looked down toward the floor.

Veve sat down on the bench next to Harley and I sat in front of Grandma's rocker at her feet.

Grandma already had her sewing kit and was hard at work; her eyes were full of tears but she kept them from running and destroying her.

"These are a mess," she said.

"I know," Frank said. "They are my work socks."

We all sat there for a good while in silence. I could hear Grandpa breathing hard, emitting a crackling sound from tired lungs as Grandma rocked back and forth, slowly sewing. I could not help but notice what I always had, that there was love and care in every single stitch. Whenever my Grandmother encountered another person's poor sewing, she would say,

"This was sewn with a hot needle."

I think that Grandma sewed those hopeless socks with longing, patience, love and resignation for things that never were. For those things made impossible by heartache and circumstance.

Finally she handed them back to Frank, neatly rolled in his little brown bag.

"There you are," she said.

"Thanks" he said, and arose to leave. He cleared his throat uncomfortably and asked,

"Dear, can I borrow some change from you till I get paid again?"

Grandma said, "I'll see what I've got."

She got up and walked to her tin can on the kitchen stove. There was nothing in it, so she went into the bedroom and returned with a small handful of change that she placed in his hand.

"This isn't much Frank," she said softly, "but we are a little short just now."

"That's fine, dearest," he said, wrapping his arm around her.

"Lou, do you love me?" he asked my grandmother in almost a whisper. She did not answer audibly, but nodded her head yes as tears gave up their stubborn battle. She cried as he gave her a tender kiss on the lips.

"Thank you," he said. Then he turned his head away from her pain.

As he walked out the front door and without looking back over his shoulder, he tapped on his pocket with the change inside and said, "I'll bring this back quick as I can. "

Grandmother waived goodbye to him and her mouth formed the words *God Bless You* without making a sound. I don't think he saw her.

When he reached the street, Harley and Veve ran to the sidewalk to hug him goodbye. That was the last I ever saw of him.

Grandmother stitched carefully with that old bent needle and a fractured longing heart. As she worked there in her rocker with the Stearman at her feet, I see now that on her face was the quintessence of every relationship of every man with every woman from the beginning of time -- all the love, disappointment and longing of wasted decades. The cherished moments and faded triumphs. I know now that the stitches were from the nights of loving, the days of laughter and those of anguish, too. Those of pain and paradise reflected in a millisecond, insinuating themselves into each stroke of her needle. Our entire world stopped ever so briefly, but none of us knew exactly why. It just did. Life had delivered the day's anticipated electrostatic package to our doorstep, and none of us could imagine its impact on us over the course of our lives.

This was my only clear memory of my grandfather. I have thought about it often in my life. Now as I sit here writing, it brings to mind the line in Zorba the Greek, where Zorba says, "Women... How can I not love them? Poor, weak creatures. They take so little, a man's hand on their breast, and they give you all they got."

With all the pain my own mother bestowed on me, I see clearly now that she gave me the most precious treasure of all — that of life — and she was always trying to give some man stitches from her own skinny, longing heart. God bless her — she gave me grief, but she also gave me a sense of humor and a sense of the absurd. Mother gave me all she could give me, all that she was able to give.

I would trade anything for ten more minutes on my grandmother's lap, or to hear her whistle just once more.

CHAPTER 27

The Tiniest Viking (Sharon De Brun; Burial in Icy Seas; Kerstin Rydstrom, the Viking Mother)

T WAS SOMETIME in September or early October in 1945 when Uncle Jimmy Brown and his wife Helen brought their new baby girl, Sharon, on her first outing. The pair delivered the child into Grandmother Brown's hungry arms. It had been raining off and on for several days, so Uncle Jimmy drove his Mercury Sedan over the curb and parked the car just in front of our stoop by the muddy yard. Within a wink, the happy new family was dry and warm inside our home.

Grandmother fussed over Aunt Helen and Baby Sharon; she held the child in her arms, talking animatedly to Aunt Helen while she rubbed the baby girl's tiny chin with her tender thumb. She had held many babies, and was smiling at the child. I remember thinking, as I stood next to her chair then, how very beautiful my grandma was. There was so much love in her eyes; it seemed boundless to me.

Uncle Jimmy and Aunt Helen Brown, 1940s

Jimmy looked at his wife adoringly, unable to take his eyes off her, as she reached out to touch his hand.

I looked at the tiny fingers and the ears and the thin little lips of the precious sleeping infant; she was so delicate. This was the first human baby I had ever seen up close, and I remember it clearly. It was during the rhetoric between those three adults that I learned storks didn't leave babies on door steps in baskets, and that infants were actually *born*, what ever that meant. Apparently it involved growing inside the mother's stomach. I gave a great deal of troublesome thoughts as to how the babies escape after they had grow in the tummies. And besides, how in the hell did they wind up in there in the first place? Someone had mentioned something about swallowing watermelon seeds, which they said could grow into babies. Unfortunately, due to my lack of sexual education, I knew nothing more than that when we ate our food, it went into our stomachs and was subsequently pooped out. My poor brain reeled a bit when I imagined everyone I knew having been pooped into this world, and that idea disgusted and upset me more than just a little bit. I felt that the idea of babies being delivered to the doorstep in clean baskets with blue or pink ribbons by some handsome stork was a far superior theory to watermelon seed poop, and for a while this confused me greatly. It was much too complex for me to ponder and it soon hurt my seven year old brain.

They tried to explain the "miracle of life" to me, although they sidestepped all the really accurate and pertinent information; so by the time they were done with their smiling platitudes, I was more confused than ever. *What miracle*, I thought to myself, *coming into the world as belching, vomiting babies made from watermelon seeds and poop.*? I, of course, asked questions that no one wished to answer in any way I could grasp. Finally, after the adults skillfully sidestepped the watermelon seed issue)and other theories), I remember asking if the stork had put Sharon inside Aunt Helen's stomach?

Something was said about Uncle Jimmy putting it in there, and I think I asked, "Why he didn't just grow it in his own damned stomach?", for which I received no clear answer, as well as a severe admonition from Grandmother for cussing, one that briefly bordered on me dining on a bar of Palmolive hand soap. Uncle Jimmy did say something about them flipping a coin to see which of their two stomachs would grow the baby. Uncle Jimmy said he lost the toss.

I honestly began to wonder if I would ever learn this stuff, and for several years the mystery of life eluded me. Anyway, after a few minutes Harley and Veve walked in and saw the infant with no signs of curiosity whatsoever. Aunt Helen and Jim let each of us hold the baby girl, and when it came my turn I was terrified of breaking her. I sat up straight in Grandmother's rocker, just the way she'd instructed me; and she carefully handed me my baby cousin, showing me just how to hold her. Sharon opened her eyes and looked at me like she was trying to focus her vision. I put one of my fingers inside her tiny fist, and she squeezed it with surprising strength. Grandmother saw I was nervous, so she gently handed the baby back her mother.

Harley was on his newest kick, calling Sharon a "little Viking." You see, he had been trying unsuccessfully to change the subject from babies to Viking fare by cornering Jimmy and Helen with his National Geographic magazine, bombarding them with the idea that we Browns — and by extension, their new daughter, were descendants of the Vikings.

After reading about them for several days and nearly camping out in the library, he became fascinated with the subject of Nordic lore, and all things pertaining to Germans, Finns, Swedes, Norwegians and so on. He told Jimmy and Helen that he was pretty sure the Brown family had Viking blood because Grandpa Brown once said something about us being of German or Scandinavian stock. Plus he had been discussing the matter with the German grocer, Hans Bearwald.

Jimmy sneered and rolled his eyes. Veve, on this rare occasion agreed with her brother, because she reasoned that we were blond and loved sauerkraut. She had just finished a pulp romance book called "Sven The Ravenous," about the sexual encounters and the morays of the Viking hordes as they "Battled all those Celts on the British Isles." The main character, in Veve's current pulp book, was a Viking called "Sven Brun"; so Veve was on board with Harley's idea. She insisted that "Brun" sounded suspiciously similar to Brown. Never mind that Harley had also read the same silly book, telling Grandmother that it was "pure addlebrained rubbish, and that little in it was in any way historically correct". But he needed to convince the new Brown parents, and didn't bother to correct his one and only ally in front of the potential converts.

I don't think that the idea sat well with Uncle Jimmy, who was left out of the war. He was brokenhearted and itching to kill "some of those Kraut-Hun-headed Nazi sons a bitches", and he winced when Harley implied that his all-American baby daughter's heritage could include German blood.

I think Jimmy's wife, Helen, felt uncomfortable with too many hands and eyes on her new baby daughter, and she had zero interest in Harley's Viking lore. The new mother was anxious to get her family back home and away from the Nordic rhetoric of Harley Brown. When the rain let up for a bit, Aunt Helen said to her husband,

"Well Brownie, we need to get our Viking Princess home to Compton."

We said our warm goodbyes, and as they walked out the front door Harley placed his fist over his heart and gave some ridiculous straight-armed salute toward the sky.

"In the name of Odin, we salute you, you mighty Viking warrior," he cried. "Brother Brun and your beautiful daughter — safe journey to the village of Compton!"

Jimmy looked at Harley incredulously. Shaking his head, he said, "Harley Thomas, you are about as much a Viking as Stan Laurel, you goof ball! And your accent is more like an Apache Indian Chief from some western movie than a Swedish meatball-Nordic heathen."

Harley, ignoring their lack of enthusiasm, glanced down knowingly at his National Geographic magazine as they left.

When they left the stoop, Harley went back out to his garage to continue building either a balsa wood Valsgaard or a Viking-style ship called a "Tune". Veve went along, promising to read to him from her newest book. It was called "Brun the Barbarian" .

Grandmother turned on the radio and took up her knitting. She asked me if I wasn't going out to visit Harley and listen to Veve's story. I replied that I just wanted to lie there on the front room linoleum floor behind her and listen to the radio and the rain.

Now, throughout my young life, I'd always searched for classical music on the radio. I was drawn to it like a new drunk to old whiskey. It was my music of choice, even at that tender age, and I wore out the dial searching for it. I cannot remember why or what drew me too this variety of music, but I always sought it out; I think in the beginning it might have reminded me of Papa's music from the old greasy turkey countries, or from Ducks cello music.

Panning across the radio dial, I hit pay dirt; a symphony orchestra was to perform from New York City. The announcer said the piece was called "Hymni, Op. 26" by Jean Sibelius, followed by "Finalandia". The radio host talked about the music for awhile, saying something about Scandinavia. The back of Grandma's rocker was facing me as I lay behind it on my side, watching her rock back and forth. I traced the pattern of the linoleum with my idol finger. The next thing I knew, it had started to rain really hard, and everything seemed just right to me. The music was beautiful, and I had the most wonderful, peaceful feeling I had ever known. It was one where everything was perfectly in unison, and I felt the earth move in harmony, slowly and correctly beneath me as I lay on my side on that cool linoleum. The thunder and lightening clacked in perfect counterpoint to the music, as the sound of thunder rang with the music and lightning lit up the sky through our windows.

All seemed right in the world, and for the first time I could recall since walking high on Papa's shoulders, I had the feeling that I was exactly where I should be, and that Grandma was precisely where she should be. I loved looking at the back of Grandma's head, and at her little round shoulders; she was always a feast for my eyes, and watching her rock back and forth as the rain accompanied by the music was priceless to me. My world, in that moment, was near perfection. I could see the back of Grandmother's head as she looked down at her work. In her low, sweet voice, almost musing to herself, she said, "Hmmm, Finlandia… Scandinavia. Maybe Harley and Veve should hear this. It sounds like it might be Viking Music?"

I responded, "Grandma, I never want this moment to end. Is there something wrong with me?" I paused. "Grandma, am I mean or selfish because I don't want to share this with Uncle Harley or Aunt Veve?"

I could see Grandmother rocking in her knitting rhythm, thinking about my question. Finally she said, "Well, no. I suppose not."

I took a breath and said, "Grandma, I just want the three of us here."

After a bit, she said, "Artie, there's just we two here, darlin'."

"Oh yeah, I forgot," I said. "But it feels like a trinity in here, only I just can't see it."

229

We said nothing more, and I lay there on my side with one of Grandma's small cushions beneath my head, just watching her rocking voyage back and forth in her chair. She moved in perfect time with the music. I felt something growing in me somehow, and could not understand it; and the strong pulse of the music grew alongside the growth in me. I looked down at my legs and feet to see if they were getting longer or fatter, watching to see if I could actually catch them growing before my eyes. Something felt large and strange and expansive. I did not understand it, but I didn't care that I didn't, either.

I briefly closed my eyes, listening to the music and the rain pounding on the windows. When I opened my eyes, there were indeed three of us in the room. A small mouse with black fur on his back and white fur on its round tummy sat on its haunches, just watching me. There was black fur on the back of his large pink ears, too. He stood directly underneath Grandma's chair, chewing something as his whiskers rose and fell in opposition. He looked serious — comically so. I did not move a muscle, and I smiled looking back at him. He saw something under Grandma's chair and skittered off, rolling back an empty wooden spool of thread he'd found at her feet. He flipped it on end, chewing its edge industriously. With the piece of wood between his tiny front paws, he chewed the edge of the spool while keeping a close eye on me; then he tipped over the spool, rolling it an inch or so deeper beneath the rocker. I laughed out loud.

"What's tickling you Artie?" asked Grandma.

"I'm just happy," I said, swallowing another giggle, and looking at the mouse's face.

Grandma kept the rhythm in her rocking, and the mouse sensed it perfectly. The rockers of her chair missed him by mere millimeters. Grandmother's skein of knitting yarn had fallen on the floor, and I watched as the little mouse scooted toward the back of her feet, standing with its tiny front feet on top of her shoe. He reached up to the yarn with his mouth. The pink yarn twisted several times around her finger, holding one of her knitting needles. Grandmother must have felt a little tug on the thread and yanked it up, thinking to unravel more yarn. She inadvertently lifted the mouse into the air, and he hung on for dear life. Finally he let go, falling to the floor and running back under her chair, hiding once again behind the empty spool.

I laughed again and Grandma joined me, unaware of the scene unfolding underneath her chair.

"Artie, you silly goose," she said. "Grandma loves to hear you laugh, d'you know that?"

The mouse continued his dangerous dance under her rocker. Now there was the rain and the music and the ballet of the mouse.

As I watched him, I thought of Vikings and such, and a fantasy was born from my joy. Perhaps this mouse was a Viking and battling the dangerous rockers on both sides. He was so very brave and swift, and I got to thinking that this must be his story — this must be his purpose in the world. This was his industry and his job, his journey. I watched him fascinated, holding my breath as he dashed here and there, peeking out from an angle behind the spool, or running around Grandma's shoe, or smelling the bolt of yarn. I got to worrying about him, and I reached into my pants pocket to retrieve a few cornflakes I had stashed there for the birds. I stretched my arm out to the mouse. He did not run away; he just looked at me with his funny black eyes and wiggled his whiskers. I slid the cornflake seductively, a bit closer along the linoleum, pushing it with the tip of my finger. I waited with baited breath. Just as I was about to give up, he ran up near my hand and took the flake, running back under Grandma's chair near his spool of thread to consume it. I watched him in fascination, well aware that I was in rare Viking mouse company. Of course I knew it was silly, but I couldn't chase the idea away. The mouse moved his whiskers and ran near my hand, waiting for another flake. This time I handed him the food, and he cautiously took if from between my fingers. Then he returned yet again to his spindle barrier, peering around the edge of it and watching me closely. I noticed he had a fat, stuffed tummy; and I thought it strange that his stomach was so full, and yet he still seemed hungry. It was then I realized that this little warrior was a princess rather than a prince; she must have had her own little Sharon in her tummy, I reasoned. I had seen other mice — heck, every time it rained they came into the house — but this one had no large "testorkills" like I had seen on some of the others, so I named her "Kerstin the Viking Mother", after Grandma's Swedish friend Kerstin Rydstrom from the Red Cross. That was the only Swedish name I knew.

As time went on, the music changed its rhythm, and I noticed the back and forth movement of the chairs' rockers, missing the mouse by millimeters. Often the Viking mouse would run directly under the rockers, dodging the back of the chair when it was on an upward roll. The skitter ballet went on for a good while, and then the rain came to an abrupt halt, almost as though someone had clicked a rain switch precisely as the rocker crushed Kerstin's back.

"No!" I yelled. I was on my feet in an instant, rushing to the side of Grandmother's chair. I immediately got her out of the rocker, trying to explain what had just happened. She got up quickly and looked down to see the crushed Kerstin. That was when a look of sadness crossed Grandma's beautiful face. She brought a large kitchen matchbox into the sitting room, and we laid the dead Viking inside.

"This little mouse was pregnant and was looking for food to grow her babies," said Grandmother.

Grandmother washed her hands and told me to wash mine, too. Now, my grandmother was not above killing a mouse or two, and she had caught many in her lifetime. She'd used mouse traps and poisoned a few others; she was not fond of vermin, and the old house drew rodents inside like a magnet. But Grandmother had a tender side, too; and many times she'd just shush the mice out of the house with her broom, or she'd put some crumbs out for them near her rose bushes.

But this one upset her.

After all, we had just witnessed a new life in "Sharon Brun", the Viking; and now this mother-Viking mouse seemed to break Grandmother's heart. This was different somehow; it had to do with motherhood and the lesson I was soon to learn about the circle of life.

I told Grandmother about Kerstin playing under her chair, and my fantasy about her being a Viking mouse.

Grandmother gave me the box and said, "Take this out to Harley and Veve and tell them what happened. Perhaps they know how to bury Viking mother mice?"

Grandmother was calm, but she had moist eyes; and I knew that on this special night of new baby granddaughters, music, laughter and Nordic thunder; this event had upset her tender mercies.

I did as I was told, and both Harley and Veve listened to my detailed story with great interest. They were most receptive to helping me honor the mouse. I left out no detail of the incident, including the music and the adventures with the spool, and that I had named her "Kerstin". It was a perfect meeting of minds, as Veve had almost finished her book, and she and her brother were both awash with all things Nordic.

Harley volunteered his Viking model boat and made the final preparations for a flaming Nordic burial at sea for sometime the next day. Veve suggested that they make a mockup of a sexual thrall, including the seven-day orgy she had just read about in her book. They soon decided, however, that since this tiny Viking was not a "Sven" but a "Kerstin" — and pregnant, and no longer living — a sexual thrall, whatever that was, was out of the question.

However, Harley said we could sacrifice several living slaves to accompany Kerstin to Valhalla. This, according to Mr. Brown's research, was the custom. Harley went to the shelf and brought a glass jar with six very large, very ugly, unhappy potato bugs trapped inside. They were trying to crawl up the sides of glass and escape.

They talked about gathering symbols of Kerstin's life to put on the barge with her, and they assigned that job to me. We talked for awhile about such things, agreeing that the tiniest Viking would have a flaming burial fit for a Nordic princess mouse. We met by flame on one of the larger ponds, made more substantial by the recent rain. I went inside to gather some stuff for Kerstin's trip — her trip to meet Odin in some place called Valhalla — looking for a few items that might work for a Viking mouse. It seems, according to Veve's book, that the funeral barge carried things alongside the departed for use in the afterlife. So my mission was clear.

I asked Grandmother, and she suggested with great aplomb and participation that I should see Papa Eudie about anything related to death, burial and the history of almost anything.

"Who knows more about death and funerals than Papa?" she asked.

I quite agreed, and the next morning, as Papa had his coffee, I crossed the street for some advice.

Between my questions, I joyfully recounted yesterday's events in minute detail, including the mystery of little Sharon's water drop size fingernails — the music and the pageantry and sad events of the evening. Papa smiled broadly and asked, "Does Harley want me to attend the Viking funeral?"

I nodded my head and said, "Gosh, yes Papa, we all do."

So Papa said he would be there to help us pay homage to Kerstin the next day.

He said,

"Ask Harley to be ready just before dusk. Anna and I will attend."

But before I got off Papa's lap, he admonished me. "Tell Harley to hold off on the Thralls. Tell him I'll be there to help a bit early"

I said, "Okay, Papa!" Then I returned home and reported all this to the rest of the family. They were all very excited.

Looking at Harley and Veve, I said, "Wow, a real Viking funeral for our Kerstin, Princess of Finland. And supervised by an actual funeral director!"

We all met about half an hour before dusk, seating ourselves either on the edge of the big swing. We sat on the stoop, too, since both the swing and the stoop were about six feet away from the biggest of the rain puddles. The largest pond we selected for our Viking lake, which the three of us named together. Veve got an idea from her book; it was some big lake in Sweden called "Takem". And Harley's choice was from another lake in an issue of National Geographic, called Lake "Sommen". I added a third name from the fertile fields of my pubescent cartoon brain, called "Lake Cucutitsettlewhat". This was where Mama Kerstin's barge was to burn. The rain pond was an oval of about twelve by six feet, and two to four inches deep. So with a few folding chairs, this became the perfect stage for our big show.

Walter Crawford, Sol Rubenstein and my cousin Leslie Dow had shown up for the gala event. Leslie sat next to me on the edge of the swing, putting his arms around me as usual. We sat there listening and waiting and grinning like two ninnies, just as we usually did.

Harley, thinking it might sound ancient and Vikingish, had phoned Sol from Papa's house, inviting him to bring his large Shofar — the mighty horn used in all those Jewish ceremonies. Solomon arrived on time, and was deep in conversation with Papa Eudie before long.

I had asked Veve and Harley what they meant by a "Thrall", but I could not get a straight answer from them. I asked Papa, too, who said that he had wanted to speak to Harley and Valera Von Brun about Kerstin and her proposed Thralls.

Papa looked at me and said, "Artie, Thralls were slaves — prisoners or servants owned by the Vikings."

Then he looked at Sol, and the group of us gathered in front of him and said, "There has hardly been a civilization in the history of mankind that has not been both slaves and owners of slaves at one time or another.

"Thralls were slaves on the downside of Nordic history. The African Negroes, here in the U.S., were slaves until the American Civil War. They, however, are certainly not the first — nor are they even the most recent — examples of Slavery. The Armenians were forced either into slavery or extinction or religious conversion by the Turks. And at this very moment, in Germany, there are untold stories of slaves from a dozen or more countries. Some were starved and worked to death by the Nazis. Even today, there are civilizations that maintain forms of slavery.

"Historically, American Indians of all varieties — both in South America and here in the U.S. — have conquered and enslaved other tribes, many of whom were sacrificed on stone alters.

"And there were dozens of Negro tribes in Africa who where themselves slave owners. It was not uncommon for one conquering tribe to enslave another; and besides the Portuguese and the Spanish and the English, the largest traders of slaves to this country were other Negro tribes, who were themselves slave traders. American slavery was just our own personal mess, and that is why we remember it more clearly."

We all listened with great interest. Sol was in complete agreement. He looked to Papa and said,

"Yes, apparently the world doesn't learn very fast. People forget about this. All slavery is evil, and cannot by its very nature work for long. It has the potential to generate feelings of resentment, hatred and ignorance. It even leads to death sometimes. So Harley, if you are going to have six living Thralls here on this barge, it is not a very happy thought.

"And by the way, if this is an homage to the Vikings, it is a bad one. You cannot honor one race — or in this case, a species — by destroying another. And Mr. Brown, your simile is flawed."

"Why?" Harley asked, his brow furrowed.

"Well, a potato bug is not a proper representation for a Viking mouse slave," said Sol. "A Viking thrall was usually another Viking in disfavor, or a foreign slave. So to make this work, you would have to acquire six live mice and burn them to death to achieve your fantasy."

Harley and Veve looked at each other, and then at the ground. Harley was about ready to say something when Papa said, "Tim has told me, Harley, that you and Artie and Walter Crawford used to enjoy pitting a spider against various other insects, or Potato bugs against red or black ants, to see who survived. Is that right?"

"Yes," Harley said, looking up.

Sol stood beside Harley as Papa continued.

"Is it also true that you three have burnt them alive with lighter fluid inside jars and watched them die?

"Well, yes Papa, but mostly I just wanted to see their reaction. Is that wrong, Papa?"

I watched Grandmother and Anna's faces as they listened intently for Papa's reply.

Eudie addressed Harley, saying, "Well, it's typical boy stuff. As to the wrong or right of it, you already know the answer. But offhand, I would say that theirs were painful and senseless deaths."

"Now then, Harley Brown," Papa said, sighing a bit. "All boys mess with bugs, usually with magnifying glasses and so on. And the fact that you have killed some bugs does not make you a beast or a monster.

"But you need to think about it a bit deeper. To insects and other weaker creatures, you must not forget that your power over them is like God's power over you. Would you enjoy it if God put you near a falling building, or in a train wreck? Or in a burning building, just to see your reaction?"

Harley looked over at Muggs' grave.

"You know, son," continued Eudie. "Every day we have the opportunity to be kind, thoughtful and gentile; and to touch upon our better selves — perhaps just to be a bit wiser. It costs nothing to be kind.

"Now then Brownie," Papa asked. "Perhaps I am misjudging you. Are you a potato?"

Harley's Brow wrinkled. Startled, he said, "What? Why, Papa — what do you mean?"

Papa repeated the question. "Are you a Potato?"

"Well, no, Papa," said Harley. "Of course I'm not."

"Well then," said Papa. "The reason I asked is that I thought that if you were a potato, a carrot or a tuber, that perhaps those Thralls in your jar might have harmed or offended you in some way. Then your actions would make more sense. Do you think these ugly thralls in that glass jar have ever bothered Mother Kerstin in the past?"

Harley answered immediately. "Well, of course not, Papa."

"Harley, you do as you think best, son," said Papa. "But remember this — and I have seen it many times throughout my life. If you get used to killing little things unnecessarily and you get to liking it, then the bigger things become easier — frogs and birds and cats and so on. When that happens, then destroying humans is only a couple steps away. Remember your little Muggs, Harley?"

"Yes, Papa," Harley said, looking sadly back over to the pup's grave site.

Papa continued, "Well, then you will remember that Bruce Tufts killed everything he could lay his whip or boot to. He killed everything he could kill, and often he got away with it.

"Eventually he killed little Muggs with a club. And the boy did near his best to kick my Whisker to death. Did you know that during our Armenian Holocaust, Turkish soldiers played catch with beautiful little babies — just like your cousin Sharon Brown — by tossing them back and forth on the tips of their swords and bayonets? They'd laugh as they threw their little half-dead bodies onto the burning fires. Those laughing Tufts brothers would have fit right in with their ilk."

Papa added," Give some thought to whom and what you kill, Mr. Brown; and more importantly, why you choose to kill. If you can't find a good reason, then turn away. If you find you must kill something or someone someday, then do it with dispatch. Do it by any means available to you.

And yet, I hope that day will never come for you. I hope that there is always food in your icebox and a friend at your flank. I hope with all my heart that you never choose to kill anything, but I have seen that there is evil in this world sometimes. Besides, some things need killing; you will know what you need to do when that happens. But meanwhile, God has given us these little creatures — like the late Muggs McGinnis and my Orange Pasha and his mouse jockey — to love and protect. These bugs need to be spared, and recognized for their worth, too. When we can, we should use them as practice for our hearts, so we know how to treat the larger things in life."

The mood changed drastically.

Sol stepped forward and said,

"May I suggest that we do honor not only this Viking Mouse Mother, but all mothers?"

Cheering spread across the entire assembly. Sol's words changed the mood, and Mother Brown and Anna's faces shined.

"The sun is setting," Sol continued. "I propose that we light the barge and sail her across the pond, and that we each — one at a time — stand and pay homage to motherhood and the circle of life as Kerstin and her babies cross into eternity."

Harley smiled broadly and agreed. He took the jar of Thralls to Muggs' graveside and released them near his pine headstone. The reprieved thralls scurried under the concrete foundation of the garage. just as the sun set. Sol blew the Shofar powerfully and long; it shook our marrow and made my fuzzy little arm hairs stand on end. I waived at Papa, getting his attention and holding up three fingers.

"A trinity Papa! A trinity!" I yelled to him excitedly.

Harley placed his Tune barge with the mouse on Lake Sommen/ Takem/Cucutitsettlewhat, with all its little accoutrements for the afterlife, including the spindle the mouse had played with and some of Grandma's yarn, plus a few of my cornflakes. Grandma made some mouse-sized pots and pans out of flower. She allowed me to put three kernels of golden corn in one of them. Then she cut little scraps of material, the size of tiny blankets, and covered the mouse.

The ship looked beautiful; Harley had done a yeoman job of constructing the Tune. Its sail was a single square sheet with a red Nordic cross painted on it. The boat was varnished and detailed, and Harley had lit it on fire, pushing it gently across the lake as the sun set. Sol blew his Shofar again. Then he stepped up and spoke, gesturing with Harley's same, silly salute.

"I salute all mothers of the world," he said. "Mothers dead and living, mothers all over the world that are being bombed and tortured. No matter who you are, and no matter what nationality, I salute you all. I salute all Life! L'chaim!"

Then Harley stood, repeating the process. "I salute my loving, other and all my sisters, who are mothers or who will soon become mothers," he said.

Then Papa Eudie: "I salute my Anna, the mother of my two sons. And I salute all those Armenian mothers that died at the hands of those motherless bastards, those heartless, self-righteous murderers that would burn my baby girls like bugs.

Then Walter: "I salute my mother Ruth and my Grandma Brown, who is our Viking Queen."

"I salute mother bees, mother spiders and mother potato bugs," said Aunt Veve.

"I salute my mother Carole Joy," Leslie Dow said, smiling and looking into Grandma Brown's eyes.

Then it was my Turn;

"I salute Kerstin, who died while she was searching for food for her tummy babies, and to Helen and Jimmy and their little baby Sharon."

I looked directly at Papa and asked, "Is that the circle of life, Papa?"

Papa smiled. Sol sounded the Shofar three final times.

Papa looked at me and said, "That's another trinity, little whisker!"

I nodded my head and said proudly, "Yep!"

CHAPTER 28

Circus Trilogy
(Part One: Bring in The Clown)

C HRISTMAS EVE, 1946, was our banner year for Christmases
— at least for us Browns there on Atlantic Boulevard. Uncle
Harley said that Santa Clause would have to enter through
the one-inch brass pipe of the toilet vent, since house had no chimney,
and only an unvented claw foot tile floor heater. The house and Harley's
garage were tacked together in about 1901. In reality, both structures
were only a little more than wood-sided sheds.

Christmas day was near, and things in paradise were more or less
back to normal. That is to say, "Johnny" and the boys had done it — we
had neutered the Nazis and nipped the Nips. Many of our lads still lay
forever sleeping in the fields of Normandy, and far too few Johnnies
had "come marching home" as the song predicted they would; but
come home they did and a new United States of America — and a New
World — had begun.

In some ways, peacetime was more frightening than the war had been.
After the cheering parades and the welcoming embraces we presented
our nation's warriors, we realized the future was uncertain. Jobs were

tenuous because of the glut of returning GIs who needed new employment. Prices where going up and income was going down.

We didn't have to rebuild from the rubble as Europe did but Rosy the Riveter was replaced by Sergeant John Doe, and there was some fear about the economy. However, the beginning our days were filled with hope and gratitude for not being forced to "Deutsch Sprechen" or bow to the Emperor of Japan. So times where happy, and when times are happy money seemed on the surface to flow more freely.

From all my previous wartime memories, this was the first and only year we were able to afford a huge Christmas tree. Previous Christmases, we did without or, occasionally one of the men on the Christmas tree trucks would "accidentally" let one of their smaller, runt-of-the-litter trees fall off their truck in front of our house. Veve or Harley would snag it and bring it in to live with us.

This year was different. We were able, for the first time, to purchase a nice full-bodied, seven-foot-tall Christmas tree for fifty-five cents, and we couldn't wait to get it up and sing around it.

We decorated the tree with popcorn threaded on a long string; Grandmother sent me to the T&T Confectionary next to the Alcazar Theater, where I bought a bag of jelly beans to string and ten cents' worth of cotton candy as a substitute for angel's hair. We strung the jelly beans as a counterpoint to the popcorn strings and found two runs of Christmas tree lights. Those sad and dangerous lights were plugged into the only electrical outlet in the house other than the one in the kitchen; and when the radio and the tree lights where on at the same time it constantly blew the fuses. Fuzzy drew a cartoon figure of all our family members and pasted them on bell-shaped cardboard backing, which we'd hang on the branches. The tree was topped off with a five-inch angel that Harley had carved from a block of Ivory soap. The tree took up a great deal of our small living room, but we loved it, huddling around it often.

That Christmas our home was full of the music of Harley and Jimmy, Eudie and young Duck, who played his cello beautifully. The music of the harmonicas, cimbalom, duduk and cello; and of course, of human voices, filled our home. We sang Christmas Carols and popular songs of the day, and Eudie and my uncle Carl Agajanian, a new relative by marriage, sang duets in Armenian, Greek and Russian. Several days before Christmas Eve, I sat tall upon my eagle's nest around Papa Eudie's neck as Uncle Harley, Papa and Hans Bearwalt, the German grocer, stood singing in front of Papa's Savings and Loan Company. Then we'd alternate our caroling to the opposite corner in front of Suekeetchers Soda Fountain, where Mother worked.

On some of the songs like White Christmas or Noel, I sang along with them and no one shushed me. Papa even told me later that I had a nice voice. I thought my chest would burst with pride when he said so. I felt like Caruso! I can still hear those wonderful voices to this day. Uncle Jimmy sometimes joined them with his trumpet, too. Those were days when, because of the European melting pot that had infiltrated the U.S., many American homes were filled with music. It was a common thing in those days to sing and play a musical instrument. It seemed essential during those war years and it bred art and poetry, tall tales, teasing, mischief and familial love.

I remember that as we sang there on the corner we saw Mrs. Manfrianni still very much alive and still calling me Marty. She still wore black, only the arm band was now gone, and she had a new boyfriend who must have been nearly ninety. We all laughed as they walked off, and her new suitor reached lovingly for her arm to help her.

Mrs. Manfrianni smacked his hand away, yelling, "Don't graba owna tah me...You fallah down ana pool me down too!"

My mother bought me a Swiss Army knife, which in those days cost only slightly little less than a brand new Schwinn Phantom bicycle. Now it is clear to me how extravagant a gift it was at the time, and that my mother must have made sacrifices to give it to me. Word was that some thought it foolish that an irresponsible eight-year-old miscreant should even possess it in the first place.

I did manage not to stab myself to death, nor did I slice a main artery or cut off a finger; but looking back on it now I can't imagine how I didn't. What ever had my mother been thinking?

But for me, the most priceless gift of all was a English Language Dictionary, which I devoured by the hour from the big swing, or perched on top of the roof. There were so many delicious words and I could not wait to impress Sol or pick an endless supply of phrases that would prove sure to aggravate my aunts. Harley and Grandmother Brown had given me the dictionary, and it must have been costly because it was a hardcover, and so large that I had to find inventive ways to get it up on the roof with me. They had all signed my book, and it said on the inside front leaf: *We love you, Artie. Merry Christmas. Don't try to use all these words in one sentence.*

Before Christmas I'd earned some money helping my Uncle Fuzzy with his artwork by leaving him the hell alone and taking a two dollar bribe to do so. I held out for three dollars but he pulled me close to him and drew a large cross-eyed bumblebee on my nose with yellow and black indelible ink, and swooshed me off two dollars richer in a promise that I not return for the rest of the day. He threatened to display more artwork on my face if I disobeyed.

I returned about four hours later and he paid me another dollar to leave again.

"Being naughty can be profitable," I mentioned to Grandma later on that day. But Grandmother told me that if I didn't stop bothering poor Elwood, that she would add another bumblebee to my little arse with her fly flap. She insisted that I return my extortion money to poor Uncle Fuzzy.

"You know, Artie," she said, "that bumblebee Elwood painted on your nose will not wash off for a month."

"Oh, good!" I said. Then I flew my Stearman happily out of the room, replacing its distinct radial motor sound with the of the sound of a buzzing bumblebee. Grandma gave me a shot with her fly flap that connected with my vertical stabilizer, so I put the "ball to the wall", increasing my airspeed. I continued gaining altitude until I flew safely into the stratosphere on the roof of our house.

I had also been paid a bit to help Sol package and mail some of his jewelry, which was inspired — at least in part — by my paper boat design I had sold to him two years earlier at the Alcazar Theater. Also, Papa Eudie had given me a crisp new two dollar bill, along with a dollar Christmas advance, as was custom; and so for the first time in my life, I actually had a considerable amount of money for gifts.

For my beloved Grandmother I bought a can of lard, a new pancake spatula and a small two-cup porcelain tea set, which I told her was for her and Anna when they "commiserated" — my newest word, and one I tried — to everyone's chagrin — to use ad nauseam and incorrectly in every sentence I could.

I gave my mother a handmade Christmas card with a little character Fuzzy showed me how to draw: a cartoon face with a skinny neck, a line for a mouth with one tooth showing and big eyes with eyelids and long lashes. The character had a bald dome head with a single hair on it. I added an arrow pointing to the sketch saying "self portrait". Then I signed it: *I love you Mommy. Love your best son, Artie.* Now, I thought, that was hilarious, since I was her only son. Inside the card I pasted four brand new quarters and a piece of double bubble gum, and one of my foil paper boats I had made out of a dollar bill. I also gave her an Abazaba candy bar with a red ribbon around it and a note that said: *To fatten you up.*

I think I bartered for something for everyone else in the family, too; and finally I was able to deliver the stick model airplane I had promised Papa Eudie year after year.

For as long as I could remember, I had wanted to build him the smaller version of the Red Barons Fokker Tri plane; and in fact, a few months earlier I had tried building it semi-secretly on my own.

It was a disaster. I managed to install the tail both upside down and backwards, and the vertical stabilizer had a distinct inclination to the port side, so each of the three wings pointed in different directions. The wings were a quarter of an inch off center and the fuselage was warped so badly that the landing gear wheels were out of place. The poor little plane wouldn't even roll on the ground without dragging the starboard wing. It was heavy, covered in too much glue and it flew like a rock. The airplane was a mess. I sat leaning against the garage, pouting — too ashamed to give the plane to the big man — so in disgust I stuffed a single marshmallow inside the pilot's cockpit as well. Then I sat it on top of Muggs' grave and lit it on fire, watching it burn to a cinder. Of course I ate the blackened marshmallow afterward, which had been my engineering master plan. As Papa always told me, "Turn a negative into a positive when you can." Meanwhile, I still had no airplane for Papa. However, fate intervened in the name of Solomon Itzhak Rubinstein, who, with great patience, understanding and logic, convinced me to try building a simpler model; perhaps a Stearman Cub, the smaller version, or better yet, why not a stubby Sopwith Camel, or even a little Piper Cub, which was the cheapest and simplest model kit to build. I agreed to go with the Sopwith, but only if we could paint it yellow and red like a Stearman.

Now, before his fateful encounter with the Brown entourage at the Alcazar Theater, Sol Rubinstein had never built a model airplane of any kind. But over the months he'd watched Harley and Walter build a half dozen or so, and so he took to it like a teenage girl takes to bobby socks. Walter, our "eggheaded engineer", marveled at him, allowing him to do intricate cuts on balsa struts and giving him very technically difficult things to do, just to test his ability, well aware that he was a novice. Sol didn't bat an eye; after all, he was an apprentice watchmaker and the son of a jeweler so intricate and delicate that work was apple pie for this very bright boy. I went to Sol with the "Sopwith" kit and we built it together in the living room, with Grandma watching us most interested while she knitted and listened to "Duffy's Tavern" on the radio. She marveled at Sol's patience with me as he walked me through every step, slowing me down and then complimenting me when I did something right, and pointing out my virtues to Grandma. When I made a mistake he showed me an "easier way to do it," finally allowing me to do it with only the minimum supervision. The final product was not bad work for a dunderheaded clown with a bumblebee on his nose, and I was quite proud of myself and very thankful to Sol. While we worked one evening, Grandmother prepared Sol's mother's receipt for Knish, adding her usual "touch of this and pinch of that." After eating four pieces, Sol said to Grandmother, "Mrs. Brown, are you sure your name is not Brownsky or Brownberg? Because — and please don't tell this to my mother because I will deny it — that is the best Knish I have ever had. I am sure you are Jewish, Mrs. Brown," Sol said with a grin.

She smiled and said, "No son, I am a Baptist, but one my best friends was a Jew."

"Really?" Sol said inquisitively. "What was her name? Perhaps we know the family."

Grandmother replied with a twinkle in her eye and said, "His name is Jesus."

Sol smiled and said, "Well, Mrs. Brown, if he has touched your hand like this in this kitchen, then I just might convert."

Grandma Brown stood behind him and reached around his shoulders. She gave him a kiss on his cheek and said, "Never mind, Solomon. We love you just as you are. And I know that Jesus appreciates what you are doing for my Artie."

"Mrs. Brown," said Sol. "Artie, for me, is a Mitzvah. You and all these giant crazies, baritones and engineers — these Harmonicats and gnomes round these woods are Mitzvahs for me. You know, Mrs. Brown, I love my parents dearly and they are wonderful people, but they are just so normal. With you Browns and that big Greek family across the street, I never know what to expect. I never know if I am going to return home dead or alive, and it's so exciting as to what lays beyond the bourn. I am blessed to know you all."

I gave the yellow Sopwith Camel model to Papa Eudie that year and he was delighted, and I think a little surprised. With a smiling face, the plane in his left hand and me tucked beneath his massive right arm, laughing and squirming, he carried me into Anna's kitchen and set me down on her countertop. Then he proudly showed her my handy work.

I said, "Sol Rubenstein helped me just a little. Gosh, he's smart, know it?"

"Yes, Timoleon thinks he's pretty damn smart too, doesn't he, Mama," Papa said to Anna. I noticed he sent a pronounced wink in her direction, too.

Anna picked me up, giving me her usual bombardment of kisses and hugs. Then she sat me down to some fudge she'd made for me. Anna set me down on her table.

Terribly formally, I said,

"Mrs. Theocarides, thanks for the fudge. It was nice commiserating with you!"

I looked over at Papa and said his name formally, which I had never done before. "Mr. Theocarides It was nice commiserating with you too, sir. We can commemorate this commiseration a bit later, if you wish. Now I am going to commiserate with Sol Rubinstein. Gosh, Papa — now Sol really knows how to commiserate, and that's for sure."

I returned home to Grandmother's arms and she said, "Your Bumblebee is bleeding." She wiped Anna's bright red lipstick off my nose.

"Guess what, Grandma," I said. "Papa liked my airplane and he said it was the terror of the skies."

Grandmother enfolded me in her arms and I napped for a bit with the back of my head against her chest as we listened to Chopin.

Then Grandmother said, "Chopin was Polish too, just like our Sol." She paused. "And guess what." Now, this was the first time in my life I had ever heard my Grandma say "guess what", just like I always did. It tickled me and I started to laugh.

"What, Grandma?" I giggled. "What?"

"The pianist's name is someone named Arthur, just like you," she said. "And guess what," she repeated. "His last name is Rubinstein, just like our Sol's. What do you think about that?"

"Gosh, Grandma that's neat," I said. "It's 'commemorative.' I can't wait to tell Sol."

I finally went to sleep listening to Artur Rubinstein play the music of someone named Franz Liszt, playing his Transcendental Etudes. What a wonderful Christmas it had been!

Hmmm, I thought as I dozed off, *"Transcendental" —what a great new word.* I decided I'd ask Sol to help me look it up in my Funk book. I wondered if I could say "Transcendental Commiseration", or maybe

"Transcendental Commemoration"? Sol would know how to spell it, but now Grandmother's bosom was calling me to sleep.

Just before I dozed off I said, "Grandma, guess what. Artie Rubinstein is my new favorite piano player."

The laughter, music and teasing had come and gone. Christmas had come and gone too, and the Brown clan's pre-Christmas wealth had disappeared. My bumblebee had almost faded. Reality was upon us, and we were in financial trouble yet again. Grandma, more often than not, failed to pay the monthly rent on time — she was always about a week late, and 1947 was no exception. Because of Tufts' beating and the fevers, I was nearly blind in my left eye. I needed glasses, and possibly surgery, only that kind of money was nowhere to be found in our house.

Our rent had gone up from $7.50 to $9.75 per month; and the lumberyard had just recently begun charging triple for water, electricity and gas, raising our total monthly expenses to nearly sixteen dollars per month.

Grandma had high school and clothing expenses for Aunt Veve, plus and Uncle Harley's high school graduation, along with a great deal of other responsibilities I didn't know much about. My mother spent all her money on doctors, throwing away a fortune on protein powder in a desperate attempt to gain weight. Nothing worked. She also drank her money away in equal proportions as she tried to find a father for me somewhere. Jimmy said her favorite search location was the Casanova Restaurant on upper Sunset Boulevard — it yielded her favorite crop of men. ·

For the first time I could see real concern on Grandmother's face; and once, sitting on the front stoop, I caught her crying. As I sat silently beside her, I saw that she had developed boils on her hands from something; she had her eyes shut, and without saying anything, I reached over and kissed her sore hands folded across her lap. She startled a bit and straightened her dress and hair, and then she quickly wiped her face and smiled. Looking at me, she hugged me and said we had to put on a happy face. "God's watching us" she said.

Two hours later, when Uncle Fuzzy came by to work at his bench, I had him repaint the bumblebee on my nose with two more coats of indelible ink, telling him that Grandmother had told me to "put on a happy face." Fuzzy said he didn't think that was exactly what she meant, but he double-coated my nose anyway.

A funny thing happened — it was a brain fart, so to speak, and one that very nearly got out of hand. This variety of divine serendipity took root not as the result of a fine active mind (like, say, Papa Eudie's), nor the clever brain of the Mighty Duck. It wasn't from the great intellect of Sol Rubinstein either, but rather as the result of a combustible mind — the idle hands of an eight-year-old with a red funk dictionary and a very expensive pocket knife; just a boy with a fresh bumblebee painted on his nose and little else to recommend him.

Uncle Harley had previously explained to me the miracle and poetry of castration as he thumbed through his National Geographic magazines. On this day, my ponderous boredom had me laying on my back on the big swing, looking up through the branches of the pepper tree, commiserating with myself as I worked on my newest word: "commemorating". I was also toying with the idea of catching and castrating Gnome Exemplumonious, with the 'Bennis' end of my pocketknife, cutting his peppercorn and throwing nuts off — then commemorating their existence by putting them in Aunt Veve's purse, and later commiserating with anyone who would listen to me. But the gnome was elusive, and my thoughts went to asking about Eudie's circus experiences in Spain. I had heard stories of him through the grapevine and I wanted some verification.

Alas, Papa was burying a family today, and Grandma and Anna were working at Red Cross. Harley was in school. I had been sent home early with a note for my mother, for disrupting the class by running up and down the aisles and pretending I was a Stearman biplane, flying around the room passing gas. I claimed that the farting noises were exhaust from straining my radial engine while I was doing wingovers and outside loops at full throttle in the higher altitudes.

Furthermore, my teacher told me that the bumblebee on my nose made it difficult for students to concentrate on their schoolwork, and that two of them had even tried to paint a bumblebee on their own noses. In the note, she stated that she had one clown too many in her class already, and that she wanted to have a word with Mom before I could "fly my little bumblebee back into class". When Uncle Fuzzy heard about the note, he defended me to Grandmother saying, "Mom, Artie is just a trendsetter!"

Anyway, I was now safely at home, and it was terribly boring. Veve was home sick, reading her pulp romances. She was supposed to be watching me, but she was enthralled by her latest book, "Love on the Flying Trapeze". So she directed me to take our newest stray pup, whom I had named Bark Grable, out to play in traffic.

I had named the female pup not after Clark Gable, but after Betty Grable; but nobody except Sol appreciated my clever thought processes.

As I lay there thinking about the cover of Veve's pulp book, I got to thinking a good deal about circuses and how I could run one.

After considerable thought, I determined that my circus would be a combination of a circus and an air show, with plenty of Stearmans a few Wacos biplanes, a few P38s, and perhaps a few P47 Thunderbolts or a couple of P51s; my pilots would all be dressed as clowns, and they would all be instructed to perform only vertical Cuban eights as they moved downward toward school teachers, city officials and Reverend, Wall forcing them all "bite the dust" for the benefit of the screaming circus fans below.

I had talked with Harley about Papa Eudie's time in the Spanish Circus in his youth, when he would throw cannon balls with a net woven into his long hair. He used the net as a sling to hit targets in floating boats ten or so yards away by snapping his head as he tossed them. Maybe Papa would join my circus, or teach me how to do it with a baseball hooked to my head. Also, I could fold my own paper boats, making them quite large by using entire sheets of newspapers, and using them as targets for the balls I would toss.

Bark Grable was mostly white with a black spot around her front left paw, and a black fur mark just above her right eye. It made her left eye look like she was always winking. She was a lady in every way, never tearing or chewing furniture, nor did she ever make a mess where she shouldn't; and for this reason alone we all loved her. I loved her mostly because she was naturally silly and did tricks. With Sol's help, perhaps she and I could even do a circus act — this got me to thinking even more about the project.

Bark jumped up on the swing with me and started biting me on the nose to get my attention. Now, Harley and I once had a flea circus, so perhaps I could develop that idea, I thought. Gosh, ideas were whizzing in my head faster than I could handle. I was really getting smarter; and it was a bit frightening to me at first, but I got used to it. I could feel it stretching my brain more and more each day. I couldn't wait to tell Grandma Brown and Sol about my new ideas; I just knew that we could make a lot of money, and that Grandmother would never have to cry again.

I took Bark out to Harley's garage — he had left it unlocked, so we both entered. Harley had left his socks and dirty underwear in a pile, which Bark promptly gathered and moved neatly to the corner of Uncle's garage.

Meanwhile, I got into his cigar box, where I found twenty or so Mexican jumping beans. I held them in my hand as they popped up every few seconds. This got the pup's attention, and she came to me curious about the beans. I balanced one on top of her nose and repeated the task, just as Sol had once shown me with treats.

"Wait! Wait! Hold on, Bark. Not yet!" I said.

Then a bean jumped and Bark caught it in midair, swallowing it whole. She looked funny for a second, and then she briefly crossed her eyes. The next time, the bean flew into her nostril sending her dashing around Harley's lair, knocking over a magazine rack filled with his naughty girl magazines.

I picked everything up as best I could, and Bark and I got out of there in a hurry. This time I took Harley's padlock and clicked it shut.

"Shh!" I whispered to Bark. "Perhaps he won't notice we've been in here?" The expression on her little face was doubtful, and she stood at my feet with her tail between her legs.

Then Bark and I headed for the swing to reconnoiter and put our heads together to think about the circus. Why, the more I thought of this circus idea, the more excited I became. I swear, I finally got a glimpse of one of Pie Exemplumonious' eyes peering around one of the top branches, and I very slowly removed my Swiss army knife and opened its razor sharp blade, rubbing my thumb sideways as the sharp edge crackled against my skin. The gnome's eye disappeared in a hurry, and shortly thereafter an idea came to me for the name of my circus. It was clearly a vision. I would call it:

THE MEXICAN JUMPING BEAN CANNON BALL FLOATING FLYING FLAMING AND BURNING SPECTACULAR AEROBATIC DAREDEVIL FLEA AND CASTRATED GNOME CIRCUS

My mind wandered like a Butterfly on straight whiskey from one thing to the next. I knew it was my brain expanding almost hourly, and I felt ever so smart.

Now my fervent mind settled on suggesting to everyone that we should put on a circus right there on our property, to help with Grandmother's finances. And, who knew — maybe we'd find a husband for my mom and a daddy for me from the Casanova Club. *Gosh, what a great idea*, I thought to myself, and said so out loud to Bark Grable, who just tilted her head and raised her unibrow.

The more I thought of it, the more I was convinced. Besides, Sol had his own successful business, and he was only a few years older than me. I was sure he'd help us. Heck, he knew how to do everything, and guess what? Maybe if I could trick Papa into telling us about the circus, then I could get Sol to convince the big man's into showing some enthusiasm about the idea. This thought cheered me up considerably.

Grandmother used to tell us all that there was "an idea growing in the garden of your brain every second, if you can just nurture it." I felt something budding in my own garden and I was determined to see it grow, but first I needed to know some things, and vowed to corner Papa Eudie and Anna.

That day came slowly — but almost effortlessly — as though the gods of my strange musings and energy had designed it that way.

CHAPTER 29

Circus Trilogy
(Part Two: Hear Those
Giants Singing?)

F
OR A FEW days my fervor for a circus wavered from one of fanciful eight-year-old exuberance to one of childish self-pity and insecurity. I was, after all, a little kid; and in my misery I reminded myself of that as often as I could. *Why should anyone pay attention to my silly circus idea?* I reasoned. *Why should they take me seriously?*

I knew my idea was a good one, but those ideas fell mostly on deaf ears. Veve said I had seen too many Andy Hardy movies.

She was correct. She, Cousin Leslie and I had attended an all-day marathon of Mickey Rooney and Judy Garland movies at the Alcazar, and "putting on a show" was indeed the central theme of those films; so those movies were absolutely on my mind, especially when it came to my circus ideas. The adults changed the subject when I started my spiel, so soon I started to lose heart; but one day, unable to let my idea go, I lay on the big swing and pouted. That was when the gnome Exemplumonious pelted me in the head with a peppercorn or two; and for some reason, that made me remember how Mickey Rooney's Mickey Moran in "Babes In Arms" persisted in getting his gang together. Now it was my turn to go into action.

I just had to know more about circuses — I needed to know about Papa and his boyhood experiences in that Spanish circus. We had all spoken about asking Papa about his circus life, but the opportunity simply never seemed to present itself. Anna had told us a bit about it, and had even shown us some old photos of Papa winning some kind of foot race against a horse — and another photo of him throwing those cannon Balls with his long hair — and yet another old photo where he lifted twelve people off the ground from the center of a carrousel (she said that he slowly turned all the folks around 360 degrees, but we never got any other details), and I thought maybe that if I could corner Papa and tell him my ideas, then perhaps I could get the information I needed to bring my project to life. And also, to find out how circuses make money.

Sol, I figured, would surely go with me and help explain it. But as I lay there, fending off the gnomes' peppercorns and my own insecurities, I pondered my insurmountable problem: how to discuss circuses with people who could actually make them happen. If I got that far, how could I suggest that we all put on a circus? What would Mickey Moran do?

One afternoon, Sol and Grandmother were discussing the Old Testament scriptures as they often did; and as usual I had nothing whatsoever to add to that conversation, so in an effort to sound wise I repeated to Sol what Grandmother had told me — that people can have "an idea growing in the garden of (their) brain every second if (they) can just nurture it"; and of course, I brought up circuses yet again.

Sol and Grandmother looked at me funny, and then at each other. Sol paused and said something odd.

"Yes," he said, "but what one actually needs to nurture those ideas in that garden is fertilizer."

Now that made me laugh, because I knew that fertilizer was cow poop, and how could I put that on an idea inside my head? Gosh, Sol was strange. He made my brain hurt sometimes.

Before he left I broached the subject of my circus idea. Then he grabbed the briefcase he always carried and turned to leave. I thought he hadn't heard me, or maybe he'd just ignored me, but when I asked him where he was going, he said,"To get some Fertilizer."

Then he walked out the door.

I looked over at Grandmothers face, and could see that she also had no idea what he meant.

Confused, I ran back to thinking about how to get Papa thinking circus; but the more I thought about it, the more hopeless and far away it seemed to be. The adults were too busy for little boys with big dreams. Plus my Stearman engine was sputtering, which made me very close to anarchy.

But then fate intervened on my behalf. Eudocio's Brother came from Philadelphia to live in LA.

Who better to talk to than Papa's twin brother, who we knew was right there with him during his circus days?

Later in the week, Grandma and some of the Browns were across the street in the meditation garden, waiting to meet Anthanasios Theocarides for the first time.

After the brothers arrived in the garden, we followed them into the house; and there were introductions all around. The brothers could not have been more different. Except for the shape of their eyes, they looked nothing alike. Anthanasios, who the Theocarides family called "Uncle Ant", was completely bald, while Papa had a full head of thick, black hair. Ant was very tall too, just a couple inches shorter than Eudie, but he was thin and wiry. His eyes were as blue as the summer sky, while Papa Eudie's were black as coal. The thing the men did have in common was that neither seemed to age; both of them looked younger than Anna and Grandmother Brown, who in fact where nearly twenty years their junior. The brothers looked like happy young boys, laughing together from the moment they entered the garden. When we sat down, the normal adult conversations seemed to go on forever, and I couldn't wait to get to the good stuff. I was nervous, anxious and ready to talk circus;

but before I could say a word, Duck said something to the brothers in Greek, and they spoke for awhile. Anna joined in too.

Finally, Duck looked at Harley and me.

"Brownie, what did you and Artie want to know about the Spanish circus?" he asked.

Anna brought the brothers a large bottle of Armenian Vodka called Oghi. She brought everyone else pastries with coffee and milk, so we ate and dunked our food, listening to Eudie and Ant as they swigged the Vodka and chattered away.

Amazingly, we learned more in the next few hours about those brothers and their lives and history than we could have imagined. We learned more about circuses, giants and strong men by listening to their conversation than we would have had Harley asked a dozen questions. I was in heaven.

They came from a wealthy Greek family, where they grew up strong headed and often in trouble. From their banter, we learned that that their father believed that if he pulled his sons hair really hard twice everyday, then their hair would become extraordinarily strong. He also claimed that it would make them brilliant because according to their father, it stimulated blood flow to the brain. Both men laughed heartily at these memories. Ant often escaped those rituals by running away and hiding behind his mother's skirts, refusing to have his hair pulled while Eudie endured the daily torture for almost eight years. The end result brought another chuckle from the brothers. It seemed that Eudie, in his adulthood, could tie heavy weights to his long hair and lift them from the ground without losing a single hair. I'd even seen a photo of him pulling a train engine with several carloads of passengers waving out the windows; and he pulled the train 100 feet or so down the track via an attachment woven through his hair. Ant, on the other hand, told us he was completely bald by the age of twenty-four.

Eudocio said, "So, Baba was right on at least one account."

"Yes," And replied, "but don't you remember you were as dumb as a cow biscuit until your smarter, balder brother started tutoring you. Tell the truth, Eudocio!"

Papa had a big smile on his face and his eyes sparkled. He said something in Greek and his family all roared with laughter, and Duck slapped his knees in delight. The brothers teased each other for the next few hours, while the rest of us listened.

As they told their stories, they acted out each part, exaggerating every gesture. Occasionally they'd jump up exuberantly, sometimes shaking the floor with their energy as those events became more and more vivid to us.

As I listened to their lives unfold, I grinned from ear to ear, sitting there like a pup waiting for a bone.

Eudie and Ant were born on August 2nd, 1880, in the tiny village of Kechries, south of Corinth in Greece. They were both homeschooled by their mother when they were young; and put in the hands of the Catholic Christian Brothers, both were pinpointed as either military material or bound for the priesthood.

Ant joked, "I think Father and Mother wanted us to either kill people or bless them, but they insisted that we do one or the other — or both if possible."

"Yeah," said Eudie. "First kill them — then read them their last rights as they lay bleeding!"

The boys rebelled against the priesthood because they cared too much for women, alcohol and fighting; and they were also growing far too large, which proved problematic when it came to the military outfitting them as common soldiers.

In those days, military officers were purchased by contract by people with political connections, and at considerable cost. The family had to furnish all equipment and uniforms, and the boys' father did not wish to sacrifice good money. So in their teens, they were sent to the stone quarry to work out their "piss and vinegar". But it didn't work.

The lads were just two inches shy of seven feet tall by their sixteenth birthday. When they were eighteen, they left home against their parents wishes and traveled to Turkey. Both had been trained their entire lives in pugilism and Greco Roman wrestling, thanks to the knowledge of their warrior father. They became boxers and wrestlers for hire through a Turkish gambling syndicate, who provided them with a great deal of women and money. By the time they finished growing, another two years had passed, and they were constantly in some kind of trouble with their Turkish benefactor, a local crime head named Osgur al Saglam. The trouble really started because they had both been undefeated for more than a year. Osgur ordered them to throw their next fight and placed a large wager against them. The boys, however, got drunk as skunks, and in order to impress two young French women, they beat the living hell out of their Turkish opponents. They'd forgotten to warn Osqur of their plan.

Osgur al Saglam lost a small fortune and sent six cutthroat henchman to find the brothers.

"Kill those goddamned Greeks," he ordered, "and show no mercy. When they are dead, cut off their heads and piss in their eyes. Then bring their skulls too me. Tell them just before they die that Osgur al Saglam bin Farouk is not to be trifled with."

Two of Saglam's henchmen met Allah in paradise that day at Eudocio's invitation, and a third received a broken arm and cracked skull. Ant had torn a large Turkish knife out of his hand, stabbing his attacker in the ass with his own blade. The brothers laughed and refilled their Oghi before moving on.

Leaving Saglam in 1902, the brothers made their way to Madrid, Spain and out of harm's way. The next thing they knew, they'd joined a circus.

The circus was called; "Severinno de La O's Circ De Doce Camisas". It was a one-ring circus, run by a cantankerous Scotsman from the Pampas of Argentina. The circus had a Trapeze act, one old toothless lion and a young elephant; plus ten sideshow booths and a horse riding act from Romania.

I sat there, fascinated, but I still hadn't learned a thing that could help me rescue Grandmother and Mom. I was learning things, but most of those things I had no real interest in, and the rest I simply didn't understand. Anna said something about the twins being fraternal, calling them "non-pathological giants". Harley noticed me squirming and explained that Anna meant the brothers were born at the same time, only they didn't look too much alike. He went on to tell me that "non-pathological" meant that the boys were big because their families were too, so it wasn't the result of abnormal pituitary growth. I really couldn't grasp that very well either, since I thought it seemed obvious that their mother and father were really big too. After all, I mused, Grandmother was small, and so were my aunts Eddie, Veve and Carole. Any other explanation would have seemed rather silly to me, not to mention the fact that the whole idea of procreation still confused me.

"I'll explain to you later, fartnick," said Harley.

I didn't care. I just wanted to know when we could start our own circus, and how a person built a circus. I wanted to know how much money we might make too.

Finally, the conversation grew more interesting. We learned that Papa and Ant worked as walking advertisements for the circus. They wore huge headdresses and enormous shoes, both of which left them nearly nine feet tall. All their costuming and platforming were designed to exaggerate; and according to Ant, it worked — they brought in customers in great numbers as they walked around town, telling people about the circus. They often left with two young women, one in each arm, and walked them down the street. The children were fascinated by the boys' great heights, while the women swooned over the Spanish love songs they'd sing in perfect harmony. The boys became very popular with the young señoritas. Ant's eyes sparkled, remembering, and he said, "The Spanish men did not appreciate our efforts quite so much."

Papa did work briefly as a Strongman, bending spikes and large nails, twisting iron bars around his neck — all the usual fare. Amazingly Papa could lift and press his brother into a hand-to-hand handstand. There were no photos of that, but it must have been a stunning feat as they made themselves into a gymnastic tower nearly twenty feet high, from the ground to the tip of Ant's pointed toes.

Over the course of their conversation, I decided that Papa's success in the circus was the result of four factors:

The first was his ability to run long distances and keep his huge mass in motion for hours at a time. Ant said that Papa was indefatigable. I

261

didn't know what that meant at the time, but I planned on looking it up as soon as I could. Papa's endurance must have been extraordinary. He raced long distances against local contenders; once he even beat a horse on a measured course. He told us he was never fast and that he did not run for speed, but only for distance and consistency of pace.

The next thing that interested me was that one of his circus acts was that Papa would run beside an elephant with a saddle, and then he'd jump up on it, mounting it like a cowboy. This, according to Ant, brought down the house; and of course sometimes Papa would do this with "Pico" the dwarf mounted on his shoulders, hanging on to his long hair with one hand and a tiny whip or pistol in the other.

The third thing that Papa was famous for, according to Ant, was that he could throw stones with astounding accuracy. Ant said Papa rarely lost to his throwing contenders, and that his aim and power proved lethal at less than 60 feet. In fact, Papa could throw stones through a double sheet of tin.

Ultimately, Papa's claim to fame was that the circus sold cheap plates with an imprint of Papa's hand. They showed the enormity of his hand, which was more than twice the size of a normal man's hand. The plates read *Circ de doce Camisas, Madrid España* in the top right corner, and apparently they sold like hotcakes.

"Papa, I thought you were just a strongman in that Circus," said Harley.

"Well, my jobs varied depending on what the big Scot needed," said Papa. "Ant and I shoveled horse and elephant manure too. But Ant and I knew some of the greatest strongmen in the world. The strongest of them all was a fellow by the name of Stanley Zybszki, who was about five-eight, and could lift several times his own weight in a deadlift. He once grabbed me round my knees, bear hugging my legs, and lifted me a foot or so off the ground. And in those days I was a muscular 575 pounds or so.

"Stanley was a Greco Roman wrestler on the world stage, but he refused to wrestle me for any amount of money, which was just fine with me."

"Was he as strong as you and Ant, Papa?" Harley said.

"Well Thomas, people don't really know about strength. They'll often confuse it with size. But real strength is different."

Ant looked at Harley and Duck and said, "Let's put it this way: Who is the stronger an Elephant, a man who can lift his own weight or a mouse who can lift ten times his own weight?"

"Or a red ant who can lift fifty times its weight?" added Papa.

I remember that it was then and there, in that simple exchange, that I understood the notion of strength. And at only eight years old!

"True strength must be qualified," Papa said.

Since our talk, I look at physical strength in a totally different way.

We learned that Ant had knocked Papa out when they fought over a lovely Flyer in the Trapeze act. They had both been drinking, and Papa told Anthanasios to "choose his weapon". Ant chose boxing and knocked Eudie out cold, or so he said. Papa said the rest was a blur.

The boys were forced to leave Circ De Doce Camisas when officials learned that they compromising the skills of two female trapeze artists. They missed many a catch as the result of nightly trysts with the brothers.

The Scotsman, who was disgusted with the boys' debauchery, ordered them to leave.

"But you guys where tougher than he was, right Papa?" I asked.

"Well Artie, maybe, but he was right," said Papa. "We were way out of bounds in those days. We drank way too much, and we were young and acted it. We were just plain arrogant and rude, and to tell you the truth, Whisker, I wouldn't have wanted to find out whether we were tougher than that leather-faced Scot. Would you, Ant?"

"Hell, I would have rather faced Saglam's killer thugs again than fight that rock headed Scotsman. I remember he nearly cut his right hand off on some equipment, and he stitched it up himself with his good hand. Then he worked a full day the next day; and it was rumored by the circus folk that in the Argentine Pampas he had once killed a full grown bull with a single blow to its head. I don't think our exploits or bravado impressed him all that much, or that he was a bit afraid of us. Do you, Eudocio?"

"Don't think so! We hadn't had the chance to tell him how terribly frightful and magnificent we were, now did we?" Eudie said.

"Why hell, he wouldn't have listened anyway," said Ant. "And brother of mine, lord knows we needed an ass kicking. That's for sure — the old Scot's Gaucho might have just done it if he'd fought us one at a time."

Hearing this, Eudie slapped his brother on the shoulder and said, "Hell, you damned bald fool — if it had come to that, I would have just pushed you on top of him and gotten the hell out of España. Never to return for your broken body!"

The boys left the circus sometime in 1904, wandering for a couple years around Europe and the Middle East, getting into considerable trouble in almost every country they visited. Finally, in disgust, their father laid down the law, telling them in no uncertain terms that they could either pursue a military career or get an education — or else! They both opted for the latter and attended university abroad.

Ant went off to Paris to attended the Collège de Sorbonne, studying law. Eudocio, with the help of his father's influence, managed to get into Cambridge, where he studied business, philosophy and music. In 1910 they both graduated with honors, only to become the apple of their parents' eyes — finally. Ant moved to Philadelphia, while Eudie had fallen in love. He moved to the small village of his beloved, at the foot of Mt. Ararat in Armenia.

Five minutes before the little conclave concluded, Sol Rubinstein walked in the door, briefcase in hand, and sat down next to me.

"Hi Sol," I said. "Whatcha got in your briefcase?"

"Fertilizer," he said, winking at me.

"Really?" I asked.

"Really," he said, opening his briefcase and handing me a little wad of tin foil. I unwrapped it and found — to my amazement — that the pinch of fertilizer was just like the kind my grandma used in her garden. Sol said softly, "Now put that in your pocket next to your chunk of Tar and hold tight."

Pointing to a group of papers in his case, he said, "I am about ready to show these gentlepeople some Circus Fertilizer."

That was when Anna introduced Sol to Ant.

Sol knew nothing of our previous hours of conversation, but within the next ten minutes he described his plan for a circus or carnival project to take place on the Brown property. My mouth hung open; as I looked around the room I found absolutely no resistance to this sixteen-year-old boy's suggestions. No one ignored Sol, nor did they protest or change the subject. I supposed the reason they hadn't listened to me, yet accepted his ideas might have had something to do with his having gone to that Bar Mitzvah, where he drank with those adults a few years earlier, when someone told him he'd become a man. Sol opened his briefcase and showed the adults loan papers from Papa's very own savings and loan company, signed by Papa's friend and general manager Yahudi Edelstein. The documents were cosigned by Sol's father.

They all agreed to have several other meetings to prepare for the actual event. Grandmother, Anna, Eudie and Ant would be on something called The Steering Committee. The rest of us were to be what he called "Kid Power". Before Sol left, briefcase in hand, he asked me about how my conversation about the circus had gone over with Ant and Papa Eudie.

"Transcendental!" I said.

When I got home, I sat on Grandmother's lap and showed her my foil of cow manure. She asked what it was.

"It's circus fertilizer for my brain," I said.

"My, my," she said. "First it's tar and now this. What ever in the world will you think of next?"

CHAPTER 30

Circus Trilogy
(Part Three: Babes in Arms)

W E WERE "BABES In Arms", just like in the movie. And Sol was our Mickey Moran.

I was the nearly uncontrollable boy in our gang, with a mouth like a treadmill. After several meetings, we decided to call the event "The Brown Festival and Fair". This disappointed me, so I said that since it was my idea in the first place, it should be called:

THE MEXICAN JUMPING BEAN CANNON BALL FLOATING AND FLYING FLAMING AND BURNING SPECTACULAR AEROBATIC DAREDEVIL FLEA AND CASTRATED GNOME CIRCUS.

As I sat on Grandmother's lap, with my back resting on her chest, I listened to the adult plans and pouted. She hugged me to her bosom, and as she patted me on the chest, she whispered in my ear that while my idea was certainly the most descriptive name for the event, she thought that it would be too many words for Uncle Fuzzy to fit on his poster. The printers might run out of ink, she explained.

I thought about it logically and agreed with Grandma.

As the adults' ideas unfolded I became quite excited. But at the beginning there was just a lot of boring stuff, like building toilets for the crowds, a task that was assigned to Uncle Harley.

Reverend Wall had volunteered a Chautauqua tent with the caveat in which he could pass out leaflets about being saved, and about his future Sunday services.

Then there were the city permits, which cost nine dollars for a single day and more for electricity that had run from the pole on Clarkson Street into a temporary junction box behind Harley's Garage. We needed extra electricity for the ice cream freezers, ice machines for snow cones and other devices Sol had rented for the day.

The glee clubs from Huntington Park and South Gate high schools agreed to come and perform show tunes on the rented collapsible outdoor stage. The Duck had arranged to rent a sound system from Bell High School. And Grandmother invited Major Drew Ponderborst from the Salvation Army to bring his red tripod collection pot and his quintet to provide music near the tent entrance, stating that her son Jimmy would play his trumpet along with them. Sol had lined up more than a dozen musical and dramatic acts to perform outside the tent on the main stage by the big Pepper Tree, and the Venice High School Champion Gymnastics team would do a demonstration on the high and the parallel bars, plus a tumbling demonstration.

The First Baptist Church loaned two hundred folding chairs for the event, and there were at least fifteen other food and novelty vendors from the surrounding cities.

I listened to the adults on our steering committee, honing and refining their objectives. I was busy organizing vendors and booth locations; ideas were coming fast and furious, and by this time Walter Crawford, our family's thirteen-year-old engineer, was on hand. I could scarcely believe that my idea was coming to life right before my eyes.

Eudie and Ant, given their age, decided to do what they had done as young men in the Spanish circus, and that was to just walk around exaggerating their height to the maximum. Papa looked at me and said to the group, "Squirt and I can walk around town and we can pass out our flyers from his Eagle's Nest."

HOLY MOLEY!

"We can?" I said out loud. "Aren't you and Ant going to those handstands and bend nails and stuff, and lift heavy things like you did in the Spain?'

"Not this time, Whisker", Papa said. He adding, "That ship has sailed, but we can still be tall." Papa winked at his brother. "You can be our dwarf, riding on our shoulders during the add campaign. That is, if you want to."

"Wow! Do I ever," I said. "And can I put Bark Grable on my back as my dwarf?"

Papa nodded approvingly. I started to wonder what my own act in the circus would be, and whether Bark and I would do our tricks in the main tent or on the main stage outside. I decided to ask Sol and Walt if they had any ideas.

Theo, a flight instructor at the Hollywood Burbank Airport, said that he couldn't promise anything, but that a war buddy of his had just bought a surplus World War II airplane, and that he would see if he could arrange a midday flyover, if the festival could split the cost of aviation fuel. I saw Sol doing some math on his pad, then tentatively nod his head in approval. I could not sleep that night and bunked with Uncle Harley in his loft bed, asking him endless questions.

"Uncle Harley, What does omnipotent mean"

"Doesn't it tell you in your big red dictionary?"

"Yeah, but I still don't understand exactly what it means."

"Well Fartster, it means that you feel GOD DAMNED powerful!"

"Really?"

"Yep, now go to sleep. I suspect that's not a word that you will need to use anytime soon."

"Harley, would Grandmother wash out my mouth with lava if I said omnipotent?"

"No, but she would if you said *god damned*. And if you don't roll-over and go to sleep, I'll fart you into oblivion — that'll be a new 'o' word for you."

I started in with another question about the word oblivion and he pulled the blanket up over my head, bombarding me with flatulence of the ripest kind to shut me. That forced me out of the bed and down to the cot below, away from the rank smell and closer to the merciful knotholes bringing in fresh air through the plank siding.

Over the following days Sol and other family members met at odd hours because life went on, and everyone still had to work their regular jobs. Sol took charge of everything; he took notes of every detail and established a budget and work order schedule. Sol gave us sixteen days to bring it together, suggesting that we each oversee a particular function, and submit all our information to Uncle Fuzzy for the master poster and flyers.

One afternoon I watched Uncle Harley building the outhouses near the side of our property beside the lumberyard fence. He and Duck had dug four holes, a yard or so deep, and Harley constructed plank style outhouses lined with old newspapers on the inside for privacy. While Harley was putting the finishing touches on his toilets Grandmother, Walt and I where admired his handiwork. He opened the door to one of the ladies' outhouses and demonstrated his carpentry, pointing to the toilet seat benches and openings with a flurry of the forearm and palm of his hand... "Voilà" he said to Grandmother, who nodded her head in approval but commented,

"Nice work Thomas, but aren't the holes a bit too large?"

"No Mother. I made a template and figured that one asshole fits all!"

Grandmother's eyes lit up and she smacked him gently across the back of his head saying, "Harley Thomas Brown... honestly!"

Harley said, winking at Walter, "No Mom, I wasn't cussing, honest. You see... *asshole* is a descriptive plumber's term referring to the entire apparatus, I just wanted to make an opening that fit everyone's fannies."

Mother Brown smacked him again and Walter the engineer laughed and rolled his eyes as Harley jumped back.

"Apparatus" stuck to my brain. I had another delicious word.

Eventually, Harley built and Fuzzy posted cartoon characters of Lil' Abner and Daisy Mae on the doors, two for ladies and two for the gents.

Everyday we completed something. It was determined that within the tent there would be a dozen or more folding tables available to vendors. The committee rented all those spaces within a couple of days and had a long waiting list. Mother Brown was delighted, and planned to use Anna's modern double oven and stove in the early morning, just before the event, to bake her fresh pies and cakes.

Sol had his bench set up where on one side he sold his jewelry and gold leaf foil boats, and next to he set up a card table with a chessboard. He also displayed a freestanding sign that stated he would take on all those who were willing to pay fifty cents per game to play, but stood to win three dollars if they could stalemate him, and seven dollars if they could check mate him. They were promised of fifty dollars if they could checkmate him in ten moves or less. Sol used a double chess clock — set at move intervals of ten seconds per move — and if either player ran long on the moves, he would forfeit to his opponent.

Anna and Mother Brown had a table full of various candies on one side and doilies and needlework on the other. Grandmother decided to wear a white apron and a large puffy chef's hat with "Mrs. Brown" embroidered on its wide brim, while Anna would be a cowgirl and charm the crowd outside.

As the days went by I had great fun watching, but I grew concerned that I had no real act for the circus; plus my bumblebee was starting to fade again. My mind was taken off my concerns when Ant asked me if I would like to ride on his shoulders and pass out flyers. At first I was resistant to mount a new steed, but Papa assured me that it would be okay. As I mounted Ant, I realized as he sat me down on his shoulders that he had no hair to hang onto, but he held my ankles as we walked. It was great fun, but I noticed right away that my new horse's gait was slightly different from Papa's; and as we walked under the awning of the State Theater, I couldn't quite reach the awning as I had with Papa, although no other person that I could see was as tall as Ant. I still felt powerful up there in the air. We passed out flyers for an hour or so, twice that day, and I noticed that on the flyer it said: "THE BELL CIRCUS BAZAAR". On the back side of the flyer, where sponsors including the Atlantic Lumber Company, the Suekeetcher's Drug Store and Soda Fountain and Papa's Olympus Savings and Loan businesses advertised their services; and I smiled when I saw a sketch of Sol's golden foil fold boat and necklace design with his booth information, plus a blurb about his chess challenge.

"Anthanasios," I asked. "How come they changed the name to Bell Bazaar?"

"Well, Artie, I think Mrs. Brown suggested that more people would be attracted to the name of the city than by the last name of her little clan. She thought it would be a bit more commercial."

"Hmmmm," I said.

On our first walk that day, Mrs. Manfrianni ran directly into, Ant almost knocking herself down in the process. Ant reached down to stabilize the old woman, who looked straight up at me and said,"Why das ah you little Marty."

Then she squinted up at Ant and said,

"Mr. Theo you no looka so to good. Whatsa happen ah you hair?"

I couldn't help but laugh, and hearing me she squinted her eyes at us both and said, "Mr. Theo, I tinka you gonna be sick you losta so much weight. What appen ah you?"

Ant explained to her that she was confusing him with his brother and she exclaimed, "Oh my goodness. I'mah so confuse. How can ah be two socha big a boys 'n now yousa gallop horse for little Marty too, eh? Whatcha doin witha dose ah annuncios?"

Ant handed her a Flyer and said, "Ma'am, this is to tell folks about our little fair the Saturday after next. Please tell all your friends to attend. Admission is free."

"Atsa goodah price fo shu, maybe I gona come and bringah my friend Mr. Boescher." She turned to leave and then looked back up at me and said, "Marty, you be cahfull upah dare ona disa big new pony 'n dontah breck yu neck!'

"Okay, Mrs. Manfrianni. Well, see you at the Circus," I said as she walked off grumbling something and waiving goodbye with the back of her hand.

"Strange little lady," said Ant. "How come she calls you Marty?'

"She just does. I guess she like the name Marty better. That's just Mrs. Manfrianni"

"Humph," Ant said.

The so-called bazaar came together bit by bit; the construction went slowly but smoothly, well in time for opening day — with the exception of what Sol Rubinstein later called "Walter's Waterloo".

About nine days before the event I had asked what my act would be. No one but me was impressed with Bark Grable's tricks, so Walt designed a gadget that would set up on a double pulley running from the highest point on backside, around the front of the house and down past the side of Harley's garage, falling to earth on the front corner of the garage. Harley built it, although the contraption was Walter's brain child. It ran a distance of eighty five feet and dropped from a height of about thirteen feet, from the front house down to about a foot-and-a-half. Its design was intended to hook a towhead by the back of his britches, enabling him to glide slowly down face-first. Over the PA Walt would announce the "Bell Bazaar Spectacular Bumblebee Stearman Air Show, featuring the candy bomber Stearmanboy". He told me — to my delight — that he would announce my flights as "Lieutenant Colonel Arthur 'Bumbles' Spelman". Walt said he thought it would add a nice touch.

Duck and Harley had built me a little costume as close as possible to the Fuzzy's "Stearmanboy" cartoon, with tail feathers and little wings, plus goggles and a leather helmet. I'd wear rollerskates too, of all things, for landing gears, which everybody found most humorous and colorful. The costume took me twenty-five minutes to get into and was really uncomfortable to wear. I told Walt I didn't want to do the act because Anna had those "devil's cards", and they'd foreseen the possibility of something dark in store for our Bazaar. I didn't wish to be the losing hand of what Grandma Brown called her "devil's solitaire".

Walt assured me that his plan was foolproof, and that Anna was just a superstitious Romanian Gypsy. Grandmother Brown was against it and was concerned. Walt overcame her objections with calm logic and engineering principles as he always had, and assured her that I would be just fine, and that my flight was a business promotion as well as a means of entertaining the masses; because dropping penny candies down on the milling throngs of children below would bring laughter and great joy. My flights would consist of just three or four of such trips. When I was done I would be free and loose to run and pester everyone.

Grandmother thought about it but was very uneasy, particularly when she saw Sol rolling his eyes at the presentation of Walt's master plan. Now Walt was bright, and he finally convinced them both that on each of my proposed flights, a few of the candies would contain a prize token good for one of Grandmother's cookies or Anna's candies. Looking at Sol, Walt said matter-of-factly,

"You see, this will draw people inside the tent and increase sales." When I saw that Sol was convinced, then I became convinced too, but I could still see doubt on Grandmother's face.

Grandmother finally compromised, telling Walt that he must test his contraption first. Walter earnestly agreed and within an hour, after giving the pulleys a good greasing, he hooked me to it. Though I insisted I wasn't going to put that stupid costume on for the test. Walter agreed but was adamant that I — at least for the test run — put the skates on for weight and balance. As I sat on the edge of the departure point on the crown of the roof, I reluctantly put on the skates and hooked myself up as I had been shown. Walter assured me that he would control the speed of my descent with a fulcrum lever he had attached to his pulley system, gently stopping me at the end so I could "Float like angel over the cheering crowd!"

Sitting on the precipice, I awaited Walter's signal as he stood looking up to me from the corner of the garage below. Finally he waived and yelled, "Jump!"

I jumped, gliding down the wire at terminal velocity. Everything was a speeding blur as I spun around on Walt's swivel connector, out of control and feet first as the crotch of my pants pulled my poor nuts up to my shoulder blades, and I crashed like a ton of bricks into the corner of the garage, entirely missing the mattress. I'd intended to cushion the landing crashing into the corner of the garage with one leg on one side and one leg on the other, almost breaking my spine by forcing me into the air. One of my skates flew off and hit me in the head, giving me a black eye and knocking me unconscious in the process. When I woke up in the hospital, I had broken my left shin bone, ankle and four toes on my right foot. The landing had taken a good deal of the skin on my upper thighs and I was unconscious for nearly half an hour.

The hospital set my lower left leg and put it into a plaster cast from kneecap to ankle. I heard in the hospital that Grandmother almost beat Walter to death with her fly flap. Fortunately for him, Grandmother struck him harmlessly, but only because she couldn't find anything heavier to hit him with. "That damned impotent fly swatter!" she yelled at him, screaming that she'd wanted him to test the fool device with a bag of flour or a sack of potatoes, and not with Artie.

Walter didn't come around for a couple of days.

I was out of commission for a little under a week, but the activity went on. I had a little set of crutches and Papa, Ant, Anna and Duck all split the duties for what they called the TTS, or "Towhead Transportation Service", by carrying me about the grounds.

Because of my cast I couldn't get around very well, and when I tried to move about the large property my crutches got stuck in the dirt and I fell a lot. I was in considerable pain because of my constant falling and my broken toes, which felt like throbbing hot marbles. I couldn't switch my weight from one leg to the other or balance very well, either. Plus my thighs felt like two giant boils, but I didn't say anything because I was afraid Grandma would ground me and I would miss everything. She had a hard time keeping me down.

Finally they suggested that I ride on the men's shoulders passing out flyers. So over the next few days I rode a half-dozen rides or more on my two Greek stallions. It was great fun, and I couldn't wait to saddle up with either of them, but I winced as my wounded thighs chafed against their broad necks.

On one of our last walks I was with Papa, who asked me if my leg was okay. I assured him I was as good as new. Then he swung me up into the eagle's nest and we walked fifty blocks, all the way up Gage Avenue to the city line, and onto Main Street in Huntington Park, passing out flyers for our Bazaar. I handed out a couple dozen of my foil boats to the people I liked and gave the giddy up to Papa's hair when I didn't like the cut of someone's jib. My horse read my mind perfectly and we galloped on to more receptive pastures.

As we walked and chatted Papa said, "Whisker, do you have any new words from your big Funk dictionary for Papa?"

"Yep, I have been reading in the 'n' words lately, some "o" words too, but the one I like best is "nomenclature. Do you know what that means, Papa?"

"Yes, I think so," he said.

"But guess what, Papa," I said. "I am okay when I look them up in my dictionary but sometimes I just hear the words somewhere and don't know how to spell very well. And darn it, sometimes they confuse me.

"So guess what, Papa. I just use them anyway until someone corrects me. Then I figure them out and then I know, See... that's a neat trick, huh?"

"You're a pretty smart boy," said Papa. "I'd say that's a darn fine trick."

We walked a long way that day, a distance of more than nine miles. As we turned onto Main Street a really pretty lady stopped Papa and took some flyers. Batting her eyes, she said, "How tall are you, Handsome?"

I noticed the music in her voice sounded a lot like a purring cat. Papa never answered that question, although I had heard it asked from my perch many times before. Papa had told me it was the plague of the tall. He looked down at the woman and said cheerfully, "I am taller than a cloud and a little shorter than a star. I am taller than a Munchkin but shorter than a man who is two inches taller than I am."

"Well, you are a good looking man, and that's for sure," the pretty woman continued, smiling as she reached up to touch his elbow. She held it there for a good while, and rolling her eyes she said, "Will I see you two handsome devils at this bazaar?"

I answered for Papa and I spoke without taking a breath. "Gosh, yes. He'll be there, and guess what? He'll be even taller than he is right now. Know why? Because, see, he's got some big high thick boots that were made just for him. He'll wear a Mexican Bandito's hat too, so he'll be even taller and even handsomer than he is right now. And guess what? He's going to carry two big guns. Huh, Papa?" I looked at Papa, then turned back to the woman. "So bring your friends and come look at him and maybe he'll show you his pistol."

She said, "Well, that's the best offer I've had today. I'd love to see his pistol. I'll see you big boys there, then."

As she turned to walk away she blew us a kiss, and I noticed that she winked at us and that she was walking funny.

I said to Papa,

"I think she had something in her eyes. Did you see her blinking them, trying to get it out? Something was wrong with her hips, Papa, did you see that? Perhaps her apparatus is broken. She kept looking back at us, Papa, but I think she liked us. Don't you?"

"She might have, Artie, she might have," said Papa. "But my mother always told me to beware of women with broken or hungry apparatuses."

"Really, Papa?" I asked. "Why do you suppose she told you that?"

"Don't know, really," he sighed. "Mother just said that a hungry or injured Apparatus could shrivel my grapes. So as you grow up, Artie, I suggest that you remember that; and when you see a lady with wiggly hips like that, and batting her eyes, just turn away and run."

"I will, Papa!" I said.

Now I had no idea whatsoever about those kinds of subtleties, since that was word I had heard from Harley in conversation about the out-houses and not from my Wilfred J. Funk dictionary. But I learned a great deal about the word "Apparatus" from Papa.

"Papa, does Anna have an Apparatus?" I asked.

"Oh my, yes, she has a lovely one," he said.

"Papa, does everyone have one?"

"I suppose so," Papa said.

"Papa, perhaps that Lady just had some faulty squeak in her nomenclature," I said thoughtfully, adding my "n' word to impress him. I waited for his reaction.

Eudie didn't answer and I felt a tremor under the saddle of Papa's shoulders and neck as we walked, and I spoke into the top of his head as if one of his ears was located there.

I said, "Papa, are you chuckling?"

He still didn't answer.

"Papa, are you tickled about something?"

Finally he blurted it out: "Yes, Artie. Papa's tickled."

I started laughing with him but didn't know why.

"Why are we laughing, Papa?" I asked.

"Artie, we are laughing because you are the whisker of old Papa's heart, and you bring me so much joy, and I have so much fun while we are walking together. You are the strangest, funniest kid and we have fun together, don't we?"

"Gosh, yes, Papa," I said, "it's practically transcendental. But Papa, guess what. My leg hurts just a little bit and my cast is all itchy. My toes throb. Do you suppose we could go have a banana split and an aspirin and just rest for a short minute?"

"Great idea! Let's take the streetcar back home to Suekeetchers and we can see your Momma," Papa said.

"Papa," I asked as we looked for a streetcar stop. "How come you named your drugstore and soda fountain Suekeetchers?"

"Well, Tim thinks I named it after the dog Ant and I had when we were boys in Corinth, but I named it after an English widow who lived in our village. She was a confectioner and always gave us treats."

"Wow, Papa. Was she neat?"

"Yes indeed, she was neat and more. Actually she reminded me a lot of your Grandmother Brown; she was the salt of the earth, one of the loveliest people I ever knew."

We caught the yellow streetcar and headed home.

Now we were all used to Papa's Mass; you see, we had all grown up with him in our line of vision. He was family to the Browns. He was like a big ole Saint Bernard among Chihuahuas, and after awhile you just see them all running in a field or in a family, as a regular herd no matter how irregular they might be. And you just get used to them, but when any of us were in close quarters with the Theocarides — but in particular with Papa — out in public, it became crystal clear that they were not regular in any sense of the word.

When the streetcars opened their doors, Papa dismounted me without taking a single step. He bent over, stuck his head in the bi-fold doors like a cat looking into a canary's cage and deposited me around the pole onto the long bench on the wall next to the door. Papa had to take his time boarding. In tight situations, he had to twist his wide body nearly sideways, struggling to enter most normal doors. And the street car door was neither tall nor wide, and so when he entered the streetcar he had stand briefly and then bend over a great deal, as the back of his head could easily hit the ceiling of the trolley. He dropped our two dimes in the money meter and took a seat just behind the bench where he'd set me down. Papa sat on the first double seat on the passenger side, taking both seats. He reached over to me on the bench, and like a bear scooping up a bullfrog, he picked me up and sat me comfortably on his lap. I could see the gaping mouths and startled faces of the passengers in the conductor's rear view mirror.

A couple of stops later, four passengers got on, and turning to Papa in the front seat, they nearly tripped over themselves.

"Pssst... Papa," I whispered. "Guess what? I feel omnipotent when I am with you... you know it?"

Eudie said nothing but he chuckled a little bit, patted me gently on the back and hugged me as we rode along, clickety-clacking towards home. Once again I was big and very proud and strong.

"Are you tired, Whisker"?

"A little bit, Papa, but just let me get a sundae and I'll be okay. Besides, we have a few more flyers to pass out."

As we walked from the streetcar toward the drug store I said, "Papa, I feel my heart beating in my toes!"

We ordered our ice cream and all I remember was taking a single bite. I was really sleepy and a bit dizzy, so when my face fell into the banana split it wasn't a surprise. When I awoke I was in Grandmother's arms and she was smiling down at me.

"Artie, how come you didn't tell Papa you were in such pain?"

"Gosh Grandma," I said. "I didn't want our walk to end so I just ignored it because I was laughing so hard. Besides, how are we going to get me a daddy or get you out of debt if we don't give out those flyers? And guess what, Grandma. I learned about hungry apparatuses and shriveling grapes and ladies with bats in their eyes. I even told Papa a new word.

"See, when we had our sundaes we were talking about Walt and Sol and words and engineering. Just before I got sleepy. The new word, well, see, the word was 'nomenclature'. I think it means 'parts of things'. Guess what I learned?"

"I can't imagine," Grandma said.

"Papa said you were as sweet as salt and during our walk I told Papa he was my Mitzvah and he told me I was a whisker on his own heart, and I told Papa that you and he are the nomenclature in the happy part of my own hairy heart. Grandma, guess what?" I continued. "It's neat about words, huh? Gosh, I love so many things: words, airplanes and you. Guess what? Papa Eudie said we were all transcendental and he told me what that meant. Grandmother, do you think I will ever be as smart as Sol or Papa?"

Before she could answer I asked, "Grandma, do you have little hairs on your heart like you do on your chin?"

Grandmother kissed my forehead said, "My, my," she said. "No, but I will soon because when I hold you in my arms I feel something growing there."

I fell asleep again.

The big day came and the circus began at 8:00 a.m.

No one came.

All the participants, vendors, musicians, security and high school helpers — about thirty-five in all — were there twiddling their thumbs, but no one entered. Both the Atlantic entrance and the Clarkson Street side entrance were deserted. There was a large sign on each entrance that said **BAZAAR TODAY - FREE ADMISSION**, but no one came. Not a soul.

Sol and Papa Eudie were expressionless as they talked quietly. The rest of the steering committee had looks of disaster and doom written across their faces.

Almost an hour and a half later, two or three people started to trickle in on the Clarkson Street side of the event; then a few more, and finally more still. Then finally, the Bell High School Marching Band bus stopped on Atlantic and the entire band began to play. Then all hell broke lose, and there were people milling about everywhere. Cars parked on both sides of Atlantic Boulevard, all the way up to Randolph Street. The tent was full; vendors where breaking out more merchandise. Uncle Paul fired up the grill and aunts Eddie and Veve manned the hot dog stand and the ice cream wagon. Food, drink and merchandise went out by the bushel. The Bazaar was rolling along and Sol had a big smile on his face. It wasn't the circus I had envisioned but it was grand fun in ways I would never have imagined. Everyone was busy and happy and I saw lots of money changing hands.

The biggest Stars of all were Eudie and Ant, who were dressed in their tall costumes.

Papa was dressed like a Mexican bandit with two very large pistols, one on each hip. He had bandoleros of ammunition crossing his massive chest in every direction ,and his special new boots lifted him another three inches toward the sky. He was magnificent and both his Brother Ant and his wife Anna where near his equal and all quite stunning. I loved looking at them and being around them. Ant was dressed as an Indian Chief and wore special elevator moccasins and a tall feather headdress that added another foot and a half to his height, as well as feathers that cascaded down his back on both sides, all the way to the ground.

Not to be out done was Anna, who without any help from hat or headdress was already taller than any of our non-relatives. She was dressed as a cowgirl and wore modified elevator boots. She towered over the crowd, as did Duck. Heck, Duck was just plain tall. Sol said to me, "One thing's for sure — the Theocarides are easy to spot in the crowd."

For most of the day I was saddled up on Anna's shoulders, because unlike the big brothers she wore no headdress, so I could easily see from my perch. We went to talk with her brother, Sergeant Zambo, at the Clarkson entrance when I noticed that he'd sent two boys marching away. At first I did not recognize them; then suddenly I realized it had been Bruce and the littlest of the Tufts boys. Anna said something to Zambo in Greek, but I recognized the English words "little bastards" somewhere in there. They rode up the Street, past the corner of the lumberyard, giving Zambo the finger. I wasn't a bit scared. After all, I was surrounded by an army of very large soldiers, plus my grandmother.

Anna had already told me that their guns were real and fully loaded. But I couldn't help but wonder what kind of mischief those boys were up to.

The pretty lady we had met during our walk was conversing with Papa and she had brought with her a half dozen other women who were all touching him a lot and looking admiringly over the Big Bandit. Anna walked up with me on her shoulders and introduced herself as "Mrs. Bandido" to the women. They lost interest in Eudie when they looked up into her piercing Romanian eyes. Grandmother always told me those eyes could melt steel. Anna told Zambo, as we walked away toward the scene, that she had seen them before, and that she thought at least one of those ladies was just a bit too interested in Papa's big pistol. But I hadn't seen any of them ask about his guns at all — sometimes Anna said really strange things.

Then Anna said something else to Zambo under her breath, some-thing about shooting the ladies' tits off, but Ant rescued Papa and the ladies left.

For the entire day I remained on Anna's shoulders, still taller than anyone attending the fair. I'd mounted Bark Grable in a sling on my back. She wore a little cowboy hat of her own and my toy Roy Rogers pistol across her body. We got a lot of attention and dozens of people wanted their pictures taken with us, and I passed out a dozen paper boats. One lady handed me a five dollar bill.

It must have been around noon while Anna and I were walking the grounds chatting with the folks when I reached down and pulled one of Anna's ears to get her attention.

"Did you hear that, Anna?" I asked.

"What, Whisker?" she asked. "What?"

"Listen, I hear someone yelling for help!" I cried. "Go over there next to the fence," I motioned.

As we walked closer to the fence Anna picked up the spoor of the sound and walked to the row of outhouses as we heard a sad little voice.

"Helpah me! Helpah me — I'ma got stuck! Helpah me! Oh Helpah me, pleese!"

It was Mrs. Manfrianni, screaming for help. She couldn't reach the door latch and her screaming became so loud that several of the people milling by heard it and came to see what was happening. Anna asked some of the folks to turn their backs and create a modesty shield; they all cooperated and Anna effortlessly tore off the door of the outhouse to find poor Mrs. Manfrianni with her bum so far down the toilet hole that she was suspended only by her armpits, and her knees nearly fell through the opening into the pit below. She was on the verge of tears when she saw me and said, "Oh Marty, Ima so stuck… you cuvah you eye!"

I did as I was told but left a little gap between my fingers as Anna bent over to pull Mrs. Manfrianni out of her predicament. I saw Anna wiping the poor lady's butt and getting her skirts and underwear in order. I was hanging on with one hand like a bronco rider as Anna bent to her work. I covered my bad eye with the other hand. I was ready to laugh but came up short when I saw that the poor lady was really hurt and badly bruised, as well as having lost consciousness. Soon Papa was there, and he picked up the little woman in his arms and carried her into our house, lying her on Grandma's bed until the ambulance arrived.

It was great fun on Anna's shoulders, and I was able to take in almost everything without walking a single step. An hour after the rescue, I got Anna's attention again.

"Listen," I said. "Listen…do you hear it?"

"What, is someone else stuck in Harley's toilets?"

"No, listen," I said, pointing to the sky.

Anna said, "Artie, you could hear a flea farting in the middle of Beethoven's 9th Symphony. What are we listening for?"

I pointed due west, but neither of us saw anything. Still, I could hear it.

Then we saw it, the size of a house fly. Then it was the size of an eagle heading straight for our noses; and suddenly there was a roar over our heads, and a beautiful P51 Mustang — painted army green — roared over the crowd, pulling up in a vertical slow rolling climb, going almost straight up. By this time, Walt was on the P.A. with his commentary, and the crowd roared and cheered as the plane circled around for another pass. Anna looked up and said proudly, "That's my Theo, Artie. That's our Captain Theo."

"He's flying one of the older Mustangs," I said authoritatively.

"How do you know that, Whisker?

"Papa taught me how to listen to windmills and motors and their music. I know that's an older Mustang because it is painted that old Army green; it's not silver like the later ones I know. That's the music of the old Alison Engine, and not the Rolls Royce Merlin. Now that Merlin engine really knows how to sing!"

Anna pinched the little white hairs on my leg just as Papa always did and said, "Papa told me you were a savant about planes and sounds. Pretty impressive, Whisker, but it's beautiful airplane all the same. Isn't it?"

"Transcendental," I said. And she pinched my leg again as the plane flew over us, this time doing slow barrel rolls. On the third pass he flew across the fields, inverted at about 400 feet; then he righted himself and did an ascending wing. He climbed out to the south west and waved his wings goodbye to the crowd as Walter solicited applause from the crowd.

For the next few hours things went smoothly, and various musical acts from the schools performed. Then someone from the Chamber of Commerce spoke over the P.A. Harley and Eudie sang some duets. Next Harley and Jimmy played the Harmonica Boogie and sang "Blue Moon". Revered Wall did a Punch and Judy show on the main stage. It was of a religious variety and it made me laugh. The vendors had all sold their wares, and I just knew we were all going to make a fortune from this festival.

Ant returned with the three ladies and told Papa and Anna that he was leaving with them.

"They want to show me something," he said.

"Oh, I'm quite sure they do," Anna said, and Papa said something to them both in Greek. Ant laughed and then he and the ladies left.

Anna said to Papa, "Do you wish you were a bachelor, my love?"

Papa said, "No, not when I have a perfect set of Greek and Romanian nomenclatures at hand."

Anna hit the big man and said something, smiling, to him in Greek.

The people started to leave and everything wound down, and just as the marching band was getting on the bus someone saw a pillar of smoke coming from the center of the lumberyard. It wasn't particularly ferocious or frightening, but the thick smoke was black and grey and yellow — it smelled like the devil's armpits — and floated over the remainder of the crowd, making it hard for us to breathe.

The fire was soon extinguished and within twenty minutes Dave Abadgian, the lumberyard security guard, was there with Papa and Sol. It was not a bad fire, nor had it been terribly exciting, but it did bring the festivities to a screeching halt. Dave himself had managed to put the fire out with a hand extinguisher; and as the men stood waiting for the white van with "city coroner" plastered on its side. It pulled silently through the gate to the lumberyard. That was when we learned that the Tufts Brothers had started a fire and had trapped themselves in the shed where the thinners, oil based paints and other chemicals were stored. Something had exploded in their faces and both boys died within minutes chemical burns and smoke inhalation.

To this day their deaths made me very sad, and I told Grandmother that I felt guilty. Guilty and mad at myself that I couldn't manage to be happy those evil little bastards were dead and gone.

Grandmother told me that "there was hope for me yet", but I wondered some about that.

Several days after the event, I came across Grandma, who was writing at Fuzzy's little alcove desk.

"Whatcha doing Grandma?" I asked. She looked up slowly but didn't answer me right away. I noticed she had some moisture in her eyes. Finally she took a deep breath and said, "Oh, I'm just writing Mrs. Tufts a little note."

"Really?" I said. "What about?"

"Well Artie, you know those boys of hers were terribly mean and badly behaved. I think she must have known that and it surely must have bothered her some, and perhaps their meanness even broke her heart and hurt her very badly. I think it must have. So I just thought she might like to hear something nice about her littlest one, the one they called Skate. You know, Artie, Grandma's lost a baby a couple of times and it hurts terribly bad. I just thought she might like to hear at least one kind word for the little one she lost. I don't imagine there are many of those words out there for her."

"Gosh Grandmother, I never thought of that. What did you say?"

"Well dearest, I haven't quite finished the card just yet, and I'm not even sure how to get it to her, I suppose I'll give it to Dr. Wilcoxen O'Connor at the newspaper to give to her. But I am going to tell her something nice about her little boy Skate knocking at my back door a few days after he and his brothers destroyed my garden and tore down our clothesline. I never told anyone this, but Skate knocked at my back door several days later and handed me three roses and a big red tomato and a pocket full of radishes.

He said, "'Scuse me, Missus... My name is Skater Tufts and well, ma'am...well, these are for you. I am very sorry about ruining your flowers and plants, honest, I really didn't want to do it, but my brother Bruce said he would snitch the eyes outah my head with his whip if

I didn't. I told him that you'd never done nothing tah us but he just wouldn't listen. But Gosh Ma'am, I am awfully sorry 'n I'm 'pologiseing if you'll let me?"

"Really Grandma, what do you say then?" I asked.

"Well I told him that it was very manly and good that he apologized, as he well should have."

"Then what Grandma, then what did you do?"

"Well," she said, thinking about it, and looking away so I couldn't see her face. Well. I looked at his scruffy little face and saw so much unhappiness there it near broke my heart. His face was smudged and there was dried blood in one nostril and the other was running down the poor child's face. He had a black eye too, and my heart just went out to him. I invited him into the kitchen and made him a peanut butter and homemade jam sandwich and gave it to him, plus a glass of milk with some chocolate powder and sugar in it."

"Bet he liked that, huh, Grandma?"

"Yes, he did like it a good deal. He said his mother didn't believe in peanut butter or any kind of sugar and only served proper food at proper times, but he added, 'Gee Lady, that's the best sandwich I ever had!' I gave him a hug and patted him on the fanny just like I do you, and then I sent him on his way."

"Grandma, was that before those boys killed Muggs and knocked my brain out?"

"Yes, it was, Artie, and I'll not forgive them or forget that. But I am writing this for his mother. Does that hurt your feelings, Artie?"

"Naw," I said. "Not really. Gosh Grandma, he and Bruce are dead now, so I suppose their feelings are hurt way worser than mine. Besides, he was always the best of those knuckles anyway."

"Grandma, are you going to tell Mrs. Tufts the whole story, just like you told me?"

"No, darling. I am going to use a lot of varnish on it and apply it with a heavy brush and a light touch, and not mention the fact that I invited him in for the sandwich, nor say anything about Mrs. Mortimer up the street, who later told me that Skater had stolen those roses and the tomato and radishes he gave me from her garden. Grandma's going to leave that part out of the story."

"Grandma," I said. "Guess What?

"What?"

"I love you, Grandma."

I put a paper boat in her hand and said, "Send this to Skater's Mom from Artie Spelman. Maybe she will cheer up." She took the boat, folded it shut into its diamond shape and put it into the envelope.

"Oh Artie," she said, "you make your poor old Grandma cry."

Three days after being extracted from the toilet hole, Mrs. Manfrianni nearly died of apoplexy brought on by the accident. Uncle Harley was beside himself and thought sure he'd killed her, but Dr. Abadgian brought her through. From that day on she never wore black again and became a different person. She was a bright and happy soul and got engaged to old Mr. Boescher. They were married in Anna's meditation garden. At the wedding, Carl Agajanian gave the bride away and Harley sang Torna Surriento accompanied by Papa on the cymbalom. I was the ring bearer but she still called me Marty.

Ant was old man Boescher's best man, and he said the two old newlyweds had a spring in their steps and love in their eyes.

We did not become wealthy robber barons as the cartoons portrayed, but the Bazaar was a success on all levels. Grandmother did receive enough money to stave off the wolves for our last months on Atlantic Boulevard; all her bills were paid and we had our cupboards stuffed with food for the first time ever. Sol repaid his loan with interest and made a tidy sum on his jewelry. He did not lose a single chess game and drew only one game to Ant. Ant put his three dollars' winnings into the Salvation Army bucket. All the vendors made handsome profits. For the first and only time during our stay there, we had a telephone, courtesy of Sol Rubinstein. I can still remember the phone number LO (Logan)-3399, serendipitously my two favorite numbers.

Theo later told me I was right on all accounts. His friend's P51 was one of the first planes earmarked to go to England, and did indeed have the old cockpit style and the old Alison engine. He gave me a big hug, smiled at me and said, "Colonel Spelman, how do you know all this stuff?"

I smiled and shrugged my shoulders.

The last newspaper foolishness Fuzzy ever did was paste a byline in Grandmother's morning paper. It was by someone he called "Philibuster". Grandmother read it to the steering committee a week or so later.

Here is what it said:

BELL BAZAAR A SMASHING SUCCESS!
By Philibuster Breathbeast Fuzzelbuttox

The Bell Circus & Bazaar held Saturday was a great success, hundreds attended. In a period of less than five hours two people were killed, one dwarf trapeze artist had broken his leg and lost an eye and fractured his brain and a section of the lumberyard next door burnt to the ground. Mrs. Rosa Manfrianni fell through Harley Brown's asshole, breaking her cocyx in Mr. Brown's outhouse. Two young boys (names withheld pending trial) — both former Alter boys and Eagle Scouts who were cruelly refused admittance to the fair — were burned to death in a lumberyard fire next door while trying to get a glimpse of a small clown with a bumblebee painted on his nose. A Mexican Circus Giant has offered to provide free funeral services for all. Fin.

Uncle Harley told me later that Papa said that the success of the circus project was due entirely to the fine work of Sol Rubinstein, who'd had the foresight to advertise on all the radio stations, and on Don Lee's W6XAO Television Station in L.A. There were less than two thousand television sets in all of Los Angeles County in those days, but they all cost a fortune and were mostly in the homes of the wealthy.

Amazingly, the greatest single moneymaker for the project was another idea of Sol's, taken from the boy's experiences in Spain. He had a large dinner plate cast with Papa's handprint across the center. In the middle of his handprint was Anna's own handprint.

That Saturday evening I went to bed and slept until the following Tuesday morning. I didn't think about the circus anymore for a long while.

Duduk
(Day One)

I T WAS WEDNESDAY, August 27, 1947. The next three days were strange. They were simultaneously happy and sad. During those dark days, I aged two or three years. Rushing headlong into my small world were cataclysmic changes that collided with my child's brain, exploding into little chunks of wisdom that stuck unevenly to my understanding, like spit wads on a blackboard. And with the shaky growth — not unlike that of a young colt inside my pre-pubescent equilibrium — my childish heart flew with a different gallop than it had before.

In addition, during those earth-shattering events, fuzzy little white hairs grew on my body in places where I had not seen them before. I also had my first bona fide erection, which scared the bejesus out of me; and what was more, my voice was lowering a couple tones three or four years too early. Harley said it was "probably from the kick in your nuts by the Tufts boys".

We had all come to love Sol Rubinstein. I adored Sol, finding him one of the wisest and loveliest friends I ever knew. He visited the Theocarides and Browns regularly, teaching Grandma Brown how to make Matzo

Ball soup and Challah Bread. He to her about the Bible and she cherished his scholarly yet respectful encounters with her.

Sol honed Eudie's and Duck's chess skills and tested their sense of humor. He could speak Greek philosophy effortlessly with Papa one minute, then to Leslie, and my foolishness would ease without missing a beat.

Sol was amazing, and with his fine intellect and wit he could easily cross swords with Duck, and was equal or superior to him in every way other than Duck's striking physicality. Sol gave the fine mind of Eudocio a workout, but Papa had a leg up with the fluency of ten or twelve languages and decades' more life experience. So Papa Theocarides was the center of our burgeoning manhood and stood there supreme.

Sol once said that Papa had lived and experienced more than ten ordinary men do in their lifetimes. He was utterly mesmerized by Eudie and loved being in his proximity. If Duck was jealous of their relationship he never let it show, and since the Alcazar incident with the Showalter boys, Duck had become a beloved friend and protector of Sol. We all spent time together and became fast friends.

During those happy years Sol traveled a good deal, lecturing and playing in chess tournaments both across the country and abroad. Sometimes he went away for weeks at a time, and though he missed much of his education, he still managed to graduate from high school Suma cum Laude just a month short of his sixteenth birthday, and almost two years early. He'd worked as an apprentice jeweler for his father since his Bar Mitzvah three years earlier, and developed a jewelry business, utilizing — among many other things — my little paper boat fold design from which he had created a myriad of unique trinkets. His jewelry was made of gold and silver or ivory and gold leaf, as well as lacquered paper and gold leaf boats. This enabled the young, chubby wide-hipped bespectacled boy to earn more money in one week than most grown men of that time did in a month.

Sol was accepted to MIT on a complete scholarship but was holding out for entrance into USC, so he could be near his parents.

On a trip back from Russia, Sol brought his little cousin Ahava Rubenstein, a survivor of the horrors of one of the death camps in

Poland, back to the U.S. She was born the same day as me, August 28, only a year earlier, in 1937. The child was ten years old, but only half my size. She was the weight of an average five or six-year-old American girl.

She had been crippled by unspeakable abuse — only she knew what that had been because she did not speak a word, and her family had all been slaughtered, so there was no one left to tell the tales. What was clear was that she had several broken bones that hadn't healed properly, including a malformed hip that made her walk with a pronounced limp. When the war ended she'd spent several months in a mental hospital in Russia, and she was still emaciated, as frail as a porcelain butterfly.

Sol told us that she had not uttered five words in the last ten months. She was distrustful of everyone. particularly adult males. The doctors gave her little chance to survive unless she learned to assimilate. Sol and his family were her only surviving relatives, so she had come to live with them. Ahava stuck to Sol like glue. He said she was put in a little bed in his parents' bedroom where they could care for her and watch over her, but he recounted to us how at first she would lay awake all night sleeping with her eyes wide open, staring up at the ceiling, both paralyzed and glassy eyed. Finally she took to crawling into Sol's bed every night to snuggle. This was the only way she could close her eyes to sleep, it seemed.

Ahava wet poor Sol's bed almost nightly, and Sol acted with unparalleled gentility. The girl was cared for with great attention and understanding by the Rubinsteins; she was well-nurtured too, although she'd hardly eat a morsel. This was complicated by the fact that she would tear off little chunks of wallpaper and eat them at night. She ate a variety of bugs as well, mostly crickets and spiders, and could not be broken from that habit.

They were told by many that she should be institutionalized, but Sol and his parents simply would not hear of it.

The vogue du jour at that time was that many people from all over the social strata were in fact institutionalized, and frontal lobotomies were performed with regularity during those years.

Solomon was trying to wake her up, but was not quite sure how to do so. He said she may have in fact been retarded, although tests showed otherwise. No one was sure. Sol introduced her to all of us, figuring that we were just the right gaggle to get her quacking again. She looked at me as if I were a memory from long ago.

She held Sol's hand, squeezing it so tightly that it became numb and white from lack of blood flow. For a long time she would not come very close to any of us. Ahava did not move with ease, and her injuries had stripped her of physical grace, but the child had the most beautiful face any of us had ever seen or could remember. Uncle Fuzzy said her beauty was ethereal and stunning. It was a face poets over centuries have tried to write about and failed. This lovely creature was the girl whom lovers of humanity and beauty cry out about in song, the subject painters dream of immortalizing on their canvas. This crippled, sad little girl was a girl for whom many men would have died. Only she knew those dark stories of love and protection that must have saved her a dozen times from the gas and those ovens in Poland.

Sol had been trying to re-socialize her for several months. She would never touch or be touched by anyone other than Sol. I cannot remember more haunting eyes; they reflected horror and sorrow, yet there was also a kind of lovely innocence hiding somewhere within them. Grandmother said she was like a one-winged sparrow praying for a breeze to sweep her aloft.

The orphan loved to sit and just look at Grandmother Brown. She followed her every move but she would not let Mom Brown touch her. The child rarely smiled and never laughed, even though Sol and Grandma tried everything. Still, nothing worked. Had she spoken, it would have been in Polish or Yiddish, so Grandmother just sang spirituals. They seemed to have had little effect — she just continued to stare as I sat watching them from the bench. When Sol and Grandmother were cooking in our kitchen she would follow them and sit on the linoleum directly underfoot. Grandmother simply didn't have the heart to move the child, and when Sol tried she pulled away, slapping poor Sol defiantly. Grandmother would hand the girl little pieces of Matzo or bread, and she would take the piece as she would a bug within her thumb and forefinger. Then she'd squirrel the food away down her blouse, saving it for later.

Once Grandmother, seated in her rocker, started to whistle one of her unidentifiable "fly fart tunes". We were astonished to see Ahava walk settle onto Grandmother's lap. She listened to every disjointed note of Grandmother's crackly whistling wisps as though she were listening to a symphony. If Grandma stopped or paused, the girl kissed her on the lips multiple times, one right after the other like a woodpecker, until my startled grandmother whistled again. When Sol told his family of this event they were delighted. Grandmother and Sol were the only ones yet to have been physically touched by her in her new world. Dr. Fine and his associate Dr. Abadjian were delighted to hear this progress report, but they were still disheartened with her overall progress since she arrived in the U.S.

Ahava was a source of great concern for our three families. Even in our company, she'd advanced very little over the past four months. Sol wanted to try everything and was frustrated. He knew that a wallpaper and bug diet, along with her antisocial behavior, were killing her slowly. He begged the doctors to let him take her to the Theocarides' home, thinking the giant storyteller might break through to her, but both of her doctors were extremely cautious about Sol taking her to Papa Eudie.

After all, it was agreed that Papa's extraordinary body mass could be disconcerting for her. He was imposing and startling to anyone who had not seen him before. I had watched many strangers take a step or two backward seeing Papa for the first time; and Dr. Abadjian was concerned that Ahava might associate him with one of the Nazis from the prison camp, aware that she could regress irrevocably. However, Sol wasn't sure, and finally the matter was placed in his hands.

Today, August 27, Sol was at our house with his little cousin; and on instinct he took her by the hand and crossed the street to Eudie's home. Grandmother instructed me to go along and help Sol with Ahava if I could, so off we went. Sol, perhaps thinking to accompany Anna first to ease her on the big man, took us through the meditation garden, peeking into the library through the back door. He saw no one and said, "Hello, anyone home?"

When he received no response he walked inside with Ahava in hand, with me trailing just behind them. Papa was asleep sitting in his huge leather glide chair with the back turned to the door. We walked past the chair as Papa opened his eyes. Sol pulled the little girl a bit closer to his side, preparing her for the possible shock. Ahava looked into Eudie's dark eyes and at his massive head. She did not smile or utter a sound but almost immediately released Sol's hand. She leaned forward and ran a few steps toward Papa, with her arms out stretched to be picked up. He reached for her and helped her up as she climbed unceremoniously into his arms, as if they were old friends, and laid her small head on his great chest.

Papa spoke to the child in Polish and Yiddish and Russian, but the girl did not respond. He had heard about Ahava's progress with Grandmother's whistling, so he started to whistle with her in his arms. She squirmed a bit and stretched and crawled up to shush his puckered lips. Papa spoke to me, pointing toward the bookcases and said, "Whisker, open that middle drawer over there, below the center bookshelves, and hand me the duduk." I went to the drawer and opened it, taking out the strange Armenian flute I'd heard many times.

"No, the larger one," Papa said.

I replaced it and handed Papa the larger instrument, the one he called "Sister", and he began to play for the child as she lay peacefully across his stomach, resting there with the side of her face on his chest, like she was listening to his heartbeat. She reached up again to touch his chin with her fingers, feeling the vibrations of the duduk pulsing in his throat; she shut her eyes, listening as they traveled together to someplace of there own, someplace between a Giant's beating heart and the ancient duduk. Someplace warm and splendid. Someplace safe.

I closed my eyes, trying to feel what they were feeling. In the beginning, as the sound of the duduk flowed over us, there seemed to be years between those notes; winters passed into summer and back again, as his music filtered in another world. It was ageless; it rang not into our ears but into the heart and bone. Even for me, it transcended time. It must have spoken to troubled things; it rubbed its balm on wounds that could never be healed. I think that duduk cried and wailed and struggled to sooth broken hearts. The little girl's eyes were closed and her patient fingertips reached up to kiss the giant's face; and while he played, those fingers seemed to search for something indefinable as she cupped his massive chin in her delicate hands. The child lay in the depths of his protective heart, a heart that beat against her wounds. As he played, I know now that it must have given her soul some peace, as surely as it broke his own soul in two. The music spoke to them both; I think Ahava and Eudocio understood each other's fears, and that music was a conduit through which they knew each other's horrors and losses. The large man and the tiny child caressed their wounds in space and time, connecting to the divine thread of music that went back a hundred centuries to the dawn of mankind. The child and the giant sang to each other. It was a song without words, one sung from invisible throats, and accompanied by the whispering of the duduks notes. The Greek Giant and the tiny Jewish girl found redemption in each other.

The pair fell asleep there, like a cub with a papa lion. Ahava slept reclined there on Eudie's chest, with the flute now clasped in her own hands. Sol had also fallen asleep in the other chair. I sa2 those three and vowed never to forget how beautiful they were, and how much I loved to see them happy to share my Papa Eudie.

Anna brought me a cup of hot chocolate and a blanket for my knees. She covered them as she turned off the small lamp and gave me a kiss on both eyelids. I think she knew we were all in a very special place, and was quite content with the view of us all asleep and dreaming. I could still hear the flute in my head and heart, as surely as if it were still sounding. Anna walked through the swinging kitchen door. Then I heard her soft, low voice on the wall phone speaking too Mrs. Rubinstein, telling her the sweet tale between the children, the big wounded child and the small broken one sleeping on his chest.

CHAPTER 32

Kanapy
(Day Two)

E VERY KINDHEARTED RED Cross volunteer gossiped endlessly about the condition of our war orphan's progress. The stories of Grandmother's whistling and the Greek giant's wailing music, and his overall tenderness toward the emaciated Ahava, grew throughout the neighborhood. They were exaggerated with each telling.

After the war ended stories of the Jewish Holocaust filtered into the American consciousness, although there wasn't much on the news media of that period. Many who heard about it just didn't believe it. Some denied it altogether.

One of the few who had no trouble believing it was the big German grocer Hans Bearwalt. He said he'd lost his entire family due to Hitler's insanity.

He blamed the loss of his only son on "Hitler Youth". Hans told Grandmother Brown that what he could not understand was how the people in Germany were still denying the holocaust when it had been right in their backyards, in front of their very eyes; and that many a German citizen knew about the euthanasia of some of their own mentally ill Germans. That had been part of Hitler's master plan.

MovieTone and Pathe features at the local movie theaters showed minimal coverage of those tragic events, really just bits and pieces of the horrors, and by that time the world was weary of war footage, so few had any real idea of what had happened in Nazi Germany.

It was my ninth birthday and Ahava's tenth. Papa thought he would treat us to a birthday outing at Will Rogers State Park in Pacific Palisades. We were all very excited. Duck and Harley were to drive Sol, Ahava and me in Papa's 1940 Packard Sedan. During the War, Eudie and Zambo had put five of his vehicles up on blocks and given the steel rims and tires to one of Uncle Sam's "Rubber Drives", leaving just two of his automobiles functional. Now the big black beauty was back on the road, and it was Duck's pride and joy. Few teenagers of that day had their own cars, and Duck and Harley were beside themselves with the opportunity of driving Papa's "extra" car.

Ahava had added nearly twenty words to her vocabulary from Papa's dreamer's lullaby the day before, and the Rubinstein family was overjoyed. During the seven weeks she had been around us, we had all fallen hopelessly in love with the waif, and there was happiness all around. Everyone had great hopes for the child and wanted to do whatever they could for her to show her that she was now in the United States of America, and that this was indeed the land of the free and the home of the brave. Ahava seemed to be doing much better but she still stayed just millimeters from Sol's elbow. She was still skittish and had not yet fully smiled at anyone; and she was still wetting poor Sol's bed almost every night. She continued eating wallpaper and bugs too. Once we had once taken her to see reruns of "The Wizard of Oz" and "The Song of the South" at the State Theater on Gage Avenue. She hated The Wizard and became uneasy when he finally came on screen; and she had an equal aversion to the Tin Man. Sol said they both frightened her, but although she didn't understand a single word she loved the song "Somewhere Over the Rainbow", and the little girl Dorothy who sang it. She responded to the Cowardly Lion and came very near laughing at him.

Uncle Clayton Crawford Near Arroyo Secco Freeway, 1940s

That progress, however, was marred because she had now taken to peeling the chewing gum off the bottom of the theater seats and eating it. Solomon had earned his biblical name from his infinite understanding and patience with this poor child.

Something about Uncle Remus and Br'er Rabbit in "The Song of the South" generated a most positive reaction in her eyes, and she made a sound that was not quite laughter and not quite crying, but one that Sol interpreted as happiness. But neither experience brought a genuine smile to her face. There was ongoing talk of hospitalization because she consumed almost no water during the day, ate like a sparrow and was still dangerously anemic and dehydrated.

So, as my Grandmother pointed out, "This child is far from being out of the woods."

Mr. and Mrs. Rubinstein thought Eudie's proposed outing might be nice for the little girl, and since it was her birthday the trip was all set.

Papa gave Duck a twenty dollar bill, he filled the Packard's tank with $2.80 and we headed toward the Pacific Palisades and the three year old Will Rogers State Park.

As we sped along, Duck drove the Packard and Harley sat in the co-pilot's seat as happy as a prince. Ahava was in the backseat with Sol and me, and she'd squeezed herself in between Sol and the right rear-door armrest near the window, pinning herself there like a sardine between books, with not even a fraction of an inch on either side of her. I sat on the far opposite end of the backseat, just next to the left rear door with a huge space between Sol and me. We drove on awhile, discussing the meaning of the word "humorist" and perusing the Will Rogers Ranch pamphlet. Uncle Harley was reading about a place that had once been the home of the great American cowboy humorist who died in a airplane crash with Wiley Post twelve years earlier.

Harley, ever the airplane expert, said that he thought the accident had been caused by a faulty pontoon, but he'd have to ask Walt Crawford.

I said to the group, "Bet if they'd flown in a Stearman or a Ford Tri-plane or a P-47 Thunderbolt they wouldn't have crashed."

I saw Duck's eyebrows rise in the rear view mirror and my eyes challenged his to a duel.

"Bet so, Duck!" I cried. "I'll betcha… betcha I'm right." He just smiled, rolling his eyes as he looked over at Harley.

Getting no response from Duck, I thrust forth yet again.

"Besides," I said, "that pilot only had one eye, huh, Uncle Harley? No wonder he crashed. And who ever heard of a one-eyed pilot? Eddie Rickenbacker and the Red Baron had two eyes and on the radio Sky King and Penny and Clipper all had two eyes. So there!"

Duck did not answer me.;

"What do you think about that opinion Rib Solomon?" he asked.

Sol answered rather seriously but with a slight smile,

"Well, Art stir," Sol said, "the P47 Thunderbolt wasn't actually built at the time of their crash. And the Winnie Mae was a far better aircraft than the Ford Tri-plane. And three for a vaunted trinity of thought here. I think Wiley Post was one of the best pilots in the world at that time, but you may have a point in that all things being equal, I would rather have a two-eyed pilot than a one-eyed pilot. And I would rather bet on a two-legged high hurdler in track and field, or watch a two-legged ballerina rather than a one-legged runner or a one-legged dancer."

"Touché," Duck said. Then he added, "Artie, I think Sol has been studying with Walt. And you've been studying chess with master Rubinstein?"

I answered, "No, but he has been teaching me how to think, and pretty soon Grandma says I'll be smarter than you. She told me I was already smarter than Harley."

"You little liar," Harley said, throwing the wadded ranch brochure at my head. Ahava just looked at us all like a sparrow eyeing June Bugs.

Out of the corner of my eye, I saw Ahava crawling over Sol's lap to the middle of the backseat; then she scooted all the way over to me, touching her left leg against my right. She reached over and took my hand, expressionless, and held it, saying absolutely nothing. Sol's mouth fell open and he said to the front seat, "Hey you guys, look at this. Artie's got a girlfriend."

The boys just poked each other, grinning, as they glanced to the back seat.

Actually, until then Ahava had ignored me completely, just as she had everyone. In that moment, however, I was added to her rare social register: Sol, Grandmother Brown, Papa Eudocio and now, me. I smiled, feeling quite special, and just enjoying the moment. Her hand was cold but it was lovely nonetheless, and it was the first little girl's hand I had ever held. I liked it.

We drove on for awhile, running low on conversation, until Duck said to Harley, "Hey Brownie, why don't you sing for Ahava. She likes whistling and the flute, so maybe you can charm her with song?"

Harley sang "Danny Boy" and at the end of the song Ahava asked something to Sol in Polish. Sol told her that the name of the song was "Danny Boy".

She said, "Denny." Sol repeated what he had told her. Once again, she said

"Denny."

Sol told Harley, "You have a fan, Brownie. She loves that song —
look at her eyes."

We all looked. Sol was right.

Ahava pointed to Harley in the front seat and said,

"Denny."

Sol told Harley, "She wants you to sing it again. "This time Harley
turned on his seat and looked right into Ahava's eyes singing the song
once again.

For the first time, the little girl smiled and Harley was admitted
into our rare group.

We entered the Park, paid our fees and looked around. There was a
huge tree in front of the ranch house, reminiscent of our own Mother
Peppercorn, only I think far younger. Inside the main house we found
various items of furniture and possessions that had actually belonged to
the humorist; I saw his hats and lariats, and thinking back to the Tufts, I
wondered if Will Rogers had ever hung any mean bastards with his ropes.

Ahava hardly responded to the artful taxidermy of a stuffed horse
standing in the middle of the main room that had supposedly been
one of Will Rogers' favorite horses. She looked at it, expressionless, but
I got the feeling that she was waiting for it to move, and she seemed a
bit sadder when it didn't.

Shortly before we walked out of the house to the grounds, Ahava
vomited green bile down the horse's front right leg, which drew a crowd
of docents. Sol took them aside and explained the girl's condition, asking
if there were any woods or paths, or perhaps a lookout, where he could
take his cousin to sit and observe nature.

Knowing that she could not walk very far, and that she would only
let Sol touch her, Sol also made arrangements for the guide to give us a
private tour of the grounds in a golf cart that held five plus the driver.

He whisked us around the grounds, showing us the stables and
the polo grounds and beyond, including places where tourists were
normally prohibited. After 40 minutes he took us up a path that led
to a hill with an overlook down into a valley of beautiful foliage, flora
and fauna of every kind with a glorious sky just above it, near or on

the ocean. Looking out on the panorama sat several wooded benches. The docent said we could sit there awhile and enjoy the view, but he cautioned us not to wander more than five hundred yards on either side of the benches and not to go off the paths. He told us that he would be back for us in about an hour.

Harley and Duck looked at Mother Nature for ten seconds before taking off almost immediately, going who-knows-where, and of course paying no attention to the guide's warnings.

Sol and I sat on one of the benches, talking with Ahava between us. Finally she tapped me to get my attention and said, "Kanapy." She pointed to the bench. "Kanapy!" she repeated, looking at me once again.

Sol smiled and told me, "That means 'sofa' in Polish, but she's talking about this bench."

"Oh," I answered. Then I addressed her as I would have a puppy. "Yes, this is a bench."

Ahava nodded her head and said, *"Tak, on jest kanapie do zasiadania w."*

"Bench?" I repeated, thinking she understood at last.

"She says 'yes, it's a sofa you sit on'," Sol said. "Artie, I think that is the longest sentence she has strung together since she left Poland. "

"Really?" I said.

After a few more audible pronunciations of "kanapy" and "bench", which drew no further response from her, I removed my Swiss Army knife. Sol took out his own knife and we compared them for awhile, examining all the blades. Harley had shown me how to hone a fine edge, so my knife was always razor sharp. I warned Sol about that. As I watched Sol's happy face as he carved his initials into the back of the bench, I thought of other's gift and the other side of her nature — the side without daemons. The side that had sacrificed to express her love in the form of this wonderful gift, and the side of her that loved me and kept me from foster homes even though that was a fashion of the day.

As I looked at little Ahava, I thought of my skinny mother as a little girl. She must have been a lot like this little waif, like this beautiful little Polish girl sitting next to us. Despite my mother's abuse, I always saw her as one of the most beautiful women in the world. Whenever I looked at her photo on Grandma's corner shelf, I saw nothing more than a beautiful lady; I did not see her shadows. I was so proud to have that woman in the oak frame as my mother, and I showed her photo to total strangers, bragging about her beauty. I once took that photo to school for a private viewing. My classmates were unimpressed. Still, when my mother was sober and rational she was funny, charming, extremely likable and very talented. She was quite intelligent, and though she was insecure, she could do almost anything she set her mind to. She always encouraged me to laugh, even if it meant acting foolish, which was an idea I readily latched on to. Whatever talent I possessed, it had come directly from my Mother.

Sol and I carved our initials on the back of the wooden bench with my knife, which was the sharper of the two. Ahava reached for my knife and cut her finger on the razor sharp blade. She did not wince or say a word, but wrote something on the back of the bench in her own blood.

Sol looked at her and said, "I think she wants her initials carved too."

Sol carved Ahava's initials on the bench. He looked at her and spoke in Polish.

Ahava looked at him, sucking the blood from her finger, and admiring her initials she tried to whistle three notes, just as she had heard from Grandmother Brown. We hugged her but she pulled away and walked to the edge of the lookout over the gully.

Sol said, "Let's spit over the edge and throw a rock for good luck."

He handed me a pebble and I tossed it, yelling, "Bread and butter, shit and jam, bring me good luck — I know you can!" Eudie had taught me that expression. Sol said to me, "Okay, we all heard you, but you for got to spit."

I spit twice as Ahava watched carefully.

She took a half step closer to the edge rail.

"Shat'nd Jam!" she cried.

Then she tried to spit and it landed on her chin, and for the first time in her life in the United States the little girl laughed out loud. We laughed with her and put our arms around her as she stood there smiling, showing no resistance to our touch. Later. that story became a legend for our families.

After that, Sol and I tried many other things with Ahava to bring out her spirit. Nothing worked and once again, with the exception of a few more attempts at whistling, she retreated into the dark spaces of her world. The docent returned and took us back to the main house where we found Duck and Harley had cornered two pretty young bobby socks-ers, showing the hapless girls all their antics and theater. Harley had chosen the very tall girl and Duck the very short girl. Sol smiled.

Seeing us, the boys danced their last peacock strut for the giggling teenage girls. They made their goodbyes and came back to us.

Duck said to Sol, "I just called Dad and we are to meet them at exactly 3 o'clock in the parking lot of the Los Angeles Memorial Coliseum, off of Vermont Boulevard. Just next to the USC campus. Someone is going to pick up Ahava and take her home to nap. Harley's brothers are going to meet us there and take us all on some important ride somewhere."

Harley looked at Sol and me, shrugged his shoulders and said, "I have no idea where that could be. I guess we'll find out when we get there".

On the way to the parking lot, Ahava asked for "Denny" and Harley complied. Then we rode the rest of the way in relative silence.

Within thirty five minutes or so we were all there in the parking lot. We met with four other cars, including the Rubinstein's new 1947 Plymouth Sedan. Papa and Anna where there in the big Cad V-16, and Helen, Jimmy Brown and their little girl Sharon were in Jimmy's fast Mercury sedan. My Uncle Paul Brown, Grandma's oldest, had borrowed the green 1930 Model A Ford with a rumble seat from Walter's dad. The rumble seat accommodated my Aunt Veve Brown and several of her pulp romance novellas.

I am sure we all looked like a group of gypsies, but I loved every second of it. I still have memories of us standing in a disjointed line in the parking lot, laughing and joking together. The Rubinsteins, after hearing of Ahava's spitting and whistling triumphs at the edge of the viewing point, hugged everyone. Ahava broke away from Sol's hand and ran as fast as her poor little legs would carry her to Eudie, throwing her small arms around his thick leg.

"*Chcę ponownie usłyszeć głos Boga*," she said to him.

Sol said something to her and peeled her away as the family took the little girl home for a rest.

"Papa, what did she say to you?" I asked.

She said she wanted to hear God's voice again."

He smiled down at us and said, "She wants to hear the duduk once again. Tomorrow we are having a little belated birthday party for Ahava and you, so I will play it again for our angel."

Finally we found out about our mystery trip. We were to caravan to downtown Los Angeles near Figueroa Street and drive through the Elysian Park art deco tunnels onto the new Arroyo Secco Highway, which was later called the Pasadena Freeway. We wanted to experience the first Freeway in the United States. We were told that it was a road with no stop signs or intersections, and that it stretched on for eight or ten miles.

I flew directly into the rumble seat of the Model A Ford next to a smiling Veve. Grandmother was in the front seat next to Uncle Paul, driving on point. Harley stayed in the Sedan with Duck, and they were number two, followed by Jim's fast Mercury. Papa, Anna, Theo and Uncle Ant rode last in the V-16 just behind them, picking up the rear.

Paul turned out of the lot, right on Vermont and then right on Sunset toward the LA train station. And soon we were on the freeway. Uncle Paul had the pedal to the floor, and once we went through the tunnels we sped along at about forty-six miles per hour, full speed for the Ford. As I looked in the front seat I saw Grandmother talking animatedly to her eldest son, Paul.

I was like a puppy with its head out the window, taking in the air and the fumes' smells and textures. As I looked over the back fender at the pavement flashing by, it reminded me of being on Papa's shoulders, running at high speed, and I could scarcely believe the velocity of the cars in the lane just next to us, and how we jostled for our position like racing cars. This was almost beyond belief, almost too grand for my comprehension. I thought to myself, *When I get big I'll buy myself a car like this one and just drive back and forth all day down this road.* I looked over at Aunt Veve to see if she was as excited as I was, but I could not believe that she was reading her pulp romance books with an expression of absolute boredom.

It was at that moment that another erection visited me. It had absolutely nothing to do with sex, and I doubt it had much to do with puberty either. It came as a total surprise. I had grown only marginally wiser about the machinations of the "sexual animal" and all that it entailed. It came for a visit when a flatbed trailer pulled by a Mack Tractor Truck came alongside us, and on the bed of the trailer was a bright blue Boeing PT-17 Stearman Kadet bi-plane Aircraft, disassembled but complete. It was sitting there only feet away from me in all its glory. The yellow wings were detached and sat in sections tied down on the other side of the fuselage. The red, white and blue striped vertical stabilizer and tail were attached. The front of the plane was facing backwards on the bed of the trailer and I could almost reach out and touch the starting crank at the left side of the radial engine. I could scarcely believe my good fortune and had never been as excited about anything before in my life. I thought I should go blind for the shear joy of it.

Other than those flying overhead, I had never seen an airplane in person. My erection frightened me and I thought something was terribly wrong and I had no idea what to do about it, and for a moment I felt a bit faint. Fortunately, Sol had bought me a red felt cowboy hat at the Will Rogers' Ranch, and I had taken it off to keep it from being blown off. I picked it up off the floor board near my feet and cleverly laid it over my bulge as I looked over at Aunt Veve. who was still reading her book; and as I turned back to the truck it started to slowly to pull away.

I tried to get Uncle Paul's attention and yelled at him to speed up, but he couldn't hear me with the wind in his face. I couldn't get enough of that beautiful aircraft in my eyes. *Wait until I tell Sol about this,* I thought, *and he'll probably know what was going on inside my pants.* I knew I could talk to him about anything.

We went a bit past South Pasadena and exited onto a parallel road that allowed the cars to leave gradually. Stopping at the top of an incline with a cross street, we made a left and crossed over the bridge spanning the freeway; then we turned left again down a gradual ramp and drove the full length of the Highway once back toward Los Angeles. I was looking for my Stearman all the way, but there was no trace of it. My shorts were back to normal. Veve was still reading. I couldn't believe her indifference to the earth-shattering road trip.

We headed back to the Art Deco tunnels and into Los Angeles.

CHAPTER 33

Flet Boga
(Day Three)

WHEN WE ARRIVED in at the Los Angeles Union Train Station near Olvera Street, Uncle Paul signaled the caravan to pull over into the parking lot. He embraced his mother, shook hands with everyone and excused himself, leaving for his home hearth in Burbank. And Jimmy and Helen returned to Compton.

Grandmother, Aunt Veve and I got into the car with Duck and Harley. It was decided that since we were already near downtown LA that the eight of us would go to the Desmond's Department Store on South Broadway to shop and then eat at Schaber's Cafeteria, just inside the same building. Anna wanted to buy one of the new Argus C3 cameras on sale there, and the ladies wanted to shop for a birthday dress for Ahava.

But first Papa dashed across the street to pick something up on Olvera Street, and when he returned the remaining two vardos took off toward South Broadway and Desmond's Department store.

Anna and Blanche had planned an informal get-together for the next day, August 29th, a day after our birthdays. We planned on celebrating Ahava's progress and my belated birthday. This was the first birthday party in either of our lives. It seems that Ahava had told Mrs. Rubinstein that she wanted to go back to Papa Eudie and listen to Flet Boga. In Polish, that means "God's Flute"; so the families coordinated a social event for the little girl.

We arrived at Desmond's, and after arranging to meet "the men" inside the cafeteria the women left to shop with Veve in tow. Harley and I entered the cafeteria first, followed by Papa Eudie, then Duck and his Uncle Ant. All heads turned to look at the three large Greeks in what must have looked to those diners like the entrance of a trinity of giant gods.

Heads turned as they always have, and I noticed that the decibel level of the chattering customers momentarily lowered. Finally we got a big, round table and waited for the ladies to return, chatting about everything. We played as men and boys are wont to do, and soon the ladies were back and as they approached our table. Papa pointed to Grandma and his wife.

"Here comes Mutt and Jeff!"

"I heard that!" Grandmother said as Anna gently cuffed the back of Papa's head.

We went to the line with our trays and selected our entrees. One of the young servers dropped her mashed potatoes off the edge of Papa's tray, missing his plate entirely when her potato scoop went awry. She looked up at Papa and Ant, startled by their stature. Another pretty young girl went crazy over the handsome face of Timoleon — go figure. Harley snuck a lima bean into Duck's pudding, and as the line briefly slowed down Duck poured salt into Harley's ice tea.

Back at our table we ate and chatted away. Finally the ladies showed us their goods. Anna bought Grandmother a bottle of Colonial Dames, lilac perfume. Grandmother purchased some material and lace to make Anna a tablecloth for her large dinning room table. These ladies did this for each other under the guise of an early Christmas gift.

Veve had a small Desmond's shopping bag full of pulp romances. One was called "Her Forbidden Loves", and another "Happiness Borrowed".

She also had two different issues of a pulp magazine called "Love Stories", volumes three and four.

Harley asked Grandma, "Mother I thought you said you couldn't afford any more of that devil's rubbish." Looking at Anna, Grandma said, "Well, you'll just have to ask Jeff here who it was that bought them for her.

Harley and Duck had put a generous dose of horse radish in Papa Eudie's coffee, and were eagerly waiting for him to take a big gulp. Eudie drank it down to the last drop, expressionless, and licking his lips at the last gulp. He didn't say a word, nor did he bat an eyelash; but as we got up to leave, he turned to me and winked where the boys couldn't see.

We finished our dessert and coffee, and then we walked to the parking garage. We were soon home, and I listened to "The Adventures of the Thin Man", and then too "The Bob Hope Show" on the radio, falling asleep alone. I was sitting in my grandmother's rocker, and I woke up when Jerry Colona started to sing something. Looking into the little alcove I could see Aunt Veve with her two girlfriends, Sally Anne and Tootsie Westerman. The girls stopped chattering as Grandmother came in and covered me with a little blanket, kissing me on the forehead. I could hear Grandmother explaining to the girls. "He's had a long hard day," she said.

Veve responded, "Oh, he's had a hard day alright."

I could hear the girls tittering at Grandma's comment.

Grandmother ignored the girls and turned off the radio, leaving her friends to their idle chatter. I heard her walk back into the kitchen working on what smelled to me like a chocolate cake. I opened one eye just a sliver, and saw the girls poking each other and rolling their eyes. Then I closed my eyes again, pretending to sleep while I eavesdropped on their conversation. Listening to the girls chatter, I gleaned that Aunt Veve had missed nothing during the trip. she told the Westerman girls about every handsome boy that had passed us in their cars and hot rods, and about some "dreamy" motorcycle policeman who looked directly at her as he passed us by. I listened to her telling them about a half-dozen highway anecdotes that she had either made up or I had missed entirely.

Last but not least, she told them about my physiological arousal over the "silly airplane on the truck". She talked about me covering my erection with my little red cowboy hat.

Veve said to them, "There is something seriously wrong with that boy."

"Yep, and that's for sure!" said Sally.

The girls chortled even more when Veve told them that my bright red cowboy hat had a rendering of Will Rogers' horse stitched on the front. It said,

"Whoa there, Buckaroo!"

The girls were hysterical.

We had scarcely arrived home, and I was sure that everyone in all the families had heard about my "woodpecker" incident. I remember thinking that Veve hadn't missed a thing on our road trip as we blazed down the highway — she still somehow managed to read her stupid romance books. I didn't understand womankind, nor did I underestimate their powers of observance ever again.

August 29th, 1947, We all arrived at the Theocrides home at the same time, gathering in the Library. Papa assumed his position in the big leather glider chair and ottoman and as he held court.

Anna said, "Before we get started I want take Ahava in to try on her birthday present, and then take pictures of her and Artie. And then some photos of all of us." She reached for Ahava's hand, but the girl would not respond. Mrs. Rubinstein said something to her in Polish and Ahava answered, saying, "*Chcę mojej dama Drzewica.*"

Sol looked at Grandma Brown and said, "I think she wants you to take her. She asked for the 'Whistling Lady'."

Ahava went to Mom Brown and offered her hand. They left as Anna snapped a picture of them walking hand-in-hand, and then again when they returned. When they came through the library door, I noticed how beautiful Ahava was. I have often heard the term "take your breath away", but this was the first time I had ever experienced its effects. Everyone in the room took a deep breath. Her mass of raven black hair was combed immaculately, and she had a little red ribbon in it that matched her naturally red lips. Her cheeks, for the first time, had just a tinge of natural rosiness, and she wore a little white dress with Chantilly lace around the collar and sleeves, and a red cummerbund sash with a bow that tied long in the back, and a pair of brand new patent leather Mary Jane shoes.

For the second time, she smiled and looked up at everyone, crushing every heart and destroying me completely. Anna snapped yet another photo. Have you ever seen anyone that was so beautiful that you just wanted to weep? The sight of her made my knees weak; I had never experienced anything like this before. The pain of it, and not knowing what to do about this feeling, was excruciating.

I was absolutely in love. But I neither had the knowledge nor the experience of such things, other than my Lorna Green debacle. And this was something different, and far more painful. I know now that what I was feeling was pure and ethereal, the kind of passion that makes little boys numb and terribly alive at the same time. It's the love that we taste just once, then look for the rest of our lives, never really finding it quite the same way again. It's that feeling of pure tenderness and connection, one absent of any of the physical trappings of the adult sensuality. It was something indefinably frightening and fragile. It felt glorious.

Running to Grandma Brown's side, I whispered my plan in her ear. She answered, "Okay Artie, but cross at the stoplight at the corner"

So I dashed out into the driveway beside the meditation garden, got into the backseat of my Stearman and rolled out at full throttle, speeding down the runway toward Atlantic Boulevard. As I hit the end of the driveway I pulled back on the stick with a touch of left pedal and a tad of left stick as I banked to the port side crossing. I forgot to reset my altimeter, so horns honked, and at least one car on either side of the street screeched to avoid killing me, but I didn't care. I made my final approach into our large lot and landed facedown into the center of the platform swing, tearing the skin off the tip of my nose as I dodged a few of Exemplumonious peppercorn sallies deplaning. I put the chalks under the wheels and left the motor idling as I ran inside the house, retrieving my bright red INJUN Cigar Box, in which I kept all my priceless papers, foil boats, special wrappers, marbles, rocks and other sacred treasures. I grabbed the box and jumped into my Stearman again. In a single leap, like the Lone Ranger onto Silver's back, I throttled up and flew across the street into the library with my cigar box in hand.

My Stearman arrived next to Ahava with a thud of gas and my landing gear tires flat at her feet. I could smell a bit of Grandma's lilac perfume on her dress. Something made my poor dumb heart race, and I opened the cigar box and gave her a little pipe cleaner engagement ring, the one I had meticulously formed into an engagement ring for "Lorna Green", the unrequited love of my Valentine's Day massacre the year before.

I asked Sol to ask her if she would marry me one day, when we were all grown up.

Sol looked at Ahava and smiling he said, *"Artie chce wiedzieć, jeśli użytkownik będzie poślubić mu jeden dzień?"*

There was a long pause and finally she answered, *"I nie, dzisiaj wieczorem I go z Bogiem."*

Sol said to me, "She said she can't, Artie, because she is going somewhere to find God."

I was disappointed, but she put my little ring on her thumb and kissed me on the top of my nose, just where I had recently destroyed it during my bad landing on the swing. And then she kissed me tenderly on the lips. I remember my heart stopping.

The Rubinsteins watched the event with great interest. Anna took a photo of the kiss, smiling from ear to ear.

Sol brought Ahava a black felt-covered jewelry box and opened it for her. Inside was a solid gold wire Star of David. On each of the six points was a minuscule gold leaf paper boat fold, hanging from six fragile golden chains at each point. Sol placed the necklace around her little neck and kissed her on her ear. She kissed him back.

At this moment Grandmother Brown brought in her cake with ten candles and showed Ahava how to blow them out. Veve brought me an envelope and set it next to my piece of cake. As I opened my envelope, everyone stared at Ahava, who was voraciously eating her piece of cake and drinking cold milk. Papa had a large smile and Grandmother's eyes were tearing up as she watched the emaciated child eat. No one said a word.

I opened the card that was handmade by Uncle Fuzzy, who had drawn a cartoon of me flying in the front seat of a Stearman Kadet. In the backseat was the caricature of Captain Stavros "Theo" Theocarides. The rest of the writing I didn't exactly understand, so Uncle Harley explained to me.

"This is a gift card for you, Artie, from all of us, but your main benefactors are Sol and Stavros. This is a certificate of promise for a two-hour flight in real Stearman Kadet biplane out of the Hollywood Burbank Airport. Your pilot will be our own Captain Theo. What do you think of that? "

I looked up into everyone's smiling faces to see if it was a joke. I could barely comprehend it. It was too grand an idea.

I asked, "A real Stearman? A real flight? Up in the air? Really?"

"Yes, sir!" Harley responded, "And you can take anyone you wish with you."

"Can I take Ahava?" I asked.

"Well, maybe not," Harley said. "It might scare her. You'll have to ask Sol or his parents about that when the time comes, okay?"

I nodded my head yes as I looked down at the card with the funny cartoon. In Fuzzy's cartoon, my guest passenger was "Andy Capp" from the funny papers, sitting next to me with his checkered hat and a whiskey glass in hand.

Taking this all in, Veve yelled from across the room. "Hey! Better take your cowboy hat with you just in case!" she cried.

I ignored her remark.

Grandmother said to Veve, "Never you mind, Little Miss Brown. You just behave yourself."

I was too shocked over my birthday gift to say another word, and before I could think of a response Papa sat another bag beside my chair and told me that he got us matching gifts and to open the bag. I pulled out a little pair of burgundy brown Mexican huarache sandals. I loved them

— everyone in our family wore huaraches — and even Grandmother had a pair. Papa said, "Artie, hand me my pair there in the bag."

I reached in the bag, and with a great deal of effort I managed to remove Papa's custom-made huaraches — size twenty-four. They were very heavy, and as I handed them to Papa one at a time, Anna said, "Mexican Battleships five 'E' abeam!" Then she turned to me. "Papa said there is one more thing in the bag, Artie," she said.

So I reached in and pulled out a bag of one hundred Mexican jumping beans and laid some out on the table. When they started jumping Ahava moved upon them like a mongoose on a garden snake, and started shoving them into her mouth a handful at a time. Sol panicked and slapped them out of her hands as if she were a wayward two-year-old, and then he reached into her mouth and pulled them out with his forefinger like she was choking on a chicken bone. Ahava's face went pale, unlike anything any of us had seen before. She looked terrified, but she did not cry out. Mrs. Rubinstein said something harsh to Sol in Polish as Ahava became very still and looked down at the last bite of her chocolate cake. She pushed her last spoonful of cake off her plate onto the table. Tears formed in the corners of her sad eyes and she looked heartbroken. Sol looked miserable, knowing he had inadvertently hurt the child's feelings.

After awhile things calmed down, and Sol held Ahava, speaking to her in Polish in low soothing tones. Later the Rubinsteins visited with Papa while Captain Stavros played chess with Duck. Grandmother Brown and Anna brought in coffee and some knishes. Harley and Sol played pinochle as I sat taking it all in, feasting on the faces of the people I loved and thinking about what a spectacular birthday it had been.

Everything in Papa's wheelhouse library was large and warm and generous, just like he was. Papa sat there smoking his pipe looking at everyone occasionally. He winked at me on occasion. I tried to reciprocate, but I winked by closing both eyes twice. Papa knew this and smiled back at me affectionately.

Giving no warning, Ahava crawled up into Papa's arms. Then without being asked I went to the drawer as I had done before to get the duduk, but Papa said, "Artie, bring Papa the large purple glass ocarina just next to the duduks."

I complied, and when I handed it up to Papa, Ahava reached down, nearly falling off Papa's lap. She touched me on the arm, but said nothing. She did hold up her thumb, showing me the "engagement ring". She had a smile on her face and held my eyes for what seemed like forever. I turned and went to sit down on Grandmother's lap as we all got ready for the music.

Papa put his long legs up on the ottoman and held Ahava, laying her just right so she wouldn't slide, keeping the child in a comfortable embrace that allowed him to play his ocarina and hold her tenderly all at once. Papa seemed to be thinking about just what to play when Ahava started to whistle. Finally Papa recognized the melody she wished to hear. She said something to him in Polish and he answered her in English, saying simply, "You're welcome, dearheart, and I love you too."

Eudie played "Somewhere Over the Rainbow" and the glass notes filled the room like a warm bath on a cold winter's day. Everyone was quiet as the big man, the child and the music met again in that special place. Then Ahava said, "Denny."

"Eudocio, she wants you to play "Danny Boy," said Sol.

Papa played it with great heart and mystery. Uncle Harley started to sing along and Eudie played perfect accompaniment as I sat listening to them, looking at Ahava, our wounded sparrow.

Ahava tucked her face deep within his chest and exhaled deeply. She went to sleep peacefully and without fanfare.

She never woke up again.

She died without a whimper, right there before our very eyes, safe within Papas loving arms. She found God one day after her tenth birthday, listening to the music and Harley's voice still singing to her:

I shall hear, tho' soft you tread above me
and all my grave will warmer, sweeter be
For you will bend and tell me that you love me
and I shall sleep in peace until you come to me.
I'll simply sleep in peace until you come to me.
I shall rest in peace until you come to me.
Oh, Danny Boy, Oh, Danny Boy, I love you so.

Ahava had chocolate from the cake frosting on her little white dress, and a Mexican jumping bean stuck in the lace around her neck, struggling to hop free. Papa kissed her cold little hands, and he noticed that Grandmother Brown had painted her tiny fingernails with clear polish. I saw him holding up her thumb with my heart woven around it as streams of tears rained down his strong face. It was then I recognized unbearable sorrow for the first time. I knew she was dead.

Papa said something to Anna in Greek and she went quietly to The Rubinsteins, whispering to them as I watched. I knew when I looked over at Sol's face and saw his broken heart that Ahava would never whistle again. Anna took the angel into her arms and laid her gently on the sofa, covering her with a blanket but leaving her face on display.

Grandmother Brown put a small white pillow under her head and spread Sol's necklace out smoothly on her chest. The child looked as though she had just fallen asleep. Ahava had a beautiful smile on her face as Sol kissed her goodbye. We called the Rabbi and had Ahava buried the next day. The doctors later said that she had died from what they called "failure to thrive." Dr. Abadgian told us that he and Dr. Fine would have admitted her into the hospital for intensive care the very next day.

Papa said that she had actually died from hate, greed and self righteousness, and from a thirst for power at the hands of monsters with no souls. The four of us walked home, holding each other as we crossed Atlantic Boulevard. None of us slept very well that night. Harley and Veve slept out on the big swing and I lay awake in the arms of my Grandmother, trying to make sense of it.

CHAPTER 34

Last Days on Atlantic Blvd.

T WAS MONDAY, September 8th, 1947, exactly one week and one day after the funeral of our Ahava Rubinstein's funeral.

Sixteen-year-old Sol Rubinstein was dead.

I could not bear it. I was disconsolate and angry, staying up in Uncle Harley's loft bed and refusing to eat or talk to anyone for nearly twenty-four hours. I could not believe that God would take such a wonderful boy and I wanted no more truck with God.

Other than Muggs McGinnes, I had never before experienced the death of a beloved. Now there were two gone within days of each other. Two ripped from my heart, taken ruthlessly from me within a week. I hated God and didn't wish to be around anyone, especially my Grandmother, because I knew she would try to take me back to sanity and I didn't wish to be sane. I wanted to be bad. I needed desperately to defy. I did a pretty good job of it for awhile, but then Grandmother's arms beckoned to me and my heart was just too tired to resist.

Sol's Mother told us that he had been depressed for days. Somehow he'd blamed himself for his cousin's death, thinking perhaps that his harsh reaction with -Artie's Mexican jumping beans may have killed her will to live. His parents told him that he bore no blame for her death, and that the Germans had killed her long ago.

Papa assured Sol that before she died, Ahava had found love and friendship and humanity in each of us. In his opinion, Sol himself had been the person she had most cherished. Grandmother agreed with Papa completely, but still Sol never quite forgave himself. Solomon, it seemed, just couldn't get back into the world; and in the days after her death his mind was simply somewhere else. It was certainly somewhere else when he walked in front of the "J-Car" streetcar in the South Gate Loop off of Santa Anna Street.

The loop was a little square store with a soda fountain and token booth inside, around which the tracks of the yellow J-line streetcar turned one hundred and eighty degrees, reversing its course back toward Alvarado and Sunset Boulevard. Because of the forty-five degree turns around the loop, a streetcar couldn't travel any faster than three to five or so miles per hour as it circled the loop and stopped to release passengers at the end of the line. A witness standing by a newspaper stated that, "The young man and his briefcase were glassy-eyed and staring off into space, just stepping directly in front of the slow-moving trolley."

Apparently he was not knocked down hard at all, but just landed badly and struck his head, killed in a freak accident. The doctor said he was dead upon arrival at the City of Angels Hospital. Sol had also had a heart attack either in the trolley or the ambulance. Heart failure was his case of death.

My world just didn't feel right. My Stearman was broken and I had no desire to ever fly it again. There would be no Ahava or Sol to fly with me in the airplane for my birthday. The days went slowly and painfully. My heart mended, but never completely, and I was pretty sure that I would never be really happy again.

Through my grandmother I came to understand that death was part of life, and that it was part of God's creation as much as birth. I learned that our death is the one thing we all have in common, and that it connects us more than it separates us because it affects the rich and the poor, and the young and the old, and both the foolish and the wise. Grandma said, "Death does not play favorites and it gives us an opportunity to love and to feel deeply and thoughtfully every moment that we can."

Jimmy Brown and Veve Brown, 1940s

She explained to me that, "When it is your time to die, nothing can save you; and when it isn't your time to die, nothing can kill you." She said Ahava died because she was ready to rest and that Eudocio had held her hand and carried her into God's arms with his music. It was her time and she chose Papa to bring her home. She died in the company of those she loved.

I questioned Grandmother about God. The whole system seemed really unfair and poorly designed to me. She agreed but said that we were all God's creation and that he was teaching us, and that one day we would understand this more clearly. She told me that she and Sol had discussed that many times and that he was a wonderful and wise boy, far beyond his years, and that she believed he was in a better place. Perhaps at that very moment was now negotiating for trinkets held in God's own "Red INJUN" cigar box.

I have no idea why but that wonderful vision made me feel better. Grandmother's loving counsels always had. I could just see Sol and God negotiating a recipe for God's Matzo ball soup, and God reaching into his own Red INJUN cigar box to give the formula to Sol.

A few weeks passed and I felt better day by day, but still my moods grew dark and my heart numbed.

Once Grandmother caught me sitting at Fuzzy's small alcove desk, fingering my birthday Stearman flight "gift card" with a look of disdain. I would slide the envelope to the edge of the desk, flicking it an inch or two with each push of my middle finger. At my last flick it toppled over the edge. As it fell to the floor I added the long, whistling sound of a bomb falling: "Bombs away, Sssssssss, Paahque-Boom!"

I did this with the disgust of a petulant child tearing the wings off a butterfly.

I picked up the envelope again and repeated the drama several times with variations while trying to be as cruel to the envelope as I possibly could be. Grandma stood and watched my ugly behavior. She chided me fiercely about disrespecting Sol's wonderful gift of flight and the effort and cost and the considerable love he had given me to make it possible. She insisted that no matter how my heart felt at that moment, that I should not pout, but honor Sol's memory.

She said, "Be a mench! Go for your flight and quit sniveling." she continued angrily, "Do you realize how few boys in the world will ever have a chance like this? You should be ashamed of yourself!"

The tone in her voice told me she was nearing a line that none of us ever crossed. I got her message loud and clear.

After giving it much thought I relented and determined that my guest passenger would be Aunt Veve. Harley was my first choice but he had an infected eardrum. To my amazement, Harley was all for my next choice because he had something devious planned for his little sister's flight.

Cousin Walter wasn't available and my Grandmother, who received my great consideration was willing but jittery, so she passed the baton to Veve. Now Veve had no clear idea what a ride in this plane was really about, and nobody had told her what to expect. I overheard conversations she had had with the Westerman girls, and her chatter revealed that she thought it would be a nice sun-filled trip casually flying over the southern California beaches, where she could spy on some cute boys baking in the sun.

Before I made another move I asked Papa if we could dig up Muggs McGinnis, and if he could get him cremated for me so that Veve and I could drop his ashes somewhere over Los Angeles County during our flight. He told me to go dig up whatever was left of him and that he would have it done for us.

Theo scheduled our flight at the Hollywood Burbank Airport and we were off to fly at noon the following week.

My mind was back to churning in more or less its normal gear, and I began "fornicating and backsliding" once again. I went personally to talk with Captain Theo about the upcoming events, and I told Stavros that I would like for him to do a dozen wingovers starboard and port a few inside loops — and an inside loop or two, one with a full twist at the top. Walt had told me that this maneuver was called an "Immelman". I laid out a whole litany of maneuvers and he nodded his head, grinning at me as he chewed on his toothpick.

"Any thing else, Colonel?" he asked me.

"Yes," I said. "While you're at it, could you scare the living hell out of Aunt Veve? He told me that Harley had already suggested something similar. He told me not to worry about it, and that he would see what he could do without killing us. He said that he could think of few surprises for her and would tell me about them before takeoff.

When we arrived at the airport we walked past a parked a Waco Zq6 Biplane with a cabin and beech cabin, a stagger wing biplane. I tripped over my own open gaping mouth and fell on my face. Stavros stood me up by the seat of my pants and said, "Artie, you better keep your mouth closed or you'll catch flies. And if you leave your mouth open like that when we're aloft you'll create drag and crash us."

Now you see, boys in Brooklyn and the Bronx before and after the War collected and baseball cards. In Los Angeles, we were near almost every major aircraft manufacturer. So Harley, Walter and I knew about airplanes. We knew the names of aerobatic maneuvers and a good number of the names of planes. Although none of us had ever seen a plane on an airfield, we had built dozens of model planes. Lift, drag quo efficiency, wing loading, stall speed and so on, were everyday words in our vocabulary and we used them like a Brooklyn Boy would use the terms Dodgers or Yankees, or batting average.

But at least the kids in New York got to play ball. We just dreamt about going aloft or jumped off roofs with our umbrellas spraining our ankles. We broke our bums and noses and imagined days like this as we looked too the skies.

Not today! This wasn't a dream! This was my day!

I could not imagine anything being more beautiful than those planes sitting in that hanger until we walked a few yards out of the open door and I saw my beloved bright yellow and blue Stearman Kadet Trainer, more beautiful than I could have ever imagined. I was stupefied; I could scarcely believe that within minutes we would fly right up in the "actual sky" around Los Angeles for two full hours. My face must have told the tale because Veve asked me, "Need your red hat cowboy, Artie?" I thought briefly and answered quite seriously, glancing down between my legs. "Not yet."

We approached the young man in his mid-twenties who was whipping down the aircraft. He turned and spoke to Stavros. "Hey Captain Theo. Is this your crew?"

"Yep, we are going to take a spin around the sun today."

Turning to Veve, Captain Theo said, "Valera Brown, this is Tech Sergeant Skipper 'Boston Beans' Bestwick. We served together during the war. Greatest mechanic anywhere!"

Veve smiled back with a warm hello and offered her small hand, smiling up at him like a duck on a cricket.

"Second greatest, sir," he said, looking into Aunt Veve's eyes. He had a mouth full of perfect white teeth. "Surely there is one better somewhere in the world. I just haven't met him yet, Skipper."

Then Stavros said to the Sergeant, "This is Lieutenant Colonel Artie Spelman." He asked,

"How's this aircraft, Beans? Will she stay in the air?"

Looking at Veve and then to Stavros, Beans said, "Captain hasn't had a bit of trouble since her wings fell off on takeoff the other day, but then there was that fire in the motor this morning. She'll definitely come down, Captain, but you might have some trouble getting her off the ground."

Veve looked nervous but I could tell she wasn't quite buying all of it and was busy preparing her own strategy for a ground attack on the "dreamy" Sergeant Bestwick, who now started to get us aboard as he said to Veve.

"I don't think you're going to have much chance to read that book in up there. And that cowboy hat has to stay or it will fly out of the aircraft the first time you turn upside down."

He winked at Stavros. Then Veve said, "Well, I think my nephew is going to need this hat in a hurry, but I guess he'll just have to wait."

I pinched Aunt Veve and she pulled away, smiling as she shook me off, almost falling into Skipper's arms.

Taking the two items from her, Sergeant Bestwick looked at the cover of her pulp book then smiled as he read the title.

"Love Takes a Tailspin," he read aloud.

Veve responded with a twinkle in her eyes. "Well, Skip. Yes, there are many airplanes in it, and lots of romance high in the skies above Paris. I think you'd like it. There is one chapter when Diedra Dearborn and Lance Stark make love in a piper cub while he performs something the book's author called outside loops over the Eiffel Tower."

Skipper looked at Captain Theo and said, "Brother... Now I'd pay hard cash to see that, wouldn't your Cap?"

Theo answered, "Which one would you like to see most Beans? An outside loop in an underpowered little piper cub? Or anyone who is able to make love inside one while flying it?"

"Well Captain," Skip responded, "I would just like to see the damned fool pilot crazy enough to attempt an outside loop in a piper cub to start, especially doing it while he was en flagrante del naughty. Oh at the same time… that would be a hell of a pilot!"

Stavros responded, "Sure would, and it'd be one hell of a piper cub too!"

They both laughed and Veve said, "For your information, gentlemen, the plane was on automatic pilot."

Stavros and Skip looked at each other dumbfounded and exploded with laughter. I got caught up in it too and laughed mockingly.

"Oh Veve, you are so silly!" I cried with masculine authority as she smacked me playfully on my head.

"Oh Artie," she said. "Just because you think you are an airplane yourself, you think you know soooo much. Honestly!"

Finally Veve told Skipper that he was welcome to read her book and return it to her at his leisure, and that her address was written on the inside cover.

Then she grinned and added, "You can return it to me when you're done reading it and we can discuss some maneuvers."

Skipper smiled and said, "I'll keep that in mind, Pretty Girl. Meanwhile, lets get suited up."

Stavros left but soon returned to the side of the plane with a garment box and handed it to us. I ripped it open and pulled out a beautiful leather flight jacket in exactly my size and saw that on the front left side it had wings in gold leaf, and underneath the wings it said: ***Lt. Colonel Artie Spelman - Co-Pilot***.

"Veve also had a jacket that matched mine only on the right side of her flight jacket. It said: ***Valera 'Veve' Brown Wing Walker***. Her jacket did not have aviation wings over her name but a funny cartoon rendering of the multi-eyed bug from Papa Eudie's stories that she recognized right away as the flesh-eating, many winged Forlornicapedes, devourer of the brains of overly romantic girls.

Theo said, "These jackets are a special gift from my Mom and Dad."

We put the jackets on and they both fit perfectly.

At that moment I was positive that we were going to crash and burn because nobody could be this damned happy and live through it. I briefly flashed back to how happy Muggs and I had been, playing and laughing in the field the day he died, then how fast it all turned ugly; and I worried something bad was in store for Veve and me now. But I didn't care. *Take me, baby Jesus. I am ready*, I thought to myself. Perhaps tonight I will play with Ahava and Sol.

Stavros gave us both leather skullcaps and goggles to use for the flight, just as I had seen in a dozen war movies.

The Sergeant showed Veve where on the wing to step and helped her up into the front seat portal. Then he took his time strapping her in tightly. After that it was my turn. Once the Sergeant sat me to the left he strapped me in, pulling tightly on both our harnesses, checking them carefully. I looked directly into Skip's face and I said with my French accent, "Vive la France, Vive l'Egalite, Veve la Fraternite! Vive mon Chevrolet!"

"What?" Skip asked.

I said, "It's a French song about a girl named Veve, just like my Aunt Veve here. Captain Guynemere sang it when he was shooting down the Huns. I am Captain Georges Guynemere, ace of aces. Up, up and away!" I yelled out loud.

Skip said to Stavros, "Captain Theo, you've got a firecracker here. How does he know about Guynemere?"

Stavros said, "He can tell you the names of most of the World War One aces their stories — the airplanes they flew and who and how many they shot down. Guynemere is his favorite of all."

I held up both thumbs with a grin that spanned from coast to coast.

Stavros stood on the wing and handed me the little cardboard box of Muggs' ashes. He told me to put the box down the front of my jacket to hold it in place till we got over the ocean, I unzipped the top of my new flight jacket and stuffed the little box down as far as I could, until it hit the shoulder harness. Then I zipped it up again.

"Are you ready? Stavros asked. Veve and I both nodded our heads and the Captain told us, "If you are okay and having a good time just give me a thumbs up once in a while, or if you are sick or anything is wrong put both your hands up and your thumbs down, okay?

We nodded our heads and he said to me, "Artie, wait until we get out over the ocean to dump Muggs' ashes. "I will go inverted and you can just open the box the let the ashes fall just as we planned, okay? Then toss the box. Got it, Whisker?"

"Yes sir, Captain Theo!" I answered and gave him a left-handed salute. Then a right-handed one. *Jeez, I never would have gotten that straight,* I thought.

He patted me on the head and got in the backseat and strapped himself in.

"Clear...contact!" Skipper Bestwick turned the crank on the side of the motor and it roared to life. The monkey in my pants almost came for a visit again but the level of my excitement now surpassed even that. How wonderfully loud and powerful the sound of that roaring motor was. There was absolutely no point in trying to talk to Veve, as not a word could be heard above the big rotor engine unless we screamed at the top of our lungs directly into each other's ears. I loved the smell of the exhaust and the trembling of the idling aircraft and the prop wash hitting our faces, even over our wind screen.

The Sergeant removed the wheel chalks and she sat on the runway, trembling, as her motor revved up. I was now ecstatic and we hadn't even rolled a foot down the runway. Finally the Stearman started to move and wound down the lanes, leading to the takeoff and zigzagging because it was difficult to taxi in a straight line. Due to the tail dragging landing gear the pilot could not see directly in front of him until we got rolling down the runway and the tail came up. Finally, we throttled up to full power and were in the air. God, I loved the sound of the motor and wondered if I would ever feel that happy again. Stavros gained altitude and I pointed to our instrument panel, showing Veve the Air Speed Indicator and the Altimeter and other gages. It was a beautiful Sunny day but I noticed that as we climbed out it got colder and knew for the first time why Papa and Anna had thought to buy us these jackets. Jeez, adults just know about that stuff.

The world looked more different than I had ever imagined it could.

Looking over the side I could see cars moving slowly and people out on their lawns or in the streets, looking like little lead soldiers crisscrossed with their toy cars. We leveled out at about 1,600 feet and I knew that we were flying toward our house, because Stavros had told us more or less where he was planning to fly. We gained some more altitude and flew over some small mountains in the Glendale-Burbank area, heading southwest. The motor purred like a lioness, the most beautiful music I had ever heard.

More quickly than I would have imagined, Stavros descended to about 600 feet and waved his wings to get our attention, then slapped his hand just behind my headrest. When I looked around I could see he was pointing for us to look down, as I did I saw a large lot with a little shack and one only a bit smaller just behind it. Suddenly it came together and I recognized our little white house, Harley's and the garage, and the lumber yard and the spot where the greasy spoon had once stood. I nudged Veve and she looked at me, smiling and nodding her head as we flew over Papa's mortuary and the house and meditation garden, banking in a tight circle to fly over the Alcazar Theater in a tight 360 degree turn, returning once again over our house and the big lot. This time Theo throttled up and did a full inside loop over the top of our house. The change in engine pitch brought people running out into the lot.

We waved at the little people down on the ground next to Mother Peppercorn. We could not see any faces clearly but we knew exactly who they each were. They all waved up at us and there stood Papa Eudie, who even from the altitude was unmistakable, holding up a little white ball of fluff I recognized as Bark Grable. We had given the dog to Papa because we were going to move away from our paradise there on Atlantic within weeks and none of us knew exactly where we were going. So Bark was now a Theocarides and no longer a Brown.

Veve and I waved goodbye enthusiastically and Stavros banked wings left, right, then left again in a so-long. Then we turned due west, flying straight west over Atlantic Boulevard toward the ocean at about 1,200 feet. This was the same path we had seen all those Army planes fly all those years ago. I thought I would wet my pants at the shear joy this thought brought me. We flew over the hundreds of oil derricks at Signal Hill and directly out over the ocean a distance of about a mile off shore. Theo banked to the starboard and gained some altitude flying north. At about 2,400 feet he did a series of right and left wingovers. I was in heaven. I looked to Veve, who was surprisingly steady. Next was a Cuban eight and I held both thumbs up and looked at Veve, who finally — after a series of a dozen or two aerobatic maneuvers — was pale. We ended it with several hammerhead turns, plunging toward the ocean and spinning as the rotary engine gurgled, catching its breath. I loved it. We leveled out and Theo did a couple snap rolls.

No rollercoaster would ever equal this. Wow! I was Guynemere, Eddie Rickenbacker and the Red Barron all rolled into one. I loved my Aunt Veve, but in the middle of our second hammer head I wished Sol could have been sitting next to me instead. I wanted to laugh with him and throw my arms around him and tell him how much I loved him, and thank him for this wonderful gift. Theo tapped just behind my seat and I knew it was for me to get ready to release Muggs' ashes. I unzipped my jacket and removed the box. Theo inverted the plane and I let the ashes fly, and in line with the diabolical plan he and I had devised for Aunt Veve, I released the cardboard box and Theo slapped his big hand loudly just behind Veve's seat. I put my mouth right on her ear and screamed at the top of my lungs to be heard and yelled, "Oh shit, I've killed the pilot with the box!"

I looked at Veve, who was ashen. As she tried in vain to look back at Stavros, the Stearman went into a dive. It recovered and did a slow roll and came out inverted at the bottom once again and stayed there for a good while with Veve screaming at the top of her lungs. Captain Stavros righted the aircraft as large flames came out of each side of the radial motor — what they normally did when gasoline built up in the cylinders after being flown inverted for a while. This was just the natural behavior of the Stearman and Veve had no idea of this, and of course she supposed we were on fire. As loud as I could muster, I yelled, "I DON'T WANT TO DIE!"

This was the "Gotcha" we had planned for.

We turned back a bit north, flew over Ojai Valley and back toward Santa Monica, then East over Sunset Boulevard. We followed it down from the

Pacific Coast Highway all at level flight, enjoying the views of Bel Air and Beverly Hills. Veve had recovered but had slugged me hard on my right arm several times because I had been laughing at her panic. For another hour we flew over The Hollywood Bowl and the Griffith Park Observatory, and then we landed back at Hollywood Burbank Airport. When Captain Theo approached the landing field he put the Stearman into a severe skid, which made it look like the plane was flying sideways. I think that scared Veve the most and she lost it as the plane dropped like a rock. But then he straightened it out at the edge of the runway and we landed.

Soon we were deplaned and Theo unstrapped us himself and. As I got out I noticed a puddle on the floorboard, just under Auntie Veve's feet. She was wearing a pair of white slacks, and I thought, *Oh, yellow river city.*

When we stood on the field I could see that poor Auntie had wet herself, and as I walked next to her I asked, "Do you want me to ask Skipper to bring you my cowboy hat?" S

She punched me again and said, "You little bastard. I'll get you for this!"

Veve never teased me about my cowboy hat again.

I came! I flew! I conquered!

Stearman Kaydet Bi-plane

CHAPTER 35

Death of a Giant

"WAIT JUST A minute! Papa cremated a skunk," Duck told me that there was so little of Muggs McGinnis to cremate that Eudocio added the ashes of an old dead skunk to the mix in the crematorium, to ensure sufficient ashes for our Stearman Flight.

That fractured my funny bone and I got so tickled that I fell to the floor of Harley's garage, hysterical, and holding my stomach as I tried to catch my breath.

"That boy is touched in the head!" Duck said as he watched me writhing on the floor. Finally, Harley and Duck blasted me with their squirt guns and we ran in the house for lunch. We blew in through the back door, laughing as Duck pulled down the back of my britches. Harley gave me a couple squirts down my ass crack and finally we all tumbled into the living room. Duck nearly knocked himself out, hitting his head on top of the door jamb between the kitchen and front room. I yelled, "Hey Bozo, pay attention." We stopped abruptly, listening to the ladies talking.

Papa Eudie was dying?

As we listened to Grandma and Anna's serious conversation, I realized this was no joke. I thought the idea of him dying now, less than three months from losing Ahava and Sol, would kill me for sure. *This just couldn't be true*, I thought. After all, Fuzzy had said that Papa would never die, and that Eudie was a wizard or something.

Anna's cards said he was dying too. Dr. Abadjian was diplomatic but allowed that the big man was gravely ill and absolutely needed to be hospitalized. Eudie had double pneumonia and had been in his bed now for nine days, but he adamantly refused to do what Dr Abadjian had told him. Grandma and Anna sat in the front room of our house holding hands. Anna looked haggard and weary.

"Oh, Blanche!" Anna said with a troubled heart; "Eudocio was once buried alive in a shallow grave, shot in the head and stabbed several times. He was run over by several soldiers on horses in Turkey, but as far as I knew he'd never had sick day in his life, and definitely not since the day we married in 1921. Not a day! Not an hour!" She bit her fingernails and squeezed Grandmother's hands.

"Blanche, Eudie retires every evening at about ten o'clock and arises daily before dawn."

She chuckled just a bit as she looked into Grandma's concerned eyes, and as some warm memory flashed briefly across her troubled face.

"My family used to worry about me marrying a man nearly fourteen years my senior," she said, "but I have never been able to keep up with him in any way. He is a dynamo and a great bull-of-an-ox!"

Grandma smiled and put her arms around Anna and said, "The big fool will be alright, Anna. God has to clear some space in heaven to accommodate men as big as your husband. Let's pray God's helpers are busy."

The women smiled at each other and held each other's hands. Grandmother was as nervous and worried as Anna. She knew from experience that pneumonia took more people in their older years than almost anything else. Dr. Abadjian concurred, but tried to remain optimistic. Still, he was concerned because Eudie refused hospitalization.

Duck handled his dad's condition by forcing himself into a state of denial. Harley told us later that night that if Papa died it would kill the Duck for sure.

When I heard Papa was sick I could not believe that he might day.

What then? Would it be my Grandmother next, or Uncle Harley? Heck, Harley wasn't much older than Sol. Maybe God would snap him up next. After all, Grandmother had told me that God did not play favorites. It seemed to me that God was attacking me personally. I felt very alone in dealing with this idea and I wasn't sure that my grandmother could help me with this one.

It was just too much for me to think of not being nurtured by this wonderful man. I wondered why God couldn't at least give me a few weeks' warning before he took yet another loved one of mine.

And why wasn't I allowed across the street to visit Papa Eudie?

As I sat on the mound of dirt that marked Muggs' grave, it came to me that this was all going to end one way or another. The lumber-yard attorneys had already given Grandmother Notice to Vacate. The property was to be bulldozed and lumber stacked where we'd once played, and where almost my entire life had taken place. We were all to leave by January 1st, 1948. *Hell*, I thought, *Maybe we'll all just die.* I put my personal throttle forward and crashed my Stearman into the wall of our living room as hard as I could, but I did not get the joy or relief from it anymore. Since I had gone on my real flight out of the Hollywood-Burbank Airport, my own "Artie Stearman" just didn't fly with the same flair it once had, and crashing into walls had lost its magic.

So I flipped a penny coin.

"Heads, I run off to Huntington Park and look in store widows and talk to people, or tails I give Grandmother's lap and counsel one more try."

I flipped the coin and it landed on tails. I flipped it again and it still landed tails. I flipped the coin one last time and it landed tails yet again. Three flips: a trinity. So I decided to ignore the signals and head to Huntington Park. Problem was I had to pass Grandmother and Anna, who were saying their goodbyes to each other on the front porch. As I passed them Grandmother snagged me and pulled me inside the house onto her rocker, sitting me on her lap. She put her arms around me in the usual way asked, "What are you carrying around, Artie?"

"What?" I responded.

"What is that heavy load you are carrying on your shoulders? Tell Grandma about it."

I laid it all out about how unfair everything seemed, and that God was not a very good planner, and that I was really worried about the big fellow across the street. Why was this happening to us?

Grandmother rocked for awhile, patting me on the chest with those gentle arms folded around me, and she said, "Artie, did you know that in England during this last war that entire families would disappear with a single bomb? Can you imagine being on Papa's lap, listening to one of his crazy tales, then walking home here and in the next minute all of us were gone forever, buried in rubble from a bomb?"

I replied, "Gosh no, Grandma."

She continued. "Do you know how lucky we have been in this country to have had these wonderful years together? No bomb can take that away. Death cannot take it away, Artie. Do you still remember Sol and Little Ahava?"

I nodded my head.

"What do you remember the most about them?" she asked.

I thought for awhile and said, "I remember how patient Sol was with me when we were building models, and how generous and kind and funny he was. I remember Ahava kissing my wounded nose and holding up her thumb with my valentine ring, and I remember her face, Grandma. How come no one else has a face like hers?"

Grandmother smiled and hugged me, saying, "We will be alright, Artie. Do you remember that your wounds healed up when you were beaten by the Tufts? Well, life works that way too. Time will cure your heart, just like it always has in the past, and you will be happy faster than you know. Besides, Artie, how can we really know great happiness if we have never been really sad? Remember, no one can take any of this away from you — not all the Bulldozers or landlords or pneumonia in the world can ever really take what you have loved away from you. Think about how lucky you are to have experienced all this, and remember that all creatures grieve.

"It hurts to lose friends, but if you remember the best of them you never really lose them, and when you show people your true heart they won't be afraid to share theirs with you in special ways."

"But Grandma, I don't want a new giant to love," I said. "I like the old one just fine."

"Well, Eudocio isn't dead yet," she said. "And remember, no one but God knows when it will happen for sure."

Grandmother sat me down, patted me on the bottom and said, "Anna said it would be all right for you to go visit Papa and see him for a short while. She says he's been asking for you. So go and cheer up the stubborn fool, perhaps with a story about happier days, or something to make him smile and get well. You might try to convince him to go to the hospital? Anyway go for your visit, but Anna said not to stay to long because he needs his rest."

CHAPTER 36

The Eighth Life of Orange Pasha (The Dream Triplex)

THE ORANGE PASHA was Papa Eudocio Theocarides' eighteen-pound orange and white tomcat. And just like the other Theocarides, he was a large glorious enigma — a perfect fit for Papa's clan. Eudie had named him 'Orange' because he was mostly Orange and 'Pasha' because as Eudocio loved to explain, the cat spent a good deal of his time with his head stuck up his own ass, grooming his large testicles and admiring the view, just like the Turkish Pashas had done during the Armenian Holocaust in 1915.

The strange cat retrieved newspapers just like a dog, and if he chanced to hear the mortuary's telephone ring, he answered it by knocking its receiver off the hook with his head, and then meowing into the voice piece. That happened often and Papa would pet him gently on his arthritic flank and say, "L'Orange, you are going to confuse the dead."

Overall the large cat was the subject of many interesting conversations. Pasha kept the company of squirrels, gophers, chipmunks and a plethora of birds, and demonstrated no aggression whatsoever. I remember watching a junebug crawl across Pasha's nose, and he patiently watched

337

that bug's journey until his eyes crossed. Pasha was simply absent aggression. *What a peculiar cat*, I thought. He loved a good many dogs, particularly Muggs, who before his untimely demise had been his best pal. Big Orange was more like a dog than a cat, and he loved to retrieve anything thrown his way.

But the most unusual thing about Pasha was that he most always carried a passenger mouse in his long cashmere-soft hair at the nape of his neck. He had carried several mice over the course of his life, but his current passenger Papa had named Iggy, after the hermit priest Saint Ignatius of Loyola.

As I crossed Atlantic Avenue to visit Papa on his deathbed, I thought about what might befall me as I looked into Papa's eyes. None of the Browns had seen him since he had fallen ill, and poor Anna was near exhaustion. I was frightened by how horrible it would be if he died while I was there, and I sorely wondered if I could bear it. Up to that point it had been the most frightening prospect of my life, and I nearly turned around to head back home. I finally decided to just soldier through. I walked around back through the meditation garden into the library, and then into the kitchen, to find Anna sitting at the small table, holding Pasha and stroking Iggy's cranium back and forth with her forefinger.

I stood next to her chair. She had no makeup and her eyes were blood-shot and sad, and she gave me a kiss without her usual slobber-coating. With little enthusiasm, she looked to me sadly and said, "Whisker, Papa's in his big leather chair waiting for you at the bay window at the front of the mortuary viewing room. Go in and sit on his lap, but don't stay too long, Artie, okay? And remember, Papa doesn't look the same, so don't be frightened."

"Sure, Mama Anna," I said. She sat Orange Pasha down on the Spanish tile, looked at me and said, "Follow Big Orange and Iggy upstairs — they know the way."

I followed the duo up the steps behind the mortuary into the funeral director's viewing parlor to Papa, who was sitting in front of the wide bay window overlooking Atlantic Avenue.

His eyes were shut and Papa looked like a ghost of his former self. There was little color in his face, and I could not believe it but some of his beautiful rich hair had fallen out. I was stunned, and for the first time in my memory he looked like a haggard old man, and the sound of his rattled breathing frightened me. As I touched Papa's arm, he opened his eyes slowly, and looking down at me he held out his arm to help me onto his lap. Almost immediately Pasha and his jockey jumped up and lay across my lap. I didn't know what to do or say to Papa. I wanted to cry but I didn't because I knew Papa hated a coward and a sissy, so I just patted his big hand and struggled to lift his forearm around me, finally I managed to lift his large arm and I kissed the back of his hands, and then Papa said,

"Thanks for coming to see me, Whisker. I have no stories today, but just sit with me awhile and rest with Papa until I catch my breath and feel a bit better, okay?"

I nodded my head and leaned back against his chest, saying nothing. After awhile I looked out the window, watching the passing traffic across the street. Soon I heard Papa's uneven. troubled snoring ,and I could see my Grandma sweeping off the little porch and Auntie Veve sitting alone on the big swing, reading a pulp romance.

Impatiently I waited for Papa to wake up just one more time before he died. I prayed for him he would awaken so that I could tell him how much I loved him and how much I hated him for not going to the hospital.

Anna and my Grandma had been furious with him when he'd first refused to go. Anna had called him 'The Great Blockheaded Greek Bull ox". Grandma just pursed her lips and mumbled, but once she very nearly called him a "Farter", only it came out; "Fah-heartnerstork-", creating a new word that we would all use to torment her.

As I looked out the window to the curb I saw Uncle Carl Agajanian pull up in front of the mortuary, parking in front of three "Ingersol-Rand" trailers by the curb, just in front of the bay window. Carl got out of his truck and glanced in our direction. I waved at him but I guess he didn't see us because he didn't wave back.

From the passenger side of Carl's truck, Sergeant Zambo got out in his blue police uniform and walked to the back of the truck, briefly stopping by Uncle Carl, saying something inaudible from where we sat inside.

Zambo walked to the Ingersols, removed his ticket pad from his shirt pocket and wrote them each a ticket ,sticking them folded into a panel vent on the side of each trailer. Carl had a hacksaw in hand and was shaking his head and pointing toward the Ingersols, and arguing about something with Zambetes. He handed Zambo a sledgehammer. Then Zambo took off his belt and dress jacket and threw them into the cab of the truck, and then the men went to work on the monstrous Ingersols, breaking all three of those frightening machines into a pile of rubble.

Carl and Zambo smashed and sawed and pulverized those mobile devils in front of my delighted eyes. Then both men picked up the smaller pieces of steel and bent them in half with their bare hands, and tossed the pieces onto the bed of the rubbish truck. Eventually with a wide shovel pan and push broom they swept up the metal bones and smaller chards of the three monsters, and put them into three big barrels sitting on the truck's tailgate, which was marked "scrap iron". Carl then turned to the bay window, made eye contact with me and said,

"Omne trium perfectum."

I heard the sound of his words coming not from outside, but from a hole in the top of Orange Pasha's head that Iggy was licking as he tried to doctor the cat's most recent wound from his nemesis up the street. *Strange*, I thought.

"Every thing in threes is Perfect," Zambo had said.

How did I suddenly understand Latin? *This was getting stranger by the minute*, I thought. And why had Zambo given the monsters a ticket, only to destroy them afterward?

I watched Carl and Zambo get into the truck and leave. As they drove away I heard the clear voice once again, coming from the hole on top of Pasha's head.

"We are both running out of lives here," said the voice. "But I still have two left and I am willing to share one if you wish."

"Interesting," Papa said, smiling. " How do you propose that?"

"Never you mind, you bullheaded Greek!" said Orange. "What you need to concern yourself with is my fee, you stubborn old Corinthian! The cost is a great one to you, Theo, in that I must ask you to be as large on the inside as you are on the outside. Maybe even larger than you are willing to be.

"You have been very kind and generous to us all, Theocarides," the big cat continued. "And because your family needs you — Artie needs you and the community needs you — to live a bit longer, and because I am near the end of my days, I'm making this offer."

"Well, you have my attention," Eudie said to the feline, who answered, "The fee is this: you must take an olive branch up the street to Mehmet's and offer him your hand in the spirit of redemption and forgiveness, and pledge to him your new brotherhood and friendship, and you must ask him for the same in return."

"Why in the world would I do that, L'Orange?" Papa asked.

"Because, laws and agencies and politics have little chance of curing the evils of this world. Heart and soul cannot be legislated, but we each have the opportunity to make this a little better world. One friend, one embrace, one acceptance of another person's right to view things differently than we do, and one handshake at a time. And this is your opportunity to make a friend of a former enemy and turn your great hatred and pain into something better, bringing a modicum more understanding to this sorry world."

I didn't really understand much Orange was saying but I could hear the sound of the gears in Papas brain rebelling with a voice like the croaking of a great bellicose frog. That almost made me laugh, and I could hear the *sssst* of smoke coming out of Papa's ears, just like when Grandma sizzled bacon on the grill or shorted out her old toaster and blew a fuse.

"What!" he said angrily, cursing to himself for a good while in what I recognized to be the Greek language.

As Papa thought about the proposal we looked out the window to see Dave Abadgian and his sons Doctor Daniel Abadgian and Carl

341

Agajanian had returned. The three men stood side-by-side on the sidewalk, just across the street. They were all giving Papa the middle finger ;they seemed to be cursing him, agitated and shaking their fists. I could hold back no longer, which mad me laugh.

I asked Papa, "Why are they so mad at you, Eudie?"

"Because they are three young Armenians and they don't understand self-righteous Sophistic proposals from silly flea-bitten orange cats who allow themselves to be led by their ears by a mouse with a brain the size of a chickpea, trying to convince me to make peace with that bastard Turk who has never wished me well a second in his miserable life. That, Whisker, would be my best guess."

"Well, guess what, Papa," I said. "There is a Trinity of those 'Ourmanians' out there and boy, Papa, they are as mad as hell about something. And that's for sure… neat, huh?"

Papa did not respond to me but asked the Orange Pasha, "What if Savas Mehmet doesn't accept this ludicrous proposal?"

"Well," said Orange Pasha. "Then the Devil takes the high ground. But you must at least try, and that is my price to extend your life a few years. Do not forget you blockhead, that there are people who love you and depend on you."

Now I have no idea why, but by then my laughter had turned to tears, and I started to cry — most likely at the prospect that Eudie would refuse the cat's proposal. I abandoned all my attempts at maturity and decided heroes and giants be damned! It was full speed ahead into sniveling childishness and immaturity for me as I let my tears flow, sobbing without shame or regret.

Gosh, I was nine years old nearly a man. I had already lost Ahava and little Muggs and Solomon. Oh, I knew Grandma had said something about Papa going to heaven if he passed over river Jordan, and that we'd meet again someday, but that did little to assuage me, since I thought I would go straight away to hell. In any case, I just could not bear the thought of losing Papa. Besides, I thought, I was reasonably sure that Baptist heaven and Greek Orthodox heaven were in totally different localities, and likely far apart within the heavenly spheres. And how could I get to Papa's, side even If I snuck?

Would they even allow Baptists to visit the Greek Orthodox heaven? I soon abandoned rational thought with aplomb and went back too sobbing and cussing in high gear. I had no restraints and sniveling felt amazingly liberating, which was my new L word.

Papa's boisterous carping, and perhaps my crying, must have drawn Anna's attention, and we three opened our eyes in unison as she gently shook us awake. There wasn't a tear in my eye or on my cheek and I smiled, realizing that the tears and the crying themselves had been just a small part of a very strange dream.

You see, it seems that all three of us had fallen asleep at precisely the same time. Only we dreamt that we were awake, and when I realized that I had not been awake at all Papa and I smiled at each other, knowing that we and probably Orange Pasha and Iggy had just shared exactly the same dream.

We spoke of it for awhile and I learned that he had also seen Uncle Carl, Zambo and those Ingersol Rand monsters that had once so terrified me, and he knew that we had both heard Pasha's offering exactly the same way from the hole on top of the animal's head.

"But it felt so real," I said.

"Yes," Papa said. "The unreal often feels real. And the real sometimes feels like a dream." Papa reached behind his neck and removed a strange misshapen amber bottle with a stone cork and turned it over to its other side.

"Is that a medicine bottle, Papa?" I asked.

"Yes," he said, "sort of. Sometimes I use it when I am feeling low, and since I have been feeling poorly I hold it to my forehead or put it on the back of my neck."

I lifted it briefly into my hands and it felt very strange — almost as if it were pulsating. It was very cool on one side and quite warm on the other. Once again, Papa placed it back behind his neck and said that when he laid it there sometimes, when he was restless, it helped him think clearly.

Hmmm, I thought, I hope Papa is not going to give me another talisman or something weird.

But instead, almost immediately Orange Pasha got up and stretched, standing on my chest with Iggy still on his back he stepped onto Papa's throat with his front paws. He leaned against Eudie's chin, biting him on the tip of his nose three times. Papa winced; I think it must have surprised him. I watched Anna's face, since she was witness to the strange scene, but Papa said nothing to either of us, nor did he comment further about Pasha's eighth life gift. None of us mentioned the fee, or Pasha's vaunted olive branch theory.

Anna said nothing about Eudie, who was cussing in Greek in his sleep. Finally Papa kissed me on the cheek and dismissed, telling me that everything would be alright and that he would talk to me later. I noticed a brighter sparkle in his eyes and that his cheeks were starting too flush again. Papa looked at his Anna and said, "Ademeni my love, will you bring your handsome husband a large glass of my Macallan 1926 single malt whiskey? A large saucer filled with boiling black coffee, and three of those red jelly beans." Anna smiled and left to retrieve the requested items.

The next day it was as though our world had come one step closer to normal. It seemed like a dream, as though Papa had not been sick for a single moment. For the most part he looked and acted just as he always had. Even his hair stopped falling out. *Perhaps he was just joking,* I thought. There was no evidence of his previous illness.

I knew very little more about the next part of Papa's extended lifeline, nor of what transpired between him and the Turk or his payment to Pasha until some years later.

CHAPTER 37

The Eighth Life of Orange Pasha (The Winged Heart)

I WAS KEPT OUT of the loop after Papa's sudden recovery, and when I chanced into a room the adults simply stopped talking or abruptly changed the subject. And for reasons then unknown to me, I was not allowed to see Papa at all for nearly seven days.

No matter how stealthy my attempts were at eavesdropping I could not guess the mystery of Papa's mysterious circumstance.

Every once in awhile I did hear a few scant words, really just bits and pieces of things, like "electric chair" or "Pasha's tail". I heard things like "a brutal murder" and "life in prison", but I could not string anything together. I didn't know for sure who or what they were talking about, but I did know that when they all talked about "little pitchers having big ears", they were talking about me.

I knew something was very wrong, but I just could not imagine what it might be, and I did not find out until years later.

It was Monday, May 20th, 1956, around 3:15 a.m. I was not yet eighteen years old at that point, and I had joined the U.S. Navy for a four-year hitch. Uncle Harley Brown volunteered to drive me from my home in South Gate, California to the U.S. Naval Training Center in San Diego.

He allowed a generous four and a half hours for the one hundred mile trip, and soon we were on or way due south on Highway One, in the middle of the night. As Harley and I were wont to do, our conversations turned to Atlantic Avenue and the life we shared there. At some point we got around to talking about Papa and his near death from pulmonary pneumonia, and Duck's anger at his father over that stupid orange cat, and the fact that while Papa had allowed me to visit him, he would not allow his own two sons to see him during his illness. Tim was quite angry with his father over that. We teased and carried on as we always had, and finally Harley got around to telling me about Eudie's promised meeting with the Turk.

You see... according to Harley Brown, through his conversations with Duck Theocarides, Papa finally accepted Orange Pasha's eighth life. I told Harley that I thought it was through the trinity of bites from Orange to Papa's nose and chin. "I'm the one who told you about our trinity dream in the first place, numb nuts ," I said. "Remember? I was there. Now tell me something I don't know, goofus head!"

Harley smiled and slowed down the car to about fifteen miles an hour and said, "Hey Boatswain Spelman, how about if I get your skinny little ass to your boot camp? Oh, say, about 2:00 p.m. tomorrow afternoon instead of 8:00 a.m. this morning, — do you think they would throw your sorry ass in the brig to start off your illustrious Naval career?"

"You wouldn't do that to old Whisker, would you?" I asked.

As Harley brought the car back up to speed he smiled and at me and said, "Artie, I haven't heard the term 'Whisker' used like that in years. That brings back great memories of big ole Papa in all his glory."

"Well, good," I said, "then you can finish your story about Papa Eudie and that Turk."

Harley continued piecing together the mystery of the confrontation between Mahmet and Papa that had eluded me for years.

This is what I learned:

It seems that after Papa agreed to Orange Pasha's terms he walked a mile or so up Atlantic Avenue, past Randolph Street to Savas Mehmet's Lamp and Carpet Emporium to pay the fee of contrition he'd promised Orange Pasha in our dream. "But first," Harley said, "you need to know, Artie, that Savas Mehmet oğlu Babacan was almost everything Papa Eudocio had hated. He was Turkish, he was a Muslim, but more than all else he was a small-minded vicious bully. And more importantly to Papa, he was steadfast in his unyielding cruelty to animals, particularly dogs — and he hated cats, and Orange Pasha with particular fervor."

Savas Mehmet denied the Armenian holocaust by calling the reports "extravagant and exaggerated", ignoring the evidence. He had in fact written several feature articles contradicting the British historians, in which he blamed the entire matter on the Jews and the weak-minded Sufis and Koptic Priests who, according to him, aided and abetted the bad behavior of the Armenians, some of whom refused to relinquish their firearms as a gesture of good citizenry towards the Pashas .

Savas, in his teens, had fought alongside the Young Turks in 1915, in the conflict that had killed at least million Armenians, thousands of Catholics and hundreds of priests and other Christians. But the fly in Papa's ointment during our time on Atlantic Avenue was he said that Savas had poisoned, stabbed, beaten and — on his last encounter with the big orange cat — the Turk had put a hole the size of a quarter coin directly in the center of the poor cat's skull. and all over the course of seven years. Likely, Papa guessed, by using something like a carpet hammer, which the Turk sold in his store. Mehmet once tried to run over Orange Pasha with his motorcycle.

Anyway, as Harley continued his story, it seemed that Papa decided to muster all his emotional strength and sally forth into the turbulent waters of the Turkish seas.

"Wait, a minute Uncle Harley," I said. "Didn't Duck ever ask why Papa had accepted the cat's proposal in the first place, given Orange's mistreatment from Savas? Why would Eudie and Pasha care to make amends with an abuser?"

"Well, Artie," Harley responded. "I once asked Duck that very question and he just said that Papa suggested that Saint Iggy, the mouse, must have offered him advice, and that in spite of his namesake Saint Ignatius did not always give the feline fellow good advise. And Orange himself must have whispered into Papa's ear, 'Remember the Winged Heart of the Sufis'. Apparently Iggy said:

> *Who sees inside from outside?*
> *Who finds hundreds of mysteries*
> *Even where minds are deranged?*
> *See through his eyes what he sees.*
> *Who then is looking out from his eyes?*

And, well, I guess that final thrust just did it for my father, but who the hell knows?"

Harley continued Duck's story: "Anyway," he said, "After attending mass at St. Sophia's Greek Orthodox Church, Duck's Dad put his best foot forward. On that very day, on his way home from communion, he stopped off and bought a five-pound bag of strong Turkish coffee beans and purchased a book from Desmond's."

Harley explained that Papa had stopped by his house and collected his son Timoleon and some homemade Greek pastries made fresh by his wife Anna, and then he and Duck headed due east up Atlantic Avenue, crossing Randolph Street toward Savas Furniture and Carpet Emporium. As Papa and Duck walked, Papa ordered his son not to speak unless spoken to, and to be ready for anything.

"Jeez Dad, I don't understand all this bizarre crap, and your and Artie's insanity about the trinity," Duck had said. "All your Armenian friends here are furious with you, Dad, and it really sounds like you and Artie have both lost a marble or two. And Papa, you must admit that if you are going to pledge your friendship, that warning me to expect the worst is hardly a great way to start out your pilgrimage."

"Perhaps you're right," Papa said, agreeing with his son. "Even a blind chicken encounters a kernel of corn once in a while, but neither you nor Saint Iggy nor Pasha know this variety of bastard like I do. I don't think that war will ever be over for him. If it was, he could not abuse these small creatures the way he has been. Pasha was one of the lucky ones, if you can believe it. Savas has killed many animals in this neighborhood."

"Papa, for God's sake," said Duck. "Why are you bothering with this fool? Didn't you ever know any Turkish people that you liked?"

"Many!" Papa said. "There were many of them — many I respected and some whom I loved. But they were the Turks of the olden days, and they were a different cut from the fanatic political party. The 'Young Turks' were self righteous idiots. But yes, there were a few I liked quite well, Tim, although I must tell you that most — even some of those saner ones — allowed themselves to be swept up into all the lies. And still others were killed for helping the Armenians escape. Some of the 'Young Turks' could be charming and convincing, but their philosophy was rotten, and that is when the world hopefully learned what the Sufis had always known: to be weary of the cult, and that youthful energy is not always wise energy."

They continued on their walk and Tim asked, "Dad, tell me something about your first wife and my half sisters and all that Armenian business."

Papa put his arm around Duck as they walked along.

"Well, son, that's too long a story for this short walk," said Eudie. "But when I was just a few years older than you are now, shortly after I graduated from university in England, I went on a twelve day trip to a small village at the foot of Mount Ararat, in what was then thought of by many as Armenia. On my first morning there I entered a coffee and pastry establishment and came face-to-face with a living angel that walked among us mere mortals here on earth. Her name was Patil Gyurjetsivanian. She looked into my eyes as if she had been expecting me for centuries. Everything seemed familiar, like it had all happened somewhere before in a dream ,and I heard an old poem by Rumi ringing in my poor head:

I would love to kiss you.
The price of kissing is your life.
Now my loving is running toward my life shouting,
What a bargain, let's buy it

"The young beauty, whose music flooded my eyes, was the only one in the village that showed no reaction to my unusual size. She smiled at me with a centuries old smile and I ripped myself open with my bare hands and reached into the caverns of my chest cavity, tearing out my beating heart and placing it in those tiny hands for her to do with as she wished. Anyway, Timmy, we were married in December of 1908 and we had twin daughters, your half-sisters, in the summer of 1909, whom we named Amtaram and Davtig.

"In 1915 the Armenians were murdered en masse, starved and worked to death. They were raped, burnt together while many of their family members were forced to watch. My wife ran away and eventually killed herself by jumping off a cliff with our girls in her arms. She preferred that to letting them be butchered and raped by the Turkish soldiers, who had demonstrated that proclivity of disgrace and horror in our villages.

"I went back to work in earnest, killing the Turks by the bushel and not caring a wit if I lived or died doing it. During a one-year killing spree I lost my mind and came to be called 'Hayeren Dramahavaki'then', later because of my ability to throw stones and tear off their heads with my bare hands. I was called 'Akanakir nav Turk'yeri' by the Armenians, which meant 'Armenian Giant' and 'Destroyer of the Turks.'

"The story will have to wait, Tim, because now we are here at the door of the merchant Savas Mehmet oğlu Babacan."

"And this story will have to stop here, Boatswain Spelman," Harley said to me, "because I have to take a leak and get a cup of coffee."

CHAPTER 38

The Eighth Life of Orange Pasha (Rejection at High Noon)

W E WERE SOON fueled up with black coffee and donuts and back on the road.

"Duck and Papa arrived that Sunday sometime before noon," continued Harley, "at Mehmet's emporium. Savas met the two men at the front door and Timoleon entered first. Then Papa did his usual ducking and sliding gymnastics to enter Mehmet's salon.

Savas and Papa greeted each other in the Turkish language. Duck said he had no idea what they were saying, but the rhythm of the language stuttered from cordial to an indifferent tone, and he told Harley that he knew whatever the subject of their conversation was, that after about ten minutes it wasn't going well. Duck said that sometime later that day he had asked his father what had been said there in Turkish, and Eudie told him that he had spoken to Mehmet about an occasion from 15 years earlier, where upon hearing of the opening of his new Carpet Emporium, Papa had become interested and actually somewhat excited about the shop's potential. He believed it could have given him a chance to see and talk with someone from the old country.

In fact, Papa reminded Mehmet that in the past, he had bought several of his Persian carpets and a good deal of furniture from him.

Papa had told him in Mehmet's native tongue that in those days he had hoped the two might have had a chance to get to know each other over Turkish coffee, and talk of things that they both loved, and perhaps seek a common ground. Perhaps, Papa said, they could speak of the great Sufi poet and father of the Whirling Dervish, Jallaludin Rumi or Hafiz al din, and his poems celebrating the love of God; or share music literature and poetry, story telling and philosophy, and all things that Armenians and Greeks and Turks loved. Then Papa told the Turk that perhaps they could try to become their better selves, living in harmony at last here in this wonderful new world, America, where we were all simply Americans.

Then Duck told Harley that something obviously went awry because the two men abruptly went back to English, and things soon went to hell in a hand basket.

As we rode along, Harley told me that he had learned that the Turkish language is spoken with different levels of formality, and that each layer presents a certain level of respect, so that there is no ambiguity. Papa spoke to Mehmet with the highest degree of formality, but Mehmet responded with the lowest level, and so Papa switched back to English and said, "It makes me sad, Savas oğlu Mehmet Babacan, that you speak to me with such disrespect and loathing. But it does not at all surprise me. I come to you in the spirit of friendship. When I bought your merchandise all those years ago, you were most gracious cordial and friendly, and now your language has either deteriorated to the growling of a rabid dog, or you have insulted me. Which is it?"

Mehmet responded, "Who has insulted whom, Greek Talos? You offer me these ridiculous gifts. A book from an infidel Lebanese poet, Jibrān Xalīl Jibrān, who dares to blaspheme Allah's messenger by naming his homosexual poems the writings of 'The Prophet'. And I was also told that you've named your filthy vermin carrying cat 'Pasha?'

"And I know you've trained that diseased creature to steal my jewels and infect my mutfak," continued Mehmet, "and my pie safe. So now my bloated self-righteous. Grecian freak — who has insulted whom here?"

Papa stood up to his full height, looking down at Savas.

"We bid you farewell," said Papa. And he and Tim turned to leave. With his left hand. Mehmet threw the book and the package of coffee at Papa's heels.

"I shit on your mother's grave," he said. "Akanakir nav Turk'yeri. Oh yes, I see you. Infidel. And I tell you now, if that filthy 'haraam' cat of yours is sent here again, I will kill him and send you his dead eyes."

"Mahmet, you may shit where you wish," said Papa. "My mother saw plenty of Turkish shit in Greece when she was but a small girl, as your ilk butchered many in her village. I believe shit and Turks of your kind were one and the same to her. But I promise you, Mehmet, that if you harm Orange Pasha ever again, it will be your last day on this planet, and you will not enter paradise because I will bury you face down inside the carcass of a pig and lay it in a coffin filled with blood and intestines.

"So you do as you must, Mahmet. Your choices are your own, but I have given you my final word."

As the two Theocarides walked back to their home Duck said to his Father, "Well dad, that went well!"

"Better than I had hoped," Eudie said, smiling. "Did you noticed he kept Mama's pastry?"

"Pops," Duck said, putting his arm around his father as they walked homeward. "What mortal man could resist Mother's pastry?"

Duck paused and added, "What was he talking about, the cat being trained to steal from him?"

"Well, Tim, he's partially correct," said Papa. "Pasha was not trained by anyone but he did indeed steal from people, and brought his booty back to us. The Pasha loves shinny things, earrings and jewelry of every kind — anything shiny. What is more, apparently while Pasha was in the act of stealing Mahmet's merchandise Saint Iggy would jump off his neck for a snack on Mahmet's baklava or kadayif — and God forbid if Mahmet had set out cacik to cool. Then there was hell to pay."

"What is cacik, Papa?"

"It's a lot like your mother's yogurt soup," said Papa. "But what Mahmet failed to mention in his tirade was that I paid him every penny — full retail plus tax — for anything that Pasha brought back to our house, and I always apologized profusely. He refused what I tried to return because the cat had touched the goods and 'tainted' the items. I paid fully for all Pasha's booty and generously for the duo's bad table manners, and for their samples from his kitchen or pie safe. Actually, Orange Pasha and the sainted mouse inadvertently were a great asset to him and made him — at least from my wallet — a small fortune."

CHAPTER 39

The Eighth Life of Orange Pasha (Murder Most Deliberate)

A S HARLEY'S ACCOUNT continued, it seems that within a day or so of that confrontation a putrid-smelling box was delivered to Papa's front door containing Orange Pasha's dismembered tail. The bottom of the box was soaked, and there was a cracked mason jar half-filled with cacik, also containing the drowned body of Pasha's jockey mouse Saint Iggy. Either Iggy had drowned by Salas's own hand or he'd accidentally fallen into his yogurt soup. Papa had some ideas on that subject.

In the bottom of the box was a stranger in the form of the worm-filled, bloody body of some very pregnant black cat. The metal head of a garden hoe jutted out from her side. But Pasha's tail alone was enough to tear it for Papa.

Duck said that he had been in his father's office when Papa Eudie called Mahmet on the telephone. Duck told Uncle Harley that during that conversation Papa spoke to Mahmet in Turkish. When Duck queried as to the content of that conversation, Papa said he told him that he hadn't wanted to be misunderstood, so he spoke to Mahmet once again in his native tongue, telling him matter-of-factly that he was going to die.

Then Eudocio apparently phoned Sergeant Zambetes and told his poor brother-in-law that he had in fact already killed Mahmet, and promised to turn himself in and let Zambo where to find the Turk's body. Tim said that Zambo asked Papa Eudie if he didn't just want him to come over and shoot him in his god damned forehead to save Eudocio from the electric chair. Eudie said no, and that some folks back in Turkish Armenia had once tried that in a trinity of bullets, and it didn't take. Papa said he just wanted to arrange his affairs and then go find the rest of Orange Pasha's body, and that he would turn himself in after he'd found the big cat's remains.

Tim knew that statement was an untruthful diversion and that Papa hadn't even left the house, let alone had time to kill the Turk, so he went to his mother and told her that he thought his father had finally lost it completely over that stupid cat, and that his recent brain fever had obviously rotted his formerly fine mind, and that he was now going to jeopardize the rest of his life and their lives for some stupid principle. Duck embraced his mother and asked her, "Maica, is this how it's going to end for your husband and my father? After all Papa's lectures on life, his noble philosophy about Brownie's junebug thralls and his love and wisdom to Artie's hungry ears, and his grandiose stories and ideas on the human condition — all his philosophical lectures with me and Sol — was this it, then? Papa is about to kill another human being and bury him in pig shit over the life of some mangy vermin-carrying cat. God, Mother! What a sad end for the great man."

Anna listened thoughtfully and responded to her son. "Timoleon, what you say is true, but remember he has also lectured us all on always keeping our word. Your father thinks that that is the most important thing a man can ever do. In all the years I've known your father, he never once made a promise, no matter how large or small, to anyone that he didn't keep. I know this makes you sad, Timo but your big brother and Uncle Ant know Papa's ways better than you do, and they allow him his space and just love him as best they know how. They each have shared different lives with Baba."

"Bully for Babas!" Duck said to his mother sarcastically.

"Listen Timoleon," she said, a bit angry with her son, "none of you know this except Ant and Stavros, but Papa had tried many times before to be noble and fair with Savas, and was turned away. Besides Tim, the damned big fool doesn't even know for sure if Pasha is dead. There was just his tail in that box, and I think that whole silly dream was part of some longing to regain part of his equilibrium or something in his soul that is missing. I have always felt a great emptiness in him."

Tim said, "Yes, but what about Whisker? He dreamt the exact same dream as Babbá. Is that possible, Mother — that kind of dreaming?"

"Yes anything is possible," Anna said. "You know that I am from Romania, and you know how I feel about those things, Timoleon. But you also know that if your dad farted and told Artie it was the West Wind Whisker, he would believe it and set his sails to catch the scent of it. So who knows what that dream was really all about?"

"But Mother! Tim protested emphatically. Anna interrupted him and said, "Tim, you know that nothing can stop your father once he has made up his mind about something and that is both a great flaw or blessing in his character, but there is something I want you to see."

Anna left for a moment and soon returned with some paper in hand. She sat at the kitchen table across from her son and said, "Tim, I want you to read something your father wrote sometime back in 1915 or 1916. It is not dated but it must have been during his recuperation in that monastery. You need to know that your father had gone stark raving mad after he lost his family, and was quite literally insane. Any other man might never have recovered from those horrors or spent their lives in a mental institution; none of us ever knew exactly what he had gone through — we can only imagine. This letter is a bit incoherent and it babbles, Timmy, but it tells something of his pain."

She handed Tim the paper and asked him to read it to her. He complied and read it to her from the dirty stained pieces of paper. As we drove toward San Diego, Uncle Harley took a great deal of time piecing its contents together and told me the gist of what he remembered;

Duck read to his Mother;

"All my mass and girth have not saved you from these terrors.

I run on endlessly with you both sleeping here across my shoulders. Perhaps if I run to the ends of the earth you may live yet again. I run ...searching for just one kind angel to feed you, my babies, and wash you in olive oil, and to bring your rosy cheeks back to me once more.

They say there is a Sufi holy man who lives in these hills near Tiflis... I will run all day and all night and lay your dead bodies at his feet and offer my own life to the gods in exchange for holding you alive and happy one more day in my arms.

Perhaps God will touch his dervish hand, and his touch will bring your burnt eyes and limbs back to me. I will carry you back to your weeping mother and beg her to forgive me for your deaths. I will return once again to the holy man and surrender myself, forfeiting my life as payment for my own murderous ways.

You see, I was ruined and I do not understand why. I loved you so but I could not save you, and so I killed them, many of them; and all of them without mercy, just as they killed you. I tore them to shreds with my bare hands because I could, and because I had no sword or gun. Where is the song in this? What is the use of being Goliath if I cannot count even one person whom I saved in my blood rage, or see what the good of my strength was? Where was I when you, my precious daughters, were maimed? The soldiers shouted and laughed as they threw our babies alive onto the flames. Where was I when they drowned you by the thousands in the Tigris?"

I was slashing and cutting and butchering the Turks. I did not care. I still don't care. I loved tearing out their living guts and plucking out their vicious eyes and tossing their cruel raping hearts to the wild dogs. I cannot care about them. Where gardens once grew near my heart now there is only sorrow and shallow graves and death. My world is no more; it has been replaced with the unrepentant joy of killing those evil men. There is no plow to level my fields of sorrow and despair, no rain enough to wash away my tears.

What is the value of this kind of victory? This butchery of the helpless, I weep for I cannot see it. All warriors kill and are killed. But not all warriors or armies devour and gnash and gnaw eating the flesh and blood of an enemy so that they are not merely dead or so that they cannot fight another day but so that they will never again procreate or exist as a national peoples but be destroyed utterly so that their heart and song poetry music and air they breath cease to exist.

There can be no warrior like these soulless bastards who do not fight for glory or cause or to defend. None of the innocents knew what they had done to die.

Annihilation... where is the rhyme or reason?

Harley said he was so taken with that message that he later tried to write it down and remember the gist of it. He believed that it would help him understand why Papa had bonded so closely with little Ahava, and why she used his arms as her portal into heaven.

But Eudie wouldn't go to jail, or confront the electric chair. Anna had different ideas, and she knew her husband's madness quite well; and she was also aware that he had never fully recovered from those horrors and pain in Armenia. Anna went to her ally in the form of Blanche Brown, and it was soon decided that they would walk up the street to the Emporium and try to convince Savas Mahmet to leave town, and fast. When Harley told me that part of the story I could just see my very small Grandmother and the very large Anna leaning forward, marching at a brisk step up Atlantic Avenue to save Papa Eudie from himself. I thought briefly that Grandma perhaps might just grab the Turk by his ear, just as she had Hans Bearwald over Harley. These where two fearsome women.

"Hell," I told Harley, "Anna could have killed him herself if she had wanted to, huh, Brownie?"

Harley laughed and said, "Yes, easily, and with her bare hands she could snap his neck like a twig."

When Uncle Harley and I where about thirty miles north of San Diego, we stopped in an old train car turned into a roadside dinner and were seated in a booth. Harley ordered me hot cakes and eggs.

"Your last meal" he laughed.

I was hungry but distracted, wanting to get back to Papa's story. I quickly wolfed down my last meal in my pre-boot camp world, anxious to get back to Papa's madness and back on the road over a cup of java.

As Uncle Harley and I resumed our conversation, Harley changed paths briefly to talk about Tufts' mock trial at Harley's hideout, just after our beating, and the fact that in those days I had also not known that he and Duck had had their hands full trying to control Papa's rage.

"Harley said because Artie during Bruce's funerary tour and his education there from Papa Eudocio, he had shown the boy a casket in the salon and convinced him that it had precisely enough space in the bottom of its cushions to hide a young bastard's body to be buried alive, just under the next corpse client, leaving the Theo & Carides Mortuary to be buried."

Papa was spoon-feeding Tufts with what Tim and I prayed was mostly bullshit and you remember of course how God damned terrifying Duck's Dad could tell a scary story?"

I responded, "Oh man, I sure do. Grandma wouldn't let me hear most of them, and he scared the hell out of her. And remember, Uncle Fuzzy couldn't handle them and used to leave the room, and he also thought Papa was half crazy anyway. So yes, I remember those stories by reputation mostly, and the little bits of those tales you told me when I bunked with you. Remember Brownie, how many nights you kept me awake?"

Harley continued. "When Eudie asked the boy how he would like that six-foot vertical slide down into hell, without waiting for the boy's answer he explained that it would be very easy to do and that the world wouldn't even miss him and that he would just suffocate until his evil little ass expired from lack of oxygen and his lungs turned blue. Papa was so convincing that even we believed him. Harley said that he and Duck just looked at each other holding their breath when Papa told young Bruce that if he repented his evil ways and apologized for his cruelty to Artie and Muggs that Papa would do him the favor of just 'bleeding him out'."

"Then what happened" I asked Harley.

"Bruce lost it and went into shock, and I think Duck and I did too, because Papa's anger over your beating and Muggs' death was way out of control. It scared me and Duck and we didn't know how to stop his rage or how to control him and the whole thing was turning from a mock trial into something really dark and dangerous. Remember Artster, Papa had zero tolerance for bullies and murderers of innocents, no matter their rank or age. Papa explained to us that to him those Tufts boys were all just Turks or Nazis in training, so Duck and I believed that there was a extremely good chance that Bruce was going to die buried alive or bled out and it genuinely scared the shit out of us, so we worked very hard to get Tuft's stupid ass the hell out Papa's clutches and back to our courthouse and just have a peaceful hanging.

"Jeez, I can imagine," I said. "Why didn't you guys ever tell me about that?"

"Well, I don't know, Artster. I guess you just had to be there," Harley said. "I am not really sure but I think Duck and I knew that this could all get ugly fast."

"I remember how pale Tufts was when you guys drug the poor bastard back across Atlantic Avenue that day. But what happened to the Savas the Turk?" I asked, wanting to get back to his story."

Harley paid the check and we got back on the road, heading into San Diego.

"Well," Harley said. "Mother and Anna had walked up to Mahmet's shop to warn him or perhaps to do something outrageous to get him arrested and keep him away from Papa. But he wasn't there, and a few minutes later when they turned to walk back toward our home they saw him tear by them on his 1929 Sunbeam Talbot motorcycle with a side car going down Atlantic Avenue toward Gage at a very high speed. Remember, in those days few wore helmets. And as Mehmet flew past the ladies, Grandma said she saw a flash of the Orange Pasha running directly into the spokes of the front wheel, causing his motorcycle to tumble end over end and crash against the brick front wall of Han's Bearwald's grocery store. Papa ,by shear coincidence, had been just across the street at his Savings and Loan offices, preparing his last will and testament and getting his affairs in order for Anna and his sons. And before he went up the street to kill or perhaps be killed by Mehmet, he heard the loud roar of the crash and walked across the street to see what the commotion had been. Savas's brains were running down the corner of the brick wall as he lay dead, his skull crushed underneath sections of his motorcycle and crumpled side car.

As Hans and Papa stood there looking at the crash site, Zambo's police car came around and parked near the crash. Zambo got out and joined the other two men, and after standing next to them awhile he said to the Papa, "Deed you keel hem, my bruder?"

"No, I think Pasha killed him for me," said Papa.

"Goed, dat'l save mi a bullet," Zambo said.

They all looked and saw bits of blood and pieces of the Pasha's orange and white fur stuck to the spokes of Mahmet's motorcycle; and ten feet from the wreckage they found the upper half of Pasha's body sliced in half by the spokes of the Sunbeam Talbot's front wheel.

Zambo's first assumption was that Mahmet had tried for the second time to kill the Orange Pasha, but soon Grandma Brown and Anna arrived to correct, them stating that it was indeed Orange who had deliberately run into the spinning spokes of the front wheel of the motorbike, crashing it into the wall and killing the Turk. Anna put her arms around Papa and said, "Pasha has saved your life yet again, my love."

Papa looked down at the two women, and then at the smashed body of Savas Mehmet.

"Alla hu Akbar!"

CHAPTER 40

The Eighth Life of Orange Pasha (The Windmills at Gopher Spit Hollow)

UNCLE HARLEY GOT me to boot camp about an hour early and we sat in the car there, talking in the base parking lot near the USNTC front gates. I knew a good deal more than I once had about Papa's confrontation and the missing information from my naive eavesdropping childhood, and as we sat chatting I found out further that during Papa's days during those great horrors back in the holocaust of 1916 Turkey, that Papa Eudie had not known exactly when — nor how — his wife and daughters had died. He had only heard that they were dead. And after he dug himself out of that shallow grave he was nearly completely insane and had lost most of his rationality.

Sometime later during that madness he found the bodies of two small girl's corpses from one of the fiery piles of dead Armenians. The two girls were no relation to him at all, but in his deranged mind he imagined they were his daughters Amtaram and Davtig. Papa placed each of their little bodies over a shoulder and ran with them for God only knows how long, trying to escape the horrors of that war forever.

Because of his ferocity and reputation in battle, the Turkish military wanted him dead — and the sooner the better.

"How far did he run, Harley?" I asked."

"No one knew for sure, but Duck heard that the monastery was more than a hundred miles from the place where he had dug himself out of that grave.

"And when he finally arrived at that monastery and relinquished the girls' charred bodies to the old Coptic Priest, whom the Turks believed was a deranged Sufi master. The Koptik Christian Priest was called 'Ashik al saz Ishq Bashad' by the Armenians. The Turks, however, called him 'Melchizedek the Juggler of Souls' and were absolutely terrified of him, and so Papa was safe at last."

"Wow," I said.

"Well, Seaman Recruit Spelman, now you know the story, and I am sure you remember that by the time you saw Papa again a few days later he was as fit as a fiddle, and it was as though nothing had ever happened. And so Mother Brown let you visit him again, remember?"

"I remember that. Thanks for telling me some of the rest, Brownie. I have often wondered about it."

Uncle Harley said goodbye and told me to behave unless there was a good deal of fun or some priceless wickedness or debauchery available in misbehaving. Then he gave me a hug and said, "You better get to the gate, boner head. It's 7:45. Don't forget these," he said as he handed me the envelope containing my enlistment papers and added, "Tell your chief boatswain not to let you play with glue or be around matches and the flatulent at the same time. Artster watch out for those drunken jarheads and those long legged women fartnick-remember you haven't had your vaccinations yet, and regarding womankind you're still as dumb as a dingleberry on an ingrown pimple. And besides, Seaman Recruit Spelman, remember that it's the U.S. Marine Corps that gets all the pussy."

"How would you know about the military you deaf bastard'-Shove off Dog Face—that's -sailor talk Uncle Harley I said; How am I doing?"

"Well Artie, yep that'll get you your ass kicked alright, probably by some skinny Kentuckian PFC from the 101st Airborne!"

Harley waived good bye and I watched him drive off thinking to myself 'I will miss that snaggle tooth baritone.' I remember thinking that while growing up was certainly exciting it had also been very painful and I vowed then and there that I would resist maturing as much as I possibly could a would try to steadfastly remain as silly as a twizzle for as long as possible, but alas just like the Turkish bullets to Papa's head had little affect on the big Greek, twizzlery would abandon me a good deal as I walked through the guarded gate and handed my enlistment papers to the engineman second class SP at the gate my foolishness was already vanishing just a bit.

Gopher Spit Hollow was indeed magic to all of us. It was our special place, our corner of the world. Our secret place. We imagined that only we knew about it and that it was ours alone. The property was located on a huge parcel of land somewhere in a place called Anaheim. The property was a mixture of several hundred acres of Southern California sage brush, Avocado trees and on my last visit there to my nine year old eyes it was a mixture of both Orchard with the Greenery of a Sherwood Forest next to a little bit of Arabian desert and sage brush so typical of Southern California in those days of my early youth.

This was the place during my childhood where I remember dozens of times Papa Eudie driving a varied bunch of us to this very old orchard where there stood two old Greek style windmills each built into the top of tall round brick towers painted white -they had once utilized canvas sails like the sheets from old sailing ships strung on eight large masts to catch their wind. The mills had long since been abandoned and where dis functional they still spun but only by the grace of God and Papa Eudie's money and the sweat and elbow grease of Uncle Clayton Crawford and his stepson Walter Watts Crawford. Papa had always maintained those windmills simply for their esthetics he just loved that spot of earth because it remind him of his own childhood and home back in Greece.

In truth we had technically always been trespassers over those five years or more, but nothing was ever said to us and we used that spot at will. I think Papa knew the owner of one of these land parcels from Anna's bridge club so our trespassing was a passive crime.

Papa and I used to walk the property by the mile, always standing to admire those sails spinning languidly and the clouds moving like puffs of cotton just behind them. I loved sitting high on Papa's broad shoulders listening to the adagio "whoosh-whoosh" of the windmills' whistling voices as they slowly turned flapping those large canvas sails as the birds sang their distant counterpoint. Papa once suggested to me that it sounded like music and maybe it was God humming or playing his duduk, from that moment onward I listened carefully to music in the sounds all around me including machinery. It was there I grew to notice the subtle music of everything even the motor voices of airplanes flying high over head on our visits to the 'Spit' during World War Two. Grandmother Brown always called the Spit our "Magic Kingdom".

But this would be our last visit too the 'the hollow for all of us. It was then somewhere around the first week of August 1947, and if I remember correctly it was only hours after I had resumed audience with the now completely rejuvenated eagle's nest that Papa invited cousin Walter, myself and my sneaky foot cousin Leslie Dow to attend the funeral of the Orange Pasha and a mouse some of us had come to know as Saint Iggy.

Anna and Grandma Brown both only told me that someone had accidentally run over Pasha right there on Atlantic Boulevard, and that Iggy accidentally drowned himself in someone's yogurt soup.

Papa had frozen the remains of the three critters in his garage freezer and Leslie and I dug the grave just as Papa instructed; and we laid Iggy, Orange Pasha and his little black wife and her tummy babies to rest. Papa didn't open the frozen box but told us about the mother cat whom he called Madam Nubia de L'Orange and he told me wanting to spare me the gory details — that she had died in grief over Orange Pasha her misbehaving husband.

It made me sad and ever so briefly I thought of actually behaving and crossing Atlantic at the bell light then I also recalled the poor Viking mouse mother Kerstin Rydstrom. Why did so many babies die before they were born I wondered and thought about how precious life was how hard it was to get born and keep breathing. That hurt my brain and I very nearly decided to give up on pondering stuff altogether.

Papa placed the cold box in the ground and laid a good deal of Pasha's shinny stolen trinkets along with it. We covered it up each of us alternately placing a hand full of soil on top of the grave.

Finally Papa laid down his shovel hand of dirt and packing it down he said, "L' Orange, thank you my fine and generous friend. You've taught me many lessons through our friendship and we both dreamed the dream and fought the good fight. The master has become the student and cost you your life through my false pride when you gave me your precious gifts.

"Merci beaucoup, le grand chat orange, and here we now finally honor you as you find your rest. God bless you my friend."

We stood around the little grave and Papa recited a poem he'd once learned somewhere in that monastery near Tiflis:

> *My love wanders the rooms, melodious,*
> *flute notes, plucked strings,*
> *full of a wine the Magi drank*
> *on the way to Bethlehem.*
> *We are Three. The moon comes*
> *One of us kneels to kiss the threshold.*
> *One drinks, with wine-flames playing over his face.*
> *One watches the gathering,*
> *and says to any cold onlookers,*
> *This dance is the joy of existence.*
> *I am filled with you.*
> *Skin, blood, bone, brain, soul.*
> *There is no room for lack of trust, or trust.*
> *Nothing in this existence but that existence.*

My cousin Walter returned from greasing the gears of the abandoned Windmills one last time. Leslie now shared one of Papa's shoulders with me as we rode the great stallion to touch the side of the Windmill and say goodbye to Gopher Spit Hollow. As we listened to its humming, Leslie had a smile that reflected the entire width of the earth and that world was new and beautiful and happy, and to us everything, even Pasha's final rest and Iggy's tummy full of his yogurt soup and kittens, seemed in those moments lovely. It renewed us, making the world for a few precious seconds perfect.

We visited each other a bit before leaving but were mostly in pensive silence there in the spirit of love and redemption and near the mysteries of men and Cats behaving both bravely and Childishly in the forest ignorance and beauty we called life.

I cannot remember exactly at which point the windmill became a metaphor for my life; I think for me it was likely sometime later in the 1950s when I chanced to see Jose Ferrar in the movie 'Cyrano de Bergerac'. It must have been during that scene in which his adversary called him a Don Quixote. Cyrano quite agreed that he was indeed Quixotic, and replied to his foe, that he had seen himself in that way on every page of La Mancha, then his nemesis warned that if he dared tilt with windmills that; "Their arms can cast you down into the mud!" whereupon Cyrano replied, "Yes... Or up among the Stars!"

I have been struck many times while tilting and whenever I was banged about always opened my eyes expecting to see the stars or the moon getting closer as I spun ever upwards.

It was also sometime near 1956 or '57 when we discovered that Gopher Spit Hollow and some 600 adjoining acres had been bought by Disney Motion Picture Studios and that Saint Iggy the wise little mouse and his cats lay in the heartland of what became Disneyland California.

Grandmother Brown always thought it funny that Disney called itself "The Magic Kingdom" since that was exactly the way she saw it there.

Twelve years after I got out of the U.S. Navy I took my wife Janeanna and my four-year-old son Lucien there. We rode on the Pirates of the Caribbean ride and as our boat rushed under the bridge looking up at those robotic drunken sailors laughing down on the cascading boats of laughing passengers I swear I saw Orange Pasha and Iggy's Ghost near the lamp post.

One cannot help but wonder if Disney Corporation is missing shiny trinkets and bright bobbles. Perhaps they were taken to the grave of a couple ghost thieves there near that bridge?

The night of the first day Harley dropped me at USNTC, I had a dream that Pasha was reborn with opposable thumbs. Iggy found another friendly cat who had an endless source of cacik to slurp on and Pasha's pregnant wife had three kitties that looked just like him and loved to retrieve things and dream with tow-headed boys and thick-headed Giants. When I woke up it was Reveille and I was rousted out of my bunk to a gruff voice screaming, "

Drop your cocks and grab your socks. Reveille Reveille! You're in the Navy now, boys. It's 5:00 a.m. and I'm your new Mama — hit the deck and grab a teet. Mama's gonna teach you girls how to march!

Now you know the story of the Orange Pasha.

CHAPTER 41

An Armenian, A Drunken Duck, and An Irishman...

A S WE STOOD together helplessly, watching the men at the old pepper tree, Grandma Brown told us that now she knew how the refugees in all those war torn countries must have felt after a bombing.

We were all being uprooted, including our Mother Peppercorn. And all of us were going in different directions. Most of the Brown and Spelman things were sitting in boxes or stuffed into pillow cases and shopping bags. The furniture was stacked in a small pile in the front room, waiting for Carl Agajanian to come with his truck and take it to Grandma's new home. She was going to be the pie lady and head cook at a restaurant called 'Queens' in Inglewood, California. There was a small one-bedroom upstairs apartment at the back of the restaurant, just big enough for Grandma Brown alone.

I don't think any of us had a clear idea of where we were going. I certainly didn't; all I knew was that we would never be together in the same way again. My mother wouldn't say much about where we would live, but Grandma said we would know soon enough and that it would all work out in the end.

Duck was distraught because the previous day mother Anna had thrown the Tarot and seen that her cards read that he and Harley may not see each other for a very long while — maybe years and likely never again. All this was hard for the boys to handle. It must have seemed to poor Duck as though everything was broken.

The big boy was spoiling for a fight with someone, anyone at all, and I heard him tell Harley he really didn't care who it was. He'd strike out at the lumberyard, or the powers for which he felt responsible. He just wanted to hit someone or some-thing. He stated openly that being hit might be just fine as well. He could handle a fist to the face. But he had told his dad that the Brown's departure was like having a kidney operation with a rusty spoon and no anesthetic.

Harley, on the other hand, had turned to sarcastic taunting humor to express his anger, sometimes turning it into a theater of the ridiculous, as well as making fun of — or belittling — everything and everyone in sight. He didn't dare try his mouth out on Grandma Brown, but everyone else soon tired of his attitude and avoided him. This was most unusual behavior for the boys; it wasn't pretty, and Grandma said that she had never seen them in a state quite like this before. She knew they were in great pain and wasn't sure what to do about it.

Sensing their frustration, and because everyone was in a state of upheaval, Grandmother let the boys slide far more than her proprieties would have normally allowed and she gave them both a very wide berth.

The two great women hardly ever fussed, but Mom Brown chastised Anna as to why in the world she would tell those two soft-headed puppies such a thing, even if it were true.

Grandma chided, "That devil's solitaire of yours told you Eudocio would die too and now he's nearly a bull ox once again. So why in the world would you say anything to those dunderheaded boys, who believe everything you say?"

Anna looked sheepish and apologized, having no good answer.

But the damage had been done and the boys were paddling upstream with a single broken paddle between them, lost somewhere between boys and men.

The sawing had gone on all morning as two men from the lumberyard murdered Grandma's giant Peppertree. One Giant had lived to fight another day, according to Papa, because of the intervention of Orange Pasha's spirit. But this giant pepper was helpless and its only defenders were a crazy gnome and a lazy French skunk from Papa's imagination.

First the four huge ropes of the giant swing were torn off; and then our big platform swing was unceremoniously tossed aside like a corpse into a ditch.

As we sat there watching from the stoop, Harley observed that the work was very slow for the two men, because they were working with only an axe and hand saws.

I added that I was pretty sure, Gnome Exemplumonious was also tormenting them and slowing them down. We all agreed because the men were being pelted with peppercorns. The tree was giving them grief at every turn.

The moment the workers had started their butchery, the boys were in complete agreement that it might be a really good time to get drunker than a neutered goat. Duck had secured a large bottle of Papa's Ouzo and they had been refilling a couple of Coke bottles, sitting on the stoop and watching it all since the workers had first arrived, parking their Model A Ford truck next to the little white house in the early morning.

Duck allowed as to how he might "just go pick a fight with the two lumberyard bastards." He told Harley that he could watch as he whipped those men, both at once, adding that he wanted to do it alone and for Harley to stay the hell out of it. Now, my uncle Harley was a singer not a fighter, who wouldn't have dreamed of arguing the point with Duck and told him so. As he patted Duck on the back he told him he would be pleased just to watch from afar and was looking forward to that happy event.

The workers started topping the upper branches and those big beautiful limbs fell one by one, crashing to the ground. With each cut or thud, our hearts tore a little too. As the tree branches fell, perhaps with their memories of our climbing feet on them, we swore we could hear them crying out us for help.

"Did you hear that?" Duck said.

"Did you hear the pain?" he asked dramatically as he sipped the ouzo from the coke bottle.

"I heard it!" Harley said in a slurred voice, taking another swig.

"Me too. I heard it; it was a groan and a squeak, then a whistle," I said, chiming in.

I tried a neat groan and a squeaking sound, like I imagined Eudie would have made, but mostly mine didn't work. No one thought I was funny — certainly not Veve or Grandma standing next to us. I had not, of course, actually heard a thing, but I wanted to make a contribution to the boy's conversation, and had as yet not practiced my belligerence.

I sat on the stoop between Duck and Harley, watching in horror as chunks of all of us fell to the ground. Finally, all that remained was the branchless, butchered center hulk of a trunk. Then the two men picked up a long timber saw with a handle at each end and went to work on its very large girth, one on each side going back and forth in perfect rhythm until at last the core toppled over in its death knell. The giant Patriarchal Theocarides across the street had recovered, but according to Harley and the Duck this old giant was dead, by "murder in the coldest degree".

The two men took a break and went over, leaning against the remaining stump. Grandma Brown managed to find some cups, a lemon and some sugar in her packed boxes and made some lemonade. She took it out to the men, handed it to them. One of the men was David Abadjian, the muscular lumberyard security guard who had brought Muggs and me back to her after my beating. As Mom Brown turned to leave, he placed his hand on her arm and said, "I am so sorry, Mrs. Brown, about this beautiful tree. It's just my job." His face was almost as pitiful as Grandma's when he said, "Mrs. Brown, I suggested to them that they just work around this big tree, but they wouldn't stand for it.

He pointed across the street in the direction of the funeral home. "Did you know that Mr. Theocarides tried everything he could to stop the destruction of this property?" he asked. "He even offered to buy it."

"No, I didn't know that," she answered.

"I understand about the tree," she said, trying to comfort the tormented man. "But all things come to an end. God will take us when he's ready. I think maybe heaven just needed this wonderful pepper tree."

"I like that big man," Abadgian said to Grandma, motioning toward the funeral parlor across the street, and toward the man looking out the window.

Sipping his lemonade Abadgian said, "He has helped everyone I know in this community and he has buried from most of our families many at little or no charge."

"Everyone loves him," Grandma answered. "We thought he was near death a month ago, but now, God willing, he has recovered nicely."

Then Duck emptied his bottle and walked over to the stump to join in on our conversation. Spoiling like a fighting peacock, he raised his big leg and put his foot up on the a small log near the men. Looking down at them Duck said, "Well sir, I would like to have seen any men who could throw my father anywhere!"

The men looked up and smiled.

The other man with an Irish accent chuckled agreeing and said, "Yes sir, Faith I would'ha loved tah see that me own self. They'd need some help for that job you can bet, I've niver seen a fellow that big," he chuckled, shaking his head.

Duck said, "My dad says F.D.R. considered himself King of America and president for life, and that his passivism reminded him of the Armenians when they allowed the Pashas to convince them to turn in all their weapons, which they did peacefully. Then they were slaughtered by the hundreds of thousands by the same Young Turks who had convinced them to do it in the first place.

"My dad saw F.D.R.'s philosophy of passivism on the war in Europe as another tragedy. Dad said we should have stopped that Nazi bastard sooner and that F.D.R. pussyfooted with the Japanese, and that the

President tried to play both ends against the middle. He believed Mr. Roosevelt was a frustrated socialist. Dad had lived through that variety of state and government control in three different countries and wanted none of it, and when Roosevelt kissed Stalin's ass, that tore it for my Dad. He hated National Socialism, the Social Democrats and Communism with a passion, as well as politics in general."

"Hmm?" the man said thoughtfully.

He then responded, "Interesting."

"Well," the Guard said to his coworker. "We better get back to work." He handed the cups back to Grandma with a thanks.

Neither man commented on Duck's tirade but went back to the stump and started chopping the roots with axes. It was a tedious job — the roots had spread long and deep over the decades, and the tree was not going out with a whimper — her half-dozen trunk and root systems went deep then came up out of the ground many feet away, and dove back down under again like the back of a sea serpent.

Uncle Jimmy showed up in his fast Mercury sedan and Veve and Grandma were to leave with a car full of boxes going to who knew where.

Grandma kissed Harley and Duck goodbye on the cheek and looked funny.

"What have you boys been drinking? she asked.

"Just Coke, Mom," Harley said, "but we ate some licorice earlier."

"Oh, said Grandma, her eyes twinkling, "I thought I smelled candy." Then she smiled and turned to leave.

She looked at the boys and asked, "Will Artie be okay with you boys for awhile?"

"Yes, Mom," Harley said. "Besides, Eudie and Anna are home and we may go over there after we finish our Cokes."

As they left, Grandma turned to the boys and said, "Take it easy on the licorice."

When Jimmy and the ladies drove off, Duck looked at Harley and said;

"Brownie, go fill these Coke bottles again."

Harley went back to the garage and filled the bottles with three quarters ouzo and the rest water, turning it milky white. Then he returned to the tree cutting.

Duck was still trying to agitate Abadjian, but he was getting nowhere. Finally Duck turned and walked back to the stoop with Harley and took another big swig from the Coke bottle. He approached the two workers once again.

After several sallies from Duck, Dave finally lost his patience, turned to Duck and said, "Son, Mack and I have work to do here. Further, I more or less agree with you, but I was a Marine until they retired me for being too old and wounded. I served proudly under a man who was simply my president. I didn't vote for the man and I care nothing for politics. I am Armenian myself and both my father and my auntie died under the Pasha's brutal hand, so again I agree with your father."

He turned to pick up his shovel and said dismissively, "Now son, leave us alone to finish this job. Go over there with your little buddies and sip some more courage and if you still want some knurled old Marine ass, come back here and ask for it for it like a man instead of trying to pick a fight like a high school boy. And then I'll take a little break and you can show me your stuff. Now, please get your big dumb ass out of here."

Duck reluctantly returned to the stoop and he and Harley played and teased each other, part of which included tormenting me. The boys soon finished the contents of their bottles and Harley went back for yet another mix.

After twenty minutes or so, Harley, who was higher than a kite, said something about the two workers being just like the Nazis, and that Muggs wouldn't have been killed if the lumberyard had hired a better guard there in the first place. This barrage went on endlessly, only interrupted by more trips to the garage and more swigs until the ouzo ran out.

The men kept working, ignoring the boys' refusal to respond.

There was nothing of the tree that was recognizable. Where the tree had once stood was a sad hole in the earth, six feet in diameter and about three feet deep.

Harley's warped, drunken mind went into action; he turned to the men in an effort at what he doubtlessly thought was facetious irony and in his most belligerent voice, he sang as loudly as he could, stretching out his hands to mock his remembrances of the delivery of one of Reverend Wall's sermons.

He sang:

> *I THINK that I shall never see*
> *A poem lovely as a tree.*
> *A tree whose hungry mouth is pressed*
> *Against the sweet earth's flowing breast;*
> *A tree that looks at God all day,*
> *and lifts her leafy arms to pray;*
> *A tree that may in summer wear*
> *A nest of robins in her hair;*
> *Upon whose bosom snow has lain;*
> *Who intimately lives with rain.*
> *Poems are made by fools like me,*
> *But only God can make a tree.*

In spite of Harley's alcohol-soaked brain, the song was actually quite beautiful. At least it was good enough that it had the opposite effect of the one intended. The two soft-hearted men just looked at each other rather sadly, and seemed to be thinking about their pitiful handiwork as they went back to stacking the branches and cutting everything into logs, somehow still avoiding the two young drunks.

Harley's attempts had failed miserably at picking a fight on Duck's behalf.

Finally Duck had heard enough, and by this time was himself "well oiled" and slurring his words to Harley.

"Brownie," Duck said. "I am going over to 'lift my leafy arms' and prey all over these stump-cutting bastard sons a bitches. I haven't killed anyone yet this week and I am out if practice."

Duck approached Dave and said, "Okay, Jughead, I am ready. I'm asking for it like a man," he said.

Dave said, "It's 'Jarhead' son, and are you sure this is what you want?"

"Yep!" he said, slurring his words and shutting his eyes briefly. "It's just what the Doctor ordered."

At precisely this time, Papa Eudie walked across the street and onto the property, and I went to him and he put me up in the Eagle's Nest and we prepared to watch the festivities together.

Dave said something in Armenian to Eudie, and he answered back in the same language,. Then, shaking his head, Dave turned to his coworker. "Matt," Dave said, "the big man won't be joining his son. He said this is between the three of us. And I am happy to say that this Armenian 'David' is not fighting this other Greek 'Goliath', period — and if that were the case and we had to fight both these two, you and I are getting the hell out of here to reconnoiter." The big Irish chuckled a bit and shook his head in agreement.

Trying to follow the gist of the conversation and getting most of it, I yelled to the two men. "Don't worry about our Papa Eudie," I said. "He's near 67 years old and he's way too old to fight. Why, he's been really sick and he might fall down for dead, so don't worry. Heck, he's likely sick right now. See, he's got some p-newmonia and might even die today or tomorrow."

After all, I thought to myself, *it was mostly true.* I knew Orange Pasha had gotten him mostly well and given him some more life, and then saved him from the electric chair, but I didn't want Papa to get hurt, so I played it safe.

Papa reached up both legs of my pants and despite his massive fingers, he managed to pinch a few of the fuzzy little hairs and some flesh on the side of each calf, making me squeal.

Eudie said to both men, "In this case, two against one seems fair to me, teach the boy a lesson if you can... you have my blessing. I won't interfere, nor will I be joining him."

Papa said something again to Dave in Armenian and Dave responded in English.

"Yes sir, I'll do my best."

Dave turned to his helper. "Give it all you got, McNamara. The big man says his son is just eighteen but can handle himself."

"Okay Dave," Matt said. "Are you sure?"

"Yep, I'm sure," he responded.

"Dave! What's this boy's name?" Matt asked.

"His name is Duck!" a drunken Harley Brown yelled from his seat on the apple box. "His name is Duck," Harley repeated, "and he's my best pal!"

"Jesus Mary, that's the biggest damned Duck I've ever seen," the big Irish exclaimed.

There was a pause and Duck, who had been patiently standing there, wobbling with his huge fists poised at the ready, put his head down and yelled, "Quack! Quack!"

Then he tore into the two men like a charging wild boar. He grabbed Dave by his belt and the back of his neck, lifting him off the ground by the shirt. He threw him over the top of the model A truck like a sack of potatoes, and then he turned and hit Matt a cracking blow to the chin. It echoed off the buildings across the street, knocking the big Irish against the door of the truck and briefly taking his breath away as his back slid down the side of the door, seating him momentarily on the Ford's running board.

Matt rose and managed to hit Duck multiple blows faster and harder than the boy had ever experienced. Duck looked surprised, stepped back and shook it off; then he answered with a paralyzing blow on the man's head that got his attention.

"Whoa, big boy," the big Irishman said, looking to Dave as he shook the fuzz out of his head.

Matt was no longer worried about his being a young boy. They had their hands full and he knew it. Matt looked over at Abadjian, shaking his head like a wet dog throwing off water, and said to him, "Whew!"

"Yep," said Dave, picking himself up. "The big man warned me for us to expect this."

Abadgian recovered and was around the truck in a flash. He hit the big boy with crushing blows in the stomach and tackled him to the ground. Now the ground was the "briar patch" to the big boy who had Greco-Roman wrestled his whole life, and who was never defeated in High School or Triple A. I heard Harley slur, "You lumbermothers are in trouble now!"

Bark Grable had come from across the street to see the festivities. He jumped on Uncle Harley's lap.

Looking down, Harley petted her on the head. He started to say something to the pup, but instead he projectile vomited all over poor Bark, and she took off like a bat. She headed under the stoop, covered in ouzo puke. Harley didn't bat an eye, and without missing a beat he just wiped his mouth on his sleeve in the fashion of the best winos of the day.

Duck was still on the ground and Dave was struggling for control. Finally, Dave twisted out and came upon the big boy's back, straddling him at waist level, and riding him in true piggyback fashion, with his powerful arm around Duck's neck, squeezing it with all his might.

But nothing happened and Dave hung on for dear life as the big boy started running with Abadjian on his back. He ran toward the house, turning at the last second, so that the man would smash against the wood siding on impact by Duck's weight and momentum. Dave had seen it coming but it was too late. It sounded like an explosion as they ran into the side of the building.

"Papa, Papa," I said, pulling his hair. "Did you see that?"

"I saw it, Whisker," he said, "but Timoleon needs to watch out. This man is a warrior and Tim is a Boy."

Then a glassy-eye Harley slurred, "Oh yeah? Well, that stupid Old Armenian better watch out for my buddy."

"Have a little respect, Harley Thomas," Eudie said. "Have a little respect!"

Harley made no response, but yelled, "Get him, Duck! Get that Jughead bastard!"

Dave got up off the ground, followed by a semi-stable Duck who landed four or five good punches to Dave's shoulder and forehead.

"Oh, that hurt," Papa said. I was swinging my fists in unison with Duck, fielding every blow along with him. Then Matt joined Dave, and while Dave worked on Duck's stomach, Matt pummeled his kidneys. But it seemed useless. Their actions weren't having the effect the men wanted. They'd been working on the pepper tree like dogs for almost seven hours now, and this large young boy was exhausting them. The men hit the kid as hard as they could, but it seemed to have little effect on him. Finally McNamara lined up between Duck's legs and punted a sixty-yard field goal — and Duck's nuts just happened to be in the way.

So the boy went down to his knees, holding his crushed peas and gasping for breath.

Papa was breathing deeply. I knew he was concerned.

Abadgian and Matt went to work on the kid's big chin and head. Finally, Duck, who was in obvious pain and at a disadvantage, shook his head like bear shaking of a swarm of bees, and managed to get back on his feet again. The two men tried to cover themselves and stepped back, exhausted and discouraged.

Duck made a sweeping left cross and hit the Irishman, standing to his right and knocking him to the ground. He repeated the sweep this time with his right cross to his left, but he missed Abadgian.

I sensed Papa turning around and looking toward Atlantic Boulevard. Apparently he had heard something, and when we turned around, we saw a brand new black and white 1947 Ford police car. Sergeant Zambo jumped the curb and drove to where we were standing.

Zambo quickly got out of the car and stood next to Papa, and as he looked over the situation he said, "Hmmm. Timoleon 'es playing with the big boys?"

"Yes," Papa said, "it's Tim."

"Dus he know who 'es Fighting?" asked Zambo.

"Hasn't got a clue," Papa said, "and I don't think he cares much. He's as drunk as a Turk."

"It's now or never," Matt said to Abadgian, "or we're doomed."

Abadgian stood directly under the boy's chin and catapulted his fist in a mortar trajectory blow that went straight up toward the sun. But

Duck's chin was in the way, and it worked. The blow almost lifted the big boy up off the ground, snapping his head back. He went pale and looked like he was about to fall backwards, but as his eyes rolled up he fell forward, like a mighty oak onto his handsome face.

Papa sat me down and we all walked to Duck. Harley was first on the scene and Zambo was on the other side of the big boy.

Duck opened his eyes, breathed in deeply and with a painful smile looked up and said, "Hi, Uncle Zambo. Hi, Brownie. Did I whip 'em?"

Uncle Harley puked on Duck and passed out beside him. Zambo brought the hose from the side of the house and sprayed the two boys into oblivion, just as Grandmother and Uncle Jimmy returned to the property.

Grandmother just looked at the dripping boys and said, "Too much licorice?"

CHAPTER 42

Baptism in the Olive Garden

B EHIND THE THEO & Carides funeral home was what they called a meditation garden. Built for the use of mourners and the recently bereaved clients of the facility, it is also where Papa's lectures and philosophical lectures took place. Sometimes in the summer, I attended Papa's knee for an extra story or two near the edge of the fishpond, which was Orange Pasha's favorite sunning spot, along with Ceszar and Iggy, and the cats' various mice jockeys. Everyone in both our families visited that garden over the years, usually around the holidays; it was a beautiful, peaceful atmosphere.

There was every variety of flowers and a half-dozen bottle bushes and honeysuckles giving sustenance to Anna's beloved hummingbirds. There were several olive trees and a goldfish pond directly in the center. In the middle of the pond was a fountain whose base was a fluted pillar on which stood the statues of two sets of twin marble imps, each one standing back-to-back and peeing four streams of water into a shell-shaped marble dish just below, which overflowed back into the pond. The inner patio was all Greek tile, and at the edge of the tiles were a series of large marble throne-style chairs and benches at various angles, some opposing each other. At the outer edge stood the trellis with pillared arches and intertwining vines.

Today it was occupied by the big man who had just returned from his home library, sitting down directly across from a battered, unhappy boy — his youngest son, Timoleon Leonidas Theocarides. The sullen Duck sat slumped down, reclining on a large marble throne chair. His chin was on his chest and his long legs stretched out in front of him. The boy had an expression of disgust and the weight of the world on his shoulders. Both of the boy's eyes were black and swollen and his nose was broken and full of dried blood. There were multiple cuts on his large, handsome face; and as he spoke his voice was a bit higher in pitch from having had his testicles relocated to somewhere near his larynx, courtesy of the big Irishman. The Duck was sore all over his body, and was defeated in both spirit and mind. As Eudocio looked carefully at his son's face he could see tears streaming down his red, hungover eyes.

"What's wrong, Son?" Eudie asked.

"Oh," said Duck. "Nothing, Papa." He shrugged his big shoulders and looked down at his toe as it fiddled with an aluminum watering can left by the gardener. "Nothing," he said, "looking away again."

"Son, can Papa help you in some way?" the big man asked, tenderly laying his hand on the boy's shoulder.

"Oh Papa, it just seems like nothing is going right in my life," said Duck. "All those grand things I said in my valedictorian speech, my big plans for med school — they all seem so far away now. Sally O. dumped me for some short little science geek from Garfield High who's going to attend Harvard. And Mom's stupid cards say I will never see Brownie again."

Tim's eyes started to well up as he continued. "Dad, when you were really sick last month, how come you wouldn't let any of us see you? But then that stupid cat and his hitchhiker vermin sat on your lap for days visiting you while we were all locked out. And then you let Artie come and bother you when you'd said you needed to rest. Damn it dad, that made me really mad!"

Eudie responded, "Well Timoleon, that's what my body told me to do at the time. And I honestly believe that old cat saved my life. Besides, I honestly believed I was dying and I didn't want any of you to see it happen."

"Dad, you're talking crazy crap now," Duck said. "I think you were delirious. How can a stupid old cat give you one of his nine lives? You are getting really bizarre in your old age, Dad."

"Maybe," said Papa. "But I had a dream and I believed it, and whether it was true or not, that dream helped me. And I honestly believe Pasha and Artie helped save me for a bit longer.

"Tim, I was ready to die in my heart, so don't you think the important thing is that I came through it all?"

"I guess so, Dad," said Duck. "I was just jealous because I love you so much and I don't want you in the funny farm or in the stupid Electric Chair over some mangy cat that licks his ass 'round the clock and some dirty vermin you call Saint Iggy. I'm just worried about you, Pops."

Tim was ready to lose it, but Papa didn't give him time.

"I think there is something else in your craw, Tim," said Eudie. "Come on and tell Papa."

"Well Dad, you're right," said Duck. "That was just part of it. Jeez dad, I don't know where I am going to college and none of the damned schools have even answered my applications. But the worst of all is that now I think you are disappointed in me.

"Are you disappointed in me, Dad?" he asked sadly.

"Disappointed in you about what, Son?" Eudie answered.

"About the fight? Are you disappointed because I lost the fight to those two old men?"

"Well, Timoleon, when you ask me in that way, yes," Eudie said. "You do disappoint me a little but only because you have no idea why I would be disappointed."

"Well, Dad," the boy answered exasperatedly. "I did my best, Dad. Those guys just whooped me, pure and simple!"

"Yes, son," he said, pausing and laying his hand on the boy's knee. "It was pure alright, but it certainly was not simple. They whooped you, but there is no dishonor in that — all of us have taken a whooping before. I have been beaten a time or two as well.

"Even you, Dad?" Tim asked, dismayed.

"Yes," the big man said. "Even me."

Duck sat up a bit and looked considerably surprised.

"But who was it, Dad? Who could ever whoop you?"

"Son," he said, "I promise you there are people who can. Take my word for it."

"But Dad," Duck said dubiously. "All those stories from when you were just a little older than me, and when you fought in Greece and Turkey and Armenia, I've heard Uncle Zambo brag about you and tell those stories again and again. Who was it that ever beat you, Pop?"

Eudie smiled softly and said, "Son, it doesn't matter. You're missing the point — all those stories are exaggerated and colored with the paint and brushes of the teller, particularly by those that love them or admire them and want to believe the stories. We want to believe our sons and dads were heroes, the biggest and best. Stories about extremely big men like we are son become most exaggerated."

Papa Eudie paused and said, "You forgot, Son. I already told you. It was my brother Ant who beat me in one of my first fights. It was over a girl during our circus days. Fights, Tim, aren't like what you see in the movies. Any fight is won only by he who was more prepared, or who happened to be the better man that day. A hell of a lot of luck is usually involved, but I want to talk with you, Tim, about some of your wrong headedness."

"What?" Duck said, dismissing the old man as he cracked his jaw back and forth and his mouth wide, painfully checking it and thinking about those two mammoth brothers in battle.

Eudie said, "I want you to listen, Tim, and listen carefully. Your notions are wrong and you need to start growing up a bit more."

"How, Pops?" Tim asked.

"First of all, Tim," Papa instructed, "do not think for a moment that just because those men — according to you — are ancient and decrepit at 40 years old, that doesn't me they have no fight in them. And it doesn't mean that because you are a foot taller than them that it always makes a difference. Because it doesn't. Where would you get the idea that they should lose to you simply because you are younger and bigger?

"Son, real men don't think in such childish ways. You need to understand that. Those men were ready for you. It's called experience, Timmy."

Papa continued, "The other man — I believe his name is Matt McNamara? — Dave told me that Matt had been a boxer in his teens in Ireland before becoming a lumberjack, so you were in damn fine company. You're lucky these Dave and Matt are just 'decrepit, exhausted old men'. Be grateful that after working their asses off for eight hours, they didn't hurt you worse than they did.

"They didn't, Tim, Papa explained, "because they are good men and they knew you were a big mouth kid and that you thought like a kid. They knew that you were not a Jap that was trying to cut their livers out and were just a big dumb ass drunk high school boy.

"But for your information, Son, you did win their respect as a fighter," said Papa. "You gave them all they could handle, and in that you have nothing to be ashamed of. You are a hell of a powerful athlete son, but they had to defend themselves and you left them no choice.

"But Tim, I am ashamed of you because you lost their respect as a man before you even started the fight." Eudie looked directly into the boy's sad eyes.

Duck looked crestfallen.

"I did, Dad?" Tim asked pitifully. "How?"

Duck sat up straight and leaned forward, looking at his bruised hands and moving his swollen fingers. He started to speak, but Eudie interrupted.

"Wait a moment, Son," Eudie said. "There is someone else I want to hear this, and with whom I wish to speak."

Eudie got up went through the French doors and said something to Anna through the doorway, and she brought out a hungover, puffy-faced Harley Brown.

Harley sat down on the arm of Duck's big marble chair and said nothing, waiting.

Eudie looked at the two pitiful, hungover boys and said, "Grandma Brown and Veve said you two were ugly and disrespectful to Dave, who had carried little Artie and Muggs home from their beatings and laid them in the arms of Mrs. Brown. And you, Brownie, he has done nothing but good for you and the Browns. Did you two drunks forget about that?"

Eudie looked directly into the swollen faces of the two pathetic boys. "Was that the only person you could find to fight, someone who had once befriended you? And another man whom you didn't even know?"

Papa gave a mocking slow applause directed at the boys and added, "Bravo. That's just what bullies do, boys. Bullies like the Tufts or your Showalter brothers, do you remember them? Do you want to be like those ugly boys?" he asked. "Do you want to go around beating someone up just because you think you can, or because something is not going your way and you feel sorry for yourselves? God damn it boys — grow up!"

The two boys looked down at their feet.

"You're right, Dad," said Duck. "But why did I not have their respect?"

"Think about it, Timoleon," Papa said. "When you and Harley graduated a few days ago, as part of your graduation speech, did you not say that when you grew up you wanted to be like me?"

"Yes, Papa," replied Duck. "I still do."

"Well Timmy, have you ever seen me pick a fight or be belligerent?"

"No," Duck responded.

"Have you ever seen me sloppily drunk and picking a fight with anyone, or bullying anyone just because I am big?"

"No, Dad," said the boy. "But what about those stories of you and Uncle Ant?"

"We were stupid like you two are now, worse probably," said Papa Eudie. "But since you were born, have you ever seen me disrespectful to my elders, or giving my opinion to someone who hasn't ask me for it without knowing how they felt first?"

"No, I haven't," Duck answered, ashamed.

"For the moment, Tim, forget all that and let's talk about the drinking," said Papa. "Why on earth would you even want to get into any drunken fight, with you not at your best — mentally or physically?"

He paused. "I'll always take a tough sober man to a tough drunken one any day.

"There you were, Tim, drunker than a skunk, a big mouth. You were an out-of-line 18-year-old ex-high school wrestler trying to pick a fight with two seasoned men. You were sloshed to the gills. Brilliant, son! What on earth would cause you to do that, Tim? Papa asked.

"I don't know what I was thinking, Dad," said Duck. "I think the booze was doing part of my thinking for me."

"Well son, you need to learn to pick your fights in this life," said Papa. "Not just pick a fight. And that is what disappointed me in you, Timmy, not your fighting abilities. You fought those good men brilliantly and they would be the first to tell you that. And I doubt many other 18-year-olds could have gone toe-to-toe with those two for as long as you did. What is more is that I told Dave in Armenian not to hold back, and he didn't. But yours and Harley's actions were shameful, unkind and disrespectful; and you should not feel proud about that.

"Now then, Mr. Brown," Eudie said, looking at Harley sternly, "you are a very talented boy. Mama Anna and I love you as our own, but you are not always as funny as you think you are. And while you are now too big for your brother Jimmy to discipline, I'm not afraid to do so. Your mother is disgusted with you and has asked me to deal with it. I have not made a decision just yet, but I hope that you will start acting like a man soon and save me some trouble — and you some humiliation. Do you understand me, Mr. Brown?"

"Yes Sir," answered Harley as Duck looked on.

There was a long, uncomfortable silence as the boys sat there, wondering what might be coming next.

"We were just sad, Pops, and mad at the world," said Duck.

Eudie took in a deep breath. Sighing, he said, "Look boys, if one of you died tomorrow, would you really lose the memory of the friendship or of what you two cherished in each other?"

The boys looked at each other, but before they could respond, Papa added, "That's life, boys. No one knows if we will see each other again at the end of each day. Don't believe everything you hear and only believe half of what you see. Remember these and cherish them right now. Didn't you two learn anything from Ahava and Sol's deaths? Or from Muggs' passing?

"Get over it," he added. "You will tell wonderful, exaggerated tales to your children one day, and all your friends will live through those stories. And Timoleon, just remember that none of us can actually be separated, even if we wanted to be. You just don't know that yet.

"Right now there is something you need to do. Wait here," Papa Eudie said, looking into the faces of both boys.

A few moments later he returned, followed by Dave Abadjian and the big Irish Matt McNamara. Dave and Matt walked into the garden looking tired. There were a few bruises and cuts on their faces, but the old dogs wore them handsomely. They both moved slowly as they walked to the concrete benches — Abadjian with a limp he tried to mask.

At first it was a bit uncomfortable for the four of them. Finally Harley stood and offered his hand to Abadjian, saying, "Sir, I am so sorry for my smart mouth yesterday, and for my actions and ingratitude. Please know that I am ashamed of myself. It was very unkind and wrong of me to blame you for Muggs' death when I know you did all you could to help, and I appreciate what you've done for Artie, too. I hope you can accept my apology."

Matt shook Harley's hand warmly and said, "I can, I will and I do. We all make mistakes, lad, even we Irish make a mistake upon rare occasion. Dave and I both knew you two were just upset about the tree. And bejaysus, I thought you puking on the big Mallard here gave our scuffle a nice touch. I hadn't seen friendship of the like of that since mi fader's pub back in Donegal. That show of drunken affection made me a little teary-eyed when I saw da boat of yas layen there unconscious."

Harley could help but smile, and was well relieved.

Duck looked at the men and shook both of their hands warmly. "Thank you both for teaching me a damn fine lesson," he said. "I was way out of line — I just wasn't thinking clearly."

Duck smiled at Dave and pointed to his own black, puffy eyes. He said, "Thank you, gentlemen for these eyes. I see things a lot more clearly now through these sober, older and wiser — albeit blacker — eyes. Thanks to you both for my post-graduate education."

Dave and Matt both smiled and Dave said, "It was our pleasure, Son. Any time. But I've got to tell you," Dave added. "Matt and I both agreed that the next time we get into a fight like that, we would prefer it with an old sparrow or a crippled dove — not with a young Duck… you're just too gah damned much work."

The group laughed and Papa Eudie broke into a satisfied smile.

Before the older men left the garden they inquired about Duck's nut sack. Duck assured the men that the little molecular Theocarides, although staggering just a bit, were still wagging their spermatozoid tails there somewhere in gonad land, and were looking forward to future trips into some woman's lovely valley of creation. Papa got a big kick out of that, and as the men disappeared into the house, Harley and Duck stayed seated side by side, on a marble bench with there arms around each other.

Duck looked at Harley and said, "I'm going to miss you, Judge Brown,"

"And I am going to miss you too, you large braggadocios, dumb ass Greek!" Harley said.

Duck picked up Harley and turned him over his big knee, and with futile resistance he spanked Harley's posterior a half-dozen times, as if he were a three-year-old.

"You may have gotten a reprieve from my dad, but not from me, you vomitus drunkard," Duck said. "You are to be hoisted by your own petard, you bloody sod."

Then he stood up and carried Harley to the pond, like a rag doll, for his baptism.

"I baptize you in the name of Papa Eudie," said Duck. "And the whisker Artie and Mother Brown."

He dunked Harley's head underwater three times. "I am only sorry that Mr. Spelman thinks he is so slick and hidden sitting over there on the roof of our tool shed, spying on us."

Harley got out of the pond and looked up at me, pointing, and said, "You're next, Archibald!"

So I took off toward home like that bat out of hell.

CHAPTER 43

The Blasphemist
(Hope Springs Eternal)

G RANDMOTHER BROWN PREPARED a beautiful celebration breakfast for the tall, very handsome Timoleon
"Duck" Theocarides on the occasion of his acceptance into
Yale. He had finally decided on Yale, although it was further away
from his parents and he still hadn't heard back from USC. The real
factor, I think, was that now Harley was moving away, and his Irish
girlfriend Sally O. had broken his heart, so he wanted to spread his
wings and fly far away.

So Yale it was, then perhaps Harvard Medical School — at least
that was the idea. Anyway, our final goodbyes were getting closer and
the pain and frustration was harder for us all to bear. Tim loved my
grandmother and was in agony over the many things being destroyed,
perhaps lost forever, in front of his eyes. Uncle Harley and Tim, plus
my cousin Walter and I, were laughing as Grandma doted over Tim,
serving him all of his favorite things as if he were royalty.

We cleared the table as the discussion came around to Yale and Tim's future dreams. Tim spoke enthusiastically of all he planned to do with his life.

Grandma Brown stood behind Tim's chair, putting her arms around the big boy and kissing him on the side of his cheek as her tears flowed. Tim was trying to hold himself together, as he stood up and reached down to hug her, lifting my small grandmother completely off her feet. He squeezed the breath out of her as he swung her side to side like a rag doll. The rest of us arose, putting our arms around the both of them. Finally Duck motioned for us to stand and sing for her, as we had planed. He said, "Mother Brown, we are going to sing a song for you from Yale. It's called 'The Whiffenpoof Song'."

Harley had already told Duck that this was one of Grandma's favorite songs; she had always loved listening to the Rudy Valee arrangement of it on Harley's Victrola, and for some reason it always made her cry.

We stood in a block of four, Harley in front of Duck and me in front of Cousin Walter, and we sang:

> *From the tables down at Mory's,*
> *To the place where Louie dwells,*
> *To the dear, old Temple Bar we love so well,*
> *See the Whiffenpoofs assembled,*
> *With their glasses raised on high!*
> *as the magic of their singing, casts a spell.*
> *Yes the magic of their singing,*
> *Of the songs we love so well:*
> *"Shall I Wasting" and "Mavourneen" and the rest!*
> *We will serenade our Louie,*
> *Till health and voices fail,*
> *then we'll pass and be forgotten with the rest.*
> *We are poor little lambs*
> *Who have lost our way,*
> *Baa! Baa! Baa!*
> *We are little, black sheep*

Who have gone astray!
Baa! Baa! Baa!
Gentlemen, songsters, off on a spree,
Doomed from here to eternity.
Lord! Have mercy on such as we,
Baa! Baa! Baa!

And after breakfast we headed for the garage with heavy hearts, looking for something outrageous to do to quell the aching pain.

It didn't take us long to find something.

My grandmother just knew things. Things I could never quite figure out.

Whenever Grandmother Brown heard my Artie-Stearman motor sputtering, she said she knew by the sound of its changing pitch that I was in crash mode, or that she would soon need to make ready for my thumping undercarriage to crash land in her lap. She told other family members that whenever she heard that special radial motor misfiring sound, she knew the first words out of my mouth would be, "Grandma, guess what?"

She said she knew when she heard those three words that something philosophically challenging was about to come forth. She always read me well, so she braced herself for the outrage that was bound to come.

On the very afternoon of Duck's celebration breakfast there was one such occasion. Grandmother had just sat down in her rocker as my biplane flopped unceremoniously in her lap.

I intoned, "Grandma — guess what?"

I sat with my back against her chest as she kissed me on the top of my head.

"I can't imagine what," she said, holding me there in her arms.

"Well," I said matter-of-factly, "I decided to name my testorkills."

Grandma rocked back forth, trying to let my it register. Then she said, "You decided to name you're *what?*"

"My testorkills, Grandma," I said. "You see, Grandma, all men name their testorkills. And since I am going to be a man soon, well....

Well, we just had a secret meeting in the garage, and well, see, Harley and Duck said that I needed to name mine right away, before it was too late!" I couldn't see her face, but I could feel her smiling as she responded, "You are going to give your testicles names — goodness gracious. I have never heard of such of a thing!"

"Yep… I've got to!" I said very seriously. This was no joking matter to me."

Grandma replied, "Really Artie, wherever did you ever get such an idea as that?"

"Well, see Grandmother," I said. "See, we were all packing up Harley's stuff, 'cause they are bulldozing his garage down tomorrow. The boys were talking about their nuts and saying something like 'testorkills in outer space'. And well, see, I was listening then. And, well —"

Grandmother interrupted, saying, "Now slow down just a minute — 'testicles in outer space'?"

Grandma slowed her rocking as she kissed me on top of my head once again, squeezing me hard. As she patted me on the chest, she said,

"Oh Child, Grandma's going to miss you so much." I could hear tears in her voice, so before I started my long winded explanation I asked her, "Mama Brown, Duck and Harley told me that when I die and go through the pearly gates that Saint Peter will ask me for the proper name of my testicles, and that if I hadn't named them I could be sent directly to hell. Grandma, is that true?" I asked, concerned.

"Oh I doubt that," she replied. "I've never seen that written in the scriptures, but maybe you should have a little name for them just in case. It pays to be safe, you know."

Now Grandmother rarely played footloose or fancy with biblical things like that, and I see now that she was just enjoying the silly child in me and making it last as long as she could.

"See Grandma," I continued. "I understood about that stuff because, don't forget, those Tufts boys made my nuts disappear, remember? And they cut off Muggs McGinnis's peter and all his stuff and then stuck them down the back of my trousers. Don't you remember, Grandmother, when you put me back together and cleaned me up? You helped change me into clean p-jays, and Uncle Harley found Muggs' peter on the bathroom linoleum near my bloody clothes and he put them in a jar of alcohol. Don't you remember, Grandma? So see, I knew all about that stuff, so Duck said that I could be a permanent charter member of The Dee Bee Bee Bees!

"The Dee Bee Bee Bees?" Grandmother repeated.

"Yes," I explained, "The 'De-balled Boogie Brigade'. And my membership means I can participate and listen to any and all conversations about the ruptured balls or other manly stuff because I have been initiated. And after all, I am nearly nine years old, and they said I could participate in ceremonies and everything," I said proudly.

"I see," Grandma said trying to understand, shaking her head just a bit. "My, my."

At that point my explanation got complicated. I cannot quite remember the construction of my conversation with Grandma, but I tried to explain everything to her while treading lightly around the exact truths of these events. I wanted to avoid being forced to eat a Lava soap or something more serious that would befall my little arse for the telling.

Here, as best as I can remember, is the uncensored version of what I managed to convey to my grandmother:

Harley and Duck were working side-by-side in the garage, packing things up for the move. Walter and I were mostly listening and trying to get the gist of the older boys' conversation. As we listened to them, Duck told Harley that his nuts were still turning purple — and other hues — and that one was now very low and large, while the other was sort of high and a bit shriveled, and that his dad had kidded him about his testicles possibly falling off and rolling down his pants leg onto the ground, and how embarrassing that unhappy event might be for him. You know — to be walking down the street one day and accidentally step on your own nuts. Eudie also mentioned to Duck not to worry too much about it because when he got to Harvard med school they could disrobe him, exposing his manhood to the class as an example of the stupidity of heavy drinking and fighting the Irish. Eudie laughed, saying, "Hell, it might even get you a couple of hot dates."

There in the garage we discussed the similarity between Duck's nuts and the chrysalis of the monarch butterfly that went from a beautiful jade color to black, eventually disintegrating. Then Harley and Duck talked about spheres, circles, orbs, marbles, grapes, peas, cherries, berries, eggs, melons, marshmallows, and stones. They discussed all round things, and so soon they were talking about the sun and the moon, about the stars and outer space. And then the conversation just naturally turned to men's testicles, which in their minds symbolized the galaxy, as well as the planetary system, which according to Duck and Uncle Harley, was obviously masculine in nature. Harley proffered that if we were made in God's image, then naturally God had huge testicles. Harley thought it likely that each of God's nuts were at least several lightyears in diameter. They talked about testicles — not the penis — as being the most prized and profound possessions of the human male animal. They said that testicles symbolized bravery, courage and shear masculinity, and said that the male testicle should even extend itself to womankind.

"You know," Duck pointed out,

"When a man is brave or courageous, everyone says 'Boy, He's got Balls!' And even when women are brave people say, 'She's got Balls!' No one says, 'She's courageous as hell…she's got bodacious ovaries!'"

Duck, with a smiling countenance and waxing poetry, went on a long tirade about "orbs" in space and what he imagined as hundreds of billions of cosmological testicles in outer space. He pictured them whirling in unison like the rings of Saturn, which he saw as a feminine planet, waiting to receive just the right testicle in her whirling womb. Duck swore that he believed that Saturn's ring of testicles were chalk full of seeds of universal energy. He pictured them as the sperm of stars, dancing just as the roosters dance around the hens, trying to impress them.

He then said, and Harley quite agreed, that there was kind of a sexual dance going on in that cobalt blue sky far above our heads. They said that it was full of courage, passion and power, and that every time we men touched ourselves between our legs we were in direct communication with the cosmos, and with God's own masculinity. Naturally Uncle Harley was in complete agreement, commenting that this was the very reason he made a point of fondling himself several times a day, and always at night and early in the morning. He also said that since the planets were named that it was obvious that men's testicles should be named too; and that we should all then and there decide what to name our own testicles to pay homage to the cosmos. Duck added that his father Eudocio had told him long ago that he had named his testicles, and that since we were all together for the last time this would be our sacred duty to do the same.

This, as one might imagine, brought on a great deal of thought from all quarters. I asked almost immediately, "Does Papa Eudie have names for his testorkills?"

"He sure does," Duck said.

"What are Papa's balls' names?" I asked, eager to hear the answer.

"Dad told me his left one he calls Mount Ararat and the right is Mount Olympus," Duck said. This brought satisfied smiles to all our faces. I think we were all more confident now than ever before that we were on the right track, and that the events unfolding would be special.

The garage was filled to the rafters with boyish delight as the molecules of male intellect collided at the speed of light.

Then there was talk of other things, like sexual references that caused the older boys great laughter. I ignored it because I had no interest in it, and even less knowledge of it; plus I had no practical aptitude for it, so I left that discussion to Harley and Duck and the giggling Walter, who apparently understood more than me.

But I had other fish to fry. For example, I wondered if God or Jesus had balls? And if so, what names had they given theirs? I found the whole subject utterly fascinating. The two older boys had stated that all real men named their balls, and Duck had assured us that if Sol Rubinstein were here today, he would tell you us that along with the custom of the bris, naming balls was also in fact an integral part of the covenant the Jews made with God. *It's in the Talmud,* he would say. I had my doubts as to the truth of that, but this was particularly fascinating to me, since I yearned to be just like Sol — wise and kind and generous, plus funny and manly. It made me sad to remember his laughing face;

I missed him more than ever and wished he were here with us to share this monumental event, whatever it was. I respected and loved Duck and Harley, but Sol would never lie to me, nor would he tease me or exaggerate. His word was golden.

But Sol was gone. So we had our secret ceremony and I fired up my Stearman, and then I ran into the house, finding my Grandmother Brown's lap.

"Well, my goodness, I think you boys have too much time on your hands," she said after I'd explained everything.

"But Grandma," I asked with absolute sincerity, "do you think Jesus named his balls?"

Now by this time Veve and the Westerman girls were in the room and had listened to just enough of the conversation to be outraged. I guess boys' testicles were of considerable interest to them because they had listened to every detail carefully.

"Well," Grandma said, "I don't know. I suppose Jesus had testicles — the Bible says he was a man — and so I suppose he did have them."

Grandma considered this carefully. She was not shocked or angry; she was just trying her best to be objective, and seemed to me to be considering all possibilities of my sincere question. In all the years I'd known her, she never once jumped on me, even over the most absurd questions, as long as she considered them innocent and heartfelt. But the Westerman girls were not quite as kind, and their faces showed anger and shock at Grandma's lack of harshness to my devilish query. I could see that they were displeased with my foolishness, and quite offended and unhappy with Grandmother Brown's ambivalence toward what they considered my blasphemy.

What Grandma didn't know, and what I had wisely omitted, was that my balls had already been christened. They were named in a garage ceremony that only we lads were privy to. We had bonded by a sanctified tribute to the peter and nut sacks of the late Muggs McGinnis.

You see, after my beating Bruce Tufts had ripped Muggs' entire package off with a pair of his bicycle pliers. Then he'd stuffed them down the back of my pants as I lay unconscious in the lumberyard.

Subsequently Harley took them into his garage, and having only a cup or so of rubbing alcohol, he had put them into a mason jar, topping it off with straight gin. The jar had been marinating on a little shelf for nearly three years. Every now and again, one of us lads would admire the jewels and think of poor, brave Muggs. I can remember laughing a guilty laugh as Harley once — very tenderly — sang "Danny Boy" to the jar of Muggs' bedraggled dogwood. It made me laugh and cry at the same time, and I hated Harley when he did that. I always tried to wrestle the jar away from him to restore Muggs' dignity. Harley loved to torment me, and I secretly loved to be tormented by him as well.

Duck, the brain of this outfit, decided that as in ancient times our little clan should pay homage to Muggs — and male testicles in general — by each sipping a toast from the mason jar containing the brave pup's genitalia. This seemed a grand idea to us all. A brotherhood was being born here and we were both ecstatic and serious. Duck and Harley made up the rules on the wing:

Each member of the cadre would drink from the jar, take one step backward and announce loudly and proudly the names of his spheres to the group. Then he would pass the jar on to the next brother. We agreed that first sipper would be Duck, then Harley, then Walt and then me.

I suggested that we each take a trinity of sips, and everyone agreed. Harley removed the lid and topped off the jar with some ouzo, stolen from Papa's cabinet. He mixed the gory mess with the lead end of a number two pencil. He broke the over-sharpened lead tip into the juice. Then, replacing the lid, he handed it back to Duck. He held it up, and we saw Muggs' shriveled scrotum, balls and small pieces of his penis floating around in the jar. For some reason this didn't bother us at all. We had discussed how this event would make us more masculine, wiser, far finer — and braver — because of the communion with the nads of Muggs, the most courageous of us all. We discussed and imagined that the ancient cults, Druids, Celts, Vikings and perhaps even the Aztec and Mayan customs were likely created in this very manor. I was a bit worried about the taste but Dr. Duck said the two-year-old rubbing alcohol, gin and ouzo concoction would kill any worm or germ in the jar. He said that anything floating in the jar was protein anyway, so we braced ourselves for the ceremony, whose rules and regulations we made up as we went along.

Walter mentioned something about swallowing the lead pellet and added, "We could all die of something from this concoction. Germs, you know, are caused by uncleanliness, and if the filth doesn't get us the lead poisoning will."

I saw this as an opportunity to assuage Walt's fears, and said loudly and proudly, "Well, guess what, Walt. Just before Muggs died — you know, before, when we were playing out in the lot — Muggs stopped and licked himself clean and chewed off some fleas and bugs from his wee-wee. And, you know, that dog saliva stuff cleans all those germs real good, huh, Dr. Duck?"

"Why, yes sir," he said to me, smiling. Then he added, "When I get into med school, can I quote you on the virtues of dog saliva?"

"Why shoot, yes," I said, wanting to quote one of Papa's favorite retorts. "Sure Duck," I said. "You lie and I'll swear to it!"

Duck said, "You've been around Papa Eudie too long." Then he turned to Walt and asked,

"Walter, don't you feel loads better now that you have that hygienic information from Artie?"

Walter crossed his eyes and said, "Oh, lord yes. Now I am nearly free of fear!"

Duck turned to me and added, "Thank you, Whisker. I'll quote you on that, should I live through this to get to Yale."

Harley grinned and Walt added, "Ah, who the hell cares? We are none too damned happy with this moving anyway, and who the hell knows when I will ever see you fart knockers in the same place ever again? So I say Mogo of the Logogo be damned — drink up, and we all die at dawn!"

Duck held up the holy mason chalice and said, "I propose a toast to testicles, or if you happen to speak only the 'Artie-sean', language — 'TESTORKILLS'!"

The three bigger boys laughed and I did too. I couldn't help it; besides, I always loved laughing at myself, particularly when there was no one else around to laugh with me. It made me feel good now, to be laughing when I felt like crying, standing proudly with those big boys' arms around me.

The Duck held the Mason jar in his hand and removed a sheet of paper from his shirt pocket. He handed it to Harley and said, "Brownie, will you please read this for our first annual meeting of the 'De-balled Boogie Brigade'?"

It was then that Walter confessed that he could not in all honesty claim membership into this elite club because he had never actually experienced the thrill of the 'castrati', as he put it. Duck said that the rules allowed as to how we three could just then and there simply kick Walter square in his nuts as hard as we could — or by decree, simply make him an honorary member. Walter chose the latter option, even though Duck told him that only full-fledged members could drink the trinity of gulps from the sacred chalice. Walt looked a bit disappointed, but he smiled when Duck told him that honorary members could still participate in the ceremony. It was just that they were only allowed one long sip from the jar. Harley punched a hole on each side of the lid — a drink hole and an air hole — and handed it back to Duck.

Harley unfolded Duck's paper and read,
"*NOUS AVONS MAINTENANT LE NOM DE NOS TESTICULES.*
By Timoleon Leonides Theocarides - December 18th, 1947."
Then Harley read with great verve and passion:
"There are mustard balls and malt balls, melon balls and meatballs. So here's to God's gift to all men.

Some are quite fat others thin, but they all swagger — left then right in strong wind.

Here's to fastballs and slow balls and tow balls and snowballs and Muggs' balls here, soaking in Gin.

Here's to footballs and baseballs, to golf balls and space balls; all balls beloved by men.

Here's to glass balls and brass balls and those ruined or trashed balls and those balls borrowed from friends.

We salute all balls in nature and from every nomenclature, balls upon balls without end.

Here's to pink ones and brown ones, the lost and found ones, or those balls made from glass or with tin.

Salut to black ones and white ones, loose ones and tight ones, and to dull ones and bright ones.

Here's to ones cut off or stitched good as new again.

But the best balls of all are our two we now call and name side-by-side with a friend.

We can cuss them or blame them, but we surely must name them, or us into hell God might us send.

So I'll name mine quite pink now;

I take one step back and drink now, as I pronounce proudly, fondling my otherwise mangled dangling fine oval good friends."

Duck took a step backwards, lifting the sacred mason jar in salute took his trinity of sips and said, "In the names of Muggs McGinnis' sacred nut, I name my left sphere Buffalo Bill and my right Roy Rogers."

Next Harley took the Jar and sipped his trinity, almost losing his breath as he spit out little pieces of something fleshy. Finally he took his step back and said, "I name my left nut Thomas after John Charles Thomas and my right nut Thomas after Thomas L. Thomas, the two great baritones."

Then it was Walt's turn. He watched the floating fleas and particles of torn puppy flesh and he became less enthusiastic about his honorary membership, but ever the good sport he held his nose and took one long swallow, and spitting something out he said, "Ah, shit! I knew it! I got the damned lead pellet from the No. 2 pencil stir-stick." Then he said, "Okay, my left is Albert Einstein and my right I name Nikola Tesla."

Now it was my turn. I thought to take small sips 'cause that stuff always made me goofy and I was in a quandary because I had been thinking about it during our conversation, and had tentatively settled on "Batman" and "Robin", although "Buster" and "Buddy" also crossed my mind ever so briefly, but I had not as yet decided for sure. I took my three little sips and finally said, "I name my left one Andy Capp and my right one Hairless Joe from the Lil' Abner comic strip," I said, handing the jar to Harley.

"Hey, guess what?" I added, looking at the jar. "This could be Kickapoo joy juice, a moonshine elixir of stupefying potency, just like they say in Lil' Abner comic strip!"

Harley sat on the stool writing something down and Walt and I listened to poor Duck spill his guts about his broken heart and the the Irish Sally O's new indifferent toward him. He said to us, "God forbid, my mother was right, and I have to start pursuing Greek or Romanian girls. God damn those Irish eyes," he said, "they are the bane of my existence." He took a second sip of Mugg's Kickapoo juice and said, "Make a note of that, will yah, Brownie!"

Uncle Harley ignored the request and looked at Duck and said,

"Okay, Doc, now it's my turn; I have written our own song for this illustrious occasion. I call it "The Whiffen Dee Bee Bee Bee Poofer's Song", By Harley Thomas Brown, December 18th, 1947. It goes like this."

Uncle Harley held the page in front of him and sang:

From the tables down at Artie's
To the garage where Harley dwells
To this dear old mason jar we love so well
See Muggs' doghood disassembled
In this jar we've raised on high
As the magic of his scrotum casts its spell
Yes, the magic of our singing in our
Last days now here in Bell
Are not wasted in the morning we attest
We will honor our dear Muggsy
Till our health fails this test
and we'll pass and be forgotten with the rest
We are four hams who have lost their balls
Baa! Baa! Baa!

We are in far too deep like a castrated sheep,
Baa! Baa! Baa!
Gentlemen gangsters of on a spree,
Soon to be turned over Mom Brown's knee
Lord have mercy on we de bee bee bee,
Baa! Baa! Baa!
Gentlemen pranksters off on a spree,
They're scant four good lads such as we
So God please show mercy won't you please
Baa! Baa! Baa!

This was just about the time that I flew my afore-mentioned sputtering Stearman onto Grandmother's tarmac.

Now, then as I have said, Grandmother heard none of our above ceremony; none of us were foolish enough to have told her all those details, and the Westerman girls who were after all members in good standing of the Four Square Baptist Church, and the daughters of the area Baptist Bishop the Reverend Nathaniel Justis Westerman. They told their father in no uncertain terms about my sinful sacrilege and craven questioning of God's and Christ's testicles, and whether or not they had named those parts of their anatomy. This information was passed on to Grandmother's Reverend Charles Wall and onto the entire congregation. Because of my inquisitive mind our Brown and Spelman families were once again in total disgrace.

Grandmother stood firm and told those girls that my query was asked in all innocence, so she saw no evil in it. She told them that as a young girl of just eleven that she herself had wondered many a night if the Virgin Mary had experienced the "curse" and discomfort brought on by the female menstrual cycle, and she told them that her pondering during those trying first days had brought great comfort to her; and at that point she was not much older than Artie. She also told those girls that there was no guile in my wonderings, and far greater evil in the mindless pulp book trash they all read and tittered over, and that before casting stones on her grandson that they should perhaps present their pulp romance books to their father and see what he had to say about those.

That was the last time the Westerman girls crossed our threshold — hell, thirteen days later we had no threshold and lumber was stacked where our house had once stood. Veve hugged her Mother and kissed her on her flushed angry cheeks as the girls stormed out of the house.

It's funny, the things we remember and the power that love brings; and those bonds that are made between boys — the ones that cannot be broken. The absurdity, the danger and the beauty that takes us all by the hand and pulls us toward ourselves into our poets' hearts, how we look back on unwise crazy things we tried and managed to live through and sometimes finding great lucky wisdom in what we gleaned from the outrageous. I remember most our heartfelt, tremulous and lavish laughter of our boyish drunkenness — not from the drink but from the core of our dizzy hearts full of unabashed pleasure at just being stupid, young and alive, laughing there with our sore hearts like a quartet of silly loons.

I think God must love a fool. That afternoon I asked Papa Eudie if he thought we were going to die from the concoction of Muggs' ball juice. He said,

"Yes, probably, but if it doesn't kill you it will make you stronger, or at least wiser. And if it does kill you, I'll give all four of you a hell of a funeral!".

Then I asked Papa what he thought God had named his own balls and he smiled shrugged his big shoulders and said,

"Alpha and Omega."

CHAPTER 44

The Last Supper
(Sunday, December 28th, 1947)

S UPPER WAS TO be served at 6:00 P.M. but guests were advised to arrive an hour or so early for chess, a game of Tavli', backgammon or checkers, and sip the thick, black Turkish coffee with Anna and Grandma Brown's baked goods.

Soon the large comfortable home was full of laughing people. I knew even then that this was a special event because the Brown-Spelmans were going off in one direction and the Theocarides in another. Tim was soon off to Yale and Stavros had already left early that morning, bound for New York City to fly for one of the burgeoning Transatlantic Airlines.

In the 1930s and 40s, those people who surrounded and loved me were mostly of European heritage — Greeks, Armenians, Jews, Germans and Irish. The custom of those days was that small children were adored but among adults they should "be seen and not heard", unless called upon.

It was rare for children of my age — and even up to the age of about twelve or thirteen — to be invited into the conversational realm of the adults. Often I would have to leave the room when adult conversations took place. Sometimes I could sit quietly and just listen from around a corner, or from another room with the door ajar. Of course, the more I was kept away the more I wanted to hear, so I learned great eavesdropping as I moved around carefully, quiet and still as a flea. This game for me was great fun and most educational.

Over the years we had participated in two dozen or more suppers like these with Papa and Anna, and nearly as many times we offered the Theocarides a humbler fare in our own small house, but of course their sumptuous meals were major events for us Browns, and those great occasions were extraordinary. But in either extreme, both our homes were sure to be filled with laughter, song and always, music.

Papa's spacious home behind his funeral parlor had ten-foot ceilings and eight-foot door jambs that fit his tall family nicely. Carl Agajanian stood in the corner next to the bookshelves, in deep conversation with Dave Abadjian and his wife Talar, who had recently arrived from Russia. The three chattered away in their foreign tongue. I wandered from group to group and room to room, and I loved listening to them speak Armenian, Russian and Greek — all such rich, musical languages. I understood nothing, of course, but I loved the rhythm and the way their words sometimes came up from the back of their throats, rolling over their tongues and then into my ears.

My Aunt Eddie stood a few feet away, holding her fourteen-month-old daughter Susan and conversing with Aunt Helen there with her Viking baby Sharon, who was now two years old.

I wandered into the library with great childlike stealth, moving silently between Eudocio and his brother Anthanasios. I stood like a chickpea between two mighty oaks, reaching upward on tiptoe and forcing each of my small hands into one of theirs. They were speaking in Greek and only paused briefly as they glanced down from the clouds into my happy face, grasping my hands as they talked to each other. The men's large hands were like baseball gloves. Finally they lifted me off the ground, swinging me back and forth in a wide arch that almost touched my feet to the rafters. I screamed with delight as Anna and Mother Brown came through the spring-hinged kitchen door, smiling at my helpless joy.

Harley and his brother Jimmy were outside, admiring Elwood's new car. Fuzzy had traded a single one of his oil paintings to some actor in Beverly Hills for this car, which was one of the most expensive production cars in America at the time. It was a 1947 Burgundy Packard Super clipper with a black leather interior.

In a short while Fuzzy gave his condolences to the Theocarides, apologizing for not being able to stay for supper, and explaining that he had to pick up his wife and children from the L.A. Grand Central Train Station and take them to their new home in Compton, just a couple blocks away from Jimmy's home. He embraced everyone and left for the station.

The big Irish stood between his daughter and Duck, who were facing each other. Duck seemed to me to be terribly nervous, and was talking boxing with him, trying to impress the young girl. He was stealing furtive glimpses at her. She was a stunning beauty, with waist-long dark red hair. She was sneaking glances at him too. I thought it was funny, and Duck sensing my awareness, scowled down at me. She shooed me away like a horsefly.

I looked around to see Uncle Harley and Dave Abadjian walking through the archway and wondered if Anna had a big enough table.

I had counted 21 dinner guests and I wondered if on this occasion I was to be allowed at the table with the adults.

Harley put his arm around me asking where my mother was.

"She had a hot date with a Navy man," I said, repeating Mother's exact words to me before she left that morning. Harley's eyes rolled a bit and he soon made eye contact with Duck, who was trying to get his attention. I watched the two boys go to the alcove wall near the bay window in the library, so naturally I followed quietly and sitting within earshot of the boys, I heard Duck speaking desperately to Harley.

"The fucking Irish!" he said under his breath, more exasperated than angry.

"Why Duck… What happened?" Harley asked, leaning forward.

"Are you blind, man? Did you not see that drop kicking lumberjack's daughter?"

"Calm down, big man. You'll give yourself a heart attack"

"Brownie," Duck said dreamily, shifting gears. "Have you ever in your songstress tweety-bird silly life ever seen a more beautiful girl than she is — ever? For Christ's sake man…Just say her name out loud … 'S o r c h a… he almost sang it… Sorcha …it sounds like an angel's wings."

"Holy crap, Tim!" Harley said. "Again? Yet Again… again, you big dumb ass Greek mule!"

"I can't help it, Brownie," Duck said. "Those God damned Irish girls are my catnip. Just look at her, did you take in that tiny waist and those eyes? Christ man, my heart could pitch a tent there near the feast of those lips. I tell you, Brownie, I am ruined! I just know Dad and Mom had something to do with the Irish inviting his daughter. Mother has long since given up on Greek girls for me. And Dad? Shit man…I guess all you've got to do is beat the hell out of a Theocarides boy and Pops invites you over for a dinner feast and a drink… they love to torment me, you know it? Those damned devil's spore Irish girls! Papa thinks my misery is great fun. It's not bad enough that the big Celt kicked my nuts up into my sinuses a couple weeks ago, but now he's got to torment me by bringing his angel Sorcha over."

Harley was enjoying Tim's misery and Duck's face was indeed pitiful. I don't think my Uncle Harley quite knew what to do or how to respond. He just stood there, shaking his head and laughing softly at his friend.

The boys had turned their backs from the people who by happenstance had walked into the large library toward the dinning room, and I debated on whether to warn the boys about their audience. But I decided against it.

Harley said, "Tim, I was saving this for later, but I think now is a good time. You are soon to be a Yale man and you know the song "Shall I Wasting", mentioned in the lyrics of your damned Whiffen Poof Song, right?"

"Yes," Tim said curiously.

"Have you ever heard 'Shall I wasting' before?" Harley asked Tim.

"No, not yet," Tim responded.

"Well, it's time you did, if you are going to be a Yale man. I think it fits your situation with all the Irish ladies you've mooned over now for years now — six of the lovelies at last count, if I remember correctly?"

"Seven, if you include this one," Duck corrected.

"What a sod you are, Duckster!" Harley said. "Sit down here and I'll sing it for you. It's about rejection — I guess Yale men get rejected a lot"

Duck sat down reluctantly and folded his hands in front of him, looking down at his own big feet like a desperate overgrown child.

Harley sang, as always, with great style and heart:

> *Shall I wasting in despair*
> *Die because a woman's fair?*
> *Or make pale my cheeks with care*
> *'Cause another's rosy are?*
> *Be she fairer than the day,*
> *Or the flow'ry meads in May,*
> *If she be not so to me,*
> *What care I how fair she be?*
> *Great, or good, or kind, or fair,*
> *I will ne'er the more despair;*
> *If she love me, this believe,*
> *I will die ere she shall grieve;*
> *If she slight me when I woo,*
> *I can scorn and let her go;*
> *For if she be not for me,*
> *What care I for whom she be?*

When the song was finished Harley and Duck turned around to find most of the guests enthusiastically applauding. In the front row stood the big Irish Matt McNamara and his sixteen-year-old daughter Sorcha, looking directly up into the eyes of the besotted red-faced Timoleon Theocarides.

Presently Aunt Veve, who was assisting Anna and the wait staff, rang the dinner bell and started seating the group. We were lead to the formal dinning room where Anna seated us as Veve took charge of the two baby girls, taking them off to the guest room to eat and play and rest away from the adults.

The couples were seated across from their spouses; I was, for the first time, at the adults table next to Papa Eudie, who sat at the head.

Grandmother Brown and Anna sat across from each other, one on either side of Eudocio. Duck and Sorcha where seated opposite each other, both trying hopelessly to avoid each other's eyes. Brother Anthanasios was at the far end of the large table, facing Eudocio.

Anna's magnificent seven-course meal went off a masterpiece of culinary arts without a hitch, and there was laughter and warm conversation and drinks all around the table, along with funny, goodhearted banter between the two brothers at each end of the table. They were full of good mischief and kept everyone in stitches. At the end of the sumptuous meal Papa proposed a toast. Looking down at me he asked Anna to bring me the thimble. She brought me a porcelain thimble that fit her large thumb and her helpers filled all the aperitif glasses and my thimble with ouzo while Grandmother Brown looked on smiling.

Papa said, "It is our custom to open the table to toasts, but first we have some music for our guests."

Harley and Duck had already moved to the center of the Persian carpet near the archway into the library, and Tim was now seated with his cello poised and ready. Harley spoke to the seated guests, who had turned to view the recital.

"Ladies and gentlemen," he said. "Someone once said, 'Never tell a secret to a Parrot'. It has come to me through the big mouth of a certain towheaded nine-year-old chatterbox that Mathew McNamara and his lovely daughter Sorcha's favorite song is 'When Irish Eyes are Smiling'.

"So Tim and I would like to play and sing this song for the four most beautiful Irish eyes ever seen: those of Sorcha McNamara and those of Blanche Louella Brown, my own Irish mother."

Tim played a beautiful introduction on his cello as warm, rich voices looked into Sorcha's heart. My grandmother had tears in her eyes as Harley's voice lilted over the group:

There's a tear in your eye,
I'm wondering why,
For it never should be there at all.
With such pow'r in your smile,
Sure a stone you'd beguile,
So there's never a teardrop should fall.
When your sweet lilting laughter's
Like some fairy song,
your eyes twinkle bright as can be;
You should laugh all the while
all other times smile,
now, smile a smile for me.
When Irish eyes are smiling,
Sure, 'tis like the morn in Spring.
In the lilt of Irish laughter
You can hear the angels sing.
When Irish hearts are happy,
All the world seems bright and gay.
when Irish eyes are smiling,
Sure, they steal your heart away.

The entire table was on their feet, joining elbows in the second-to-last chorus:

"When Irish Eyes are Smiling sure 'tis like the morn in Spring." Tim and my Uncle Harley were a smashing success. Applauding loudest of all and raising her clasped hands to her smiling lips was Sorcha. I can remember my Grandmother Brown speaking of that duet and that moment until the day she died.

Papa Eudie thanked the boys and raised his glass.

"I propose a toast," he said. "Here's to all our beloved friends, the old and the new. God bless and keep us wherever we may be. Here's to the Browns, The Spelmans, our missing Iris and here next to me the Whisker on the face of my heart Artie Spelman."

"To the Agajanians, the Abadgians, and to our new friends, the McNamaras," Papa sighed as he continued. "Here's to the friends we have recently lost, too our beloved Ahava Rubenstein and to Sol — the brilliant, generous Sol Rubenstein. We feel both of you with us here tonight and bid you both peace and Shalom.

"Here's to the Future and the Past, the first and the last. God Bless us one; God Bless us one and All."

Everyone raised their glasses.

"Here, here!" cried someone from the group

The only woman to offer a toast was my Grandmother Brown She arose, lifting her glass of tea and saying,

"Here is a toast to my wonderful friend Anna Theocarides. I am proud, honored and grateful, Anna, to call you my friend. Prosit!" Anna's face shone like sunshine as she reached across the table, touching glasses with Grandma. She said, "To Blanche Brown, the loveliest woman I have ever known."

The others toasts were courteous and thankful, addressing the New Year just ahead. And then it came round to the Duck. Tim stood up to every inch of his full majestic height and swept back his coal-black hair with one hand and raised his full glass of ouzo in the other, first looking into his mother's eyes an then into Papa's. Then Duck looked directly at Mr. McNamara and said, "I would like to propose a toast to my future father-in-law, Mr. Mathew McNamara. Here's to you, Sir, and to the best straight jab and left cross ever thrown. Thanks for teaching me a lesson in respect and thank you for helping me become a better man.

"But most of all, thank you for the feast: the sight of your daughter Sorcha McNamara, who graces our table this evening, and whose countenance makes this world more beautiful. I will always endeavor to win your respect sir, and if I am able to do so, perhaps one day soon I'll win your daughter's affection. I realize that neither will come cheaply and that I must earn them, perhaps even fight for them."

After a clumsy silence he said, "Next time I won't drink." Then he smiled broadly, winking at Papa Eudie.

Duck said, "Yes, both God and Harley Brown know me for the frightful fool that I am, but God bless this foolishness in me, and may God bless and keep you Big Irish and your lovely daughter.

"Thank you both for coming this evening and God bless us all. To my mother and father, the best and wisest parents anyone could have, and to you Mrs. Brown. We the Theocarides thank you for your wonderful family and for my best friend, your dunderheaded son Harley Thomas Brown. Sante!"

Then the big Irish stood up, glass in hand. I saw Duck holding his breath wondering what might be coming.

We awaited a toast, but instead a story was forthcoming. McNamara told us in his thick Irish accent about his father, who once owned a pub in Donegal in the north of Ireland. The pub was called "Sticky Milkey's", and he told of how his father had once put a sign above the bar that read:

TO ALL OUR IRISH PATRONS: WE HOPE YOU'LL NOT EVER ENJOY YOURSELVES HERE IN THIS ESTABLISHMENT BECAUSE IF YOU DON'T, WE KNOW YOU BULL HEADED DUMB IRISH WILL JUST KEEP COMING BACK UNTIL YOU DAMN WELL DO ENJOY IT — MAKING ME A FORTUNE.

TO THE NON-IRISH: DRINK UP, ENJOY YOURSELVES AND NEVER RETURN AGAIN.

TO THE BRITS AND OTHER FOREIGN HOOLIGANS: BLOODY WELL PAY UP IN ADVACE… DRINK UP THEN BUGGER OFF UNTIL YOU CAN SPEAK THE GAELIC OR JUST SIT THERE ON YOUR IGNORANT ARSES AND HAVE SOME MORE PINTS 'TIL YOU DAMNED WELL ARE SPEAKING IT!

Sorcha smiled but looked a bit embarrassed. The story, however, grew great favor with Timoleon as glasses clicked all round.

"Salut," someone said.

"Sainte," said another.

Finally the toasts came full circle, and I tugged at Papa's sleeve to get his attention. I stood up on the arm of his chair and reached up as far as I could to whisper into his ear. Finally Papa stood, tapped the end of his glass with his spoon and announced to the guests:

"Ladies and Gentleman — Master Arthur Spelman would like to propose a toast!"

I was ready for this; I had been practicing for this moment with Uncle Harley, Duck and Walter for years, awaiting the opportunity, and now I had it. I stood tall up on the seat of my stool, raised my thimble of ouzo and said:

"Here's to you as good as you are and here's to me as bad as I am but as good as you are and as bad as I am, I'm as good as you are as bad as I am... Here's to yah!"

Then I swigged down my thimble of ouzo with great panache and wiped my mouth with my sleeve, just like my favorite barfly Andy Capp did in the funny papers.

Finally desert was served and folks began leaving the table. The guests started seating themselves all over the house, particularly in the library and salon, where the jukebox was. They sat in little groups of three or four. I felt for sure that my great toast had made me the cock of the walk because as I walked through the ranks of guests, someone always reached out to me pull me close with a hug. For the first time I felt as though I must be growing up. After all, I had drunk the ouzo just like the older men, and I had given my first toast, which had been a smashing success. I was wearing my flight jacket that said "Lieutenant Colonel Artie Spelman" under golden wings on the upper left side and I felt life couldn't get much grander than that.

I saw Papa at his Wurlitzer Model 1015 jukebox, selecting tunes as Harley and Duck rolled up the Persian carpets and rearranged the furniture.

The first tunes were some swing music by Count Basie. Jim and Helen, along with Carl and Eddie, jumped to their feet; and I remember them as better than average dancers. They were young, all wonderfully gymnastic, and the boys twirled the girls around their waists like batons, or over the shoulder and in the slides between their legs and the assisted flips. They all said in those days that they were "cutting the rug with the best of them."

I was sitting between the Irish and his daughter, enjoying the energy of the Boogie Woogies when Sorcha pulled me up to my feet. I had no idea how to dance, but I jiggled pretty good and made funny faces, and as my face came into her blouse my nose was starting to bubble and I decided I was not going to miss this for the world. She smelled like heaven on earth and her hands were like silk. I remember thinking to myself, *she must be wearing Chanel number two hundred*. I fell hopelessly in love with her right on the spot. She was Sorcha Ruari McNamara, destroyer of men and small boys. And I became the most requested dancer in the house.

After awhile Papa grabbed Anna, and everyone had to clear the floor because of the combined 850-pound mass of moving flesh. There was no fancy footwork between the two of them, but it was still magic to see Papa doing his best as he moved really smoothly for someone his size. Broken furniture was usually a concern whenever he danced telling his stories or imitating some character from one of his tales. Their dancing got a great round of applause. Then Anna and Mother Brown took the floor, and now Anna was very tall and Grandma Brown very short. Uncles Jimmy and Harley doubled over with laughter watching them dance. The stars of the show were the bouncing dancing genius of little Veve with her sister Eddie, dancing to "Sing Sing" by Benny Goodman. "Now those girls can dance," Anna said emphatically. And she was right — it was like watching Mickey Rooney and Judy Garland.

In the waning hours of the morning there were just two dancers on the floor. The music changed to some romantic music of the day and I stood between Mom Brown and Anna, listening to them talk and watching Duck and Sorcha dance slowly, lost in some world of their own as they danced to "Peg Of my Heart with the Harmonicats", the current 78 smash hit of the day.

I heard Grandma Brown say to Anna, "The Irish girl is a willing passenger in the arms of our Duck, don't you think?"

Anna smiled and said, "Oh my, yes, but not half as willing as Tim is to have her there."

Finally the music ended and the laughter and warmth of the perfect evening turned into goodbyes, and as the sleeping baby girls were about to leave Papa Eudie asked their parents if he could carry them out to the cars and into their mother's waiting arms. Eddie and Helen smiled and acquiesced. Papa took the baby girls and put one on each shoulder, and then he walked slowly out to the waiting parents. By this time most everyone had heard those stories of his heartbreak and tragic loss in Turkish Armenia, and our hearts stood still as we watched this scene, imagining what Eudie must be feeling. He gently kissed each child as his huge hands deftly laid his precious cargo into their mother's arms and he waved good bye.

We few Browns were all that were left; Duck and Harley sat against the Bay window and I was under Papa's desk on my last spying mission.

I heard Duck say to Uncle Harley, "Great night, huh Brownie?"

"I'll never forget this night, you pitiful romantic Greek," Harley said.

"Hey Bozo, how come you didn't make a toast?" asked Duck. "You've blathered on endlessly during every other supper — why not tonight?"

Harley responded, "What would have been the point? Arty de Farty stole my best one. Besides, after your bombshell I thought I better keep sober in case that big Irish made mincemeat out of your dumb ass."

Duck smiled and said, "Well, well Brownie, I am touched. You mean you wanted to be there for me in case I needed you?"

"Not so much, Duck," Harley said, "but I didn't want to miss watching him beat your dumb ass to death this time. And besides, on the positive side your dad would hire me to sing at your funeral."

"Thanks Thomas, I knew I could always count on your support."

"You're welcome Duck, but jeez — you're such a fiend when it comes to these god damned Irish girls!"

"Yeah, old man, you know what an ass I am, but I damn well meant it. She touches me in some special place from another life or time."

"Yeah Duck, I know you always want them all to touch you in special places, alright."

"I'm serious, Brownie," said Duck. "I want to spend the rest of my life with her, and I just wanted to warn all the damned Irish in Los Angeles County. And I thought I might as well show my intentions by warning her tough ass Irish father."

"Well Buddy, you were a hell of a hit with them, I'm sure," said Harley. "But what are you going to do about Yale and Med School and the rest of it?"

Duck shrugged his shoulders and said, "Hell, who knows. I think I am doomed."

Harley started to laugh out loud and Duck took offense at his tone and said angrily, "What's so god damned funny?"

"No, big man, It was nothing you said — except the word 'doomed'. It made me think of Artie's toast. As the little fart stood up I was really afraid he was going to use his second favorite toast, which would have been:

'A Whiskey glass and a Woman's ass made a Horse's ass out of Me!'"

"Can you imagine the consequences of that with him sitting next to my mother?" Duck asked. "Boy, now that would be doomed alright. Does he even know what that means?"

"Hasn't got a clue, he just knows it's naughty and that we all laugh when he says it. Artie would do anything for a laugh."

Then Duck snapped his fingers and said,

"You know, Brownie, it's funny you mentioned that. Because I swear to you, I saw something in Artie's beady little eyes as he listened to the Irish telling that story about his dad's pub, and for some reason I thought right then, watching Artie's face, that I hoped to God Artie wouldn't relate the story about our Dee Bee Bee Bee's drinking Muggs' ball juice from the mason jar in front of Sorcha.

"Holy shit, Brownie, can you imagine if he had done that, what my chances with her would be? Whisker would have had so much soap shoved down his throat from Grandma Brown and up his ass from me that he would have farted Palmolive until 1967. And somehow that image makes me feel much better."

The carpets were put back down and the table leaves removed; things where more or less back to normal.

Veve, Grandmother, Anna and the crew were nearly done, and I — for the very last time in my memory — was sitting on Papa Eudie's lap, chattering away and looking up to the big man's handsome face.

"Gosh Papa, guess what," I said. "I never ever had so much fun, you know it?"

"Artie, you say that every time you have fun," said Papa.

"I know, Papa," I said, "but I really mean it this time. See, even Sorcha even danced with me. Darn it, Papa, she is so beautiful and I think Duck likes her a lot. And me too.

"Papa, know what? I'll bet I danced with every lady here, even my Auntie Helen and Grandmother. I got my toaster up and everything... did you like it Papa...did you like my toaster and do you think I am handsome in my flight jacket and my blue bucks? I was going to wear my corduroy suit but I just felt military tonight, you know?"

"Why yes, Whisker, and I certainly never heard a better toast. You were as handsome as Iggy sitting on Pasha and as military as Jimmy Doolittle. And just think of it, Colonel Spelman — Sorcha the fair only danced with you and Timoleon. Now that was something, don't you think?" he asked, smiling. I could not recall ever having felt so adult, nor so handsome.

Finally I looked into Papa's eyes and said, "Why is everything so complicated, and yet happiness is so simple? How come it goes away when you don't want it to?

"Artie," said Papa. "The simplest things are often the most beautiful, but they still seem complicated sometimes. Fifty years from now those will be the things you'll remember best. Do you remember last year when Papa showed you the monarch butterfly? Remember when Mama and I had the leaf with the chrysalis pined to our library curtain and we were waiting for the butterfly to break into life?"

I nodded my head yes and Papa went on. "Do you remember what happened next, Artie?"

I did remember. I had gone almost daily to see the chrysalis, and it had turned into a brilliant jade jewel, then jet black; and finally it opened slowly as we all gasped at the beautiful butterfly emerging. I cried when I saw it. I felt like a sissy and was embarrassed, but then I looked up at Papa's face and saw moisture in his understanding eyes.

I told Papa what I had remembered and he said, "You see, Artie, how simple and beautiful that was? You will remember that your whole life, won't you?"

"I think so, Papa, but I'll remember you for sure," I said. Then I looked at him and casually but seriously said, "Papa, see, that's one thing about you being so god damned big is that people will remember, and that's for sure!"

I thought Papa was going to fall out of his chair at my commentary; he was laughing so hard that Anna and Grandmother came out of the kitchen. We all hugged and Grandmother whisked me out of the house as fast as she could before the tears of laughter and remembrance started.

Soon we were home and I lay in bed inside my grandmother's arms, chattering away.

"Grandma, is Mom coming home tonight?"

"I don't think so," said Grandma. "She is staying with her new friend in San Diego. I think she'll be home tomorrow."

"Hmmm?" I said.

"Grandmother, wasn't Veve great tonight? Her dancing, I mean."

"Yes she was. That little pulp fiend surprises me every once in a while. I was so proud of her for taking care of the baby girls — she didn't even have to be asked and she pitched right in. Maybe she does learn something from those silly books."

"I guess so," I said. "Gosh, Grandma — I had so much fun!"

"You little rascal, you where everywhere at once," she said.

"Grandma, did you see Duck and that girl fall in love?"

"What do you mean, honey?"

"Well, at the end of the night after the dancing and everybody had left, that girl and Duck where sitting next to each other on the love seat and, well, I just happened to be underneath the piano, watching.

And I saw the side edge of Duck's left hand touch the edge of her right hand, and guess what, Grandma! See, I know all about what that means 'cause Ahava's hand touched mine once just like that, and my nose had bubbles and I felt dizzy."

"Do you think Tim's nose bubbled?" Grandma asked with smiling eyes.

"I don't know for sure 'cause it was dark in that alcove, but I saw Duck kiss the palms of her hands once. Now, why do you suppose he did that?"

"Did Tim say anything to her?" Grandma asked.

"No, they just looked at each other for awhile and sat there. Gosh, they were so quiet, and they just looked at each other, Grandma. Maybe she had something stuck in her eye. And guess what — Duck didn't wrestle with her or touch her boobies or chew her bubblegum or anything like those other girls at the Alcazar. This was way different Grandma. What do you suppose they were thinking, and why was she just looking into his eyes? What was she looking for, Grandmother? Do you think that was love? Gosh, Grandma, that was neat, huh?"

"Yes, dear heart," she said. "Love is always neat."

I started to get tired and said,

"Grandmother, will you sing me to sleep? Sing me the garden song!"

I went to sleep in her arms as she sang:

> *I come to the garden alone*
> *While the dew is still on the roses*
> *the voice I hear, falling on my ear*
> *The Son of God discloses and*
> *He walks with me and*
> *He talks with me and*
> *He tells me I am His own*
> *And the joy we share as we tarry there*
> *None other has ever known....*

I was asleep but sobbing throughout the night. You see, I knew I had lost my Eudie and Duck and Harley, and that this loving woman who held me in her arms was moving away to Inglewood. My life would never be the same again. But I tried to think of what the big man had told me about the simplest things as I held my Grandmother close.

CHAPTER 45

The Trinitarian Bottle

THE TRINITARIAN BOTTLE was an object of startling proportion. To this day I cannot fully explain it.

The bottle, as it could only loosely be described, was my last gift from Papa Eudie. It remained with me for the better part of forty years. The bottle touched my heart and spoke to me many times, but as with all beautiful things, I did not always appreciate it as I should have. Although I found it amusing, I most certainly did not "get it" until decades latter. I sometimes misused it as a paper weight or a doorstop and once I used it as a missing foot on an old sofa and on at least one occasion wedged it under a rear tire of a vehicle with a bad emergency brake. My relationship with this unique gift was one that vacillated between utter distain and indifference to dependency and love. I felt a deep appreciation for the curious bottle that was genuinely profound and that could only be explained as mystical.

While I can physically describe the bottle to you by telling you that its form was a misbegotten amorphous mass of glass with a crooked spout somewhere near its malformed top. It stood about six inches tall, amber in color, and it seemed to change shape in front of my very eyes.

It lived under my pillow. I wondered why in the hell Papa had given me the damn thing in the first place.

All the sadness, music and joy of our gathering a few days earlier had come and gone, and I was numb. Today was my last day there in Bell, California. This was the death knell of that wonderful house on Atlantic Boulevard we had loved so much. The home where I had spent the first nine years of my life beside Mother Brown, or at the knee of my protector, Eudocio Theocarides.

Grandmother and Veve had already moved out of the house which was now still and lifeless. The dying house contained not a crumb of food, but only a single tin cup for drinking water and one roll of toilet paper. Grandmother's old Ice Box was now empty, standing askew with broken doors and an open box of baking soda inside. There was no furniture anywhere in the house with the exception of Harley's old apple box sitting in the middle of the front room floor and Grandmother's broken down double bed in the small bedroom on which lay a blood and urine-stained mattress with some springs popping through. At the foot of the bed were a white sheet and a grey wool blanket with many of my mother's cigarette burns on it. On top of the blanket lay two soiled feather pillows with no cases.

My mother and I were to spend the last night there, and then in the early morning hop on a big red electric street car that would carry us across town onto Abbott Road in Lynwood to my cousin Walter's house. He lived with his mother, my Aunt Ruth, and his stepfather Clayton Crawford.

As mother and I both dressed that morning she instructed me to go across the street and visit Papa Eudie for awhile. She told me that she thought he might have something for me and to visit him as long as I could because she had a lunch appointment with a friend in Huntington Park and didn't know when she would be coming home and so I should entertain myself the best I could. We had her little suitcase and two large shopping bags full of our miscellaneous items in the corner of the bedroom and we were both dressing from them. Mom put on her best dress, a large sun bonnet and white gloves for her luncheon. I put on my second-hand tan corduroy suit with the matching vest and my salamander brown dress shoes to show Papa Eudie.

Mother finished putting on her lipstick, admiring herself in her little pocket mirror, and she asked me as she folded it up, "Isn't your mother beautiful, Artie?"

"Gosh yes, Mama. You're about the most beautiful-est lady in the whole world!" I said sincerely.

She smiled at me and put a drop of her perfume water on the end of my nose and a drop on each ear. She called it her "Chanel Number None". I accompanied her to her streetcar, kissed her goodbye and asking if she could bring me home a sandwich. She boarded the streetcar with purpose, smiling at the conductor without answering me. I waved as the streetcar pulled away, but she did not look out the window to see me.

I really didn't wish to go across the street to the big man again because I had said all my goodbyes and had cried all night the night. I didn't want to move away, nor did I want to snivel in front of Eudocio again.

I bit my lip and walked slowly across Atlantic Boulevard toward the meditation garden. When I entered the back of the house I found Papa sitting behind his desk in his large throne armchair. He asked me to sit down opposite him and I pulled up a stool and seated myself. We looked at each other but didn't speak for a long while. I knew I was about to cry again and I thought of running home as fast as I could when Papa reached across his massive desk and covered my head with his. Then he lovingly scratched the top of my head with his big fingertips as he would have a puppy.

He said, "Artie, you look very handsome today and you have on your nice suit and your white shirt and tie and everything. Why, you are as handsome as Mickey Rooney, and you smell like a little lord too."

"Thank you Papa I am wearing Mothers -Chanel number none!"

"What's that in your watch pocket?" he asked, pointing to my vest.

"Oh, that's the boatswain's whistle you gave me, remember?"

He corrected me,:

"That's a boatswain's pipe — never call it a whistle. Can you still sound the calls?"

I told him I could remember and demonstrated the four hand positions that changed the tone: open, curved, closed, clinched; then I blew the 'all hands on deck' loud and clear.

"Great Artie, why, that was perfect, son. You could summon John Paul Jones up from the deep six with a call as good as that."

Papa smiled, and in his smile I sensed the place where my heart had camped out in a safe world of things manly and good. This was near those things I craved and cherished, and I heard real pride in Papa's voice when he praised my small actions. I felt as though I could conquer the world, kill any beast or fend off the foulest enemy with my boatswains pipe alone. I remember so clearly looking at this man's massive head and loving face, fighting back my tears and wondering where in the world I would ever see his equal again. Where would I ever hear stories like his, or stand safely at the foot of a mighty oak of a man? On whose shoulders would I sit, reaching up to touch the clouds and laughing at the sky and listening to the windmills? I had been through this a dozen times in my mind already, and my eyes must have started to well up because Eudie read my face and said to me, "Be a man, little Artie. Be a man."

Then he changed the subject to get my mind back in the moment and said, "Yes, you remember those boatswain calls, but I'll bet you forgot poor old Exemplumonious?"

I am sure at that moment I went pale, because the big pepper tree had been destroyed now for more than fourteen days, and I had totally forgotten to send the gnome on the journey to his new home as I had once faithfully promised Papa and Anna I would.

My mouth was hanging open and Papa reached across the desk, and with his big forefinger he lifted my chin off my chest and closed my gaping mouth. I was mortified; I had thought of this possible event many times since my introduction to Exemplumonious more than three years earlier, and had promised myself to be vigilant and prepared. I had vowed on my solemn oath to be ready, since I was imminently qualified and fully credentialed for the job, and had completely accepted the responsibility for the dreaming transfer; but when the moment came to hand and I had totally forgotten to send him to his new tree, I was so ashamed.

"I am sorry Papa Eudie," I said. "I guess when Tim got in that fight with the Irish, Mr. Abadgian and I just got distracted and forgot".

"Well son, the lesson of the gnome then is that sometimes when you forget to do what you've sworn to do, people can die or get hurt. It is very important to keep your word, did you know that? And if you can keep your word on the small things, you will be able to keep it on the large things. Never give a man your word if you cannot keep it, son."

"Yes, Papa," I said with my head down. Do you think I am too late?"

"Well, I suppose not. We will talk about that in a few minutes, but right now I don't have a lot of time, and I need to talk to you about something else, okay?"

"Sure Papa. What?"

"Artie, Papa's got to conduct a funeral today, so I won't be able to spend much time with you, but I have something for you that I want you to keep to yourself. And I need to tell you something important about it, okay?"

"Sure, Papa. What is it?"

Papa reached back to one side of the bookshelf and behind a large book he retrieved a small bottle and set it down in front of me. I thought I recognized it from our Trinity dream with Pasha, but I wasn't positive — in any case, I couldn't take my eyes off of it; it was the strangest looking object I had ever seen. For some reason, I laughed out loud when he set it down in front of me. I have no idea why, really, but I just couldn't seem to help myself. It just plain tickled me to my core and I had no idea why. I looked at it long and hard then noticed Papa carefully watching me looking at it.

As I studied it, it reminded me of something from "ACME HARDWARE" in one of those 'Warner Brothers Looney Tunes' Cartoons — perhaps something that Bugs Bunny or Elmer Fudd would have utilized. It just didn't look real to me; it sat all askew, leaning much too far to one side and it was sort of melted and misshapen in the middle. It sat as though it would topple over on its own, and I got the distinct feeling that something inside of it was looking at me. I just couldn't tear my eyes from it. Finally I asked Papa incredulously with great childish curiosity, "What is this, Papa?" I said, unable to look away from it as I spoke.

"Artie, in ancient Greece it was sometimes called 'The bottle of Winter's dusk,' and the Armenian singing historian storytellers called it 'The Soldier' or the 'The Gilgamesh Flask.' Some of the Coptic Christian Sufis called it a 'Trinitarian Bottle.'

I stopped laughing when I noticed Eudocio was quite serious, and was staring into it with great attention. It was opaque and amber in color, but I could still see my own reflection in it when I noticed something unrecognizable inside the bottle, moving just behind my own image.

Finally, he said to me very seriously,

"Artie, I am going to speak for awhile, and Papa wants you to just listen very carefully. You won't understand all of it, but don't worry, you don't have to understand it. You will know what you need to know as this bottle travels through life with you. This bottle was given me by a Koptic Christian Priest in Turkey during the Armenian holocaust in 1915. This good man saved my life from the wrath of the Turkish soldiers. You see, Artie, Papa's soul was damaged and didn't function very well — you see, my mind and heart in those days got lost and I could not find them anywhere. Papa was a very sick man and that priest cared for me and gave me hope after I lost everything. Everything I loved had been destroyed. I lived with him under his protection and studied the funerary and stone cutting arts while he studied me. I was with him for exactly a year and three days. He worked chiseling my new heart while I chiseled stone, and the day I left his care he gave me this object that I now give to you. From this day on the bottle is yours until it opens to you or until you decide to give it to someone else — you will know to whom — when and if that will ever happen.

I listened, but he was right; I really didn't understand very well and asked,

"Did you ever find your mind and heart, Papa Eudie?"

Papa was very sober and very serious for awhile as I waited for his answer, and finally he said slowly and thoughtfully, "Well, yes. The priest found them boiled them in gold dust frankincense and myrrh, and put them here in this bottle so I wouldn't lose them again, and so that they could have a safe place to heal and scab over."

"I don't understand Papa," I said, still not looking away from the bottle.

"You will understand enough someday by experimenting with it when it becomes yours, but for now Papa has got to transfer the core of it to you. So we are going to do this just as the priest and I did thirty-one years ago. Do you see the stone cork on top of the bottle?"

"Yes," I said.

"Turn it left and then to the right, just to see how it feels."

I did as I was told and was amazed to feel no resistance whatsoever, neither to the right nor the left.

"Okay, now try as hard as you can to pull out the stone cork," said Papa. I did as I was instructed and the cork floated up easily, a quarter of an inch or so, as if it was sitting on an air cushion or a spring. But no matter how hard I tried the cork, it would not come out any further."

I sat the bottle back on his desk pushing it toward Papa and asking him to remove it.

"Artie, neither I nor an elephant, nor even Hercules, could remove that cork," said Papa.

Then he added, "Okay Artie, now here is what Papa wants you to do: Turn the stone cork to the right three times, then left five times and then back to the right three times."

I did as I was instructed and looked at Papa for my next instruction.

"Now lift the cork straight up very gently, like you were lifting a cornflake off the kitchen table," he said.

I did as I was told and the cork came out effortlessly. As it did, I could hear the soft wisps of laughter that sounded like two little girls at play somewhere in the distance. The sound was clearly audible and seemed to be coming from inside the bottle, as well as from inside our room, and again from outside in the street — all at the same time. The sound was a very strange trinity.

"Now take the bottle and empty its contents on the floor just next to your chair," Papa told me. "Shake it three times, just as if you were shaking pepper or salt. Shake it three times to your left, three times in front of you and three times to your right."

I shook out the bottle and Papa watched me carefully; and as I did it, I heard the same little feminine voices singing softly in what I knew from eavesdropping during our last supper as the Armenian language. It was coming from that strange little bottle, just as I had before. I told Papa about the singing and realized by the expression on his face that he had not heard any of it, and he seemed a bit startled when I mentioned little girls' voices.

But then he said,

"Now put the cork back in and press it down very gently with just the weight of your forefinger."

I replaced it just as he had told me, with a feather touch.

"Now Artie, what are your two favorite numbers?"

"Gosh Papa, I guess, three for the Trinity. I am nine years old now, and besides I always liked nines," I said, looking at him for a response."

He said,

"Then turn the stone cork to the right three times, then left nine times and then back to the right three times"

I did exactly as he instructed, while Papa Eudie made the sign of the cross.

"Now then, Artie, you've poured me out and the bottle is now yours."

"But Papa," I said, thinking this must have been a joke. I looked at him with great doubt.

"What's in it?" Papa paused for what seemed like a long time. His face was pleasant and his large, expressive eyes sparkled.

Finally he smiled slightly and said slowly,

"Why, you are Artie. You're in it... all those you have ever known and loved and all those you will ever know and love are in it with you. But only those whom you've loved and only those who love you or will love you someday are in there. The bottle will not hold evil or truck with demons or enemies, so it is a fortress, and a safe place for you."

"Are you in there, Papa?

"You already know the answer, Artie. Just think about it."

Then Papa smiled at me, studying my face carefully.

"Do you believe this, son?" he asked.

I hesitated, remembering what my grandmother had always told me: "Never lie when the truth will do and the truth will always do."

After taking a deep breath, I exhaled and shook my head with a guilty grimace on my face, as I looked down at the palms of my hands, clicking my fingernails nervously. I said slowly and regretfully, "No Papa, not really. I think you're joking with me, right, Papa? This is one of your stories, right, Papa? Is it a trick?"

"No, Artie, I am not tricking you. But it's good that you doubt things, and always remember that anything in your life that is real will prove itself genuine in the end. Remember, Artie, I have always told you never to judge a person by what they say — rather, judge them by what they do. Do not judge this gift by what I say it does, but rather based on what you see and how feel about it for years to come. And I want you to have this old bottle anyway, okay? At least it will remind you of old Papa and Anna, Sasha and Iggy."

'Sure Papa, but you said *old bottle*. Is it really old?"

"I was told that it dates back many centuries before Christ and has likely been passed from person to person, just as we did here many hundreds of times over many centuries."

"Really Papa, will I be able to open it, using my numbers?"

"It may open or it may never open for you, Artie; mine never opened for me when I turned my own numbers. My numbers did open it just now; but remember, you had to turn the stone for me using my numbers, that is the ritual of transfer. My own numbers never opened it for me when I turned them, but perhaps one day yours will. The priest told me that it will open only if it should; and when and if it ever does, it is said that there are other treasures within. But if it doesn't open for you, Artie, it has other worth, uses and dimensions that you will discover."

"Papa," I asked, "is this the same bottle you put behind your head when we had our trinity dream there with Orange Pasha?"

"Yes, Whisker, it felt like the right thing to do at the time. Remember the Trinity, Artie, but its contents also contain what in ancient times was called the Law of Five. As you grow into manhood, look now for fives. Also, your first five to think about are all the senses -- sight, sound, smell, taste and touch."

I suddenly felt this was no joking matter to Papa, and that for him this was a monumental offering, and not a small thing. And I felt a bit guilty and disrespectful doubting him.

Papa looked up at the grandfather clock and said,

"Artie, I am running late. I have to get ready for this afternoon, so I am going to have to leave now. You have what you need to know about the bottle, and I suspect that you will discover more about it; but before I go, there is something else you need to know. The bottle has its wonders but it will not protect you, nor will not make you smarter, or stronger or wiser; it will not make you richer or more powerful; it won't make you more handsome or famous or talented, but it sometimes will make you a great deal happier, and often very nostalgic. And it's full of dreams and will sometimes play them inside your head. Grow as a man, my whisker, but always keep your child's heart. Strive to be wise rather than sly. The bottle cannot be broken or lost or destroyed except by fire alone; and it will disintegrate at very low temperatures, so keep it away from flames. As Papa got up to leave I asked, "Papa, why did you give this to me instead of Duck or Stavros or Harley?"

Papa replied simply,

"I just knew it was for you.

"Now then," he added, giving me the bottle which he had placed inside a red velvet drawstring bag," do Papa a favor. Leave me now and go back home; don't hug me or kiss me as you leave. Just shake my hand now then turn around like a soldier, without looking back. Can you do that for me?"

"Sure, Papa," I said. "And thanks for the bottle." I gave Papa my hand to shake before turning and walking out into the meditation garden, swinging the bottle carelessly and letting it bang against the doorjamb like an ungrateful, thoughtless child. Then I noticed for the first time how very heavy it was for such a small bottle and was surprised; it felt like a bag of our leads used to make our soldiers. As I stepped out and walked away I heard Papa's loud voice.

"Papa loves you, Whisker!"

I didn't look back because I had promised, but I yelled,

"Me, too!"

Then without looking back I yelled loudly,

"Papa Eudie! Is the crows nest here in this bottle?"

But no one answered. He had gone into the funeral parlor at the front of his house. Those were the last words we ever spoke to each other, and the last time I ever saw his face in the real world.

CHAPTER 46

Anchors Ah-Waitress

I NSIDE OUR LITTLE white house it was deathly silent and sad. Immediately I remembered my debt to the Gnome Exemplumonious, and took up the task with a new sense of urgency and responsibility.

Papa had forgotten to get back with me on the dream transfer for the gnome, but I felt confident and had decided to man up and take responsibility, so I spread the sheet over the mattress and laid out the woolen blanket on top; then I stacked the two pillows one on top of each other, placed the bottle in its velvet bag under the pillows and lay down on my back with both my hands folded behind my head, interlacing my fingers as was my custom for dreaming or thinking profoundly.

I fell asleep almost immediately and in an instant I dreamt that I was there with poor Exemplumonious, who had been hiding, shivering in the crawl space under our house, snuggling in an erotic spoon position with "Mouffette Superbe du Pew", I suspected something naughty had only just then transpired between them. The gnome, you see, cussed like a sailor and was pure mischief on fourteen toes. He was a troublemaker, and a mixture of all races and sexes, as well as having three kidneys made from a small part of greasy chariot wheels. And remember, Muffy was, after all, French, so there it was! Plus I remembered Harley and Duck's frenchy tongues and paddy fingers with their girlfriends in the Alcazar theater, so just naturally I had my nine-year-old suspicions.

Artie and Mom, 1940s

When I crawled upon them I blew my boatswain's pipe, shrieking both the calls of Lay Up and Lay Out directly into their ears to discourage their libidinous behavior. As you might imagine, both were surprised as well as relieved that I had at last found them, and finally remembered to do my duty and to pipe them to a new home. After a few moments of contemplation, I remembered what Sol had laboriously taught me about the names and sections of the human brain, and I decided to implement my intellectual, fancy footwork in this ritual. It was then I determined that this Balzacion duet's new home would be one of the giant Redwoods in northern California; I knew they liked oaks, peppers and elm trees, but beggars can't be choosers. And after all, it was *my* dream, and Papa Eudie no longer had any say in this fantasy. So a Giant Redwood it was, full speed ahead and damn the torpedoes.

In my mind's eye, I folded the three large paper boats using the opposable thumb and forefingers of my parietal and frontal lobes; then I envisioned waxing their ground hamburger-looking countenance with just a dash of Corpus Callosum in the same way Grandmother Brown would have rubbed a stick of butter over the naked skin of a plucked chicken. Then I added just a pinch of the hypothalamus, threw some salt over my shoulder and sent them on their way, baking them happily into the oven of my fantasy until the concoction grew crisp. It was that simple; my mind seated the gnome at the stern of the Trimaran and Muffy at its helm, as they set sail up the California coastline toward Redwood State Park. As I watched the two disembark I awoke, immediately engaged my boatswain's pipe sounding the trinity — All hands — Small boat alongside — and Hoist Away three times in a row, mathematically creating number nine by using three trinities. The deed was done.

I awoke, fidgeting for a good while, and trying to kill time. But the time died slowly and painfully, and I started to worry about my mother as my stomach growled its empty chant. We had no clock, but I looked up at the position of sun and guessed it was about three p.m., which meant that the combination of my ritual dreaming and nap had taken the better part of two hours. Looking for something to do, I grabbed the Trinitarian Bottle from under the pillows and sat inside the small closet, my refuge. There was nothing in it, no clothes or those vicious wooden hangers or shoes, and it felt peaceful sitting there. As I sat inside the closet with that ridiculous bottle pressed to my chest, I heard a gnawing, crunching sound; and when I looked down at the hinge side of the open closet door, I saw a hole smaller than the diameter of a dime just behind the door moulding. As I watched in the direction of the sound I saw a tiny pink nose, as well as whiskers chewing through the small hole.

I held my breath and watched as the hole doubled its diameter. When the mouse came out I could see it was very young. It ran up my leg, put its forepaws on the bottle and sniffed briefly. The mouse scratched the surface of the bottle like a puppy trying to get inside a kitchen door; then finally turning away, it skittered back down to the floor, sitting upon its haunches and looking at me.

As I looked into his eyes, I heard a voice inside my head say clearly, *I'm hungry!*

"Me too," I said out loud.

Then I remembered my inside suit coat pocket and looked in there to find a single inch long, individually wrapped three-for-a-penny Abazaba candy bit. I unwrapped it, broke it in half and handed a piece to the mouse.

"Thank you!" sounded my mind — or perhaps I heard it in my fingers as I held the bottle to my chest. I didn't speculate, or even really care that this was just really enjoyable as I watched the little creature chewing happily, not breaking eye contact with me.

"You're welcome," I said out loud to the mouse. "Are you any relation of Kerstin Rydstrom, the Viking mouse? Or Ceazar Pasha's first jockey, or Iggy?"

"No, I don't think so," said the mouse, finishing his morsel.

Then he said politely,

"Thanks for the food. Goodbye!" I watched him turn away and run back through the hole, quick as a wink.

I wandered around for awhile, looking for something to do. I finally decided to get up on our favorite spot on the roof of the house for what I knew would be my last time there.

Many times I had laid up there looking at the clouds or the stars, dreaming. I had even fallen asleep up there once, ultimately tumbling to the ground and nearly knocking my brains loose. Now I climbed up the trellis on the side near the stoop, carrying the bottle up to my old familiar spot. I put the bottle in my inside suit pocket, just over my heart, and lay on my back looking up at a beautiful blue sky filled with puffy, floating clouds. It was a perfectly breezy, comfortable day. I looked up and began to think of all my memories there over those years. The more I thought about them, the more I began to love the idea of the stupid bottle in my chest pocket; because I reasoned that if all those that I loved who loved me back were indeed inside it, how lovely that would be to always have them - and my memories of them — with me. Specifically, I would have Ahava and Sol and Muggs near me; nobody I cared for would ever disappear, not even the dead ones. I suddenly became very pleased and enthusiastic about the weird little cartoon-shaped bottle, and I said out loud to the testicle shaped clouds floating just above me,

"Don't touch my Twinotwainian Fwask yu Waskely Wabbit!"

I got a real kick out of myself creating a dozen more of such accents, voices and scenarios. I yelled them into the sky, trying to make the clouds laugh with me; they resisted my efforts, but my joy increased until my belly ached. I had, in that moment, a terrible sense of freedom and power, and a real appreciation for what Papa had done for me over the years. I reasoned that even if all this bottle stuff was a trick or a joke or simply a tall tale from a very tall man, that it was at least the best lie I had ever heard. And that very moment, I think, was the beginning of my enjoyment of the Trinitarian Bottle, and my relation with this mysterious artifact.

As I looked up at the clouds and thought of all the things that flew in God's blue sky, I thought about the Stearman and Waco biplanes AirCobras, Fokkers, Stukas and P-51 Mustangs; I thought of sparrows, woodpeckers, bats, hummingbirds, fleas, bumblebees, gnats and balloons.

I wondered about God and bubblegum. I wondered about the Devil and my grandmother's pies. I gave some thought to my penis, Iggy and Gopher Spit Hollow; to Puppies and to my Uncle Fuzzy and Auntie Carole. I wondered some about Viking mice; I thought a lot about all those sexy things I didn't know much about — was it as naughty and disgusting as some around me thought it to be? I wondered if the word sex was one of those four letter words Reverend Wall carped about, or was s-e-x just another trinity, since it only had three letters? I thought about when I kissed Lorna Green, how her bubblegum kiss twitterpated me, and I wondered if that was evil. And when Ahava kissed me, why did it send little bubbles into my nose and make my heart beat faster and my brain fuzzy? And what was that shock up my spine when I looked into her eyes? Was it a sin? Was that evil? Did the devil do that?

I wondered about little girls and boys and what I would be when I grew up, and if I would even live long enough to grow up; and if I did, would I be a good man or a disgrace? Would I be kind and generous, and noble and funny like Papa Eudie? Or would I be vindictive, hateful and brutal like Bruce Tufts? Would I be brilliant like Sol Rubenstein or dumb as a rock like the Showalter Brothers?

I thought about testorkills, and if our fraternity of the Dee Bee-Bee Bee was to ever hold its second annual meeting. I thought about the Muggs McGinnis gin-filled Mason jar now sitting in my shopping bag, waiting to be delivered into the hands of Walter Crawford — a parting gift from Uncle Harley.

I sat up to jump down and scooted my butt to the edge of the roof; and as I looked down I laughed out loud, remembering filling those things called condoms with water in order to drop them on Veve and the Westerman girls' heads as they walked around under the eaves near the rose covered trellis just below. Only by chance, it was Grandmother Brown that walked into harm's way and got soaked. I remember how Grandma chased Harley and Walt around the property, hitting them with her broom as I hid in the closet, escaping the thrashing straw.

I wondered if all those tears of laughter were in the bottle. *Likely not*, I thought.

There just wasn't enough room in it for them all.

I got down off the roof and went to the front stoop, looking toward the street and waiting for Mother to walk up the sidewalk.

There wasn't much of the day left when a yellow cab pulled up to the curb. My mother and a naval officer, whom I recognized by the sleeves of his blues was a Lieutenant Commander, stepped out of the cab. He was two inches shorter than my mother, had a pencil line mustache and wore horn rim glasses. They were fussing about something, but I couldn't hear what they were saying. I wanted to impress him by sounding my boatswain's pipe. I removed the pipe from my vest and blew Mess Call three times. The man extended his arm, pointing to me as he yelled something angrily at my mother. They raised their voices and my mother slapped the man hard across his face, turned her back to him, leaned forward and stormed away, staggering up the pathway toward the stoop.

He got back in the cab, slammed the door and left.

I followed my mother into the bedroom. She was still seething about something, and I could smell whiskey heavy on her breath. I immediately went on guard. I had seen this scene many times before. Mama had returned without her gloves and bonnet, and I knew instantly that this was not the same mother that had left me nine and a half hours earlier. Suddenly I felt very queasy. I knew from my earlier visit that there were no wooden clothes hangers in the house and took some solace in that, but I also realized that there was no one in the house to act as a buffer between me and my mother's demons.

I noticed my mother's wrinkled dress, smeared lipstick and messed hair. Her cheeks where flushed, but her forehead and chin where quite ashen and pale.

I knew I needed to tread lightly, and I asked her gently if she had brought me any food. She looked at me disgustedly and asked why in the hell I hadn't eaten at Papa Eudie's. I explained that he had a funeral and had to leave. She was angry, but I felt safe, and thought I might escape her wrath — and very nearly did — until she saw my suit.

I had ruined my suit lying on the asphalt shingles, wallowing and laughing up there on the filthy, deteriorating old roof. My shoes had scuffed into the raw leather and my suit had tar from the asphalt, from one end of it to the other. My coat was ripped, and the suit was indeed hopelessly ruined. I saw my mother's face and immediately held up my hands in front of me to protect myself, but it was too late. On the window sill my mother found the stick that was used to prop open the broken sash window in the summertime, and she struck me with it hard several times across the back and head. One of the blows knocked me completely across the bed and up against the wall, and I briefly lost consciousness. I was hurt and in real pain, and struggling to get on my feet and run, but I refused to cry. I thought to stand my ground and take what might come, and I scowled at my mother, choking breathlessly.

"Oh yeah, well I'm hungry!" I screamed defiantly.

"Quit sniveling," my mother said, "and get in there and take a shower. Then get your smart little ass in this bed this very minute!"

"But Momma, there's no soap and the hot water has been turned off."

"Tough titty, what a pity!" She said, mocking me and raising the stick to strike once more.

"You should have thought of that before you ruined your damned clothes," she said. "Don't you dare come into this bed unless you are spotlessly clean. Do you hear me, Arthur Spelman?"

I didn't answer, but I did run into the bathroom and shut and locked the door behind me. I managed to find a sliver of Palmolive soap under the clawfoot tub and got in the ice cold shower.

On the small wall mirror I could see two knots the size of large grapes bulging, one on my shoulder and another near my spine just above my buttocks. They hurt badly and when I got in the shower, the ice cold water hit them like a sledgehammer, and I started to sob peeing myself. I sobbed uncontrollably into the tub. There was nothing to dry myself with, and when I got out I took handfuls of the roll of toilet paper, trying to dry myself with it as best I could.

When I returned to the bedroom, Mother threw some PJs at me. As I dressed for bed, she was still in a foul mood and I sidestepped her as best I could. I noticed she had the Trinitarian Bottle from my suit coat in her hand.

"What is this rubbish?" she asked angrily.

"Papa gave it to me," I said.

"For Christ's sake," she said, "he couldn't have given you a god-damned ten dollar bill or something? This is the ugliest thing I have ever seen. This is just what we need, more junk, just a bit more crap to carry to my sister Ruth's!"

She held the bottle up to the light and said something about it containing whiskey. She showed me, but I saw nothing in it other than a milky substance.

"Christ, now there is a hell of a gift for a nine-year-old boy," she said. "BOOZE!"

Mom tried to get the cork out several times, but it would not budge even a fraction of an inch — not in any direction. She cussed the bottle and threw it as hard as she could through the bedroom doorway out into the empty living room. It caromed off of the corners of the far walls and wound up knocking over Harley's empty Apple box, landing inside like a dead soldier in a trench. I thought briefly to brace for round two — it had happened before — so I jumped into bed and covered myself immediately, waiting for the blows. Mother smoked for awhile, sitting out on the stoop before coming inside to bed.

I could not lie on my back because the painful knots were growing worse by the minute, so I turned on my side, ready to spoon mother. I did not dare touch her or get close, but when I heard her soft crying my heart melted, and I decided to give her a back rub, just like the ones Grandma Brown used to love. I started to rub. At first Mother was cold and stiff, but finally I could feel her relax just a bit. That was when I said,

"Mama, I am sorry I ruined my suit. I should have been more careful."

Mother made no response.

I rubbed her back for a good long while until I felt her quite relaxed.

"I love you Mama. I am sorry!" I said.

"Go to sleep, Artie!" she said coldly.

Finally, she fell asleep, and I lay with my arm around her.

Sometime in the middle of the night, I felt her pat my hand as it lay across her tummy. The devils had departed.

The morning came early and we were awakened by the motors of the bulldozer and workmen's trucks just next to the house.

As we dressed for our trip across town, we gathered our things into the bags. Mother noticed the Mason jar with Muggs' nuts in it and her expression was priceless.

"What in the world is this?" she asked. I explained the contents and that it was a gift from Harley to Walt. A smile broke over Mother's face and she said,

"Oh my! No, no, no! I have a much better plan for this little treasure."

When I complained that Harley had told me to give it to my cousin Walter, Mother said,

"Mr. Spelman, I'll explain later to Brother Harley. Sisters trump nephews, you know."

Mother searched through the bags a bit and found just the right sized box, freeing it up by removing its contents and placing them at the bottom of the shopping bag. She put the Mason jar in the box and told me to go get the roll of toilet paper. I retrieved what was left of it and watched her pack the four corners round the jar with the toilet paper, but it wasn't enough packing, so she went into the kitchen and returned with a piece of semi-old wet newspaper from under the sink and brought it to her package.

"Mom," I said, "there is mouse poo poo all over this newspaper, and it smells!"

"Perfect!" she said. Then she finished packing the jar and sat the box back down in her shopping bag. I could not imagine what my mother had in mind for Muggs' chalice.

As we walked out the front door I carried the small suitcase and Mom hefted the two shopping bags with a self-satisfied grin on her face. As we walked through the front room, I glanced at Harley's apple box and saw the Trinitarian Bottle resting inside. Mother saw me looking at the bottle and read my thoughts perfectly, saying,

"Don't even think about it!" She spoke firmly.

We walked out, leaving Papa's precious gift to die along with the house. We walked out the front door, down the path to the sidewalk. No sooner had we reached the curb than the big CAT started pushing down the house. We stood there watching for a while until the old house was a pile of rubble, just like Harley's garage behind it. Nothing of our Eden existed any more. We turned our backs on it and sadly walked up to Gage Avenue, going past the streetcar stop by a couple of blocks. I followed Mother into the post office and stood next to her on a little oak step stool for the customers next to the marble table. Mother instructed me to borrow a couple pieces of paper and a pen from the clerk; and when I returned with them, Mom took the box out of the bag and sat it on the big table.

Now my mother always had a way with the poetry of the English language, but she also cussed like a sailor. As I stood next to Mom, here is what she wrote on her missive to her Navy boyfriend:

"Dear Rosy, Here is a little thank you gift for the lovely lunch and our romantic afternoon. The contents of this jar are to replace the gonads you lack and your fear of meeting a nine-year-old boy and for lying to me about how you felt about us. Good luck and good hunting, you cowardly, thoughtless, grandstanding weasel, user prick son of a syphilitic Jarhead bastard.

Semper Fidelis Asshole-and Sweet dreams, Anchors ah-waitress, Iris Spelman.

Mom slid the note over to me and said,

"Artie, draw your little cartoon that Fuzzy showed you. You know, the one you always call your 'self portrait,' with the one tooth and the big eyes and the skinny neck?"

I did as she asked taking great care to draw my best, and signing it Artie Spelman. Mom took the page and folded it neatly, placing it inside the box.

"Wait just a minute," I said, putting in three of my small paper fold boats on top of the jar.

"What's that for?" Mother asked.

I scrunched my shoulders and said,

"I just thought he might like some of my boats, being a sailor and all."

"Artie, you are really weird. What a strange little kid you are, do you know it?"

She taped the box shut and wrote on the label:

To: Lt. Commander Rosemead J. Skullnick
Enlisted Personnel Distribution Office-Pacific EPDOPAC
North Island Navel Air Station
Coronado, California.

She paid the twenty-six cents and sent it on its way.

Our trip into Lynwood was enjoyable, and went off without a hitch. When we arrived on Abbott Road we had to walk a little more than a mile to Aunt Ruth's house. Walt was delighted to see me. Auntie Ruth fed us, too. I ate like a ravenous vulture, while Ruth looked questioningly at my mother, who just hunched her shoulders.

We put our things away in our tiny room. I was given one of the small drawers on the mirrored dresser in which to put my things. As I put my belongings away, I took out my treasured bright red INJUN Cigar Box. And as I went to set it in my drawer, I wanted to check see if I had remembered to put my Swiss Army knife inside. I opened the box, and it was there alright, lying right next to the Trinitarian Bottle that I had personally seen laying around in Harley's apple box as Mother and I walked out of that house.

I was stunned. I removed the bottle and looked at it carefully. There was no mistake; it was the bottle alright, but I couldn't help but notice that now it was as light as a feather. I replaced the bottle, putting it back in the cigar box. And as I did, I swear I saw Papa Eudie's big smiling face reflecting there.

Epilogue

PAPA DIED IN 1958 at the age of seventy-eight. Anna's cards had been right. None of us were ever together again — at least not in the same way. Harley did see Duck just once again that day in 1958, at the his father Eudocio Theocarides' funeral. There Harley sang Ave Maria, while Grandmother Brown played the Piano and sang 'Just a Closer Walk with Thee.'

Eudie's ceremony was attended by almost four hundred people, most of whom he had helped in some way. When Papa died, he weighed almost 720 pound, and his weight — combined with the large specially made casket — required eight pallbearers. The great loving oxen who hefted the great man that day were the Big Irish McNamaras: Dave Abadjian, Carl Agajanian, and — insisting on breaking tradition — were Papas two sons, Duck and Theo, who helped shoulder their beloved father. Eudie's brother in-law, Zambo the cop, and Uncle Jimmy Brown and Butter Guest, the big footballer from Mississippi who had once offered Tim his support at the Alcazar Theater all those years before, were the two extras.

The first I heard of Papa's death was just before I left to live in Mexico City, when Harley told me that Papa had died and was buried with the

Duduk he called "Sister". Papa had carved that flute while recuperating in a Turkish abbey. Harley told me that he had carved it from the femur bone of an Armenian Holocaust victim.

Uncle Harley told me Anna wanted me to know that in the breast pocket of the suit Papa was buried in was a trinity of my first foil paper boats. I had given them to him when I was just four years old.

The Duck never made it to Yale. Timoleon Theocarides and Sorcha Ruari McNamara were married in 1949, and both attended USC. Tim went on to the Cooper Medical College near San Francisco (now Stanford Medical School). After he graduated, they moved to Long Island, New York. That was the last any of us ever heard of them.

Anna liquidated all her possessions, which were considerable. It was said that she lived with Ant until he died a year after Papa, and then she moved to Bath, in Somerset, England. She lived near the Royal Crescent, and that was the last anyone ever heard from her. Anna had always talked about Bath, but Papa would never leave the United States. He considered the U.S. the greatest country on the face of the earth.

The End